I MIGHT GET SOMEWHERE

I MIGHT GET SOMEWHERE

—— ORAL HISTORIES OF ——

IMMIGRATION AND MIGRATION

*Gathered, recorded, and edited by students
at Balboa High School, San Francisco*

826

PUBLISHED IN CONJUNCTION WITH 826 VALENCIA

Published May 2005, by 826 Valencia.
Copyright © 2005 by 826 Valencia
All rights reserved by 826 Valencia and the authors.
ISBN: 1-932416-43-9

Volunteer editorial staff:
Shannon Bryant, Ian Carruthers, Sekai Chideya, Katrina Dodson, Norman Patrick Doyle,
Alison Ekizian, Doug Favero, Linda Gebroe, Sarah Gibson, Alanna Hale, Heather Hax,
Pamela Herbert, Sasha Kinney, Chad Lent, Eric Magnuson, Amy Miles, Keri Modrall,
Walt Opie, Brian Pfeffer, Mark Rabine, Lily Rosenmann, Heidi Schmidt, Gordon Smith,
Maya Stein, Caitlin Van Dusen, and Liz Worthy.
Proofreaders: Jon Kiefer, Maya Stein, and Eric Wilinski
Book design and production: Alanna Hale, Maya Stein,
Taylor Jacobson, and Alvaro Villanueva.

Front cover depicts interviewees who lent their personal photographs for our use.
We thank them for their generosity.
Back cover depicts several of the Balboa High Shcool students who participated in this project.
Photographs courtesy of Lisa Morehouse.

Printed in Canada by Westcan Printing Group

OTHER BOOKS FROM 826 VALENCIA

Talking Back:
What Students Know about Teaching

Waiting to Be Heard
Youth Speak Out about Inheriting a Violent World

THE VOICE AND THE LISTENER

by AMY TAN

Voice—that's what I look for first in a story.

A strong voice is half the story. It is the essence of self and soul, mind and what matters. The voice determines what kinds of stories will be told. Often the voice has a secret past, what has never been told, but usually because no one has asked or no one was there to listen. So much about storytelling depends on an interested listener.

The voice also has a particular way of viewing the world, through eyes that clearly see what happened in the past. Some eyes never blink or turn away. Or sometimes they are squeezed shut. Even so, the narrator still sees what he cannot forget. There may be bodies in a field, the same field he is running through to escape the soldiers. He sees something and dips down closer to see. You, the reader, must dip down, too.

The voice has a perspective. It may be looking behind or ahead and then behind again. It can look sideways and consider how things might have been. The perspective might start off by peering into the past through a small crack. It might widen, allowing us to step in further and even experience the visceral aspects of the story, the humidity, the stickiness, feet sucking against mud, the air in a crowded space growing rarer by the minute.

The voice often has particular reasons for telling a particular story. They become a story within a story, related to one another, like the egg white suspending the egg yolk. The reasons can be urgent. Someone needs to know the truth before it is too late. Or the storyteller has a confession of love and is bursting to say it. Or the reason is as simple as a grandson asking his grandmother to tell him why she came to America and how and is she glad.

The voice can be in another language. Through the magic of translation, we, the reader, can understand it perfectly. I am quite fond of this technique. Yet, with the best of translated narration, the story retains its tone or emphasis. It may be more reserved or more intimate than we are used to. And the imagery can be startling and fresh, giving the reader a new sensorial experience of the imagination. When I come across those images, they are like gifts from the universe.

Some of the strongest voices are personal testimony. Fiction writers often employ that voice as well—I certainly do. It is a first-person voice, and the narrator is often chatty and spontaneous. She may ramble from time to time or interrupt herself to go on a detour. She often offers up strong opinions, some of which can be offensive. She often has linguistic tics, the repetitive use of a bit of this, a bit of that, which is a bit unnecessary. In fiction, those narratives strive to sound like the real thing, naked personal account with ums and ahs, not dressed up to hide the flaws or made more presentable. Some critics say that this is an artless form—artless meaning both without application of refined literary skills but also without guile and manipulation. There is no hiding behind craft, no prettying up the sentiments. The voice is direct, plainspoken, spontaneous, and flawed. Its best attribute, however, is honesty.

The stories in this book contain all these elements of voice. They are artless yet stunning, full of startling imagery. If ever there were reasons for telling stories, they are here. Many of the storytellers have survived terrors and difficulties beyond our ken. One woman hands over her one-year-old daughter to a border coyote who will bring her to America. Another witnesses the Khmer Rouge's complete disregard for human life and escapes from Cambodia. We want their observations to enlarge ours. The voices are fathers and mothers and grandmothers and friends, and they are talking to daughters and sons and grandsons and classmates. They confess missing home while being grateful to have found a new one. We are sitting with them on a couch at midnight. We are in the kitchen, listening as dinner is being prepared. We are watching the Super Bowl, cheering victory when we are not moved to tears over loss. They are telling stories and we are listening.

STORIES OF REAL LIFE

by

JACKIE CHEN, VINNIE COLLIER, JIMMY MEAS, MIKKO DELOS REYES,
ROGER LE, TEPORA MALEPEAI, ROBERTO ORTEGA, SHARON OU,
GABRIEL PADILLA, DEXTER PASALO, KYLE PINEDA, JENNY TRAN

I Might Get Somewhere is a book of oral histories. These oral histories are not *based* on true stories; they *are* true stories. Each came directly from a person one of us knew, talked to, and interviewed. The stories in this book speak from each person's point of view, his or her past and background, country, family, journey, and experience in San Francisco.

We interviewed our parents, friends, uncles, and grandmothers. Most of our interviews were conducted in person with a tape recorder, each filling about an hour of tape. After we transcribed the tapes, volunteers from 826 Valencia helped us edit our transcripts, suggesting places where we needed to go back to re-interview. Some of the second interviews took place over the phone. (In fact, one of us did the whole interview over the phone because the subject, her father, had moved back to Mexico.) Re-interviewing helped shape the stories to give them more depth and direction. Always, we organized our interviews into three sections— the homeland, the journey, and the new life in California.

During the process of interviewing, we learned things from our storytellers that we hadn't known before, even if they were close family members. And sometimes our storytellers told us things they had never said to anyone. Often, we were surprised by the answers.

Oral histories are different than written stories. When one interviews someone for their life story, one gets to hear what they are thinking. They give certain details and memories. Sometimes, they get sidetracked and start to tell about something else, maybe unrelated. But mostly, it's the individual's personality that comes through. They laugh or sigh or look sad at certain things they remember. They give you the raw material, untouched, unedited.

Our book is not written in perfect English because we wanted this collection of stories to convey the language of the person telling them. We tried our best to keep as much of the original content in. We wanted to use the original grammar, to write down our storytellers' specific way of speaking.

Of course, many of these stories come from people who did not speak English as their first language. In some cases, we conducted our interviews in the native language of our storytellers, and then translated their words to English. It was important for us to keep the stories intact, as they were told to us, to write them down in the way that we heard them. So a minimum of edits was made in terms and grammar.

All the stories in *I Might Get Somewhere* are about moving from one place to another. They tell of the journey from one homeland to a new, often completely unfamiliar home. And while the stories of these journeys are often similar, they are not the same. Each of our storytellers is an individual who came from a different place and life. They've had their unique families, hometowns, travels, work, and experiences with their immigration.

These stories here are also unique from each other because of the distinct relationship between the interviewers and the storytellers. In each case, we interviewed someone we knew pretty well, but the better we knew our subjects, the more open they seemed to be with us. Not always, of course—if we interviewed our parents, they didn't necessarily want us to know everything, and sometimes people left things out because they knew it was going to appear in this book. But in all of the stories, the people we interviewed spoke their minds. They spoke from their hearts. And so the oral histories in this collection are the best kind of story. They are stories of real life. They are stories of truth.

CONTENTS

LEAVING FOR A BETTER LIFE

HERE YOU FEEL RICH

IT'S ALWAYS RUSH RUSH

I DIDN'T WANT TO COME

OH, I WOULD FOR SURE GO BACK

MY THUG LIFE CALIFORNIA DREAM

I MISS THE SIMPLE TIMES

DON'T FORGET WHERE YOU COME FROM

PART I

ONE OF
THE LUCKY ONES

A MEMORY THAT WILL LAST FOREVER

MARIA REYES MEZCALA, JALISCO, MEXICO
INTERVIEWED BY VERONICA REYES

I interviewed my mom in my room, on Friday night after dinner. We were both wearing our pajamas. —*V.R.*

I was born in Mexico on August 19, in Tepatitlan, Jalisco. I have seven sisters and four brothers. I lived in a ranch, about an hour from the town Mezcala. I liked it because there was a lot of freedom there. We didn't have stoves or microwaves. Our stove was made for firewood, and was almost like a chimney. Our fence was made of bricks, and some of the rooms had doors, others didn't. We had to share bedrooms and beds. I shared with my twin, and my sister, Alma. We were able to make a lot of noise because we didn't have neighbors. We didn't have electricity, so we heard the soap operas on the [portable] radio. We used our imagination. When the batteries died we put them in the sun and they would work again. When I was ten, I started working, milking the cows. I woke up at three in the morning to help my dad. I would get paid one hundred pesos. We had no other choice than to work, or else we couldn't eat.

I went up to [the] second grade. Oh yes, I loved going to school. Even though I remember that once they hit me with a ruler because I didn't do my homework. We couldn't afford to buy pencil and paper. We were all together in one class, all fifth graders, fourth graders, third graders, second graders, and first graders. We had no other choice; there was only one teacher for about twenty-five to thirty students. We also didn't get fed at school. We made it fun. We got divided and we played soccer, the big students against the small ones. I didn't like to go home, in a way yes and in a way no. Yes, because it was quiet and peaceful. No, because I had to work to feed the animals: cows, chickens, and donkeys.

Dinner was always the same thing, since we were a big family. When my mom cooked we had to get just a little bit of food because others won't be able to eat. We had beans, tortillas and soups. My mom never let me go out because I had to do the cleaning. The only time that I was able to go out was when we went to Mezcala to buy the groceries. We had to walk an hour to get back and forth. When we left the house it was early, and when we came back it was dark. I was scared because there was no light.

The traditional party came on August 24, called *La fiesta del 24 de Agosto*. It was pretty to me. It has two plazas where you and your boyfriend would go and talk. He would give you flowers. This happened on the traditional parties—it was the best part of the years. *Bandas* would go and you would dance. You could also go and see *el rodeo*. They would sell *churros*, *tamales*, *posole*, cotton candy, drinks. I know that now they take roller coasters, but when I was there they didn't.

Well *mija* [my daughter], I never thought that I would end up married with your dad when I was nineteen. We got married in Mexico. I met your dad through my twin, Juana. She was going out with your uncle, Raul, and one day she invited me to go to the dance with them. So I wouldn't feel lonely, he invited one of his brothers. I didn't like him because he was so serious—he didn't talk at all—so I got mad and got up and danced with someone else. Yes, I realize it was wrong. Then later on he asked me to dance. I said yes. He was here in the U.S. most of the time and only went over for traditional parties. He told me that he would write to me and asked if I will write back. I said sure. We went out like three times in like two years. On our honeymoon we went to the cathedral in Mexico City. It was so nice, wonderful. I enjoyed looking at the Virgin Mary. We stayed in a hotel, which was so different than the ones here, of course, because they are poor. I didn't eat—oh my god (laughs)—nothing, because I was so embarrassed of your dad. I was shy to eat in front of him. My honeymoon was one week. After that I went home, and your dad came to the U.S. He was not a U.S. citizen. It took us a couple of months to fix the papers, and he was also helping his cousin get wedding arrangements.

The day I left Mexico I believe that was one of the saddest days of my life. I packed my clothes and then I took an airplane to Tijuana. I got here by a *coyote*. Vero, you have no idea how much I suffered to get here. You can't even imagine. The *coyote* was such a bad man. I stayed in a hotel at first in Tijuana a couple of days. The man went to the hotel and took me to his house. The man would tell me to go to the living room, I would sit down in the corner sofa. Then he will go to the store and buy cigarettes and bring movies. I was scared because he would put his legs on top of mine. He would put porno movies and *make* me watch them. I called your dad to tell him that I was in Tijuana. But I never talked to him. I talked to my father-in-law. He would ask me where was I at. Nobody had any idea what I was going through. The man tried to rape me if I said that I was in his house. I had to say that I was in the hotel. I had to lie. An old man came to his house in San Diego on the second day. He looked so much like my dad. That man saved me from the *coyote*. He told the *coyote* that I was his daughter and that he had no reason to make me do the things that he was making me do. That old man was like a guardian angel. Because of him, I'm here. That man brought me all the way here to San Francisco. He made sure I was in the right house, because he had already talked to your grandpa.

I thought it was so ugly here at first. The food, the streets, the people, the houses, everything seemed so ugly. When I got here I lived in the same house that we still live in. I didn't like it because I saw so many stairs up and down. I didn't like anything. I ate a *burrito*, which got me sick. I would cry all day and night. I was sad because I missed my mom. I had no family here, but I know I won't (laughs) go back, because I got used to the life here in the United States. Now I like the city and I enjoy it a lot.

It was hard working here because I had to fill out papers and I didn't know how to. I was shy to tell your dad to do everything for me. I worked in a flower shop, starting at three in the morning until six in the afternoon. I would always get soaked wet. I got paid $4.50, then they raised it to $5.00. I worked there for nine years. I met friends, yes, a lot of people. Once in a while I would get a ride or I would have to get the bus. I was scared to get the bus at three in the morning. Then the schedule changed. We started working at six. So I would leave for work with my mother-in-law. Later I learned how to drive, like eight months later. At first I was scared, but then I got used to it.

I was twenty-one when you were two. We decided to go to Mexico. Your dad drove all the way over there, took us three days. I thought Mexico was ugly. I didn't like anything. The food got me sick, whatever I ate. It was really different at the ranch, lots of things changed. My parents looked so different. All my sisters were teenagers. We planned to stay there for three weeks, but we came back on the second week because [you got] very sick. The doctors couldn't give you anything because we forgot to take the immunization record.

I would never go to live there—just for vacations. All my family is here. My parents live in Los Angeles, so I really have nobody over there. My mom was over there in Mexico with three of my sisters. Two of them are married, and my dad came here to work with Hector her oldest brother. He was working with him for two years until one day something bad happened. Dad got shot by an African-American guy. My dad was watering the flowers and the man told him to give him money. My dad dropped the water hose and put his hand in his pocket, but the guy thought that my dad was going to pull out a knife. He was really going to give him money. He got shot in the stomach and until now he still has it, the bullet in the stomach. We all thought that he was going to die, so we all got together. He said that he wanted all of us to stay together.

Translated from Spanish

NEGATIVE TENSION

Tina Heard Speaking about Nathaniel Heard, Domino, Texas
Interviewed by Robert Rodgers

Tina Heard is a thirty-six-year-old, church-going, loving, caring mother. She has a wonderful, fun personality. Without her, I wouldn't be where I am today. She told me the story of her grandfather, Nathaniel Heard. —R.R.

My grandfather came [to California] because he wanted to make a better life for his family. The opportunities weren't as great in Texas as out west in California. One of the main reasons he moved out here, was that back then there was a lot of racism in Texas. My grandfather went in the store with my dad and his twin brother, my Uncle John, and the Caucasian store clerk said something racist and derogatory to my grandfather. And he responded verbally—and firm—that he should not have been spoken to that way. It really, really disturbed the white community, and they wanted to do something like hang my grandfather, so his relatives had to get him out of Texas. So they got him out, and he came out here to California with some relative who had just came from Texas also. We had relatives out here in San Francisco, so they had some place to stay while they got back on their feet. He worked hard, and in a short time he had sent for my grandmother and my dad and uncle John to come out here. They came by way of train.

You have to remember their train trip took place in the 50s and down South was a lot different than out West. Our people weren't even voting in the South yet. My grandmother told me stories of how it was back then. If it wasn't for God's mercy, grace, and loving kindness, and the closeness and love of family, it would have been, I don't know… I shiver to think. She picked cotton for meager wages as a child. They were still saying, "Yes sir," "No ma'am." African-Americans had a tremendous fear of white people back there then because they treated us so bad. There were hangings and cross burnings. We had to come in through back doors. My grandmother was around nineteen when she and Dad and uncle John took that trip out here. My grandmother says that the train ride was pretty scary because there was a lot of racism down South. They were very open with it, very open with it back then. And she remembered that the KKK was outside the train station, so she took my dad and my uncle into the bathroom and they were just sitting there. She remembered this white lady walking by, saying how cute my dad and my uncle was, you know. She just said, "Thank you ma'am," and they got themselves up here to California.

They had more opportunity [for finding work] out here. They worked really hard, my grandparents, and they bought a house here in San Francisco, in Bernal Heights. The house is still the family house. My uncle John is there and all my children are there often, quite often. They wanted to come and make a better life for their children. They just wanted a better life and they needed for my grandfather to stay alive, so they had to get him from down there. He's visited many times down there since then. He's taken me down there. We hope to take Robert down there this year to Texas. It's a lot different and it'll be a change. The kids will see a whole lot of differences.

My grandparents, your great-grandparents, who you had the pleasure of being able to know, Otherma and Pop, always had a nice time when they visited Texas because there's still a lot of family still there. I know it [the story] seems like a lot of negative tension; however, that's just the way it was told to me. I can't wait to visit Dallas this year, and meet Dad and Uncle John's sister that we just found out about last year. This is going to be amazing.

[Otherma and Pop] were really sticklers on education. My grandfather, Pop, he didn't have more than maybe a fifth-grade education, you know? That was far as he went in school, so they were tough on my parents and on Uncle John. And then, in turn they were tough on us, and that's why I'm tough on you. Because education will take you everywhere. I'm really glad they came to San Francisco so that my dad could have a better life. And not only that, so that years later my dad could meet my mom and have me, and then, years, years, years later, I got to have you. And you are such a wonderful son. You are smart, and you are intelligent, and you are charismatic, and you are wonderful, and I know that you're going to excel. I guess that's it. I can go on and on and on, but the hour is late and I won't. I love you, and I hope you get a wonderful grade on your report.

HE NEVER DID, SO I AM STILL WAITING FOR THE SILK DRESS

Rose Camilli, Guanajuato, Mexico
Interviewed by Aida Guerrero

My grandma is a really loving and caring person. She loves talking and gets along with everyone. I did this interview in the kitchen. —*A.G.*

I am seventy-one. I was born in Guanajuato, Mexico, in 1933 and I had a wonderful childhood. I was always on the ranch, with a lot of animals, and all my grandparents. My toys… they were pieces of wood, rocks—beautiful rocks—and it was like a collection to me. *Mija*, my grandfather used to make dolls for me. He used to put on (touching her face) eyebrows, everything. He used to sew so beautifully. But when I knew I was coming to the United States… well, I didn't want those dolls any more because they said that they had everything here. So I left my dolls behind.

Guanajuato is a beautiful state—beautiful land. They call it "green valley" because everything is green. I used to ride the horses, the donkeys, and I used to milk the cows. I wish my kids would have had that opportunity so they can appreciate everything they have in this country.

Well, you know, my mom used to say (laughs), "When you were born, I paid a chicken." That was what they paid in those days. There was no money so they paid that way, with a chicken or a pig or whatever. I was five years old in Guanajuato. I used to go in the fields with my grandfather and I used to put the seeds in the ground. They call it the *yunta*... I don't know how you say it in English. We would go to work when it was dark and come back home when it was already dark. There'd be times when I got really tired and I would tell my grandpa, "Grandpa, when are we going to go home?" "Oh, when you finish your seeds." "Oh really?" So I would go and walk three or four rounds, make a hole, and I would throw the seeds in there. In three or four days, all the seeds would come up, the corn and the beans, and my grandpa would say "Oh! I think all the rats grabbed all the corn and beans and they put it there." He never complained. He was always happy. He kept saying to me, "Do it right and I am going to buy you a dress, a silk dress!" But he never did, so I am still waiting for the silk dress.

My grandmother used to make I don't know how many pounds of flour tortillas every morning at four o'clock. She used to get up and make them and I used to help her. She stretched the tortillas, [then] rolled the tortillas, and I used to turn them on the *comal*. (Pointing to the stove) How do you call it? On the stove to cook, and I'd turn them. I helped my grandma to wash because in those days the washing machines weren't like they are right now. We might not have a car, we might not have a bank-book but we have a horses, donkeys, cows, pigs, chickens. When the men used to come to the ranch, my grandmother used to exchange eggs, or chickens, for clothing. My grandfather used to plant tomatoes, lettuce, chilies, onions, garlic. So we had everything. We had plenty to eat. We had milk, a lot of milk, but when I came over here, I went to work and my husband and I bought our homes and nice furniture. I had my car, he had his car. It was different and I've been back in Guanajuato for a few months, but I don't know... I like it here in the United States.

My mother used to teach me the letters, ABCs and my name, my last name, all my uncles' names, my grandmother's name, where I was born, and stuff like that. I went to second grade to the fifth grade. When I went to Mexicali, I never went to school because it was too far for me to go.

When I was moving to the U.S. I was excited to see my grandmoth-er, my uncles from my mother's family, but I was really sad because I left my other grandmother in Mexico. She practically raised me, too. That's the thing that I miss because I left them there, but I was coming to live with the other family. I came with the sister of my mother, with my grandma, and I started to work immediately. I came with a permit, and then I stayed. I came with one of my mother's brothers. They all lived in Salinas. All of them worked in the fields. My uncles, my aunts—they worked in the factories so I decided to come to California.

I was 16 years old when I decided to go to Salinas, and I started working in the fields. I worked in the carrots, I worked in the lettuce, in the tomatoes and garlic, and the onions. To me it was beautiful to be in the country doing all those things. For me it's not hard to learn because when I see things I can copy right away and do things. I can cook. I cannot read directions or anything but when I see somebody doing anything I can copy right away so I enjoy doing. I've worked in the factories. I worked in the corporations where they use to do all the tops for the Cokes.

I was working in the fields and I said, "This is not for me." I wanted to go to beauty school. I went one year to beauty school in Salinas and I got my licenses. I never went to school to learn English because I was working daytime and I was always in nighttime in school. Soon as I finished my school I went to work. In my mind since I was five years old I always said, "I am always going to have my own business, I am not going to work for anybody!" So I had a little bit of experience—about six months, eight months—then I took my own business and I worked forty-five years in my own business. I enjoyed every minute.

I worked six months in Emporium and then a lady saw me working there, and she asked, "Why don't you come and work with us in 22nd, 23rd and Mission?" and I did. Then the owner sold the shop a year and a half later, and then I had my own shop. Then I sold that shop, Rose's Beauty Salon, and then I got another shop in 22nd. I had six girls working for me. Different tops, black skirts and it was a beautiful. I don't know, it was like a family. People would just come to see how we were dressed, how our hair was combed, because I used to tell the girls, "Before you start working on the floor, you have to have your make-up and your hair done, because we're selling beauty." And everybody was really, really nice.

I got married and we moved to San Francisco, and then I have three children. My first one died and then I had another two girls. Then I got a divorce. Then I got married again and I had two more children. The second time I was thirty-three years old. Now I've been a widow for sixteen years.

San Francisco was so beautiful in those days. Women would not dress with pants. The women [wore] gloves, with the hat, the coats. Beautiful! We used to dress so beautifully and go dancing Friday, Saturday, and Sunday. We used to go dancing on South Van Ness and Market. We used to go to the Sachieo, we used to go to the Sinaloa. They had a floor show. San Francisco was a beautiful city in those days. You can walk in the dark in the night and no one would bother you. We went to 365 Bimbo's and Columbia. Oh my God it was so beautiful there! They used to have a lady and she was there with just a bikini. She used to be inside a ball, and every hour she used to come in. You should see all the people looking at this beautiful girl in the ball with all the mirrors all around. My husband was a musician. We used to go out a lot; we used to *love* to dance. We used to have a lot of orchestras come from Mexico, big orchestras, not like now. We [would] dress up so nice, high heels, no pants. I never wear pants until your grandfather died. He used to say, "I didn't marry a man, I married a woman."

Sunday I used to go to mass with my children. If we didn't have enough money, then we would do breakfast at home, and if we had money we would go to a restaurant. Or if we had money then we would go to the movies and if we didn't, we came home and listened to the radio.

I would send money to Mexico to help my parents. I was working and since I knew a lot of people over here I had a lot of connections. They helped me fix my relatives' papers. I had a lot of friends that had businesses. So when my father came he had a place to work, my mother, a place to work. My brothers and my sisters, they all had a place to work.

I never had a problem getting a job or doing anything that I wanted to do. I always remember my grandmother saying one time to me, "If you do wrong, you always be doing wrong, so try to be positive in this life and whatever you want, you can have it." Whatever I wanted, I had it. And I think I accomplished a lot in my life. Now I travel. I've been going to Europe every two years. I always took my kids back to Mexico, so they could learn the language, and to know what is Mexico. Because being an American citizen you have an opportunity to vote, to do things for this country. And when you travel, you're really proud to have the American passport. I feel that way. I love living here in San Francisco and I have everything here. Really, I have all my family here. I have cousins and uncles still in Mexico. I go once in a while but here's my home because my kids are here.

Translated from Spanish

ONE OF THE LUCKY ONES

SONIE KHATH, BATTAMBANG, CAMBODIA
INTERVIEWED BY STEVEN KHATH

When I interviewed her, my mom was wearing sweat-pants and a sweater. She was on the couch in the living room under a blanket and looking very tired. —S.K.

I was born in Battambang, Cambodia. I'm the only child. Lifestyle back in Cambodia? Hm, let me see… [I] don't remember much. There's no lifestyle. Pretty much grow up with not enough food, not enough clothes… um, just nothing much.

I was growing up during the communist Khmer Rouge time. Pretty much I didn't get to stay with my parents. They keep me in one of the places… you should call it [a] shelter. They kept a bunch of kids there—like twenty, thirty children there—and they sent both parents separate ways to work [at] different places. You work without getting paid, you just exchange it with food. I don't know if you call it food—basically you just get a bowl of rice porridge, a few beans, and water. And you work day and night. I had to work even though I was just five years old. I had to wake up early in the morning, and they send me to the rice field. Chase the birds, make sure the birds don't eat the rice.

I remember one night I missed my mom so much I sneak out in the middle of the night just to go see her. On the way there, I have to go through the jungles and water, and it was really dark. I thought I could get to see my mom that night, but I got caught by the… I don't know what you call them. Guard, security, one of the Khmer Rouge. I got caught, and they tied both of my arms behind my back. And another girl got caught, too. They tied both of us with [a] long towel; one end tied me and the other end tied the other girl. They also drag me, whipped me with the rope, pushed me into the water, and told me to swim through that dirty water. [They] punish me because I sneaked out, and they said I shouldn't do that.

After that they took me to this very dark place [and] they kept me in there. They lectured me all kind of things I didn't even understand. But you cannot answer, [or] they're going to hit you. And they kept me there for about an hour or so, and somehow my mom knew about it. So she rushed over and looked for me, and she knew I was locked in that room. So she was begging the Khmer Rouge to release me, 'cause I'm just a young little girl, and promised that she will talk to me [and] that I won't do that again. Then they released me, and they kept me in that shelter for a few days.

Somehow my dad got sick, so my mom also requested that I be with my dad for a while during that time. They agreed. A few days later my dad picked me up from that shelter, and I stayed with him in another jungle. He was sick. It was no disease or anything, it's just starvation. I stayed with him for a couple weeks, and he go[t] skinnier and more tired. I remember one morning he woke up. He told me that he was very hungry, and he asked me to go get food. They give food at a certain times. So he told me to go to that place and get some food for him. Anything, 'cause he's really hungry, and he's not feeling good. So I did. I went [and] got a little bowl, and when he told me to hurry up, I went on my way. I ran along and I got some food, but when I came back he [had] passed away already. But I can see he's still breathing a little bit, and his eye still open a little bit. He hasn't completely passed away yet. But the problem is, there's nobody helping him. So [when] I came back [and] saw him, it looked like he was sitting down on the bed, but his head was down on the floor like he's trying to reach for something but couldn't get up because he's tired and hungry. So I tried to pick him up, but I couldn't do it. I was screaming. Yelling to the neighbor to help me pick my dad up. And they did, the neighbors heard. They came and helped me, and then somebody ran to the nearest Khmer Rouge people [to] tell them that my dad was really sick. He need a doctor or something.

I don't know what they said, but [after] about a good twenty minutes or so, a few guys arrived with a long stick that they used to carry him. Just one stick! They tied both his hand [and] legs together and put the stick in the middle and carry him like you carry a pig. And just took him away from me. I don't know where they taken him, but they told me that I can't go with them, just stay here and wait.

Yeah, just stay there and wait. I never seen him again. And they left me in that place for a good two days by myself before someone pick me up and take me to my grandma's in another part of the jungle. They said I can stay with my grandparents for a while, but it wasn't any luck for me. When they send me to my grandparents' house, they're both sick, too— the same problem. I got there just one night [and] my grandmother passed away. A few days later my grandpa passed away. I have one cousin left, about the same age. We don't have anybody else but my mom [who] is still in another place working so hard. But after both of my grandparents passed away, my mom came to pick me up and bring me to stay with her. And wherever she go, I follow her, and from there I was really skinny 'cause not enough food and all that.

When I went with my mom I got better. I gained some weight. No matter what, my mom always tried to feed me, even though we don't have much food. She picked some leaves, boil it, or sometimes in the middle of the night she would just sneak out to steal a chicken for me. The worst part is, when you steal a chicken, even though you ate all the meat, you can't throw the bone outside, 'cause if you get caught, both of you going to get killed. [So] after we ate the chicken, she buried the bones under the place where we sleep. It's not a bed or anything, just a cloth or a blanket or some kind of fabric (pauses). Yeah, that's how I survived. If my mom wouldn't do all of that, I wouldn't make it today.

I wanted to have a better life and an education. I wanted to get out of that horrible place. I knew if I stayed there any longer, nobody would survive. The next one's going to be either me or my mom (pauses). There was a lot of people during that time trying to escape.

We ran, basically, all of us. I think I remember my mom used to say that she put me in a bucket and carry me—one side with some pots and rice and stuff, and on the other side me sitting down in that pot. We went through water, we went through the jungle while the people—I think the Khmer Rouge—are shooting and bombing. A lot of people got killed. I would say more than half of them died. Not many of us survived, but we managed to escape—one of the lucky ones.

[I was] scared. You can hear the bullets and the bombing, and my goodness, everything. You name it. All you hear is gunfire. It's like you're in World War II or something. We tried to cross to the Thai border, the closest place we could make it.

Well, we got into Thailand and they put us in the camps, a small camp with all the refugees. They told us to all stay there and gave us a certain amount of food. Vegetables, rice, some fish and stuff like that—different kinds every week. Not a whole lot, but at least better than the Khmer Rouge time. In that camp I started school. I think I was either eight or nine years old. I don't remember.

I stayed until '83, and then I don't know exactly what happened. One day we had an interview in Thailand, not in the camps. They brought us to one of the cities and we had interviews to go to America. That's when I heard about America. It was a very hard interview. They interviewed me about three times. They gave me a hard time about me and my mom. We had different last names, so they didn't believe that I'm [her] daughter. But [to] us Cambodians that [is] normal. My mom used her father's name as her last name, and I used my father's name as my last name. I had to go back and forth three times for an interview just because of that. They wanted to make sure that we didn't lie and that all of our answers were true. After the interview we waited a good three months or so to get to the answer that everything is clear. They said, "You're ready to go to America." I came by airplane [to] San Francisco, my destination.

When I got to the airport, everybody got out. We claimed our luggage and everything. We had to get on the escalator—that was the scary part for me. I [had] never seen anything like that before. Oh no! My mom didn't know that I was scared of that escalator. She got her bag and was already up there. When she got up the escalator she turned around, looked down and said, "Where's my daughter?" I was all the way down there. I didn't hop on that escalator. I just stood there crying. My mom got so mad. She said, "What are you doing? Why don't you just come up here?" I said, "No, that thing might eat my leg or something. I'm not going to get on that thing. What *is* that thing?" She was kind of mad and laughing at the same time. So she had to come all the way down and hold my hand and drag me up there. Everybody was just looking at me. It was a scary moment for me.

[When] I came here, I stayed with my cousin in a small room, not all that big. I stayed with him for a good year before we found a new place, just [for] me and my mom.

I never saw white people before. Blonde [hair] and blue eyes, oh, that's something very strange to me.

The first time I arrived here, everything is exciting. Everything is just... to me, it's the best. It's everything. It's paradise compared to what I've been through. Everything is different: the culture, the food, lifestyle. Nothing compares. It's one of a kind.

I don't miss anything [back home]. I just remember the horrible things that happened to me. I don't want to remember, but it's always in my head, in the back of my head. It will never go away.

I recommend watch[ing] the movie, "[The] Killing Fields." That's what Pol Pot, [the] Khmer Rouge is all about. They don't really show everything, but most of the things that have happened [are] in there. It's a true story of what we've been through. If you watch the movie, you will understand more about how I survived.

TROUBLEMAKER

PEARLA GUERRO, NICARAGUA
INTERVIEWED BY KEVIN HOLLINS WRIGHT

Pearla is forty-nine years old. She has known me all my life. She has been my mom's best friend since they were in high school. She is Nicaraguan, and she speaks Spanish. She has been through a lot, such as changing countries and changing schools. She seemed very happy when I interviewed her. —K.H.W.

I was born in Nicaragua. There, it is tropical—palm trees, coconuts. It's kind of like Hawaii in my point of view. I really liked it there, and my parents liked it there. It was just great. I really didn't want to leave. I had one sister and one brother. My sister's name was Guadalupe, and my brother's name was Michael. We always hung out and did a lot of things together. We tried to get jobs together, even though we couldn't get jobs. We still went out for jobs for fun. We got in a lot of trouble. We were not the kind of people that took the blame for somebody else. If you got caught, then you were on your own. If one of us did something wrong and didn't confess, then we snitched on them so we wouldn't all get in trouble. [When we got in trouble] we got hit with things. We didn't like that. And we had to do more work than everybody else. We always had to do work. It was boring, but we still had to do it. My mom was hard. You couldn't mess with her without getting a beating. It was like we had to do everyone's chores, and when we whined we also got beaten.

My sister and brother, we wanted an adventure, and we were going to get it one way or another. We never liked staying inside the house. We always went outside to play, getting on peoples nerves. We always got in trouble and we got punished for that. We were considered troublemakers. None of other the kids liked us there because we were making all the boys look at us. Our parents separated me and my brother and sister because we were so bad. We broke everything and when somebody else broke something they would blame it on us. So they split us up in everything— schools, churches, and sometimes people's houses. If we were in school together we would do a lot of damage, and we would get expelled.

My family needed money, so I thought that I could go to California, get an education, get a job, get some money, and come back here to Nicaragua to help my family out. Go back there and teach my family something I picked up in school. My parents didn't get that high of an education, and I really wanted to help them. They thought that I couldn't do it, but I wanted to show everybody that I could, to prove everybody wrong. I liked to prove people wrong and show people that I was the best at everything I did. So I wanted to come here, and get some money and a job, and go back and help my family with their money problems. [My uncle] said that we could move in there anytime we wanted to. So we came here. My plan was to make a living and stay alive. We went to school and we got jobs and we made some money. I wouldn't say it was a lot of money, but money is money.

We went on a sailboat with a lot of other people who were going to California too. We were loud the whole time. We were the loudest ones on the boat. It took a long time.

My uncle lived in San Francisco, California, and when I first got there

I thought that we were going to move right when we got to San Francisco. My uncle is a shoemaker and he makes the good-looking shoes. He don't make ugly shoes; he says it is against his religion. I just didn't want any shoes. I liked my shoes the way they were.

I thought that it was going to be dangerous, and that we were not going to be able to do what we came down here to do. At first I wanted to go back [to Nicaragua], and they were not taking anybody back for a few days.I thought that this place was going to be a bad place to live. Then my uncle showed me the ropes to San Francisco. I got used to it, and it really wasn't that bad. The school was great, and the people that were living here was good. The food was good, the houses were big, and there were a lot of restaurants. I liked that because I love food so much. One of the schools I saw was a school named Balboa High School, and that school looked huge. I thought that was one of the biggest schools in San Francisco.

San Francisco was not what I expected it to be. I expected it to be really bad, people shooting at each other, and people dying every day. But it wasn't like that at all. It was not that bad. So San Francisco is great. The weather is great, too. It's not too hot, and sometimes it's cold, but not most of the time.

We had a lot of fun. We went to the snow for the first time. Then my uncle took me to the mall and I had a lot of fun there. We left my sister and my brother at the house. They didn't feel like doing anything because they thought that the place where my uncle lived was going to be boring. They said that no place was more fun than their own home. So they stayed inside the whole time we were down there in San Francisco. We went shopping and then we met up with some of my uncle's friends, and they had some kids for us to play with. We had a lot fun with those kids. Sometimes they could get annoying, but other than that they were all right.

I was going to school, then I got suspended. I was minding my own business when this bully came out of nowhere and tried to pick on me because I was the new kid. So she pushed me. I wasn't any punk, so I pushed her back. She hit me in my arm, then I hit her in the mouth. And she fell to the ground and started crying like a baby. Then everybody thought that I was the bully, all because I made the bully cry. I got in trouble then, that's when I was called a troublemaker. I finished out the rest of the school year as a troublemaker. Nobody picked on me after that day I beat up the bully.

I'M A LUCKY ONE, THANK GOD FOR THAT

ALFRED HUNKIN, LEONE, AMERICAN SAMOA
INTERVIEWED BY ANGELIQUE UGAITAFA

My uncle is seventy-four years old. He is very easy-going and fun to be with. He was very cooperative during the interview. —A.U.

Samoa is contained in ten little islands. The largest one of American Samoa is Tutuila. The second one is Manua. Ofu, Olosega… lots of them.

In Samoa they have plantations: taro, coconuts… that's the most favorite food in Samoa. Very important food, taros. Cobra from the coconut, it takes a lot of work [to make]. It's the thing [flesh] in the coconut. You got to cook the coconut and dry it and, when it's dry, they take it to the store and measure how heavy it is, and then you got your money, maybe two dollars or three dollars a pound. That's another way for Samoan to get money, that Cobra.

Samoa is now changed. So all the things they have in Samoa are just like in here. Everything's the same. But there's not much work over there, so that's why I came from Samoa.

When I was there, I was a student. Samoans, they eat good, drink good. If you're working hard in your plantation, you're the rich one. You sell, got money, eat good every day. You go fishing. But they don't have much people working, the pay is too low, the education not so good.

We have our high school, our first high school, in the year 1946, with a lot of students over fifty-years-old, forty, thirty, not like here. Kids in the high school are fifteen, sixteen, graduating at seventeen, eighteen. They look for another step, go to university or look for a job. Some families, they send the people to here, and some of the people, they stow away on

the steam ships that came to Samoa to bring the merchandise and everything like that.

So we appreciate our life, we like it here. You need a job to have
money, to feed the family, put food on the table. In 1952, the Navy drafted Samoan men. They were called *Fita Fita*. So they send a ship over there
to bring all their dependents. So that is how I got a chance to come,
because my uncle just retired from the Navy after thirty years and came
over there as a postmaster of American Samoa. He's the highest man in
the post office. So he asked me if I wanted to come. I say I wanted to
come, so I came, called his brother over there in Hawaii to wait for me [at
the airport].

So I went out there and I was very happy and my uncle was waiting
down the ramp to receive me. He paid [for] the apartment for me, and he
paid his own apartment. I got a job he set up for me working at the gas
station after school [McKinley High School]. But all of that I still don't
want. I wanted to join the armed forces of the United States, so after
about a week, I went to the Marine Corps recruiting and took the test.
So about a couple weeks later I received a letter from a Navy shipyard
down in Pearl Harbor, and my uncle read it to me, "This is your letter
from the Marine Corps. You going to join the Marine Corps? I told you
go to school." He wanted me to go school, but I told him to please understand. So I joined the Marine Corps for four years, and got out in 1956,
and went back to Hawaii.

I was a driver for the Com-Section, you know, the radio receiving.
I receive the notice that I was going to Japan. Well, I went to Japan in
1963, and I stayed there about two or three years. That was the time of
the Korean conflict. We [were] stationed in Japan waiting for [the call for
their group to go to war]. We had three divisions in the United States
Marines: First, Second, and Third. I was in the First Battalion, Third
Marine. But we were lucky. Before we went in [to battle] the war was
over. I'm a lucky one. I thank God for that.

The reason why I came [to America] from Hawaii in twelve hours
was that the plane was too slow, not like the jets. The jets started, I didn't
know, maybe 1968 or 1970, the first jets running between Hawaii and the
United States. But at that time, those planes had a propeller. It's very slow
man, very very slow. It was a long, long trip. I sat with a lady, she says she
was going to Iowa, so we talked, talked until the plane stop.

Samoa is very different, very, very different from the United States. The people of Samoa you almost know from one corner to the other; it's not a big place. On the island where I came from, all the people are social. Samoa is just like Puerto Rico, they are two territories of the United States. That's why we are free to come here to the United States without passports. But not from Western Samoa, because Western Samoa is under their own government.

I WAS SURPRISED TO SEE A LOT OF FILIPINOS WORKING AT THE AIRPORT

Shiobee Ann Refol, Visayas, Philippines
Interviewed by Amy Paningbatan

Shiobee Ann is my sister-in-law. She is so nice that everyone wants to be her friend, and she is so smart that everyone wants to be like her.   —A.P.

My name is Shiobee Ann. I'm twenty-six years old. I was born and raised in the Philippines, Visayas, a province of Aklan. I didn't have to make the decision but it was up to my parents, because we were petitioned by my auntie. It was actually my dream to come here to the United States because of the opportunities, you know, it is a great place. Oh I miss some of my friends and a lot of relatives, and all the memories of college years. College years were the best part of my life because I made a lot of friends, like popularities at my school.

I think more about my friends. All I remember is that my parents spent a lot of money just to immigrate to the United States. Actually it was a pretty good journey. I was excited during that time. The only transportation we used coming to the U.S. was a plane. It was December 15, 2001. I was about to turn twenty-one years old. I was with my mom, my dad, and my two sisters. I was actually surprised, when we stepped out of the plane, because we were greeted by [a Filipino]. I thought here in the United States we would be greeted by a Caucasian, you know? I was surprised to see a lot of Filipinos working in the airport. I was in culture shock.

We also had conflicts with my dad, my family, and my aunt who petitioned for us. So there was a mixture of a lot of things going on during that time. We really thought about going back to the Philippines. We were actually expecting my aunt to be at the airport, but she wasn't there. We were looking for her and consider the fact that, you know, coming from the different place, we knew nothing about this place. We were looking for her. Luckily my grandfather my mother's father was there, waiting for us. He helped us get a taxi and he helped us to go the apartment where Auntie lives. When we came to the apartment my aunt wasn't actually there. She was actually in Reno. We didn't know what she was doing there, just like we're not welcome. My dad was like, "Oh my gosh!" My dad was really angry. Imagine her just leaving us alone to take care of ourselves. We were like, "Oh," you know? What if we only have money for today? We would've went back to the Philippines. It was really a sad experience and I'll never forget that.

I wasn't supposed to stay in the United States for long. I was planning to go back to the Philippines because I have to continue my studies there. I was in college, taking occupational therapy, and I was about to graduate the year after. Unfortunately, we had difficulties, like financial stuff, so my parents weren't able to allow me to go back there. I'm doing good now, but if I went back, then I could finish my bachelor degree there and take the board here in the United States, and work here as an occupation therapist like my friends and classmates.

I worked in a department store. You know where Howard Street is? In Burlington Coat Factory, I was working as a cashier at first, and they promoted me to be auditor, and after that the store manager promoted me to become customer service manager. At first I really had to work, because we were trying to pay back the money for the plane fare and we really have to work our tails off to pay. After a year I decided to go back to school and I tried to enroll at City College in San Francisco, actually planning to take nursing courses. Actually [now I'm] working full-time as a nurse and studying full-time.

There is much more freedom here than there. I guess I had everything there, except for a car actually. My life here is harder than my life over there. We had maids that would do, you know, house chores, do the cleaning, do the laundry, and other stuff, but here you do everything. I'm actually married now so happy. I have a daughter. She is twenty-one months old and she is pretty like me, hahaha. I'm just kidding, but she is really beautiful. Let's just say she is cute. Her name is Shelly Shaine. Right now I'm thinking of just finishing my school and work as a nurse.

You didn't ask me about my love life! Jose P. was my first boyfriend. I was scared. I'm actually a Filipina-type girl who is shy and not talkative. Simple, it's just, you know, I feel awkward if some one sees me [with him], like, of course my classmate, or any person who sees me, who knows me. You know, [if you] go out with a guy, they would think or say something. Jose P. is sarcastic and a happy person. We worked in the same store. Actually, I didn't like him at all. I didn't like him at first because I'm kind of a person who sets higher standards. I wanted an intelligent, smart guy you know? Sorry, he's dumb.

Okay, my first date. Actually I was, at that time, I was really shy to go out with him. He asked me to go out with him. Yeah, I think he said, "Can we eat dinner together?" he asks me, you know? Uh-huh, I told him, "okay," but I have to bring my friend with me. So I bring my best friend with me that time on our first date. Her name is Armida. I brought her because, I don't know, I wasn't used to going out with guys. Um, I was actually just not comfortable at that time going out with guys, and I think we went and see the movies.

I can't even believe I have a baby! I married Jose P. Already it was really hard for me. I had a difficult pregnancy. It was really hard, yes. I had a complicated pregnancy, some diabetes. She was just brought out early, premature. She can say "apple" and "Barney's," and she can even operate the computer, the DVD, and VHS. She can eat by herself. She knows how to handle the spoon, and she knows how to do all that stuff.

Parts of this interview translated from Tagalog

WHAT IS IT LIKE BEING
FROM TWO DIFFERENT STATES?

ARLENE M., MANHATTAN, NEW YORK
INTERVIEWED BY DEVIN MELVIN

Arlene is a very funny person and even when she's in a bad mood, she still gives a good impression, so you'll think that she's happy. She is also a great supervisor and she's always there when you need her. —D.M.

I was born the year 1981, in Manhattan, New York. It was cool. It was rough but it was cool. I had a good childhood. I had both Mom and Dad, yeah, like most anybody else—I assume. I mean, the area we lived in was rough, like when it comes to people robbing each other, and there was tons of jacking, so my parents was always worried about us. They were always like not letting us go out and stuff, because it was so crazy. It was actually my grandma and my mom, they had got robbed, and it was just crazy. Like when they got robbed they just realized that it wasn't good to raise two young girls there, so they just moved.

My dad didn't want to raise us there 'cause it was so bad. He got offered a job out here, actually, by his friend. His friend had quit his job and said they were looking for a hotel manager, which is what my dad is right now, and so we moved over here to California. Oh, we (laughs) hopped on a plane. It was the first time we ever rode a plane in our life, but yeah we hopped on a plane. I thought it was the coolest thing in the world 'cause it was the first time I've ever rode a plane, so yeah, most everybody was scared. We were all saying our Hail Marys and stuff (giggles).

I don't think we left anything important behind. I used to live in Palestine. I only visited Palestine once, about last year. I visited for the first time and it's crazy, like checkpoints, soldiers, gunfire in the middle of the night. It was occupied territory that we were staying in. Yeah, like if you want to be in Palestine out at night, it's not going to happen. Like out here, anybody can just go out at night and nothing's going to happen to you but over there it's like you'll be stopped by soldiers, 'cause soldiers will stop the Palestinians and question them. Like, what are you doing out so late at night, you know? Are you causing trouble, you know? They will check under your car. They will put mirrors under your car to check for bombs and all of that, to see if you're a terrorist. Most of Palestine, most of them are medium-skin Palestinians but otherwise—no, I mean you see tourists walking around—but otherwise people that live there, there isn't any black people out there. There's black Palestinians; they're really dark.

I traveled with my mom, my dad, my sister, my grandma, and my pet goldfish, who committed suicide on the way over here. (Sad voice) I'll never forget that goldfish (giggles). Basically [my dad] needed a job, so he came out here to California. I mean it's pretty much all around not safe to raise kids [in New York] 'cause it's rough. Plus, my dad couldn't get a job there anyway. So those are basically the two biggest reasons that we moved out here. I had my cousins who live in Los Angeles and we lived with them for like a few months.

I was born in New York, but when I came out to California I was eleven, ten or eleven, something like that. While there's black people in New York, I didn't really see a lot of black people until I was like ten or eleven. I only heard about 'em. I had this kid who was half-black, half-white in my class, but never really seen a black person, like full black, until I was like ten or eleven. No, I think I might have seen one or two, but they were not older, they were younger kids, like they wasn't our age, so we didn't really talk to them.

I thought [California] was going to be rough, rougher than New York. I think it's just more diverse out here, which is nice. You can actually talk to people of different races.

We found a place where my dad managed. He managed a hotel. They needed a live-in manager. He lived there and worked there at the same time. So as soon as my dad had the job, he found a place. It kind of just fell into place. My dad needed a job out here and there was one open for him. Like, here's a job, and my dad was like, "Oh, we might as well go out there."

I was about thirteen when I had my first job working under the table, at a little take-out place on Market Street. It's closed down now. It was cool 'cause they just gave you money when you left, they gave you what, twenty-five dollars a day. Back then it was 1995 or '93, something like that, and back then twenty-five dollars went a long way compared to now, where you can't buy nothing with twenty-five dollars. Like, you can't even buy a jacket.

I had two parents, which is the thing that probably nobody had, and it made everything a lot smoother. When you have two parents you have a mom and a dad as a role model. We were poor as hell, but we had a mom and a dad too, you know what I mean. Whenever times got rough, we were hella poor, but a mom and a dad makes you rich. And that's rich in love and rich in affection, you know what I mean? Well, in our culture—we're Arabian, we're Palestinians—our parents don't believe in putting your children with baby sitters because you just don't do that. You want the love of the child to go to the mom and the dad. You don't want the child to pour his or her love inside a stranger. My mom would always take care of me and my sister, so we would be in the house all the time with Mom. That's why we was kind of poor.

My second job was at Jamba Juice. I worked as a person... what is it called, like, a *barista*—a regular person there. Then I moved up to supervisor there. Yeah, Jamba Juice. That was my first time actually being a supervisor. I liked it a lot because it was a position of power, like you're not being told what to do. You're actually helping other people do their job, you know, by showing other people what to do. So I kind of like that because it gave me a sense of leadership, a sense of responsibility. Instead of being just part of the crowd, I kind of ran the show. So that was better.

I had a lot of jobs. I was always about work. Right now I am the Youth Coordinator and Associate Editor at the *Beat Within*, the place where you work too. And we go to juvenile halls all over the Bay Area. We talk to kids and they talk to us. And then we help them write a piece, or they write. And then we take the writing back to the office, we type it, and then we edit it—take out the gang stuff. We take out the stuff that will incriminate them, and then we put it in a weekly publication.

When I first started I was an intern like yourself. It was right after September 11 took place, and I needed a job real fast. What's crazy is my best friend Manen, the Asian dude who does the layout, he hooked me up with a job. And I did what you guys did, except I was more of the boss' assistant. Dave [the boss] was the one who started this up. One day he was like, "You want a full-time position?" And I was like, "Hell yeah, I do." Then I became the youth coordinator over here. Yeah, I love being a supervisor. It's always fun to do that.

I was always a good worker. My family said I always knew how to work. I never thought I would go to college. That's something I never thought I would do 'cause I always thought I wasn't smart enough or something, you know what I mean? Or I always thought I would work just like my parents had worked. I'm the first generation to graduate from high school in my family. I'm the first generation to have a college degree, so I'm really proud of myself. My mom is really proud.

I went to City College for two and a half years, and S.F. State for about two and a half years. I majored in Criminal Justice and Administration of Justice 'cause I always wanted to be a Probation Officer. That's what I really wanted to do, but this job fell into place—and yeah, I liked it more. I don't want to be a Probation Officer no more. I just know I want to work with youth that are struggling. When I was a youth I had somebody help me, so I really want to give that back to other youth in the world, like other places out there. That's what I'm doing right now, helping the community. You know they say those who've been there and done that give back. And that's what I want to do, give back to the community. I love kids, I'm telling you, I love kids. I mean, youth at least. I like working with teenagers and I hope they like me (laughs).

I got a bunch of goals that I recently accomplished, like I graduated from college, and getting a job that I like, and getting my own place and stuff. Now that I have all these goals, I'm kind of like stuck, like, what am I going to do now? I really want to get a better paying job so I can save money, so that I can maybe one day, instead of rent, maybe own a home, you know? I just hope I can be there for my family. I mean, I am there for my family right now, but I just want to be able to be there from now till the end.

IT'S HARD ENOUGH TO LIVE IN AMERICA
WITHOUT HAVING TO MISS YOUR CHILD

ZARINA SANTA MARIA, BUANG LA UNION, PHILIPPINES
INTERVIEWED BY KRISTOPHER CASILLA

My cousin is a quiet person, but when words come out of
her mouth you want to listen. My interview took place in
my bedroom. —K.C.

Since I was a child, I knew that I was coming here to America because of my grandmother, my father, and mother. And that's why we came here to San Francisco.

The Philippines is a beautiful country. There are beautiful places. And I love the Philippines because I was born there. Being one big family is happy because there we can talk about [so many] things. We can tell them secrets. We can have fun, we can laugh like that, and we can help one another. I have three brothers and two sisters. My two older brothers live back at home. Because my older brothers and sisters were over age, they could not come with us. My younger brother, my sister, and I arrived here in San Francisco, California.

It first started with grandma Gean, she came here as a tourist. Back then it was hard, because tourists like grandma Gean didn't like to go back home. Grandma Gean then went back home to the Philippines so that she could petition for grandma Rose, your mom, uncle Joven, auntie Myrna, and all of them to come to America. Then grandma Rose petitioned for us to come here. The process took eighteen years. It took long 'cause we have to start from when we were young. Our information was ready, we just wait for the interview and the examination. My sister, who is the oldest one, helped me with the papers. But with money, no. My sister tried to take our money, but I tell her no 'cause the money belongs to us. Our visa was the last thing.

The first thing I did when I stepped on the plane was say a prayer. When I was in the Philippines I heard that America was like El Dorado. The first time I came here I saw what America was like. I can't explain. It's hard here because we have to start again, and I don't like it here. I want to go back someday....

Before, I used to work in the Philippines. I didn't interview, I'd just go to work because somebody got me in there. But here they interview you on the spot. One time I go into the interview and they say they're going to call you but they don't call you. It's hard to get a job. If you have no connections you cannot get a job. But I work. I get paid very little. One hour is ten dollars. I have only twenty-four hours a week. That's why I'm looking for another job. The job is I.H.S.S. provider, in-home supported service, for helping elders. They call me a "companionship and personal care giver." Over here you have to pay for a lot of stuff, and over there you only pay for the land. It's like taxes, but you have to pay the house. You don't pay electricity and water, but we mostly use the well.

I plan to continue my nursing. At first I had two things on my mind. One was hotel management, and the second one was nursing. This was during college. When you have friends that go to the same school with you it's hard, 'cause you always want to be with them. So I decided to go with them and take nursing. My mom told me to take what I wanted, so I did. But I didn't get to finish. I'll continue if I get money. I have two years. I might take medical assistant first, then take two years nursing.

Before, I was scared to go outside because I heard that a lot of people were bad outside, that they were going to jump you or hit you. That is why I don't like to go out without company. It's hard to live here, even though I am lucky to come here. I'm lucky, but I have to work hard for the money, food, and clothes. I want to go back, but I need to stay here because I have a child back in the Philippines. She's only three years old. My greatest importance coming here was for my daughter. I needed a job so that I can work for my husband and daughter at home. My husband works, but he doesn't get paid a lot of money, and every day he takes care of our child. It's hard [enough] to live in America without having to miss your child. I want to go back just to see them again. I don't like it here, but I'm doing something good for my daughter so that she can better herself when she gets here. I want them to come here because I want them to see what I see, and I want to give my daughter what I could never have. As soon as I get a good job, and money, I plan to bring them to America.

Definitely money is crucial when coming here to America, because you can't take the plane here, you can't process your papers, without money. It took us eighteen years to come here, and only three of us got this far. If you have no money, you can't come here.

AVOID THE CROSSFIRE

Hoa Huynh, Dilinh, Southern Vietnam
Interviewed by Jeffrey Huynh

My dad is fifty-five years old, and he's full Chinese. He's been through a whole lot, and he seemed quite sad as I interviewed him about the war. —J.H.

My full name's Hoa Huynh. I was born and raised in a small town [Dilinh] in southern part of Vietnam. The population was about twenty thousand something. Mainly, the small town was only for planting coffee and tea and some small crops. It was a very peaceful town when I was a young boy living there. The weather's good, almost like San Francisco—foggy. People are very honest and work hard. The school had only about hundred kids. In elementary school, we learn general education: art, math, and also we have some English. By middle school and high school we have about ten hours of English in one week, and twenty hours of math and science. Every day we have a very good, very peaceful life, even though at that time the Vietnam War is still going on—but mainly in the jungle and border area. That town was mostly Vietnamese, some Chinese, and some minority people.

The year I was born is the year the country divided into North and South. The North was communist-controlled, and the South still enjoyed freedom and democracy. But the war never stop since the country divided. The war only moved to the jungle side. But, year after year, the war escalated. The North side getting stronger and stronger, getting help from the communist bloc. And the South kept defending. The war was escalating and getting closer and closer to the urban area. At one point, the enemy attacked my town, and we needed to get into the underground shelter to avoid the crossfire.

By the end of my high school year, the war became serious, and a lot of young men got drafted into the army. I was lucky, I stayed out of the army, but I joined the local force. All over the country, the war was getting worse and worse. Some of my friends already lost their lives on the field. Finally, in 1975, the North army take over the whole country. And because the North is communist, they bring in communism to apply on the South, for every small town, small village, to the big city. They send whoever is working for the South government to the education camp. The North army applied communism everywhere and to everybody. They took over all the personal property, like businesses, or farmland. Except the house you're living in, there's no personal property, and life became harder and harder, and no more freedom. In 1975, I was twenty-four or twenty-five years old, the war ended.

Even in the war-time, we still had some personal property. We could enjoy freedom. We had enough food to eat. When the whole southern part collapsed, the whole country collapsed. Not enough food to eat, no more freedom. You can't even have three or four friends talk and stay together. The government would be suspicious you are saying something to oppose them. But because we already enjoyed freedom, I really could not blend in with the communist country. So I planned to escape. That's the right term, "escape."

I am one of twelve brothers and sisters. Our family is made up of three boys and nine girls. After the war ended, we were living under a tough communist government for three years. Most people, especially Chinese, decided to escape the country by any means. By boat was faster and safer than going on land. My family decided to send me and my younger brother and younger sister together to leave the country. Of course we don't want to risk having the whole family to go on the same boat. On the open sea, a small boat filled with hundreds of people is very dangerous. Also, the boat is not built for ocean.

When we escape, we don't carry any money at all. When we were living under the communists, they took over our property, so we can hardly get living. We put all our savings to buy gold, to get a seat on the boat. That's only a small boat for river cargo. Normally the boat can carry only ten to twenty. But we put 150 to 200 people on the boat. It is way overloaded. When the boat gets in the ocean, you don't know what will happen. Sometimes there's shooting from the government's navy. If you put the whole family to escape together and the boat sinks, the whole family is gone. That's why we separate to let somebody go first. If successful, the family can wait for a second chance or get sponsored.

The rest of the family stayed in Vietnam, living in the same town. I took my younger brother and younger sister. We go to the seaside and join the people there, escape on the boat. By four o'clock in the morning, we quietly board the bigger boat. It took us five days and five nights from the southern part of Vietnam to cross the ocean into Malaysia. We end up on a small island, and that's the refugee camp [that] the United Nation set up. The island is very small and green and bushy.

They put us on that island to wait for a third country to accept us. The [number of] people escaping from Vietnam keeps increasing, and they end up on that small island. At one point, the population in the camp reach 60,000 and the condition is very, very bad. We don't have enough water to drink, we have no food, and we have no shelter. Because that island is about thirty miles off shore, there are weather conditions preventing the supply coming in steadily. So a lot of young people— babies—cannot survive. Finally, after eleven months, the U.S. government sent a delegation there to interview us, and I was the lucky one who got picked to [go to] America. When we escaped from Vietnam, our minds were blank. We just want to get out of that horrible country. When we get to the camps, we were hoping to go to a freedom country, but we cannot choose the country we want. Some refugees end up in Europe, some in Australia, some in Canada. But for me, it's lucky I got chosen by the U.S. I was very excited when I learned I can come to the U.S., and especially California.

When I escaped I only took my younger brother and a young sister. My mom, two elder sisters, and four younger sisters still stay in Vietnam. At first I miss the peaceful countryside living, and all the business, the property from my family and all my friends, and of course my relatives left behind. I don't have anything to bring with me on that journey. We spent all our belongings to get on the boat. Then, in the camp, we don't have any money to spend. So I only have two pair of jeans and a couple T-shirts. That's it, that's all I have.

[I first step foot on California soil] around January, 1980. I don't know anybody in the U.S. when I got accepted by U.S. government to come to California. So when we arrive at California, the church and some agency from the government help us to get a place to live. We're coming to a brand new country. It's totally different from home. The culture, the lan-guage, they're all different. We had a lot of things to learn.

In the homeland, that's a small town where people not that open. Also there's wars going on. Coming to California, especially San Francisco, we see it's very peaceful and the city is very mellow. People over here are more friendly. Maybe because they live in a peaceful environment. They are very kind. They are almost ready to help you when you need it. We can enjoy a new life here with freedom and new opportunities, and it may be extended to the next, next generation. Life becomes easier and easier. Back home I was already learning some English in my school. We still cannot communicate with the local people here. We only can read. It become really hard to talk to people on the street.

When we first come to this country, we don't have a job and we don't have income. We live in a very basic, very minimal level. I keep moving from apartment to apartment, just because the rent is getting cheaper and cheaper. We are lucky coming to this country as a refugee. The U.S. government gave us a very big assistance, like supporting the daily food, giving us some money to spend, and paying some part of the rent. Language is very necessary to start new life. I went to adult school to learn English, to learn how to speak, how to listen, how to understand. I spent six months in that language class. But the future is a job, so I cannot just learn the language. I need to get some skills.

I went to a training class for basic electronics. After that, I move to an academy to get better training in electronics. I spent one and a half years learning the whole course, and got my associate's degree in electronics. The school helped us to find jobs in electronics companies. My life became easier. I could buy my own car and start saving to get a house.

[Me and my wife] met in the company. We worked together. One year later we get married. We started a new life, with two boys now. Also we bought a house. Then life becomes much more enjoyable.

Two years after I settled down in San Francisco, the U.N. and the whole world keep pressuring the Vietnamese government to stop people escaping by boat. They started letting the relatives living outside to sponsor, and get the relatives and whoever was left behind to come and reunite with the people already settled. In 1980, I filed a petition to sponsor my mother, my sisters, and my brothers for a family reunion—to come join me in San Francisco. It was approved by the U.S. government. The rest of the family members came to the U.S. by air. I already had a job, and now my family members could come over and I can at least support them a little.

FROM PHYSICS CLASS TO McDONALD'S

CAN PEI ZHANG, CHINA
INTERVIEWED BY YUE HUAN ZHANG

This interview was held at my house. The interviewee was my uncle. He was wearing white pants and a gray shirt. He felt that this assignment was interesting. —Y.H.Z.

When I was young, I studied in primary school. I remember one of my physics teachers. One day, when he was talking about technology, he also talked about technology in other countries. I remember he said that technology in Japan and America was advanced, but in my home country, China, it was still the same, not improving. He suggested we learn more about things in other countries. He had just finished talking; then students got together and hit him. We weren't allowed to talk about the things in foreign countries, especially at school. People from China were not ready to accept things from foreign countries. They were patriotic and believed that their country was the best. They didn't have enough education—it was limited.

I was in the army when I was eighteen. If I had talked about this at that time, I would have had no chance to be in the army. Becoming a member of the army was my dream.

At that time, to be in the army was lots of people's dream. I was so lucky I passed the physical check. It's not easy to be an army soldier. I felt proud of myself when I was allowed to join the army family. I joined the army family in Guang Xi. Interestingly, because education was not enough, some of the people didn't know how to write letters. They always asked me to help them. They would say something, and I wrote it down. It felt good to help them. After I finished the training, I became a headmaster of a primary school because I had studied until ninth grade. At that time, it wasn't easy to study for such a long time. They considered my record of formal schooling and chose me to do this job. I was twenty-one years old. I worked in my village, Shan Sha. If students didn't pass the test or received a low grade, their parents would buy me things such as tobacco or ask me to have a big dinner. They would also ask me to let their children keep on studying.

These things always happen in China, especially today. If I hadn't come to America, maybe my life wouldn't be bad, because I was a head-master. But I chose to come here and now I have a good life anyway. I believe that if you are hard-working, you can have a good chance no matter where you go.

People who worked in China at that time went to work, but in fact, they did nothing. You just needed to let people know you had arrived there, even if you were late or did nothing. You could earn the same money as the people who were hard-working. You could read the news-paper, have a cup of tea, even sleep. The country was backward. In China, by 1985, people began to accept the ways of foreign countries. Also, they were interested enough to hope to go abroad, to have a look.

The Chinese wanted to go to America because gold was found in America. They believed that San Francisco was Gold Mountain—they thought there must be a lot of gold, and it was as big as a mountain. This was the reason they wanted to come here. They thought that I must be rich if I went to America. They never considered that the gold belonged to America, and I was just an immigrant and had nothing. I heard some-body say that the life in America was free, and it would be easy to earn money. Because we couldn't talk about the things of foreign countries when I was young, America was unfamiliar to me. I didn't know anything of America before I came here.

I came to America on January 26, 1985. At that time, I was thirty-five years old. The reason I came here was because my wife's family was here, and we wanted to bring the family together and take care of my wife's parents. I think it was a good chance for me to experience a new life and let my children have a good education. Also, I wanted to earn more money so that I could afford things here and enjoy my life when I went back to China.

The first job I found in America was working in a restaurant, and then I found another job working in a factory. So I had two jobs from 7:00 AM to 11:00 PM. I kept on working like this for eight years, and I had no time to take care of my children. Maybe they felt lonely at that time. Today I own a moving company.

We have a festival in China just like Christmas. It's Chinese New Year. Before the New Year, people are busy preparing for it. They will go to the flower market to buy some flowers and a tree called *Daji*, just like the Christmas tree here. After fifteen days, they will pick the fruit from the

Daji tree and cook it. It tastes delicious. Also, people will go to their cousin's houses and say something good to them during New Year's. They will give children lucky money—including the people that haven't gotten married yet. They will have a big dinner together, and eat something sweet. In the evening, children will go outside and light fireworks with their friends. It looks beautiful at night. During New Year's, people wear new clothes and join the movement outside. It's exciting. America is different. Few people go outside at night. It's quiet.

Chinese food is my favorite, but I also like American food sometimes. It tastes good. I like to taste new food. Eating the same thing for a long time is boring. When I tasted McDonald's for the first time, I loved it and it tasted fresh.

I have lived here for twenty years. Now I am fifty-five years old. My children both got married and have their own children now. I no longer worry about my life. Once, I told myself, if I can earn thirty thousand dollars, I will leave and go back to my country and not come back to America again. But I consider my life full of happiness now, and I can't leave. I think I'm still a Chinese immigrant. I just moved here and live here. I feel proud of myself because I'm a Chinese and I love my country. Several years ago, a book author interviewed me and wrote my story in her book. That book was called *The Way to San Francisco*. It covered the stories of Chinese immigrants.

I've worked so hard for such a long time, and I think it's time for me to have a breath now! My brother and sister have both moved here and we get together. They also have a peaceful life. As for the future, I plan to have a tour to other countries and enjoy my life.

Translated from Cantonese

STIR-FRIED PUMPKIN

BONNIE TONG, VIETNAM
INTERVIEWED BY DARRYL KENDRIX PENG

This average-looking woman on the bus is no ordinary person. The things she's been through are highly commendable. She may not be the wealthiest, strongest, or even the happiest person in the world, but she's one who kept fighting. —D.K.P.

I lived in Southern Vietnam. That's why we had to leave, after the war was won by North Vietnam. It became one big communist country, and my dad didn't [want] his children raised in such a place.

I didn't have too many emotions [when I first came to the U.S.] because I was very young then. But the culture is a lot different. I remember I did very well in school in Vietnam, but when I came here to the United States, because of the language barrier, I kind of struggled through in the beginning, because like I said, I was still young. But it's easier to adapt when you're young. In the beginning I struggled, but then maybe about a year or two later I started meeting new friends and kind of started my life here. It went fine from then on.

We came here in two groups, you know. I came with my grandma, my nanny, and my three other sisters. The other group was with my mom, my dad, and my two younger sisters, and [I think] they came by boat, too—to Indonesia first and then to America.

My dad found a job, like, on the second day after he arrived in America. He's [a] grocery helper. I mean he works within the grocery store to stock up fruits and vegetables. He found that job in Chinatown.

My parents had this contact in Hong Kong. They had this relative in Hong Kong, who they kept in contact with us, and he would write to our relatives really often to see where we are and how we are. And occasionally we talk on the phone too. I don't know if it's illegal, 'cause we came out of the country without permission. I mean we were refugees. We were just running away from our country, so I don't know, [but] maybe it's not legal. My parents thought that we would be better off at a different country because Vietnam was turning into a communist place.

I've been living here for twenty-something years, so I'd like to stay in the city. I love the city and, you know, I went to Vietnam to visit once, and I don't think I would like to stay there.

My dad and my mom rented this place on Pacific Street. There were three rooms in this place and ten people lived there, I believe. Yeah, ten people just crammed in that place.

I remember sharing a room with my five sisters and my nanny, so there were seven of us living in one room. My parents got one room, and my grandma got one room.

I don't remember how long it took me to speak fluent English. I guess in middle [school]. I remember even when I was in Spring Valley and Marina Middle School I met a lot of Chinese friends, so we spoke Chinese most of the time. Of course in class there they taught in English, so I was semi-fluent then still, but I guess there's more to practice. The more practice you do then the better you are with it. So maybe like middle school I became pretty fluent. In the beginning there was freedom, but later on because of the Vietnam War, Vietnam became one country and it became a communist country. So we had to run and find a better place to live.

The main things [differences] that I noticed were freedom, and the money value was pretty different. The cost of living is so high in America, versus Vietnam, [where] everything is pretty cheap.

I think I bonded with my three other sisters. We were very close because we practically grew up with each other. The other two younger ones came with my parents. For a few years we were apart, so I felt that I'm not as close to them as I am with the other three.

I was scared because when we were on the boat—it was a really small boat, and there were maybe 300 people on there—there wasn't a lot of space to sleep. I remember sitting up all the time, and I just felt tired and exhausted. I didn't know where we were going or if I would ever see my parents again.

I remember there was this guy that we used to play with [on the boat]. He was maybe five years older than I am. I still remember his name, but I don't know where he is now. I don't remember his face or what he looked like anymore. I just remember we played together. I would like to meet up with him today and see how he's doing.

On the way over to the U.S., I didn't get sick, but my oldest sister did. She got really sick. She needed to be sent off to the hospital. She stayed there for maybe a week. Then she got sent back to us.

All I remember was taking the boat and that it was really crowded. It was a long trip and we saw our parents at the airport. [I was] so happy to see them, but that was it. I mean that was all I remember about the trip here. On the boat we had fried chow mein, but it's not really good because you know there's so many people, so they had to cook it in big batches. It wasn't that tasty. I remember when we were in China we had these food coupons that we could exchange for our meals. Every night we had the same lunch and dinner, stir-fried pumpkin. I don't remember if there was any meat in there, but I do remember that it was stir-fried pumpkin. I don't remember eating any meat, no. I mean we were okay, I guess. At least we weren't starving. I was chubbier than I am now, so I think we were okay. We had food to eat, but it's just not a variety of them because we just keep on eating the same thing over and over again.

I probably [would have gotten] married early because that's the culture in Vietnam. The girls get married a lot younger than people here. I probably [would have gotten] married and had kids even like, you know, have my own little family. It's like I said, there's so much freedom in this country, and that's one thing that I really like here. I mean we get to say what we want, and you don't have to hide about it, you know? So this is a better place for me.

Now the U.S. is more welcoming to anyone who wants to come in because the U.S. is already so diverse, and everyone is willing to accept one another as human beings.

I can't remember any racial issues, not that I can think of. Maybe it was because I lived in a community with a lot of other Asians. That way I didn't feel like a foreigner in the city. The one lesson that I learned from my parents was that they were very brave. It took courage to take your family with you on a journey to the unknown, hoping that the grass on the other side truly is greener. They sacrificed the good they had in Vietnam for a brighter future for their children. I feel as if my future couldn't get brighter.

KID TO ADULT

GRANDMA, SAN LUIS RIO COLORADO, SONORA, MEXICO
INTERVIEWED BY MONICA LARA

*I chose my grandma because she is an interesting person to
know about. She has the best personality I know. —M.L.*

I was born in San Luis Rio Colorado, Mexico. I have a big family:
uncles, aunts, and cousins. Mexico is a pretty big country. It's full of
lots of cultures. There are a lot of poor people but there are some
that are a little wealthier than others. It is usually hot. The women would
wash their clothes outside on a rock, and the guys would work on the
houses. Sometimes the men would sit around and drink (laughs).

I didn't go to school in Mexico. The schools were poor. They would
only have a small piece of paper [to write on]. Schools had electricity—
some had petroleum lamps—but during the day they didn't need it
because it was so bright out.

I don't really remember much. My house was kind of poor-looking
(laughs). We only had two rooms and there were six of us altogether. I was
five when I came here. My sister was three. We always played in the dirt.

My mother died when I was five. I was seven and my sister was five
when we were adopted and brought into the United States. That's when
I started school. I was in kindergarten at the age of seven (laughs, embarrassed). I had met [my adoptive parents] before because we knew [the
stepmother's] sister so they introduced us. My adoptive mom's name was
Balbandea, but they called her Nelly. My dad's name was Bernardo.

My [birth] dad was alive when we left. He signed the papers for us to
leave, but I think he really didn't know what was happening (sighs). We
were too sick to stay in Mexico. And my dad didn't have no money to
take my sister and me to the doctor's to get help. My sister and me were
so weak that we couldn't even walk. I don't remember anything. All
I remember is crying. He was very upset, because he was never going to
see his kids again. He recently just passed away.

I guess I can say I was happy moving to an exciting place, because we
weren't healthy. We were weak and very skinny. We thought [our new
home] was nice and big. But we were scared to go into the shower 'cause
we had never taken showers like that. I remember my sister went in and

ran out, 'cause she was scared. She thought it was raining (laughs). We were very scared but also excited. We were very confused.

It seemed like forever sitting in the car. I remember thinking of a lot of things. At this point I was very emotional. I was scared and confused, a little excited. I was thinking about how much things were going to change. We were still in Mexico while my mom in the U.S. was fixing the papers. She would go back and forth from Mexico to the U.S. It wasn't that hard to cross the border 'cause we were smaller, I guess.

We didn't know anybody. The first [things] we saw were the big buildings, big streets, all the cars, and all the (doesn't know what to say, starts laughing) lights, a bunch of lights. There weren't a lot of stairs where I grew up, and my adopted parents had a big dog that kind of scared us.

We didn't speak any English. We only knew Spanish. We started speaking English by going to school. We start meeting people by my adopted mom's friends, and by the kids at school.

Our adopted mom was very strict. We had a pretty hard life. She wanted to adopt just me, but the [orphanage] people said that we were sisters so she had to adopt both of us. But you know what they say, "You can't judge a book by its cover." I say that because we thought she was nice, but we were wrong. Every time she could yell at us, she would. We hated it! Sometimes she would even say, "I should've just left you and your sister there to die," and I would say, "Why didn't you?" That's when I would get hit. My stepmom would clean us and feed us. She would rub us down with a lot of alcohol, and my adopted mom's sister would say, "You're going to kill them." Then my mom would say, "At least they die clean." My mom would make us run all the time to make us stronger. At night my sister and me would cry 'cause our legs were so sore. She would put alcohol and egg white on them to make them better. She only did this so we could walk and be strong again.

My sister and me were always cooking for everyone. When my mom had parties, we were like servants. If our chores weren't done we were in trouble. For example, if our beds were messed up a little she would come over and mess it up and make us do it all over again. We hardly went out because my mom was really strict. We were trapped! We just went to school and went back home.

The only job I really had was cleaning for my mom. My mom was too strict to let us out the house, so I really didn't do much in my teenage years. I felt like I went from a kid to an adult.

On March 11, 1961, [I got married]. I was only seventeen and he was twenty-seven. I didn't really want to get married; I was just trying to get out of the house. Well, my mom was just trying to get rid of me.

When my sister turned seventeen, my stepmom sent her back to Mexico and took the papers away so she couldn't come back. So we were separated for a while. Later, when she took my sister to Mexico I was already married.

But now that I have came to the United States my life has changed a lot. I am very happy that it did. I like it very much. It seems like I have more freedom, more transportation, and more friends. I mostly miss the people the family. I mean we can still visit, but it won't be the same!

SOMETIMES YOU HAVE TO GO THROUGH A LOT TO GET WHAT YOU HAVE

DUNG VAN TRAN, CHAU DOC, VIETNAM
INTERVIEWED BY JENNY TRAN

I love my dad, and I know he has been through a lot. That's why I asked him to tell me his experiences and life story. My dad is a survivor, and for that I admire him. I am happy to have him as a father. Throughout the interview he referred to himself as "Ba" [father]. —J. T.

From small to big, from birth, *Ba* never saw my father. My mother is Vietnamese and my father is American. My mother did say that, a long time ago when the U.S. came to Vietnam to fight, my mother was friends with my father. When my mother was pregnant with me, he went away; he returned home overseas. He went home to America, but *Ba* don't know why he didn't take *Ba's* mom too.

In Vietnam *Ba's* family was poor. I went to school for two years only, grades one and two. *Ba* didn't have money for school, didn't have money to even stay alive. I showered in the dirty lake. My grandmother went to sell stuff so *Ba* could buy food to eat. When I was young I was starving because there was never any food. It was always the same. I always slept every day, and when I woke up I went out to look for food. Back then *Ba* didn't have money, so I broke bananas from a tree and ate them, and I went to go pick up fish. In my house, looking up at the ceiling, all I could see was the sky outside. *Ba* went to the street and slept on lots of banana leaves and sugar cane sticks.

I have three *anh* [elder brothers], two *chi* [sisters], one twin *em* [sibling], and one that went with me to America. Some of my *chi* and *anh* are in Vietnam. My twin brother is in France. *Ba* saw him when I was young; now *Ba* doesn't now where he is. Before, I had a younger sister. She was born and got a little older, then she died in Vietnam. She died because she was sick. My mother had no money to take care of her. I remember when I was younger, how sad and poor life was, how people would harass me and hit me. Other than that, *Ba* doesn't remember anything else.

The place I lived in Vietnam is called Chau Doc. A long time ago the place I lived was very poor. It had only one lake. The place I lived was in the poor streets. There were no mountains or cities. I lived in a place with rice fields and farms. My mother did housework for people; *Ba* stayed home to take care of the house. People in Vietnam hit me a lot, people my age. They saw me playing with my friends, so they wanted to torture us.

My grandmother paid money for the paperwork for my passage to the U.S. A lot of money: one million in Vietnamese money. One million in Vietnamese money was one hundred dollars in American money. I was sixteen years old. *Noi* and *Co Tu* [came also]. At that time *Ba* wasn't thinking anything. I just thought that living would be better in America than Vietnam. I thought that coming to America, I would be living a different lifestyle. The family was so poor. When I came to the U.S. long ago, I went to the hospital to get my feet fixed. *Ba* was born like that; they were swollen, black-and-blue swollen. They were like [this] before your grandma gave birth with me. It happened inside her.

I thought that [America] was neater and bigger and more crowded than in Vietnam. Beautiful, yes. Living here is much better, with more opportunities than in Vietnam. When I came here I saw a lot of things, like how you could rent a house, and how it was so damn expensive. But living here would be a good life, better than in Vietnam. Here there are a lot of buildings and clothes, a lot more than Vietnam. *Ba* didn't have clothes to wear. Blankets, curtains, and clothes—I saw they have so much [more here] than in Vietnam. They [our sponsors] gave us food to eat. *Ba* got off the plane and went to live in Vallejo, lived there for two years. Then *Ba* and mother moved to live in San Francisco, in the Tenderloin, for, like, seven years. Then *Ba* moved to Third Street.

Ba did work in Goodwill for two years, like going to school then going to work after school. *Ba* went to school at Mission High School for about two to three years, up to the eleventh grade, and when I couldn't handle going to school I dropped out. Only, when I was in school, *Ba* fought with people. People made fun of me and they were just looking for trouble. Also, I didn't speak any English and was new to the country. Since I didn't know anything, it was hard to answer, and when I answered they would be mean and just hit me. All you could do was just take it. I just told the principal, and they caught the person. It wasn't my fault.

The school helped me during summer school to get a job. Then I would work for like an hour, and they paid me five dollars for every hour I worked. I just worked there, like, one year during that summer. They paid everyone all the same. People helped to make things better, and did not dare to hurt me or do badly towards me. In high school, I had a lot of girlfriends and many friends. When *Ba* came over, they put me in the ninth grade. I met this teacher who didn't understand, and he would yell and holler. After all that, I couldn't take it anymore. I quit school.

I want to go home to Vietnam and visit. If I want to visit my family, I can go once or twice. But I'll still come back and live in America. If I go, I'll stay there two to three months and visit my *chi* and *anh*. Yeah, but now *Ba* doesn't have a lot of money in the bank. And I don't have citizenship and such papers to bring *chi* and *anh* over. If I had this stuff, and if I had money in the bank, it would be easier to bring them over. But I still don't have money to go back home to visit my siblings. Plus, I am still trying to get a house.

Ba has more than in Vietnam, and I think that it's better than in Vietnam. I have a bathtub, I have a toilet. In Vietnam, we didn't have that. [It is] very different in America. In America, it is beautiful, everything is beautiful. Vietnam is poor, but still it was a home to us. We still like it in Vietnam because we grew up there. Our hearts are there. We don't have beds, we don't have tables. We just lie down on banana leaves. We don't have good food to eat. No, there's no good food. We eat what we have. In Vietnam *Ba* didn't have any electronic stuff. I had nothing. I didn't have a machine to listen to music, didn't have anything. And coming to America, I got all I needed—this and that stuff, I have it. It makes me happy. I just live a relaxing life. *Ba* doesn't go do bad things. *Ba* doesn't have to go around looking for food. *Ba* is filled with joy. Like before [in Vietnam], your grandma was really poor. She would go to work and waitress for people, cleaning tables and such. And the little kids would curse at her because she was poor and they were rich. Grandma would get drunk because she was depressed. Now that she is in America, *Ba* sees her happy, and she's relaxed. In Vietnam we had no money to fix my feet, but in America we did. Yeah, I am not going to go anywhere else. Anytime I go anywhere I have to return home here to San Francisco.

Ba is scared of what would happen to the kids. And I'm scared that they would go out, do bad things, and not listen to us. What parent wouldn't be scared that their kids would be bad? And we worry about them—scared that people would trick them to do stupid stuff. And scared of all those guys that just have sex with girls—just get them pregnant and that's it. I want my kids to go to school, and not fall into bad situations, and not listen to people who tell them to do terrible things, and study hard, and not follow other people's footsteps that are going the wrong direction. *Ba* wanted kids and *Ba* didn't want them to be bad. Because I see a lot of girls on the streets, and I see them go play, and they smoke drugs.

Anytime I'm sleeping, I really think of my girls. *Ba* is scared that guys would trick them and take them to do bad things. And your little brothers, they have bad legs with their muscular dystrophy. *Ba* is scared that they might go to school, try to socialize, and people will hit them. I'm scared like that. Like I'm thinking, my legs are messed up and people will treat me badly. I'm okay with it, just as long as it isn't my boys. *Ba* can handle it, but not my little boys. My little boys want to run. They want to be like regular people.

My name is Dung Van Tran. I was born on August 22, 1968. Yeah, [this is my life] and I am done. Like if I have it, I have it.

Translated from Vietnamese

PASS THE BACK DOOR

YONGYI WU, GUANGZHOU, CHINA
INTERVIEWED BY WILLIAM WU

My mother was born in Gaozhou, China. She came to the United States in 2001. She is a serious person with many emotions who has always been pessimistic. Now she owns her own acupuncture office. She is a hard worker. Let us listen to her story. —*W.W.*

My childhood was very hard. Not enough food. People had to stand in a line to get meat from the government. We could not eat meat every day. We ate meat about three times a week.

When I was ten years old, there was the great Culture Revolution. People had to work. I went to the field to pick grain. After turning seventeen, I went to the countryside to work. The government chose the students who worked in the countryside. After smashing the Gang of Four, the government ended the Culture Revolution. Then the government resumed college examinations, so I finally had the chance to go to university. This is my deepest experience.

I moved to Guangzhou to go to university, and then I worked.

In the morning, after I woke up, I went outside running. Then I had breakfast. After that I went to work from 8:00 AM to 12:00 PM. Then had lunch and rested. In the afternoon, I worked from 2:30 PM to 5:30 PM. Then I had supper, watched TV, and went to night school.

I went to the continuing education classes in order to improve my professional job skills.

The people in China were friendly, but they didn't show their emotions openly. They're different from Americans. And people rarely say hello to strangers.

At that time, the government was so poor. There was not enough pork. That was the unstable period of China. Not like now, it was not easy to eat fruit. Even the powdered milk was scarce.

I thought the U.S. was a very developed country. Very technological and very free. I thought it was a very good country. It was a place that many people wanted to go.

My move to America was unexpected. One of my friends invited me to come travel. At first, I just wanted to come here to travel and then go back to China. But I liked the U.S. very much, especially the environment.

The people here are friendly and polite. Americans usually say hello when you see them, or give you a smile. They treat the strangers the same. Americans are passionate and unrestrained.

In China, there's no freedom and no human rights. It was dark. Many people collude with officials. It is called "pass the back door" in Chinese. It means that human relationships are important. For example, if you know your boss very well, you can get promoted. Or, if you have money, you can also get the special "help" from superiors. No equal opportunity.

Before I came here, I thought, it's easy to earn money in the U.S. But in fact, the immigrants work hard, though the chances here are equal. The immigrants here go all out and they are very thrifty. They go back to China to spend money [that they saved here in the U.S.]. So the Chinese thought the "San Francisco Gold Man" was very rich. In a word, it's not as easy as earning money in China.

Not knowing English was very inconvenient. I didn't know how to talk, I was, like, dumb.

I haven't gone back to China because I like it here very much. I like the freedom and the environment.

I still think it's a busy country. The people here seem to be very busy.

When I first came here, I traveled around, met your stepfather, married, then looked for a job. First, I worked in a Chinese pharmacy, as a Chinese doctor. Seeing one patient could get eight dollars. It took me about ten minutes. But there were not many patients. The business was not very good. The work was not very hard, but there was not enough work to do. I also taught Chinese. I could earn more than one hundred dollars per month. It was not very much.

I earned less than thirty dollars per day when I worked in the Chinese pharmacy. And I had to read books. I prepared for the license test for acupuncture, primarily. So, the first year, my goal was getting the license. And I was successful the first time.

I lived in Daly City during that period. The rent was 1,050 dollars. I was not able to pay for the rent. I had to ask my relative who sent the money to me from China. I wasn't able to pay the rent until I established my own business—an acupuncture clinic.

Translated from Cantonese

PART II

I WAS EXCITED AND SCARED
AT THE SAME TIME

HERE IN SAN FRANCISCO
I'VE NEVER SEEN A SNAKE!

ANONYMOUS, SURABAYA, INDONESIA
INTERVIEWED BY GLENN SETIONO

The person I interviewed now lives in San Francisco. She is forty-nine years old. She is Indonesian-Chinese. We did this interview in my living room at about 9:00 PM on January 30, 2005. —G.S.

The weather in Indonesia is really hot and humid. I lived there ever since I was born, until I was thirty-four years old, when I moved to this country.

Most of our food over there is spicy. That's why they call our country a spicy island. We always need spice to build our appetite because the weather is so hot and most of the time you just lose your appetite.

We only have two kinds of weather: hot and rainy. Rainy season starts around September, all the way until maybe March. During rainy season of course there is a lot of rain. If it's raining it's normally pouring, pouring heavy rain. And we have thunder and we have lightning a lot. It's scary.

For fun we went swimming. All the time we went swimming because it's so great to go swimming over there. The weather is so hot, when you jump into the water you feel so great. Other than that we went shopping, because we really cannot do anything outdoors, because of the weather. So outdoors is more like swimming and indoors is like shopping (laughs). The malls over there are *huge*! I think the shopping mall over there are really pretty—everybody spends their indoor activity in the mall most of the time, because they're air conditioned and cool. Plus, if you're walking outside—lots of crimes. You just can't walk around your neighborhood or any neighborhood comfortably, because there's so many robberies and so many thieves.

The reason why I left my homeland was, well, a lottery first. Back in 1985, I think, I read the newspaper and there was an advertisement from U.S. Embassy saying that they will accept 5,000 immigrants from Indonesia. So all you need to do is fill out the name and the number and they will go by lottery—first come, first serve. They took the first 5,000 people that mailed their name and the address and all of that kind of information.

So I thought it was for fun. I want to see how far my luck goes, you know? So I was with all of my co-workers, writing and sending our names putting it in the envelope. But I guess I was the only one that seriously mailed the letter, and I didn't hear anything from them until 1989. I forgot all about it, and all of a sudden, I received a letter from the U.S. government that I was one of the lottery winners. I thought, I want to know how far I can go. So I filled out all of the application and turned it in. Then I got accepted, and so I thought, this is really not that bad. Since I got accepted, I might as well go for an interview. Again, I wasn't really serious about moving to this country, because I had a good job over there. We had a good living; we had a house already, so I wasn't planning to move anywhere. But after we went for an interview I just realized the consequences if I didn't accept the visa: in the future I couldn't come to this country. So I thought, okay then, I'll just take the visa and come to the United States. So I left you guys, you and your sister, back home because your sister is already was school. I didn't want her to, you know, get behind with the school if I took her to this country. So your dad and I decided to just both of us come to this country, and we did.

After I came to this country, I came to San Francisco and I fell in love with the weather right away. That was the one thing that made me really change my mind. First, the weather is so beautiful and then second, the traffic, and then third… and so on—everything else. I mean, here in San Francisco I've never seen a *snake*! So I decided to stay. We petitioned [for] you guys, and four years later we were able to bring you here.

My expectation of California in the beginning? I didn't have any expectation. I was just thinking, just looking around, and seeing how is this country? And I liked it. But I left you guys behind because I was so afraid that we couldn't survive in this country, and I did not want to involve you guys in this situation, you know. So I left you guys behind for four years, almost four years. If I had known that I could just bring you to this country and bring you back home, I would have done that. But I didn't get enough information. So when I had to petition it was so painful, because I was separated from you guys. That was the hard part of moving to this country. That was really hard for me. At that time you were only, uh, one year old. So planning to move you with my parents was also a hard decision because you were not so used to Grandma and Grandpa. All of those little things that I needed to think. And after I got the visa, that's when I just did it. The flight didn't do much to me. It's only twenty-four hours. The preparation to move to this country was difficult. I had so many things to do within a very short period of time—from selling the house and those kinds of things, and your school, I mean your sister's school—and everything else, you know? How was I going to handle the financial things?

So why did I choose San Francisco out of everywhere else? I had a best friend, auntie Miranti. She lived in San Francisco. And it's not that I was choosing San Francisco. It's because auntie Miranti is the only person I knew in this country. And well actually at that time I had "*Om Kuse,*" you know, uncle Kuse in L.A. But after asking so many people at home—I mean back home—they were like telling me about the weather, the city is beautiful. And it just so happens that auntie Miranti was here. So I started by sending her a letter to ask her whether or not she could help me out, moving to this country. You know, picking me up from the airport, or giving me a place to stay for a couple of days. Stuff like that, and she just helped me out with all of that stuff.

We didn't get settled in until recently, the last, maybe, seven years. The first couple years it was just learning a lot of stuff. Like learning how to get a better job, learning how to speak the language, learning the culture, so it's like everything has come at the same time.

Taking transportation in San Francisco? I think San Francisco is the best for public transportation. You know, I think ninety percent of the city is covered by public transportation. So I really think that public transportation in San Francisco is the best. I don't know, I've never been to a lot of places in this country. I took a trip to L.A., and I thought I could take public transportation like over here, but it appeared that there was no bus, like one an hour, every hour.

But there was a funny story, when I first came to this country, Glenn. Because I thought that if I took a bus, any bus, it would bring me back to where I was. So I took the bus until the end of the line and I thought, oh well, if I sit in the bus and I pay another fare, the bus driver would just, you know, let me sit in the bus without getting out of the bus. And I took the bus on 19th Avenue, but I don't remember [if] it was twenty-eight or twenty-nine. It was going to Daly City. So I thought that Daly City was a different city so… let's go there, and I rode the bus to Daly City. And at the end of the line, I was just still sitting over there, and all of a sudden the bus drive came up to us and said, "This is the end of the line, you guys have to get out." And I said to myself, "Oh my gosh." I did not see a bus station (laughs out loud), and riding a bus was kind of like a new thing to us because back home we never rode the bus. I always had, you know, a car or a driver or something like that. So I finally had to get out, and there was one man, an old guy, sitting in the bus also when the bus driver was talking to us and asking us to get out. I told your dad that we should follow that guy, maybe he was going in the same direction as we were. And we followed the guy; all of a sudden the guy was going inside his house (laughs out loud). We were lost.

My first job was, oh gosh, I never imagined I would take this kind of job, you know? Back home your dad and I had a good job. And when we moved to this country—and of course language was our first barrier, without the language people wouldn't believe in what we could do—I started working. I went to the agency and they sent me to this chocolate factory [Schmidt]. And it only lasted for one day because I thought that that was the stupidest job that I have ever thought [about] in my life. The chocolate just came out from the tube, or something like that, and I had to take out all the bubbles. The whole day I had to take out the bubbles. And I thought to myself, I'm not coming to this country just to do this. The next day I didn't show up. And I thought that if I couldn't survive with a better job I'd rather go home. You know, and that was my first job. And then at that time I was still going to City College to take an English class.

I liked America because of the information—the information in this country. Because it's a free country, you can have any information you ever wanted to know, any information you need to know. Only this country can provide you with all of that information. Okay, books, computer, television, everything is just full with information. That's what I liked about this country. And the freedom of speech.

The most exciting thing that happened to me was, of course, when I got my first job in the office. And it was like one of the happiest days ever since I moved to this country. That's the only thing I wanted, you know? At least if I have a job I can survive in this country. And I got hired with the insurance company. And after two years working with the workers' compensation insurance, I got promoted. So that was the most exciting, exciting moment.

The interview was really hard for me. Again, with the language barrier, I didn't know how to sell myself, you know. Without good language, people kind of doubt about you, if you really know how to do your job according to your resumé, you know? I went to a couple interviews before I got that insurance job. And I did not get hired until probably, say, ten interviews. Finally I got so frustrated and I talked to myself. If I did not challenge whoever interviewed me, then I wouldn't ever get a job here in this country. So when I was interviewed by this insurance company, that's when I really spoke up for myself. I said to Debbie, the person who interviewed me, I said, "Why don't you give me a chance to perform my ability, you know, just hire me as a temporary. If I can't do my job, then you don't have to use me." And she liked that challenge from me. She hired me, and then on the first day it only took me an hour to prove to her that I could do my job. And she said to me, "Okay, you are hired permanently." I think that was my biggest accomplishment. I really wanted to get a job in this country—that way, I knew that I could survive—and I was very proud of myself.

I decided to move to this country because I thought that we could do better with your education. So that's what is always in my mind, that I can give my children a better education. Hopefully my dream will come true. I can't wait until you graduate from high school. You start to think about college, and going go college and stuff like that. That's the biggest goal in my life. I moved to this country because of my children.

FLY TO THE SKY BY MY LOVELY BIKE

ZHUOJUN PAUL LEI, GUANGDONG, CHINA
INTERVIEWED BY YUK MING EDMOND TANG

Paul Lei is a Chinese teenager who always goes around with a smiling face and his lovely bike. After seventeen springs and autumns, he started on a brand new road from China to the United States. —*Y.M.E.T.*

I was born in Guangdong, China, in 1986. I do not have any brothers or sisters because there is a one-child policy in China. Therefore, people can only have one child, and if you have more than one child, you have to pay a fine. I lived in a house that was not very big, but also not very small. My family was not rich, but also not very poor. Everything was fine in my family and we did not need to worry about our food supply and living conditions. The life of my family was fine, but the main problem was I didn't have a very good relationship with my parents. It was because my father was too passive and quiet. Therefore, we did not have much conversation between us. On the other hand, my mother was the real leader in my home. I did not have much power in the house, and I needed to obey her orders all of the time. It was because my mother always liked to hold her power in her hands and my father was too shy, and [he] did not care much about this. Therefore, my mother was the king of my house. There was no fairness in my house. In my own opinion, I believe that it is difficult to have equal opportunity between men and women, and women usually have greater power than men in Guangdong.

I spent all of the time with my family and studying, especially when I came to high school. It was a whole different world compared to the life in middle school. It was very hard and I needed to have a lot of study to maintain good grades. My life was very simple. I would ride my bicycle to my high school every day. I needed to go to school six days out of the week. There was less entertainment in my school life because the only thing in my head was study. When you are in Guangdong, you can go see some cultural buildings on the street, and eat those traditional Chinese foods such as dog meat and spring rolls. Or you can go to the cinema to watch a movie. There are so many places you can go in Guangdong.

Sometime I would go shopping and sing karaoke with my friends on holiday. We would take many nice photos and enjoy these times.

I came here on February 15, 2004, and I will never forget this date. My parents decided to go to the United States because they wanted us to have better lives in a better country. But I had heard this news before. When I was a little kid my parents always told me that we needed to immigrate to America. Therefore, I was not very surprised to find out I would come here two months later. Actually, I had two different feelings before I came here. I was very excited about the immigration, because the United States is the country with the most freedom in the world. I would get a lot more opportunities than in China if I came to America. And it is very exciting to experience another life in a foreign country. But, on the other hand, it would be very sad to leave all my friends and come to a new country. I had lots of wonderful memories with my friends. And I don't know when we will meet again.

I thought a lot while I was waiting to fly on the plane. I saw my friends' letters and presents, and I was so happy to read these letters because they gave us lots of energy and love.

When I came to San Francisco, the sky was deep dark already, and I didn't notice a lot about this new city. After several days, I started to walk around this beautiful city. I found that the houses were only two to three floors and I believed they were more beautiful than the houses in Guangdong. And I noticed that the weather of San Francisco is very cool and sometimes there is fog all around the coast in the morning. This was a special surprise to me.

After one year, I believed I was more mature than I was in China, and I thought I could face more challenges in the future. Some of my studies were not as hard as when I studied in China. But it is difficult to get a high grade now because the studies are becoming harder. I believed I could face them [the studies], and go to a good college. However, I also noticed that I didn't have a smiling face, like I did when I was in China. Maybe it was because it is not much fun in San Francisco. But I still have a lot of good friends right now, and I quite enjoy life going around with them.

It is very difficult to decide what I will do in the future because I still need to finish my studies and I hope I can go to college and have a better education. I want to do this so that I can have a better career and help my parents to change our living conditions. Therefore, maybe I will choose to stay in America now and go back to China only when I become an old man. Because I would still like to live in China more than in the United States. There are more friends in China; there is more fun, and I can feel warmer there.

Translated from Cantonese

CHINA TO MACAO
TO HONG KONG TO SAN FRANCISCO

WAI NA IAO, CHINA
INTERVIEWED BY MEI TENG TANG

My mother is a hard-working woman. I interviewed her while she was reading a newspaper, sitting on her bed.
—*M.T.T.*

I was born in China. I lived in Guangdong. When I was little, China was not that modern. All the food, like rice, oil, salt, fish, meat, etc., was rationed. The government gave you tickets to get food. If you lived in a city, the government gave you meat at a cheaper price. It gave you some meat tickets to get meat, and rice tickets for you to get rice. If you lived in a village, you didn't have tickets to get any food, because the people who lived in the village bred pigs, chickens, and fish for their food. If you didn't breed anything, then you needed to pay more money to get food. The people who lived in the city needed to have tickets to get food, but there was a regulated quantity of food, and the government would mark down your name and how much you took. I had to pay money. It's just cheaper. If you had the ticket you paid ten cents to get a catty of rice [about 500 grams]; if not, you needed to pay second price. "Second price" means you need to buy food from the farmer, and it would be more expensive. The Chinese economy was not that good, and there was not enough food for the whole country. And the government used the tickets to control all the food.

School was very simple and crude. There were fifty-something students in one class. I had Chinese, mathematics, something like that, but

I didn't have English. But I also needed to work on the farm, because the government wanted the people who lived in the city to go to the village. They dispersed your family. One of my family members could work in the city. Then the other members needed to work on the farm.

My family was not rich, so we didn't have enough money for the entire family go to school. I have two sisters who are smaller than me, so I went to work when I was eighteen to give my sisters a chance to go to school. The wages were low. I needed to work in a factory like a student to learn the things that I needed to do. The first year was sixteen Chinese dollars per month. The second year was eighteen Chinese dollars, and the third year was twenty dollars. After you had been there three years as a student, the factory would let you work by yourself. Three years! It was so stupid. I needed to stand eight hours a day and didn't have one second of rest. You needed to be a student first, but I think it was just a trick to get us to work cheaply.

In 1983, China's economy was not good. So when I was twenty-one I went to Macao with my second sister, because I wanted a change. It was easy to go to Macao. It's not easy to find a job in Macao, but easier than China. I met your father, and then I married him. One year later I had your brother, and one year after that I had you. At that time your father lived and worked in Hong Kong, so we moved over to Hong Kong. Macao is like Hong Kong, but Macao has more interesting places that connect to history. It's really a great place!

Hong Kong is a modern city and it is a good place for shopping. When we bought something, we didn't have to pay any tax. We had freedom in Hong Kong. We could do whatever we wanted, say whatever we wanted, go wherever we wanted. It was easy to buy anything, and the food was yummy. It is totally different from the U.S.

Your aunt, who is your father's sister, applied for us to come here. She had lived in the U.S. for twenty years. Because your aunt was in the U.S., I thought everything would be fine, so I just left. I didn't prepare for leaving. The trip was almost fifteen hours.

It was not easy to get used to the U.S. I came here for education. It's good for my children to have a better education. So the first thing that I planned was finding a school for you, then finding a job.

I had lived in Hong Kong for fifteen years and I just came to the U.S. as a total stranger. How can I compare it to Hong Kong? In Hong Kong

I had a good living area, so I always prefer Hong Kong. The food is very different. In Hong Kong, different kinds of food are clearly separated in the stores. In the U.S., they're not. The vehicles here are not a convenience. In Hong Kong it's more a convenience. It is also easy to speak in Hong Kong, because we can speak Cantonese everywhere. I have a job now working in a restaurant, and it is harder than Hong Kong. The first thing is language, because I don't know any English, so it is harder to find a job. I don't have a car, so I can't go somewhere to make more money. If I could, I would like to have a more comfortable job. I think I will go back to my homeland later.

Now, I don't know if I will travel or just go back to live in Hong Kong. I communicate to my friends and watch the news about Hong Kong. I also use the Internet to meet my sister via webcam. I think I am Chinese, because if you don't naturalize to America or live in America more than ten years, nobody will think you are a part of America.

Translated from Cantonese

I MISS THE SMELL OF THE FIELD

JU SON, SEOUL, SOUTH KOREA
INTERVIEWED BY HONG SON

I interviewed my dad at 7:30 PM at his work. He looked very tired but happily answered my questions.   —H.S.

My name is Ju Son. I was born in Korea. I had a lot of brothers and sisters so I never got bored. I have three sisters and two brothers. Back then in Korea it was hard for us. The war just ended so there wasn't a lot to eat. We couldn't go around to ask for food, so if my brothers had something to eat we would always fight for it. It was very hard when I was little.

When I was little we didn't have basketball courts, cement grounds, or a nice field. But we had a yard that was big enough for us to play soccer. It was dried grass, and we put our clothes where the goal was. We would all take our shirts off and play. We would play till nighttime. I was the best one there. The thing I miss most is the smell of the field. When I saw a ball, like a soccer ball, I would go crazy. I really liked playing sports when I was little. I played soccer and I was really good at it.

I was very smart when I was to elementary school and middle school. I was the smartest in my school. But in high school I started hanging out with bad people, and I started smoking and drinking and got bad grades. But I graduated and went to college. I went to college for about two years. I still had bad grades. After school I just started working.

When you're eighteen, you have to join the army, or you will go to jail. But I was twenty-one when I joined the Korean army, and I came back when I was twenty-four years old.

In Korea I worked at a business called Evergreen. I made clothes and I sold them. I had to go around to towns and sell to clothing shops. I had to work very hard. In Korea it was a lot hotter than here. It would be extremely hot in the summer, nice in the spring, chilly in the fall, and it would snow in the winter.

When Park Jeong was president we didn't have a lot of freedom. Like during 1979, people were kidnapped by the government and were beat up. Also, this kind of made me want to leave. I didn't want our family to fall apart. I felt very uncomfortable hearing these rumors around our village.

It was hard to save up money because you worked really hard and you didn't get a lot of money. The land was small, so there wasn't really that many places to work. Also, the government asks you for money. When my parents passed away, it was really hard for me and my brothers and sisters. So I decided to move to America. I believed that it was a nice place to live with the family. I heard rumors that it was an easier place to earn money because you would get paid more.

I chose to come here because of you, your brother, and your mother. In Korea, the land is really small. There are a lot of people, and it would get really crowded in the streets. It was hard to go to college and to get a good education. That's why I came here, so you guys would get a good education. I wanted you and your brother to have a good future.

I had a friend in California and he owned a Korean restaurant. Because my friend was in California, he wanted me to come here, so he could help me out. I felt like coming here because of my friend. I got here by plane. I came to San Francisco in 1993. I came alone because I thought it would be hard for me to bring you and your brother, since you guys were so young back then. So your mother stayed in Korea with you guys while I was looking for a job in San Francisco. I left behind my whole family. It was just me. It wasn't until 1994 that I thought it was okay for you, your brother, and your mom to come. So you guys came a year later. But when I first got here I felt scared. I was very lonely and missed my family. [When] I got here, I first stayed at my friend's house. He let me stay in one of his bedrooms. Then I moved out when I had enough money.

The streets downtown were very noisy because there were a lot of cars and trucks. In Korea, it was never that noisy. Most of the people I saw looked like they were in a hurry. The streets looked very busy. I got a job as a contractor. I helped build and paint houses. It was hard for me. I did what I had to do. I had a lot of different kinds of jobs. I was working as a contractor, I was working for a clothing company, and I was selling some clothes in the free market. It was so hard back then, but I didn't give up.

Sometimes I felt like going back to Korea, but not to go back and live there. I just wanted to visit, but I never got the chance to. I just want to go back [to] see if anything has changed. I want to visit my friends and see if they're doing okay. I want to go see my father's grave and my mother's grave. The way people live in Korea is kind of similar to the way people live here. It's just that education is free here until you go to college. In Korea it's more expensive to send your kids to school.

A couple years later, after I settled in America, my relatives in Korea were having a hard time. So I told them to come here and settle. I had to help them settle in by finding them a home in San Francisco, and finding them a job. Now we can reunite with our family and I can at least support them a little.

Translated from Korean

I STARTED TO COOK
WHEN I WAS NINE YEARS OLD,
AND I'VE BEEN COOKING EVER SINCE

DOROTHY ANDERSON, INNIS, TEXAS
INTERVIEWED BY CHEMIKA HOLLIS

My grandmother is a nice lady who has taken good care
of all her children. I interviewed her in her room, while
she was lying in bed. —C.H.

I am Dorothy Anderson, age seventy-one, born on March 10, 1933 [in] Innis, Texas. Well, I say, it's like this: my parents were kind of tight on me. That was just their way.

I used to go to the cotton field with my grandmother and grandfather, and I used to pick cotton, pull cotton, and chop cotton. My father used to work at the cotton field and my mother took care of houses for white people and worked at the restaurant.

I never got in trouble [when I was young], besides fighting with the little kids around where I stayed, but that wasn't nothing. Oh, I loved to cook, and clean house. I started to cook at the age of nine years old. I've been cooking ever since. The school system was alright—very good teachers.

[We lived] in a big brown house, with white trimmings and with beautiful vines—three bedrooms.

[When we left Texas], we just packed our things and took a hike to San Francisco. I was scared when the train came across Salt Lake City, that big ol' tall bridge. I was scared (laughs), all that. My step-grandfather was already out here and he had got a job and sent for us to come out here and stay.

I had to leave [Texas] with my grandmother because she was the one who raised me. I was scared of the water when we came across on the ferry. [I left behind] cousins, friends. I was just a kid. The hardest part was packing all our things that day and having to move it the same day. [I was] twelve, when it was decided to move, in 1944. I was hoping I would enjoy myself here [more] than I did in Texas. I was just glad to be away from there. I have never been back. I used to say, "I want to come back to California." But I never did think we would. But when I got here, I never wanted to go back—me or my grandmother. We stayed and I'm glad I'm still here. That's how well I like it here. And I still love San Francisco.

I DIDN'T EVEN KNOW
WHAT AMERICA WAS

AMY PANINGBATAN, PHILIPPINES
INTERVIEWED BY JALEACE SMITH

This interview took place in the Balboa High School library. —J.S.

I live [on] Naples Street, in San Francisco (laughs). I'm from the Philippines. Filipino. I moved because I was with my dad. My dad immigrated. My dad petitioned, I mean, so my dad brought his family. And I'm one of them.

I miss going out with my friends and going shopping. And riding this tricycle—a ride that you have to pay, like, five bucks for. It's been five years [since I came here]. I was with my dad, and I had no choice, like I didn't even know I was going. My dad just told me, "Oh, we're going to live at your aunt's house in America." But I didn't even know what America was.

[I left on] June 5, 1999, six years ago. My dad waited for twenty-one years. Then they sent us the papers.

I have a story. My mom was next to me [on the plane], right? And then I was dizzy and I wanted to throw up. And my mom said, "Just drink that water over there." I didn't know it was a coffee. And then my mom just grabbed this thing; she didn't even read it. I thought it was a sugar. My mom put it in, and then she started drinking it, and she was like, "What the hell... what kind of food... what kind of drink is this?" I was like, "Okay Mom, just drink it or whatever." It was really hard in a plane, 'cause you don't know what kind of food they gave you, especially if you're coming to America and you don't know what's going on.

At first, it felt sad, 'cause I left my country, right? But then if you stay here like one or two years, it's your homeland. Like you own it—not that you own it, but like you're used to it already. I have a lot of opportunities to do anything I want, make lot of money and, you know, go to school and stuff. In the Philippines, there's a lot of poor people.

The biggest difference [is] weather, style, clothes, and stuff like that. Oh yeah, attitude. There's more freedom here.

I want to go back because it's been five years since I have been back there. I miss my sisters, my two sisters that we left there. Of course [we use] phone cards, email. We send food, money, and clothes. We send clothes by this company called Bayanihan Cargo. I think next year we're going there with my whole family. My auntie who lives there sent us money to get our passport, and everything.

I can't wait to go back to the Philippines. We're going back there to get [my sister]. And my other sister, I think she has to wait for ten years to come, 'cause she's over-age. There's a limit to come here—under twenty. There was a problem with her passport. They put male instead of female. We couldn't wait for her. My dad thought if we waited, we would not be able to go.

My dad is a security [guard], but my dad is sick now, so he stopped going to work. My mom works at this restaurant. She cooks their food. I didn't have all the things that I wanted in the Philippines, but now I get whatever I want. I ask for it. In the Philippines it's really expensive. Here it's cheap. Not cheap, but you know, yeah…

I WAS EXCITED AND SCARED
AT THE SAME TIME

ANONYMOUS, MANILA, PHILIPPINES
INTERVIEWED BY JASON PAULAR

My auntie is a good, kind, careful person. She works as a sales clerk to support her family.   —J.P.

I grew up [in the Philippines]. We came from a poor neighborhood. My father died when I was three and my mom worked hard as a hairdresser to support us. We were nine kids. I'm the oldest. When I turned eighteen years old I was able to help my mother. I got a job from my university to help enroll the students. I helped them with the enrollments and I issued them permits.

[In the Philippines] there are a lot of poor people. They show only the poor people [on TV], and the kids rummaging through the trash. But I've never seen that because my family lived in the city. So I've never seen that. In the Philippines, I never saw people begging for change or sitting on the street. I never really saw the poverty in the Philippines. Because we were poor, but we [were] kind of making it. Also, my aunt was very helpful, so she helped us with the grocery and other expenses. My dad died when I was three. We were doing okay with my mom. She was a beautician. She was supporting us. When I was still in college, my aunt got me a job with Philippine Airlines as a clerk in the auditing office, chief auditor. So I'm a big help to my family. As the oldest, I'm like the breadwinner, and my mother's strong and very grateful for me.

I didn't experience having a father. My mother remarried and then I was abused. I was beaten by my second father. My stepfather was mean to me, and then, when he was sick, I remember he threw his slippers at me. He's a big guy, has big feet, and his slippers were big and heavy. And when he couldn't get up anymore, and was lying down, he would ask me to sit by his feet and stay there. And I could only get up to go to the bathroom. That was my worst memory that I can remember.

I moved here when I was thirty years old. I came to the U.S. on vacation, and then my aunt wanted me to stay here because she was sick and wanted me to take care of her. When she got better, she took me to Seattle and Canada. Then I came over [to San Francisco]. She enrolled me in a beauty college. I enjoyed it, and liked taking care of the customers. They give me tips. Back then one dollar was big money. I wasn't able to finish [school] because I got married. I got pregnant and then my belly was so big and heavy and gasping for air (laughs).

I enjoyed the trip from the Philippines to the U.S. It was kind of rough and scary, but I still enjoyed it. I also enjoyed the food in the airplane. I was kind of excited, but I had kind of mixed feelings. I was excited and scared at the same time.

I like living here because people are friendly, and you can buy anything here as long as you have good credit. You can live like rich people. You can buy a car and house. You can buy anything you want. And also I kind of like the weather. I got used to it even though it gets cold sometimes. But I like cool weather better than hot weather. The Philippines is so hot and dusty you need to take a shower twice a day, like in the morning before you go to school or to work, and at night before you go to bed. It's very comfortable here because there are a lot of Filipinos. That's why it feels like home. There's a lot of Filipinos and Asians.

My job as a sales clerk is a pain, and you have to get along with everybody because some people give you a hard time—employers, customers. Customers acting like spoiled brats, like they own the world. To be honest, I don't really like my job, but I'm stuck in it. I'd really like to be a singer and a dancer (laughs).

I picked San Francisco because it's an exciting city. It's a nice city, and especially [because] my family is here. I'm very comfortable living here. I'd like to go travel around the world, but that's in the future. Those are my plans, my future plans. I'm going to get there. I'm going to see the world. I promise that to myself (giggles).

IT WAS NICE TO LIVE IN THE PHILIPPINES BECAUSE IT WAS FREE

GRANDMA LYNN, PHILIPPINES
INTERVIEWED BY KEVIN SAN JUAN

I chose to interview my grandma because she's a caring person who cares about her grandkids and would do anything just to make them happy. —K.S.J.

The Philippines, Cardona, that's where I'm from. My dad worked at the docks as a fisherman. My mom was a housewife taking care of the kids.

Our town is a very small town, with a very quiet neighborhood. Everybody knows each other. The most memorable place in Rizal was our town plaza and the church. The plaza is the same thing as the municipal building.

There was always something happening over there, like activities and fiestas. There was dancing. I loved that place. That is my hometown.

Every day was normal in our place, there were no special days except Sunday. On Sunday nobody does anything, nobody works. They go to church every Sunday, and after church everybody goes to the town plaza [to] watch whatever is playing there. The town plaza—it's a small place where they perform things to entertain people.

Yes, it was nice to live in the Philippines because it was free.

We decided to move because we had a lot of kids, and it's hard to find a good job to raise my kids. I want my kids to be raised [in a] good place and have a nice future. I'm sad, but I'm happy because we moved with all my family.

I had relatives in California. They moved earlier than we did. I have four kids, three boys and one girl. They were sad [to leave], but at the same time they were happy because they knew that we'd have a good life [here]. They all followed us, and soon we had no more family in the Philippines except some cousins, but no strong-blooded family.

In 1969, we had to apply to come over, and we had to go through all the necessary paperwork. We took a boat for eighteen days, and we stopped in Hawaii to meet our in-laws. And in a week we took a plane to San Francisco. Thank God there were no problems, and we had a lovely trip.

[Our kids] had no idea they were coming to a new country because they were still kids. The oldest was nine years old, then seven years old, then four years old. We had money, [but] just for our immediate expenses. [Our] relatives here gave us money. My husband looked for a job right away. He didn't pick any [particular] kind of job just as long it was a job. He worked as a custodian at Golden Gate Elementary School. My parents followed us [in 1971]. We stayed with my sister, who had already been living here for a few years.

In 1973, my husband got a permanent job, [and] we got our own place. My parents lived up the block on Banks Street with my younger sister.

LIVING IN HEROIN CENTRAL WAS HARD

Erik Haeberli, Providence, Rhode Island & New Jersey
Interviewed by Diona Knowles

I interviewed my journalism teacher, who is a fun person who likes to talk... and he has to have his coffee! —D.K.

I was born in Providence, Rhode Island. I lived there until I was eleven. Providence is a city, and I grew up in a suburb outside the city, on the water. I had a lot of friends, and I had a lot of fun there. We grew up on the water and in the woods, where we built tree forts, and did a lot of fun stuff like that. My neighborhood had a lot of kids—there were probably twenty or thirty kids on three blocks—so it was like a party. It was a lot of fun. So I was really sad when we—my dad—found out that his company was transferring him to New Jersey. So when I was eleven I had to leave all my friends behind and go to a whole new place and a whole new school, so that was a big transition. [But it was also good because] my dad got—his company, his whole division—got transferred. We had just bought a house out in the country in Rhode Island. They were going to move, and my brother and I were so depressed because we didn't want to live in the boondocks. And so a week after they bought the house my dad found out he was being transferred, so we were really happy and were like, "Oh yeah, we don't have to move out to that stupid place in the country."

I lived in Narragansett Bay. Narragansett Bay was the scene of a very famous battle between the Pilgrims that were living in Rhode Island at that time and the British. There was a famous ship battle—and of course I should know this but I don't—it was a big battle, and it was right where I lived. So there was a lot of historical significance to that area, and a lot of history. That is what's very unique to the East Coast compared to California. Because that's where people settled. They're very old and they value tradition more than out here.

I'll tell you, there was a journey when I left. We moved from Rhode Island to New Jersey during a humongous snow storm. There was so much snow that we had to go five miles per hour the whole way down. So, normally, it's like a four-hour trip, and it took like twelve hours. There was so much snow that all we could see was the lights on the moving truck. We were stuck in the car and my cat was in it too (laughs), and we couldn't see where we were going. It was very exciting, actually.

When we got to New Jersey it was a different kind of neighborhood, because where we grew up in Rhode Island people were very open-minded and they accepted a lot of people, and in New Jersey people were very conservative. So you had to wear a certain brand [of] jeans, otherwise you were a loser. We weren't used to that. So I hated New Jersey when I moved there, because people were very superficial. Then of course after living there it kind of grows on you. But I hate New Jersey.

I ended up going to three colleges. My first college was U.C. Santa Cruz, but I hated it, so I dropped out after the first semester. Then I spent a lot of time backpacking around the country for a year. Then I went to school in Vermont for two years, a very small school. There were only 200 students. It was an art school where you could make up your own major and stuff, in Vermont's countryside. Half the year there's snow on the ground and it's freezing cold, so there's not too much to do. And I think people just sit around and drink. That was my East Coast experience. I hated it; I came back to California, and I made up my mind that I wanted to be an art major. At the time I was a literary criticism major. I transferred to the San Francisco Art Institute, and that's the school I graduated from.

The trip that I actually made from New Jersey to San Francisco was fun because I had my car. I put all my personal belongings in it, with my chair and my stereo, and all my records—that's old-school, having records. I put [them] in my car and it was completely packed, and I drove across the country. I did it in like three days, and I felt like I was one of the pioneers that would go across the country. I would sleep at the truck stops in my car, and of course it was snowing, and I had a sleeping bag with all the blankets on top of me. So it was a big journey, I guess.

I remember, when I first moved to New Jersey, my brother and I were very apprehensive. We didn't want to move because we thought we wouldn't have a lot of friends, and all that stuff. So we were kind of scared and worried. Then when I left New Jersey to go to college in Santa Cruz, it was the first time, and I was very excited because I wanted to get away from my parents (laughs)—as far away as possible. And then the second time I came to California, from New Jersey, I was very, very excited because I really wanted to go to art school. I visited San

Francisco the week before and I fell in love with it so I was very excited about a new beginning.

My stupid mother got me some tickets to fly from New Jersey to San
Francisco. Not knowing that Santa Cruz was really close to San Francisco, she bought me a plane ticket to fly from San Francisco to somewhere
near Santa Cruz. The plane arrived at three in the morning in San Francisco, and then my flight that flew to Santa Cruz was like at seven in the
morning. So my mom didn't want to get me a hotel room, 'cause she
thought I would miss my flight, so I had to sleep on the floor in the airport. I got to San Francisco airport at three in the morning, and I had to
lie under the chairs because the lights were so bright. I was just lying
there and the guys were polishing and vacuuming the floors. And
I thought, "Oh my god, this is horrible. I'm lying here sleeping on the
floor in the airport." All this noise was so loud, and I was like, "Why am
I doing this?" I kept saying, "My stupid mother." It's hard to say this—it
was a very bad trip.

U.C. Santa Cruz was a lot of fun because it was my first time in college. I had a lot of freedom, and I did things I probably shouldn't mention.
I dropped out, which was very exciting because I hated school, and my
friend and I decided we were going to buy land and move to the country,
like Wyoming, and live off the land. We had these crazy ideas. When
I dropped out, we saved money working in construction for a year. Then
we went out to Wyoming, out to live off the land. It didn't work (laughs).

Then we moved back to San Francisco. When I was in college in San
Francisco it was totally different because I was living on campus. I was living in an apartment, and it was a small art school—a very different experience. I was older, so I had more experience. [The school I went to was]
the San Francisco Art Institute, in North Beach.

The first time I came here I was in the San Francisco airport, so that
wasn't such a good impression. But when I came to Santa Cruz it was
beautiful, because Santa Cruz is on the water and you can hear the sea
lions. It was beautiful. I remember it was around Thanksgiving. My friend
who went to college in Illinois sent me a postcard, and he was saying it
was freezing cold and I had a picture of him with a jacket and scarf and
all that stuff. I had just gotten back from playing tennis in my shorts. I was
like, "California is amazing! Why would you ever want to live somewhere
where it's freezing cold?"

I had some friends that were living out here in San Francisco, and that's where I stayed when I moved out here. It was a broom closet— I paid one hundred dollars a month for it. It was a little cot I found on the sidewalk, and I would lay in bed and I could touch both sides of both walls with my hands. It was four feet wide and nine feet long. It was tiny. It was like a cot. I had my clothes in a pile and one window. That's where I lived in San Francisco in 1991.

[It was located at] Sixteenth and Mission, which was heroin central. I would look out my window and there were mattresses on the parking lot next to my building, and all these prostitutes took all their johns and they would just have sex with them in broad daylight. Then I would see junkies shooting up all the time, because it was heroin central. I saw people shooting up under their fingernails. I saw an old man, a ninety-year-old man, and someone was shooting into his aorta in his neck. I saw people get shot in the chest right in front of me. It was just insane. I grew up in the suburbs and I never experienced anything like that before. So that was a very unique experience when I moved out here. That was because it was a very poor neighborhood, but it was the only place I could afford.

[I don't have family out here,] but my brother found out that he is being moved from Colorado to San Francisco. My mother said that if my brother moves out here, then she and my dad will move here. I used to be the only person, but it could be the whole family moving out here.

A lot of people come to California because the weather is very nice and it's supposed to be the land of golden opportunity, and with the high-tech boom, a lot of people moved out here. In the end it crashed, and those dreams kind of crashed as well. Even though some good and bad things happened out here, I think it's a better place to live. It's just getting very crowded, and as you know, San Francisco is very expensive now. That's the only downside.

MY CHINESE NAME IS LEE FONG YEE

CATHY CHAN, CANTON, CHINA
INTERVIEWED BY WESLEY CHAN

*I interviewed my mother in our livingroom one night,
with the television on in the background. We were dressed
in our pajamas.* —W.C.

My English name is Cathy Chan and my Chinese name is Lee Fong Yee. I was born in 1952, in a small village in Canton, China. My dad was a mechanic and my mother was a housewife. I had two older sisters, two younger sisters, and two younger brothers. My grandfather had passed away, but my grandmother was still alive. My mom always stayed home, took care of the family, and kept the house clean while my dad went to work to raise money for the family. When I was little, I helped my mom take care of my family and did household chores, like washing dishes and sweeping the floor. We also had to help cook dinner each night.

I enjoyed going to school. Although the teachers were very strict, I got very good grades. When we got a good report card, my father would reward my siblings and me with gifts. He bought us small gifts, like bookmarks and notebooks; he wrote small messages complimenting us. Even though it wasn't much, it meant a lot to me, because it showed that he was very proud of us. When we had free time, we usually played together outside of our house. Sometimes, after dinner, our neighbors would come over and we would just hang out and chat. We also played a Chinese game called *mah-jongg*. It is a game played with four players and blocks with different symbols on them, similar to American playing cards and poker.

In China, I liked my family and I being so close. We had a very good relationship. What I did not like about living in China was the government. They limited us to very few rights, and we didn't have much freedom. For instance, if you got good grades in school, they wouldn't let you continue schooling because they didn't want you to become too educated. Also, when I wanted to go visit my father at work in Guangzhou, they wouldn't let me, because I lived in Canton.

I moved to the U.S. in 1982. I moved here because my husband lived here. He came to China to marry me. After the marriage I moved to the

73

U.S. to live with him. I traveled here alone by plane. I remember, when I was on the plane crossing the border, I had to fill out forms about where I was going. I didn't know any English, so a passenger next to me, from Sausalito, helped me fill them out. She helped me fill out my address, which was on Divisadero Street, in the Marina district of San Francisco. She said she was familiar with that neighborhood—she drove by there each day when she was going to work. She told another passenger about me just being married and moving to the U.S. The second passenger wished me luck and said that I was lucky for living there. Because of this experience, I became even more anxious and excited to live here.

When I got here for the first time, I thought it was very beautiful compared to China. I had a lot more freedom here than at home. The streets looked much cleaner and the buildings were a lot newer. My first home here was the home of my husband's family. I lived with my mother-in-law, father-in-law, sister-in-law, and my brother-in-law. We were one big happy family. We got along very well and had many things in common. On the weekends we always went shopping together, and went out for *dim sum*. Most of the time at night we had good conversations. We were very comfortable talking to each other.

Coming here for the first time and not knowing any English was very hard for me. I didn't study any English in China, so after one week of getting used to my new home, I decided to start going to school to learn. One time when I went to the grocery store to buy some chicken to make dinner, I didn't know what chicken was called, so I pointed at it to the butcher. I remember the butcher was very nice and taught me what it was called. This was one of my first experiences of learning English. I got my first job in 1983. I worked for an antique shipping factory. It was very hard, because I didn't know much English. Now I work as a nanny.

Ever since moving here, my life has really improved. When I first arrived in the U.S., I liked it. Now that I'm used to living here and [I'm] more adapted to the American style, I love it here. To me the American style means that I can do certain things without being judged, unlike in China. Everything is also so high-tech and convenient. I have no regrets about coming here to start a new life. I would never want to move back to China. I wouldn't even go back for a vacation.

Translated from Cantonese

ALL-NIGHT DINERS

JAN SASSANO, MANHATTAN, NEW YORK
INTERVIEWED BY JACKIE CHENG

Jan is a writer, editor, and researcher for Too Far, a pro-duction company. She has an incredible personality that has taken her very far in life. —J.C.

I lived in Greenwich Village, in Manhattan, a place where you could go to a different restaurant every night for your entire life and only exhaust maybe a fifth of them. It's got a wonderful theater scene and film scene, and I was pretty into the arts. My career in casting for film was [in an] incredibly culturally rich environment.

I didn't know any different until I moved here, but New York apartments are generally really, really small, and you just make do with these small spaces. And you generally live high up, so the buildings are higher than they are here. I got used to living in a small space and not going outside of a three-mile radius, ever. The air was polluted (laugh), you know? It's maybe not the healthiest place to live. But I liked it there.

I was a pretty happy child. I had lots of friends and usually one or two really, really close friends. We were always doing enterprising things, like putting on a show in the backyard or teaching nursery school to the kids on the block. I guess the hard part was that my parents separated twice before they finally divorced, and so you know there was a little bit of moving around. My mom would move out and then I would go live with her, and then I'd come back and she'd come back and we'd all come back, and then she'd leave again. And so that was a little bit trying.

I was a casting director in New York, and my job was okay, but I found it frustrating in a couple of ways. It wasn't intellectually engaging or challenging to me. I felt as if I was very much anchored in New York, that I couldn't leave if I wanted to live anywhere else. I'd have to start from scratch because the casting director needs to know the names and talents of actors in her location. And I knew New York actors. For me to move to L.A.—which I would never do—but to move to L.A. would mean having to relearn the actors who were there. I knew I didn't want to stay in New York forever. New York has a way of kind of anchoring you to it (laugh), and I've always had a little bit of wanderlust.

And when I was sixteen, I went to San Francisco for the first time with my mother to look at colleges. We looked at Berkeley and Stanford, and I really liked San Francisco, and I thought I'd like to live there some day. The other part is that I had a boyfriend who was here after he had been in New York. He moved to San Francisco, and so I thought I might try it out for a summer.

When I was in fourth grade, I was always very good at grammar. That was my thing, grammar and spelling. In fourth grade my teacher, Miss Lamonte, was having a relationship with Mr. Denoply, another fourth grade teacher, and everyone knew it. She came in very upset one day, and it was pretty clear to us, even though we were just nine, that they'd broken up. And she was in a very, very bad mood. I was a shy kid—and I think this is also the year, the first year, that my parents separated. So I was going through that at home. But I remember we were having a grammar lesson and she was very angry, and she said, in kind of a squawk, "So, class, what is a noun?" And no one wanted to respond because they knew how she could be temperamental. No one wanted to cross her. Then she looked at me, her eyes stopped on me, and she pointed to me and she said, "Jan, I know that you know what a noun is. Can you tell the class what the definition of a noun is?" I was really, really nervous, but I kind of mumbled. I said, "A noun is a person, place, or thing." And she screamed, "Nooo! A noun is not a person, place, or thing." And I looked at her like my whole world was caving in on me. Like, what do you mean a noun is not a person, place, or thing? It's always been; it always will be. She said, "No it's not. Don't you people know anything? It's the *name* of the person, place, or thing." And with that she threw her chalk at the chalkboard and said, "I can't teach this class anymore," and she walked out of the room. And I don't remember what happened afterward, but about five or six years ago, my mother and I were talking about that day, and she said, "Well, you know what happened next, right?" and I said, "No, I don't." She said, "You fainted and I had to come and pick you up at school" (laughs). So apparently I couldn't believe that a noun was not a person, place, or thing.

In my twenties I would stay out really late (laughs) at night, and sometimes I'd stay out all night. And there are these all-night diners that were on every few blocks, and you could have bottomless cups of coffee. They just keep on pouring you cups of coffee when you are done with your cup, so you stay awake, and you just have these great conversations about the reason we're here, politics, philosophy, you name it, the arts.... And we'd talk about it through the night on these epic conversations. It's something I really miss.

My friends and I were all in our twenties, figuring what we really wanted to do with our lives. In the beginning we were all assistants in various offices, many of us in the film industry.

We had actors who were very good actors, and good actors are always sought-after actors. We couldn't pay our actors very much. So if they got something better they had to take it. We sort of had our A Cast. One actress was offered a major movie, and another one had a better paying play, and so we'd lost some good talent and that was frustrating. I found that it is a series of compromises, it's a team effort. Sometimes you don't get along with every member of your team. Sometimes you have to hash things out with them, and there are tensions where you finally come to a head and you have to talk it through. But we were very lucky; we had great costumes—beautiful costumes—and amazing sets. It took a lot of work to pull all of those pieces together.

I traveled [to San Francisco] by plane because it's quick (laugh). I didn't have a car. I didn't feel like I had the time to drive cross-country. While I was traveling, I was very much in love. I was thinking, is this the one? Am I gonna get married? Are we gonna get along, you know? What's gonna happen? If I get married, will I have to give up my career in casting?

My very first impression of the West Coast was when I was sixteen. I couldn't believe all the open space. The East Coast is just more developed. You don't see these huge expansions, undeveloped coastline, like you do here. My mom took me on a bus tour from San Francisco down to L.A. and we went along the coast, and I just thought, these cliffs are so beautiful, and wow, the Pacific Ocean is so exotic. 'Cause I grew up by the Atlantic. It's funny what you remember as a kid, but I remember shopping at Banana Republic, which was brand-new at the time. This is dating myself, but it had just opened, and it was a safari clothing place. There were these giant giraffes and huge displays, and it was amazing. I couldn't believe how cool this place was. And I remember going to Fisherman's Wharf and loving Chinatown. I was so into Chinatown.

In New York, buildings are gray. They're very, very high; everyone has a little corner of the sky that they can see. You can't see the whole dome of the sky. San Francisco has all sorts of flowers, and the beautiful pastel houses, and the Victorians.

I remember walking around Telegraph Hill. I just walked around Telegraph Hill, North Beach, by myself. And I got to Coit Tower and I looked around, and I said to myself, "I have got to live in this city. This is the place I am going to live." It was funny. When I got here I was still very [confused about] where I was. I started to notice that I didn't know the good areas versus the bad areas of San Francisco. It all just seemed so good to me compared to Manhattan. And I found myself walking through a neighborhood—like the Tenderloin, you know—at night. I was just wandering and walking. In Manhattan we'd walk a lot. I think San Franciscans walk less because of the hills. But I just walked all over the city, and I ended up in the Tenderloin at night. It was pretty scary (laughs) because I didn't look like I knew the city. I could walk through bad areas of New York because I knew there were bad areas, but I also knew where I was going. In San Francisco, I gave people the impression I didn't know where I was going. I was completely lost in San Francisco, and I remember getting a little scared about where I was. I remember once I was walking through Hayes Valley, and all of a sudden I noticed that people, like everyone, was missing a lot of teeth, that no one had teeth. They had like one tooth or three teeth. And there were some gold teeth. I was just walking along. I must've looked a little scared or disoriented and a guy came up to me. He came up really close to me and said, "What's wrong, girlie? You think someone's gonna rob you? No one's gonna rob you." And I was like, "Ahh, (laughs) I've gotta get out of here."

I miss the theater in New York a lot. There were hundreds of plays happening simultaneously. Great, great plays—very interesting, experimental plays. There were great actors, a lot of recognizable actors, a lot of not unrecognizable actors who were just really good. I miss that scene a little bit. I also miss my favorite film festival. I miss the all-night diners. I miss having friends who were doing the same sort of thing that I was. I miss the local dog run. It was a very social time for both the dogs and the people. It was kinda cool.

There's a difference in senses of humor [here]. New Yorkers can be more sarcastic, more edgy in their humor, dark. California seemed as if the whole culture is based on the climate and sort of the natural resources in the area. This is a very outdoorsy city. In New York we have seasons. In the winter it's very cold. You just don't see many people out running. You see people in the gym certainly, but it's different. I think my general impression is (laughs) that Californians are just a lot, (pauses) they're a lot happier in a way (laughs) that New Yorkers aren't. New Yorkers are used to really bad weather, you know? Thunderstorms, dramatic things, which drives them inside. When a culture's driven inside, the arts torch. I see that in London, where I lived for a little while. Because the weather is raining almost always, people just manage to bring all their interests indoors, create great theater, and great plays. If I had my greatest wish it would be to take the places and put them right next to each other, so I could go back and forth very easily.

I can't imagine this as my last stop. I love the art scene, and I actually love the food [in the New York]. Most people say it's terrible. I don't think it is. Also, the East's a jumping-off point to Europe, and I love the idea of being able to go for a weekend to France, or to a province in Austria.

FROM THE PHILIPPINES TO AMERICA

AMY PANINGBATAN, MANILA, PHILIPPINES
INTERVIEWED BY VIVIEN PAULAR

My friend Amy is a cool friend with a good heart. She's very funny, nice, and smart.　　　　　　　—*V.P.*

My name is Amy Paningbatan. I live with my three brothers, my father, and my mother. I am from the Philippines. It was cool and it was hot over there, but if it's very cold there, it rain also.

The family gets along really easy and cool sometimes. They argue, but it's cool. They don't take it seriously. When I was little I mostly played with my brother and my cousins. I played a lot of games like jump-rope and stuff like that.

I would go back to the Philippines because I miss it. But I'd rather stay here because I like it over here. I have a lot of cousins I love who live here.

[In the Philippines] it was kind of bad because if you didn't listen to the teacher, or did not pay attention, you would get hurt by a stick. That's pretty scary because I saw one of my friends get hit by stick and by ruler. It really hurt and you wanted to cry. After that you learned more and listened to the teacher. Sometimes you went home if you couldn't take it.

Most of the people there are really nice if you get to know them well. I think some of the similarities and differences between the Philippines and California are… I don't know, I think [there] are a lot of Filipinos here, just like the Philippines. And the difference is that I guess there are a lot of other ethnicities here.

I was with my family, but I came here by plane. It was really funny because I was excited coming here. I had seen the Golden Gate in the Philippines, and I was really shocked that I was here now. I was thinking, where are we going? (Laughs.) I didn't know at first that we were going to the country. I moved with my uncle and my auntie. We had a big house. I live with my family now.

I WANTED TO BE BRAVE FOR MYSELF

M. I. RECINOS, GUATEMALA
INTERVIEWED BY MAYRA RECINOS

My mom is a wonderful person. Once you get to know her,
you'll see how fortunate I am to have a mom like her.
—M.R.

I'm from Guatemala City. I was born there. It's like a village, like a little town. I still have some special memories from when I was little. I remember when I was four years old, and I was playing with my little sister. She was two or three years old. And I was playing that I had a store… a bakery. And I also have another memory—when I grew up and went to school. I had good friends. We shared everything, and we were very close friends, best friends. We played on the same block where I lived, and we grew up together. We shared many memories. Their names were Olga and Laura—or Aura—and we had good moments that we shared in the neighborhood. We played "hide-'n'-seek." That's my favorite game. When I reached my fifteenth birthday, my sweet fifteen birthday, I didn't have a fancy party, but I still remember it. It was a nice celebration. We weren't very established people, so we didn't have much money to have a fancy celebration, but I invited some friends to my home and we shared a cake. I didn't get too many presents, but I remember that I had a good time.

It's amazing that in my life, until I turned sixteen years old, I never wished to come here, or ever expected to come here. I once heard my older brother say he was going to come to the United States. He planned it one time in a conversation with my mother. I heard my uncles were planning to come and live in Boston. But my life changed when I turned seventeen, because I met my boyfriend, Yony, in Guatemala. His father was very close to my stepfather. When we became boyfriend and girlfriend, he was already planning to come here with his family to San Francisco. So when we started a relationship, he told me that he wanted me to come here with him. But *no sabía*. I didn't know where San Francisco was. I'd never heard of San Francisco until my boyfriend mentioned it to me. He said that he was going to San Francisco, and he was going to take me with him. Of course, with the permission of my stepfather and mother; he was waiting for me to turn eighteen to ask permission to be my boyfriend. Then, a year later, he proposed to me. And both of our families accepted. We decided to come here, plan our trip to get our visas, and then come to America. We came here in 1980, when I was seventeen years old and he was almost sixteen. So when we came here, we planned to get married after we got our money together to arrange our stuff and our marriage here.

At first I was scared because I had never been out of my city, or my country. Never. But I wanted to be strong and brave, knowing that I was coming to an unfamiliar place. I think it's because I learned from my mother. She never gave up on herself. She was always brave and always a hard worker. So I learned from her that I can trust myself to do it—trust that I can have the self-confidence to get back up when I fall and start over.

We took an airplane to San Francisco. It was beautiful. I remember when I saw the city from up there. I started to see the bridge, and the foggy city. Finally, when we got to the airport, one of Yony's cousins was waiting for us, with a warm coat for me and a jacket for Yony. When I met Yony's family, I was very surprised. Everything was new for me. Especially the city, the weather. It was very foggy when I came here, in January of 1980. So then I started wondering about how to live here, and how to get things. I learned, and I am very happy to live here in San Francisco.

In the beginning, I was sad because it was my first time that I had to live without my family. That was a hard time. It was very sad, especially since it was hard for me to know if I was going to be okay. I had to get used to the people here because they are very different from what I was used to. The people that I came here with started to change.

That's when I started to realize that if I had to be here, I had to work. And since I was going to work here, I had to learn to speak and comprehend this language. I only knew a little bit because in our country they taught us a little bit, and we studied it in our schools. I got a job very fast. The second week I was here I became a housekeeper and a babysitter of three kids. I remember that I loved that job and how happy I was to work in that house. Sometimes a job is hard to get. But I think it depends on you. If you want a job, and keep looking around for one, you can get it. I remember that I didn't give up. I kept looking around and I got one.

The first three years were so hard for me. The first year was so hard, to the point where I felt that it would've been better for me to stay with my family. A few times it was because I was alone, and got lonely. But I learned to live by myself, to be independent, and to fend for myself.

I think it's easier to live here [than Guatemala], and I can explain why. It's easier because you can find as many jobs as you want, and you can decide if you want them to be full-time or part-time. You can make good money easily. Then it's also easier to support your family. I remember I did that a lot. When I started working here, I sent money to support my family. Then it's easy to make future plans because you can work on doing your best to achieve them. Whatever you wish you can make happen over here, but you have to work at it. If you work hard, you can have everything you want.

My life was different. I think a few times I talked it out with my husband, Yony, just thinking about living in Guatemala. We compared our lives here and there, and we looked at how they're different. We didn't have things that we have here. My husband started a business in shoe repair and upholstery in 1997. And I started my business in 1998, as a housecleaner. I remember I had more than twenty houses to clean on my own. More like twenty-five houses, because I counted the small ones. So sometimes I worked with him, and we shared our time together in many ways. I started driving in 1990. If I had stayed over there in Guatemala, I wouldn't have a lot of things that I have here. We have a lot of material things here, but in Guatemala, we don't have anything like the things we have here.

I'm so happy with how my life has turned out. I've got a great job as a certified nurse's assistant. I work in a hospital, knowing that I can feel good because I can make a difference in someone's life. I love the idea that I can tell my children that I've made it this far.

Parts of this interview translated from Spanish

PART III

LEAVING
FOR A BETTER LIFE

WHEN I LOOK AT THEM, I THINK OF US, WHEN WE WERE SLEEPING AT NIGHT IN THE WOODS

SAO MEAS, SVAY RIENG, CAMBODIA
INTERVIEWED BY JIMMY MEAS

My dad is a survivor—a proud and great man. I did this interview at midnight, right after he came home from work. Both of us were tired. —J.M.

Back in the day, Cambodia was good. Everyone was happy. It was peaceful. I was born on March 5, 1953, in Svay Rieng. I liked it because there was no war. There were a lot of trees and empty land. And in the southern part, there's the beach. There are a lot of abandoned temples but there is one that is very popular, and that is the Angkor Wat. It's a very big temple full of monks and statues of Buddha.

When I was a kid, I took care of cows, and I went to school. I was your little brother's age when I was doing this. I walked two or three miles from home to school. I was very tired. And when was the rainy season, it is just got worse because I would get wet and my sandals and feet would get dirty and muddy. School was fun, though. I had friends to play with. The teachers were great, and I wish that I kept going to school. But when the Khmer Rouge came, that's when the schools were being burned down, and the teachers were killed. School was fun, though, and we did a lot of activities like playing outside in the fields. It was hard because every day I would stay in school for four to five hours a day, and then come back and farm, grow rice and raise animals. It's almost like having two jobs, but it was good exercise.

My school was in the plains. It was in the middle of the land. So it was just an open field when you looked out the window from the classroom. But if you went to the rear of the school, there were woods, with a lot of trees. The school wasn't made of concrete or bricks. The walls and floor were made of wood.

In Cambodia, when I was about sixteen, I was a farmer. Four years later, when the communists came, I became a soldier. This was in 1975. I think I was twenty at the time. I was a soldier for the Cambodian army, not the Khmer Rouge. I was just doing stuff like patrolling areas, almost like a lookout person. Then the communists came, and they were Cambodian people who were working for a guy, Pol Pot. He was killing everyone and didn't stop. Pol Pot and his soldiers were not good people.

I was captured along with other soldiers I knew, and the Khmer Rouge killed many of my friends. I had one family member killed—my brother. He was a soldier fighting against the Khmer Rouge. We split apart and I never saw him after that. I guess he's dead now, because I never heard from him [again]. I also had a lot of friends that they killed, a lot of my friends. Most of them were people I knew from the army camps of Cambodia, soldiers who served the country.

The day the communists came, in 1975, maybe the month of March or April, they came with red rags on their heads, with jeeps full of young soldiers that Pol Pot sent out. They were armed with guns, and they put a lot of landmines near the forest and along the border of Thailand.

I left Cambodia because of the communists taking over the whole country and killing people. It was war. The communists captured everyone and anyone, and they would make us work all day and all night with nothing to eat but soup. No rice, just soup. I was doing their work for them, and I was very tired and afraid because if I slowed down, they would do something to me, even execute me. They would kill you in a big field with mud. They would execute you in many different ways. They would get a blue bag and wrap it tightly over your head, they would shoot you, or they would hang you. Sometimes there were little boys and girls that they put in charge, and they, instead of the adults, would kill you. The fields were known as the "Killing Fields" of Cambodia. That's where you would go if they executed you.

If you didn't do what they told you, they would be rough and hit you. They would torture you, and if you were lucky, you wouldn't get executed, because they didn't want people dying on the job. So no one refused what they ordered, because everyone was scared of getting killed.

There were many, many dead bodies in the fields. I don't know how big the fields were. They were probably about two miles long. But yeah, a lot of people were killed. And it was the victims of the Khmer Rouge, because mostly the bodies had blue bags tied around their heads. That was how they would kill you. I almost cried when I saw those bodies because my people were dying. The soldiers were also being bombed by U.S. airplanes, and there was no food.

I escaped at night with your mother—I met your mother when I was about nineteen years old and she was farming rice in the fields—and we ran to the forest. That's all I can say. It was dark and cold, windy, raining… You couldn't see anything because there were no lights, and our blankets were the clothes we had on. It was scary because I didn't know if soldiers were patrolling these areas, and I was scared we were going to get caught. I was also scared of bombs, because the Khmer Rouge put landmines all over the country.

If you got caught or seen by the Khmer Rouge, you were killed. Or they took you back to camp and asked questions and killed you there. When I was walking through the forest, there were many people that had already escaped, and there were dead people and people dying of wounds. Everywhere, I saw were people dying and dead bodies left behind. Some tried to help, but they weren't doctors and there wasn't anything they could do. But people's heads were bleeding, body parts were missing, people were wounded from bombs, and there was a lot of blood gushing out. There was nothing they could do about it. There was no food to eat, no food for your mother or me, no food for them either, and many died of starvation while they were escaping. And that's why I wanted to leave and go to Thailand—go some place that was peaceful, to get away from the war and killing.

We slept, but it was in the middle of the woods, and I wasn't comfortable because it was cold, dirty, itchy, and the soldiers could come out of nowhere and catch you. But we took a quick rest, and after that we walked for several days and finally made it to Thailand. It took about a week to get there. Some nights were sleepless.

In Thailand, I stayed in the camps for about six or seven months. The camps were separated by sex and age, so adult men stayed in one camp and stuff like that.

When I got to Kouida, Thailand, there were many people from the camps, from different camps, and they were trying to leave on a plane. But they only let a few people at a time go, so you can imagine the commotion and everything. But I was riding in a car and drove to the airport. Usually, they would only use a helicopter to transport people to the airport. When I got to the airport, there were people trying to get a plane ticket, and we had to wait. Then we needed a passport. So I got one for your mother and me, and then we were able to get on the plane.

After that, your mother was happy. No more worries about running and getting caught.

We first went to Iowa, and after that we took the next plane to San Francisco, California. Iowa was nice, but I had heard of San Francisco and that was where I wanted to go.

I wanted to come to California because I had looked at a map, and I had heard that California was a good place to live, and that the weather was good—it was warm, no snow.

I had a sponsor from the IRC [International Rescue Committee] who helped me find a house. We stayed at Eddy Street, in downtown San Francisco, with your mother. She was pregnant with your sister, Alina. It was difficult to find the room number because we didn't know English well. And there were toilets here. Back in Cambodia there were no toilets. Here, you could go whenever you needed to.

Only a few people were bad. But there were people walking around at night. You didn't see many people in Cambodia walking at the night. And I thought that was good if people walked at night, because it seemed it was safe. But I didn't go outside late at night. I stayed inside because there were bad people on the street corners trying to rob you.

I didn't know how to speak English, and I needed to learn how to write and fill things out. Plus I needed new clothes, a new car. But every month, once a month, the IRC would send us stamp cards, or food coupons. It took me about two and a half years to find a job. I had to go to school first to get a job, so I could understand the language spoken here. At first I didn't know anything about California, but after going to school, I knew more. And I was nervous when I went to school. I went to some kind of elementary school; then I went to Mission High School, and then to a school in Chinatown. I learned how to read, write and speak English, do math, and a lot more.

I like Cambodia because it is peaceful and relaxing. There is no war over there now. So everything is back to the way it was. But if you tried to move there, you wouldn't be able to buy a house because there is no land where you can build your own house. No land—there are mostly trees. You can only vacation there. You can stay in a hotel or something, but you can't move there. If I had the money I would go visit, because we still have family there, but you need a place to stay first.

I like California because there is work that pays and we have a house to live in. And there is no war here, whereas in Cambodia there was war all over the country. And here, there is a lot of transportation. There are streets, highways, food, and houses you can live in. There are more buildings and a lot of people walking from place to place. So it's better here in California.

The only thing about California—it is very dirty and I see a lot of people sleeping in the streets. When I look at them, I think of us, when we were sleeping at night in the woods.

Translated from Cambodian.

LEAVING FOR A BETTER LIFE

ILTIFATH SHAREF JABBER, SAMAWA, IRAQ
INTERVIEWED BY RASOOL ALGAZAWY

My mother is always wondering about life, about her family. But when she does, she never looks at the bad side of things. —R.A.

I'm from Iraq, from the southern parts. I lived in a small city called Samawa. Iraq is about fourteen million square kilometers. There are about twenty-four million people living there. The religions are Islam, Christianity, and others, but over ninety-five percent are Muslim. Iraq is a bountiful place, and the land is rich and clean. Also, the people are nice and helpful and they like peace. Iraq was always under bad leadership, so the people were often really miserable, especially under the dictatorship of Saddam Hussein. But people are trying to make life better.

I remember a lot of things happening. I remember going to school and having a good time. I also remember having a good childhood. [Education] was important; everyone had to go school. Schools were really strict because the people just wanted you to learn and be worth something. I was registered and I went to school. After all, it was a requirement. People liked going to school, especially if you had a chance to go to the University of Baghdad. When you finished high school, then they gave you a workshop for the job that you applied for. You also need to remember that school in

Iraq was much harder than here in America. First we had to go to school, then finish homework. After finishing homework, we did the chores that needed to be done. Then if time was left you could do what you wanted. Life was easy and not complicated. After all, Iraqis had gone through tough times, but they survived.

As a teacher I taught Arabic, sports for girls, and history. We also taught reading, writing, and math. English was easy because it doesn't have that many rules. Also there are two Arabic languages—the new one and the old one. But I remember a lot of my students falling behind because they had to support their families. Some were fourteen or younger. I think the youngest ones were about ten years old. They worked on the streets selling groceries and whatever else they could sell. A lot of them worked in their family stores and shops. But for the people who had nowhere to go they could always join the army. Of course Saddam loved it when they did.

No one could leave Iraq, only if you were in high power. But everyone really wanted to leave. People got their chance in '91, in the Gulf War. The people who left thought of America as a free country. To be free of power, religion, speech, and to just be free. Also to have free education.

When we crossed the border [into Jordan], it was the happiest moment of my life. I also felt free and safe because if I had been caught, then I would have had to go to prison. And God knows what happens in prison. I wanted to go to the U.S. because my husband was there. I just couldn't stay by myself. I had to get some papers, passports and other things. Then we moved to Jordan, where we stayed for about six months. It was a wonderful yet miserable moment because I left my country and my family. The U.S. embassy helped me the most. My husband was waiting here, and he greeted us. There were also some friends and family members.

At first I hated living in America because I felt like a loner. I really hated to see the homelessness and the gays because it was a surprise to see them here. Gays went to jail in Iraq because Islam did not tolerate same-sex marriage. But after I got used to it I began to see a different side that I liked. I also loved the American people because they were so nice. The first days and weeks were hard, but after a while I began to get used to it. I loved how things were—schools and hospitals were so organized. It was also different how people could say what they wanted. It felt like freedom to me. I loved the atmosphere here and it was just beautiful.

I'm Arabic and a Muslim, so I tell people I'm Arabic even though I'm an American citizen. I still know and think that I'm an Iraqi because that's where I was born and raised.

I did go for a visit, and that was about four months ago. I saw people who were still struggling to get food, gas, and also electricity, but things hadn't changed. They were still the same. The only thing that did change was the leadership. The visit was mostly for my family and friends. I called from time to time to check on them. If they were in trouble I tried my best to see how I could help them, whether they needed money or they just wanted to talk. I also went to visit some holy places in Iraq, like Najaf, where Ali was killed. He was the prophet's cousin. I loved how some soldiers treated Iraqis. They treated them nicely and with respect. I also loved how things began to change. Hospitals were cleaner, and a lot of little things were being improved on. People built new houses and buildings, also some schools. But the thing that made Iraqi people mad at that time was when the British troops robbed the museums. It was true because after the war, about seven months afterwards, the Iraqi museums reported missing items that were found in Britain later on. They couldn't get them back because they said that they had no evidence to prove it.

The Iraqi food was better because it was healthier. And there were not a lot of restaurants there, because people mostly cooked at home, especially if they had a big family. We can't eat the meat in the normal restaurants here because it's not Halal meat. Halal meat is meat that was killed in a sacrificial way. But we do go to Islamic restaurants, maybe every Friday. It is also hard to buy Halal meat because it costs triple of what they sell in normal delis.

There is more freedom in the U.S. than Iraq, but I also felt free in Iraq because it was my home. I think it was better for me in Iraq, but it is better here for my children. I really don't expect anything but for them to get their education and have a better life.

Translated from Arabic

I WANTED TO STOP THE DAYS

Yolanda Cortes-Lara, Mexico City, Mexico
Interviewed by Luis Lara-Cortes

*After my mom crossed the border, she knew what she was
coming here to do. Now she owns her own business in
financial services. She is a very smart lady and she has
a big heart.*   —L.L-C.

Mexico is one of the biggest countries in the world. It has an immense population. On a daily basis you live on the run. [Mexico City's] a hurrying city. The [public] transportation is always full. You never have the luxury of finding a seat and being comfortable. You have to run to get in front of the bus so you can be able to hop on. Every day it's bumping into each other, in between people, people always arguing. It's a city with a lot of smog and gangs. It is really a big country, with a lot of interesting places to visit. I crossed the boarder on December 27.

When you first arrive in Mexico City, you can see the whole city. All you see are houses and houses and more houses, some on top of the others. Just imagine how many people live in each house.

Conflicts that go on in Mexican culture are the same ones that have been existing forever. There is a lot of discrimination in the workplaces. Sometimes they discriminate against you because of your looks, or because you don't look attractive. There is a lot of discrimination at restaurants. If you don't dress decent you won't get hired. The waiters at restaurants will sometimes treat you bad because it doesn't seem like you have money, or if you don't dress elegant they won't pay attention to you.

I always dreamed about going to school. Every morning I woke up wondering when I was going to go to school. At the age of ten I still couldn't go to school. I don't know what happened, but it seemed that my mom was too busy working to send me to school every day. I guess she forgot that I had to go to school. At the age of ten, I started being uneasy about going to school. I told my mom that it was time for me to go.

It was a bit difficult, but I always kept a positive mindset that I was going to overcome it. I had plans that I was going to go to school and take courses on air flight. My area of expertise—what I studied for—was tourism, so I was developing in the areas of flight agency and hotel and restaurant management. And I had to finish the area of airlines. I wanted to go work at an airline company. The opportunities for me to do that weren't that good because I had necessities at home. I had to work to be able to pay for food, clothes, shoes, and I had to make the choice to work or to study and fulfill what I wanted to accomplish.

I dedicated myself to work, but then my life suddenly changed, because I got married and my plans to go take those courses just went away. Then my husband said "Let's go get ready, it's time to go [to the United States]." Since he was already here, my mentality was, "Oh, I can find a lot of opportunities over there. Maybe I can continue studying over there to become a professional."

I left because I got married. That was the first thing that made me think I had to come here. I had the feeling I had to come with my husband because he lived here, and then, thinking about it, I realized I really did want to come here. Because we could both fight together for a better life.

There have always been people leaving Mexico. In every decade there are people leaving the country. There are always people emigrating, because to me the people that emigrate are the people that aren't happy with what they have. They have that right to go and look for a better life for themselves and those that they love.

I believe that to be prepared, you have to be prepared mentally and materially. It was hard for me to prepare in any of these areas, because mentally my mind wasn't ready for change. I had to leave my life as I knew it. All my life was gone now. My childhood, my family, and that was very hard. I don't think that anyone could ever prepare themselves mentally to leave their family and start a whole new life with people you have never seen or been with in your life. And to be able to interact with those people you have to adjust to their ways, because here it's not only made up of Mexicans. There are people from all over the world, so you have to find a way to not offend anyone.

That week before we left Mexico was going by so fast that I wanted to stop the days. But I couldn't, so I had to say goodbye to all of my family members.

Well, I had to take a plane from Mexico City to Tijuana. When I got to Tijuana I had to wait for the people dedicated to passing people, even those who don't have papers. I had to contact them so they could help me pass, because at that time I still didn't have papers. We had to find a way for me to come and be with my husband.

The whole border-crossing was simple. We found someone that knew everything on how to cross people—a *coyote*—and basically, I met this person and got in the car with her. She made me some illegal papers by getting real papers and switching the name on them to mine and making me borrow someone else's identity. She prepared me for some questions that the immigration officer might ask. When it came to the official stopping us right on the borderline of the U.S. and Mexico, he asked me if I was the person on the papers and I said, "Yes." Then he asked me why I had gone to Tijuana. I told him that I had gone shopping. He then asked me where was I going, and I told him that I was going home to the address that was on the papers.

Some of the risks involved in crossing the border with someone you know or love are that that person might not make it and you might not be able to see that person again. But if I had crossed the border with someone I loved or knew, it would have been so much easier. I would have felt less sad, more accompanied, and with more will to make it, because I would feel so much better.

Well, the first thing I wanted to do after crossing, of course, was to hug my husband!

The thing that surprised me the most about California was how it was very organized, the way cars ran. The transportation didn't seem so full or packed. The streets were clean and well-paved. The street lines were painted. The city was full of lights, and just a lot of fancy stuff. When everybody gets to San Francisco, they have the same impression, that it is a very pretty city, very elegant. The first time I crossed the Bay Bridge it was so beautiful. I was crossing a path to excellence.

My first week was a bit of getting to know people. The first people that I met were people that my husband knew. My first month was a day-to-day thing. Each person I met, I tried to listen to what they had to say. All I heard was English. And my limitations to understand were great. My English wasn't well-developed, even though it's spoken in Mexico with the people I knew. I didn't practice English the way it's spoken here. Here you have to speak it every day. And you have to dominate it, because it's very important.

[The obstacles that I faced were] the languages, because it wasn't only English. You heard all types of languages, like Chinese, Portuguese, Vietnamese, Spanish, Italian, so it was a lot. And I thought to myself that I had to dominate at least one, besides my language. I knew that besides Spanish the most spoken language was English. I had to dominate English.

I met people by going to church, where the mass was done in Spanish. I think that's the best place to meet people. I started going to some community meetings and that's where my first relationships with people outside of my husband's family circle started. That's where I met a lady that I know. She's a very nice lady. She was the one who helped me find my first job. My first job was to work with an old lady, accompany her. She was eighty-something years old. The things that I did were to help her take showers, heat up her food, take her shopping, drive for her. That was it. And take her and bring her from her doctor's visits, or any little thing she had to do.

Life in the U.S. has no comparison [to life in Mexico]. Family-wise, I'd stay in Mexico, because that's where all my family is. That's where you get family love. You get more help from your neighbors. So if you need any help, you can always turn to your father, mother, brothers, neighbors, friends—just about anybody. And in the U.S., it's not the case, because definitely you have to fight for everything. It's you against everyone because you don't want to ask for help. That might affect you in the future. So you have to find a way to succeed by yourself. And you have to fight very hard to pay off all the debts you have to people. I will always be Mexican and I will never stop being Mexican. I consider myself a Mexican, fighting as an American. Because I think even though I am Mexican, I have the instinct in me to fight like any American. And not only with fists but with the mind. I believe I am capable of learning anything. I want to be better every day.

Well, I have to say [that the things I miss most in Mexico] are the streets, the music, all the things that come with having all your family with you. And being with your family on your own soil. Because you're never treated like a stranger.

Translated from Spanish

OOTYBOOTY

PAUL DUNBAR, OPELOUSAS, LOUISIANA
INTERVIEWED BY MIGUEL DUNBAR

I interviewed my grandfather in the livingroom of his house on Third Street at about three o'clock in the afternoon. He shared his story of coming to California from Louisiana in the '60s. —M.D.

I moved to San Francisco in December, 1960. I came to California on a bus. All the way from Louisiana to here—three days, two nights. To get here it was fifty-five dollars, if I remember right, and by the time I got here I was broke—no money in my pocket.

I worked on the waterfront [at] the navy yard [as a] longshoreman. Unloadin' and loadin' the ships and stuff. I worked with all kind of races—white, black, Chinese, Mexican. [The ships] came from different places. They came from Japan, Hawaii, Germany. They came from all over the world.

I didn't know no other states (smiles). I came to California first. I heard it was a little bit more slack on the race thing. The money was better. It was a big decision, a hell of a decision, because I didn't know no one out here. I came out here, just me and my brother, and we struggled.

My mama didn't care too much about [my decision to move to California]. I don't know how much my daddy cared. But they told me don't be no fool or no follower, go out there and be a man, so that's what I came out here to be. At first I went back for a lil' while to see if I really wanted to stay out here [in California], and when I went back over there [to Louisiana], I couldn't stay. I couldn't stay because the people had changed, and it wasn't the same place. The whole place had changed, and the weather was hot, so I came back to California.

The racial makeup in Opelousas was white, Creole, and black. It was hard to get along. Everybody was hard to get along with. It was just rough. If one skin was darker then the other, or if one skin was lighter than the other, you had a problem. We had a lot of fights because of that; a lot of the people got hurt over racist things.

There's racism everywhere. Don't get it twisted; there are racists every where. But you gotta deal with it, you know? In Louisiana, you know who's racist, so when you go there, you know you're dealing with racists. Over here you don't know until it really comes out and slaps you in the face. So that's the difference.

They'll call you a n****r, or they'll call you a bunch of names. It's a racist thing. And when it gets like that it always makes you mad. You do your best to hold your peace, but sometimes you just can't hold it, and next thing you know it just blows up on you, or him, or her. It's not so much the ladies. It's the men who are the biggest racists. But I dealt with it. I guess I could say I was a racist too, back when I was in Louisiana, 'cause there was so much of it. Maybe when I got here I had some racism in me, you know? I can't say who was wrong, who was right.

In Louisiana, there was black-on-black racism. If you didn't have really light, light skin like white people, straight hair—black folks couldn't go in that area. And it was all black folks. They couldn't [pass] for white, but they didn't wanna be black, you understand that? The family would deny their son or daughter if that girl or that boy would go with someone darker than them. It was black-on-black. Still got it like that. You can't go into an area if you're dark, you can't. And that's black folks, them black folks will beat you to death. See how dark I am? I couldn't go in some areas. Your hair had to be straight, just like white people's. People got into a lot of fights because of that, you know? Being black and white, we got into a lot of fights about that. But they got good people on each side. Both sides is "ootybooty" (laughs).

[First, I lived] on Kiska Road, up in Hunters Point. My brother's wife's uncle had a house, and that's where we were staying for about five or six months. You gotta know people—to get to know people—to get a job. It was real tough, but we made it. We made it, and after about six months I moved out of Kiska Road in Hunters Point, and onto Divisadero. That's where I was staying until I got married.

It was a big difference, because when I came out here the people was different and I was around more of a variety of different nationalities. And that was strange to me because I hadn't been around, like, Chinese, Mexicans—different kinds of people like that. That was hard to adjust to. I had to adjust to that, you know? And learn and listen to different languages.

My grandmother had long hair. She was part Indian, [part] French. My grandfather couldn't speak English. We was all French, my whole family. My mama was French and would talk in French. She was Creole

French. I was used to speaking French until I came to California. After I came to California, I had nobody to speak it to. I lost it. That's why my English is so messed up right now.

Louisiana is a good state. I love Louisiana; it's nice. It's a lot of fun, you know? People are much friendlier even though there is much more prejudice over there. But people over there will help you faster than people will help you over here, you know? Let's say something happened to you on the road or something like that. People will stop to help you. Over here, people run over you. They won't help you.

What's my best memory of California? Meeting my wife… um, what's her name? Winnie? [Laughs, because she's right next to him.]

FOLLOW THAT BALLOON

Anonymous, Michoacan, Mexico
Interviewed by Zulleyma Franco

My mom is the greatest person I know. She is hard-working and can manage a family. She has gone through so much to be where she is now. I truly look up to her.

—Z.F.

I was born in Artiega, Michoacan, but I lived in Uruapan. Over there people are very *amable* [kind and respectful]. You can walk through the streets freely. In the *pueblo* you can walk to different places. You don't have to use cars or buses or anything like that. It's a small town, where everyone walks from one place to another. It's a very nice place because there are a lot of animals, there's a lot of houses, and there are many beautiful places where you can go have fun, like swimming pools, places of *artesanías* [where you can see art], and recreation parks. The most beautiful things that I remember are the people, as well as the education over there, and traditions like Christmas, *El Día de los Reyes.*

My life in Mexico was good. My parents always had money. I never had to work to get money. My father always worked and gave us the best life. We were a family of nine kids. All nine of us got the same opportunities. My father never let us work, because he was always in a good economic position. My life changed when I got married and I had many problems. That is why I had to come to the United States. Here my life has been better because I've learned how to work. I've learned how to take care of a family. In Mexico I would have never been able to do that. I would have never been able to survive with my kids.

I went through a family problem, which is why I had to come to the United States. My father tried to tell me not to come—mostly because I was very young, twenty-one years old. I also had a daughter. She was one year and seven months old. He especially tried to stop me because of that. I was also seven months pregnant. He said that it was very hard here. He had already come many years ago and he said it was very difficult. I had already made the decision that I was going to leave. If I stayed over there I don't know what would have happened, so it was something I had to do, not what I wanted to do. I worked and I could live there but unfortunately that didn't happen. I worked in a deli where we sold sandwiches, drinks, smoothies and fruit salads. It was a little store that I owned, in a place called *La Charanda* [a market place] in Uruapan, Michoacan. What I was making there wasn't enough for me and my daughter, and I was going to have another daughter. I sold my store. From there I got the money to come. I also prepared myself by bringing some clothes, things for my daughter.

The person who brought me was my brother-in-law, my sister's husband. They were coming to Tijuana because he had a sister living there. They drove to Tijuana and I came with them. I crossed the border but I had to pay someone to cross me over. People that don't have documents have to pay someone, called *coyotes*, to cross them over illegally. That person prepares you in order to pass you. They put makeup on you, change your clothes, and dye your hair. They take pictures of you and put it onto a passport where they change your name, and you have to memorize some facts about the person that you are pretending to be. They have you memorize some streets of Tijuana so that you can say that you live there and you're just going to see some relatives or something. I was very lucky, they just asked me for my passport and I showed it to them and they just told me to go ahead.

The *coyotes* didn't let me pass with my daughter. They said it wasn't easy to pass two people at the same time. They passed my daughter in a car and said I would have to walk across the border. Just imagine that—putting your daughter in the hands of a person you don't even know. To come to this country, I had to risk my daughter because we couldn't pass together. I was afraid that they would steal my daughter. When I passed over, a lady told me, "When you see a red balloon outside a restaurant, follow that balloon. Your daughter has that balloon tied to her hand." I followed that balloon and my daughter was there.

When they gave her to me she was all peed, and had been crying for a long time. She was cold and hungry. They hadn't been taking good care of her. After they gave her to me they put me and two other people in a car and drove us to Los Angeles. I remember that I was very hungry. I hadn't eaten because I was very worried about my daughter. The two men that were bringing me to Los Angeles bought themselves some KFC, and ate it in front of us. Every time I smelled the food I wanted some, but they weren't even kind enough to offer us some. We did not eat until the next day.

I was planning on going to Washington. I had no money so I stayed in a hotel in Modesto, California. I had no money to keep on going so I called my cousin. She came to pick me up from Modesto and told me that I should stay in San Francisco. She said that there were a lot of jobs and many more opportunities. I wanted to go to Washington, but then I ended up staying here in San Francisco instead. [San Francisco] was very pretty. The big buildings, the freeways, the stores—so big—and shopping malls. What surprised me was the way people were living here. I never imagined that there would be cockroaches and rats here (laughs). That surprised me, that people were living in some really small apartments with a lot of kids, up to five people, filled with rats and cockroaches.

The first week, the first month, or maybe even the first year, is very difficult. You come and you don't have anywhere to live. I'm telling you, people are living in really small apartments. They don't even fit in them. I was only here with my daughter. And if you have your family or your relatives here, not all of them will try to help you out. Some won't help you at all. Others don't let you live in their houses because they don't have room. That was something that was very difficult and very hard during the time I was first living here. Nobody can help you because everyone is living in the same bad conditions. It was very different than how I had imagined it. Even your own people change here; they treat you differently.

When you are in Mexico, the impressions that people give you about the U.S. are, oh, it's something marvelous. They tell you that life over here is much easier, that over here you could make a lot of money, that everything is different. They tell you a lot of lies, really, because when you come here, it is very difficult. It's not as easy as you thought it would be. I thought it was real, what they told me, that it was going to be easy to come here, and it would be easy to survive. But no, it wasn't true. We had to work a lot. Mexico is where there is more tradition and people are more united with their family. That is something very important, and I see that in this country people lose out a lot on *union familiar* [family unity]. Here in this country, what mostly matters, unfortunately, is work. It takes away all your time to be with your family. What matters more here is not the family, but what can I have and what can I make. Because we can't live here if we don't have money and if I don't have a job to make money. That is where I see that there is a big difference.

I have thought many times of returning to Mexico, but for me personally, I think it will be very difficult to return. I have been here for fifteen years now. My four other kids were born here. This is where my family is, and I think it would be very hard to return. Mexico now is a very hard country to live in. It is very poor. It has always been poor, but right now it is worse than ever. Now over there, there are more people than available jobs. Comparing the United States and Mexico, you could not really describe it. Life in the United States is very different. Life here is always in a hurry, and everything is work. Time is limited for everything. You get stressed out and you get a lot of sicknesses, because here, you are under a lot of pressure. Life in Mexico is calmer. Maybe it's not better, but it's calm. But I am very happy. I like California very much, and I would like to be here for a couple more years.

Translated from Spanish

I STILL PREFER THE PHILIPPINES

DARRY CRISTOBAL, MANILA, PHILIPPINES
INTERVIEWED BY MIKKO M. DELOS REYES

Darry was just sitting there in the old clothes that he wears to sleep. He's your average Filipino male living in San Francisco. He has his ups and downs, but still manages to be a cool, outgoing, and fun Pinoy.—M.M.D.R.

My name is Darry Cristobal, from Manila, Philippines. For me, my childhood was good. I enjoyed everything, and back then my dad had a good job. I was growing up all right because I wasn't poor or rich. That's it.

When I moved here I think I was twenty-six or twenty-seven, something like that. It was hard for me, because I couldn't get a job since I wasn't a high school graduate—I mean college. I decided to move from Philippines to America.

I lived in Manila but I went to elementary school in the province we call Bulacan. But we ended up moving to Bulacan. I grew up there. I stayed there for six years. Then we moved back to Manila. Manila is where I went high school. So I went to two places, Manila and Bulacan.

I wasn't really enjoying Manila because I didn't really know that many people. I didn't have a lot of friends. In the Bulacan province, I had a lot of friends because that's where I kind of grew up. I knew a lot of people, so I really enjoyed Bulacan more, because there I got to play and stay out later. In Manila I couldn't because there were a lot of cars. A lot, you know? So it was not safe. The province was safer. And the air was fresh and you could stay out more.

Sometimes we would eat only two times a day—not three times a day—'cause we didn't have that much food. There wasn't enough food for us, and then I experienced us having to share food. Like my mom cooked only one *bangous* and we had to divide it into four pieces. I also experienced not having money. As in no money. I wanted to buy food but I couldn't. I wanted to buy candy. I couldn't buy it. And I also experienced having to sleep at other people's houses, because they had money and that's where I ate. Yeah that's what I experienced in the Philippines.

The education in the *Pinas* [*Pinas* means Philippines for short] com-

pared to here is different. When you finish high school or college, you still
don't have a good job—even if you graduated college and got a degree in
nursing or computer science. Whatever you could study there, you still
couldn't get a good job. You would have to wait four or three years. But
the education was still good. The subjects and the teachers, they were
good, and they had good decisions for teaching the students so that they
could learn.

I left a lot of things there in the Pinas, like my friends and my best
friends, and all my relatives. My best friends were Cheska, Yoyog, and my
aunties, my dad's sisters, my other cousins. I left a lot.

I didn't encounter any problems on my way here. Actually they were
nice to me. All the people were nice and had good manners.

The person who paid for my ticket was my aunt and Lola. If it weren't
for them I wouldn't be here.

I stopped over at Japan. It was cold there, and the people are always
smiling and they greeted you nicely. They were clean. They were always
bowing when they greet someone. I traveled by myself, but there were
these Americans that were going to Cali too.

I was scared and lonely because I left my family in the Pinas, but I was
also excited it was a new country. It felt like I was a newborn.

At first I was thinking San Francisco was a nice city. A lot of tree,
cars, and big freeways. To compare it to the Pinas, it was bigger and less
pollution.

What I miss from the Philippines is the food that they sold on the
street, like *ballot, banana que, camote que.* And I also miss the jeepneys. And
I miss my friends.

In the Pinas I would just kick it with no work. Here, I got to work at
Fisherman's Wharf, the Aquarium of the Bay, and Alcatraz.

I felt like I was at the Divisoria when I went to Chinatown, because
there's a lot of people and it's loud and there also Filipino grocery shopping there. It's like the Pinas because there's also a Chinatown there in
the Pinas.

I love it here. It's the best. But I still prefer the Philippines. Because
that's where I grew up; it's my culture. And the weather there is tropical.
I miss the marketplace were all the people shop. It's all messy, you know?
I miss the neighbors. Everyone knows each other. And in the morning
you can eat breakfast outside, like right in front of your house. You can

chitchat and *chismis* [gossip], and you can't do that here. People are too busy. Time is too valuable here. In the Pinas it's not. Life there is easygoing, like, easy-go-lucky.

Translated from Tagalog

LOCKED IN MY ROOM

EDUARDO CISNEROS, MICHOACAN, MEXICO
INTERVIEWED BY FRANCISCO CISNEROS

My father is very responsible because he cares about his family. He always keeps his promises. If I ask him for a favor, he'll do it for me. We conducted this interview in my bedroom. He was relaxing after dinner.

—F.C.

In Mexico there wasn't any life, no work, because you got paid very little, even if you did a lot of work. Mexico is very poor. I am from Brisenas, in the state of Michoacan. It is a very small place, surrounded by water. The only thing you can survive on is land farming because there are no industries, nothing like what America has. But I liked Michoacan because it was free, and nobody had to listen to the laws because there weren't any. My place, where I was born, is very small, but it is very beautiful because there are rivers and farms. It's very beautiful.

Back then, every parent wanted their child to live somewhere else. The parents didn't want them to stay. My father didn't want me to stay with him all my life. He wanted me to have a better life than he had had when he was a boy. My parents and I worked on a farm, but we didn't own one. We would get up in the morning and every day we would work until night came.

In Mexico there is nothing but fields. Where are you going to work? You can't work because it is very poor. You work very hard but still you get the same amount of money. I only went to school from first grade to third grade. I wanted to be in school, but I couldn't. My family was poor, but I really liked school. My father told me that the farm made it hard to go to school. And then I told my father I wouldn't go to school because I would help the family.

My mother left Tijuana because she had two sisters living over there. I had brothers over there too, my sister Ramona, and my sister Carmen. I lived in Baja California, in Ensenada, with my sister Carmen. My brother, who was living in Vista, sent someone, a *coyote*, to get me across the border. I waited for hours, just sitting, for the man to pick me up. My brother had to pay him, because people didn't cross people for free, so that man brought me here to America. I didn't want to come. I missed my country. I missed my horse, my dog. Coming to this country was hard for me. I was sad because in Michoacan there wasn't any life, and no food, but it was my home. I always went to the river, I rode horses. Like I said, life was free. We could do whatever we wanted to do. When I came to San Francisco I was stuck in my room—which my sister gave to me to stay in, in her apartment. As the days passed, I kept crying because my family wasn't here. I missed my home because here in America life was different.

I always stayed locked in my room until, some days afterward, I went to school to learn English. I was maybe six months in school trying to learn the language. By then I was getting used to America. I was getting to know it better, and that's how things started for me. What I like about California was that work isn't as hard as when you live in Mexico. Life is very comfortable here in California, and it has more opportunities. For me, life is better in America because you live better, there is more community. When I came to this country, I was eighteen, nineteen years old. Now I don't want to leave here because I've been living here for thirty years.

Translated from Spanish

WE ALL STUCK TOGETHER

ROSA RAMIREZ, LEON, GUANAJUATO, MEXICO
INTERVIEWED BY RAUL RAMIREZ

*Rosa is a really great and fun person who has been there
for me every single day of my life. I'm glad to have her
as my mother.* —R.R.

My name is Rosa Ramirez and I was born in Mexico, in Leon,
Guanajuato. I was raised there till I was ten years old. The
experiences I had in Guanajuato were very nice since I only
was there when I was young. I went to a Catholic school, and it was a very,
well, what they taught there was hard. They were very strict, I remember
that. If you disobeyed the teacher, they would make you actually sit in a corner. No, they wouldn't hit you with a ruler, but they would scold you. It
was good in a way because you would learn and you would have a lot of
discipline.

The school provided good discipline. They wanted you to be in uniform, and clean. They made sure you brought your books to class. When
you were in class they would tell you not to lay on your desk, to sit straight
in your seat. They especially wanted your writing to be very neat. They
did not take sloppy work. Some parents would buy their kids new books,
and the parents that did not have enough money for new books, they
would use old books. It was okay in a way, when I was going to school.

Fortunately [my parents] did provide me with what I needed, everything new. It was hard for them, but, uh, I had new books. Anything the
school wanted us to have, I got new. Some children didn't have new stuff.
They had used stuff, and some of the stuff was ripped, but they had to
live with that.

My neighborhood was good. I would say it was a middle-class neighborhood. Some of my friends lived in a bad places and [were] poor. My
neighborhood was okay. We had running water, flushing toilets. Electricity we had. Some kids did not have that. But even though all of us didn't
have money, we still got along. I loved my neighborhood. I had fun.

Some people lived in tents, and houses made from sticks and straw.
The houses in Mexico were built differently. They're usually built with
brick instead of the way they are built here in the U. S. The buildings were

about fifteen stories high in the downtown area, [and] built of brick, so if one fell down, it would kill a lot of people. In the U.S. you have more of a chances of surviving [earthquakes].

My mother worked at home. She was a seamstress. She would sew wedding dresses in Mexico, and my father had a butcher shop. They would spend a lot of time at work, but they would still make time for us. I have one brother named Ernesto and two other sisters, Maria and Teresa. It was kind of hard for them to move because they had already made friends.

We, uh, actually, my father decided to move us to the United States. The idea was for him just to come and visit for a year or so, [but] uh, it happened that it wasn't a year. It extended to more than a year. My father went ahead and just registered us in school. We just ended up staying, and my parents sold all their stuff back home.

We didn't get a *coyote* to pass us through because we were fortunate that my father had an uncle in California and he helped us out in fixing our papers. My father didn't want to put us in any danger because we were still small. We actually drove here. We took all we could in the station wagon, like clothes and other belongings. It took us five days to get to the U.S., and from there we ended up staying [in California]. One thing I remember leaving behind was a doll that I loved, and also some of my clothes and my toys.

As I remember, we didn't have too many problems [immigrating to California]. Of course every border [guard] asked us to bring our luggage out. They wanted to see what we had. Some of them didn't care, some said, "If you don't want to take your stuff out, you could pay us and we will let you go through." I remember once they thought we had drugs. They made us take out everything. Dogs were smelling the car. That stuck in my head. Knowing we were Mexican, and they were Mexican too, they thought they could treat us bad.

At first I wasn't upset [when we started our trip]. I was happy because of the way people said the U.S was beautiful [with] lots of bridges, and that's what I wanted to see. I was excited to see lots of buildings and lights, and how the houses were and also the apartments. In Mexico things were not built like they are here. I was scared because I didn't know if I was going to get lost. [Also], I didn't speak English that well.

[When we got to my uncle's], we settled in and we went sightseeing.

I remember the Golden Gate Bridge. I remember going across it, and it was scary for me because I had never been so high over water.

My dad decided to stay [in the U.S.] because there wasn't enough money to go back to Mexico, and my dad had a job that could provide us with what we wanted. He knew that if we went back we wouldn't get what we wanted, so that's why we stayed.

It was hard [when we first came] because my father had his own business. My mother still [worked] as a seamstress, but the money started running out. And of course my father did not want to live off my uncle, so he took another part-time job. At this time my mother didn't speak English and didn't know where to find a job.

When we came to California, I didn't know how to speak English. I was made fun of, but we all got through it. At school I learned [to speak English] because they helped me out a lot. I would say it took me about a year to learn to speak English well.

After my father saved enough money, we ended up moving into an apartment. I thought it was really nice because we were on the third floor. Back home I never lived so high up. Then my mother finally got a job, [but] it was hard for her, 'cause it was with all Chinese-speaking people. She didn't understand, and of course they gave her the s***ty job. Excuse my language.

She was hired to sew shirts and stuff. But instead they had her doing the janitor's job. She stuck it out because we needed the money, and after a while she gradually moved on to sewing.

Yeah, sometimes it was hard for my mom. We barely had furniture; most rooms were empty. Not like back home. All our rooms had furniture. And it was hard sometimes for me to see my mother cry. And it was hard for my father too, because he got another job to get what we needed. I remember shopping at Salvation Army because we needed new clothes and we barely had money. And I'm not ashamed to say it, because we all stuck together and we had a roof over our head. And thank God for that. We pretty much did it on our own. The opportunities here are big. They offer a better education and better jobs, a better life for us.

Even though I love my country, I would [only] visit to take my family to see where I was raised, and where my husband was raised. I haven't been there for a long time so my life is set here. I have a good job, same as my husband, and a good family. I would not [move back to Mexico].

For the people who think Mexico is dirty and stuff, it's really beautiful. Yes, there are poor places, but it's great. And before you listen to other people you should go see it yourself. Leon, Guanajuato is a beautiful city.

I FORGOT HOW I FELT BEFORE

Maurizio Zegarra, Lima, Peru
Interviewed by Gabriel Padilla

Maurizio is one of my best friends at Balboa High School. He likes to joke around, but he still gets his work done. —G.P.

I was born in Lima, Peru, in a clinic called Javier Prado. It was far away from my house. It was the best place my parents could afford. It was one of the expensive clinics in the city, and it was a really good clinic.

My homeland was there. There weren't that many buildings because it was a new area under construction. We had a normal size house, but my mom made it bigger later, because then she got a new job. There was a new school that I started going to, but then it was too hard so I was failing. The beach was three blocks away from my house. I was living with my mom, my dad, and my sister. And sometimes many of my uncles would come and visit us or we would go and visit them. We had a lot of family back in Peru.

Every morning I used to wake up at 6:00 or 6:30 with my sister. We used to get dressed, then breakfast was ready for us at the table, then we just walked to school. Then, after school, we walked home, we did our homework, and sometimes my grandmother would come and take us to the park to play. When we got back we just did any chores we had to do and waited for my dad and mom to get back. The one that was making breakfast was actually our servant because my mom had a really good job at the bank as an executive. We were in the middle-high class because of her. She had a lot of money, but we really weren't that rich, until the economy went down and then my mom was getting paid less.

What I liked the most was the Carnival month, which is February, where you could just get water balloons and throw them at anybody you like. In the streets they wouldn't get mad because it was just part of the game. I remembered I used to go sit on the street in front of my house, get some water balloons, and, with my cousins, we used to throw them at the buses. We used to hit the drivers on the head. We used to give money to whoever would hit the driver. I remember once going to my cousin's house in Carnival month. People around would dig big holes, fill them up with mud. They would just get anybody in the streets and throw them in it, and they used to throw powder at them. It was just part of the fun. But then some people would just get mad because they just don't have the spirit in them.

I traveled to California with my mom and my sister. We went on a plane and [I was excited about] basically everything. I was really amazed because we were flying over the clouds and it was all beautiful in a way and it seemed much warmer up there. There was also a movie showing on the plane. It was *A Bug's Life*—I liked it back then. It was the first time I was on a plane. We had some turbulence and I thought the plane was going to fall down.

[When I arrived in California] I liked the freeways because there weren't that many freeways in Peru. Cars are not allowed to go over forty miles per hour, but in California they were going about seventy miles per hour. I also liked the streets because they were actually bigger, and they're smooth. And I remember we went to Mitchell's Ice Cream that first day. I like that because I had a lot of ice cream. And then we went to my auntie's house, which is bigger than my house.

I had a lot of family in California before I moved here. I had a bunch of uncles, my godmother, my cousins, and my grandmother, because she was here visiting. She went back, though. I also had a couple of cousins in Las Vegas.

In the beginning I did like California, because it was cool, you know? And I liked the trips my dad took me on, like to Yosemite and a bunch of other places. I liked the trees because of how green they were, because I never really seen a forest, at least that big. Also the big waterfall, which is really nice. And I saw a bunch of birds, too And there were also little houses where people would stay, and I remember they used to store food in this little place next to the campgrounds, and you have to lock it because... I asked my dad why, and he said because the bears would come and eat it. I went to Lake Tahoe, Reno, Las Vegas, Lake Berryessa, and Lake Livermore. We went to Great America and Marine World. It was really nice, but then now that I am in school, I can't go on that many trips anymore.

School was much harder in Peru. In California, school was easy because I already knew what I was learning. In Peru, when I was in the fourth grade, they were teaching stuff from the eighth grade here. It was like four years advanced, and that's why it was pretty hard for me in Peru. But I was always trying to do better in school even though I was failing.

I guess what I miss most would be my friends and all the things we used to do together. We used to go around at the park and play soccer. We also used to go to each other's house and play around and find anything to do. In the summer I went to camp and it was three days a week. It used to be kind of like school, only we had to do sports and arts activities. We used to ride our bikes every day, but this one day was completely different because there was a swamp nearby and we went in there with our bikes. Our parents would have been mad. But then we went anyway and then we started racing with all the dirt flying around and we were having fun. And then we went down to the beach and we just started racing there, too, next to the water. Since the sand there wasn't smooth, but is really hard, we could ride our bikes there. But then my friend fell down and he messed up his leg, and we got home. We had to tell the truth, and we got in trouble, but the grounding went by really fast.

I basically forgot how I felt before I came here. Back then—because I hadn't seen my dad for three years, he left before us—I was just really happy that I was going to see him again.

At the beginning, I felt kind of messed up because I was leaving the rest of my family. But then I didn't feel all that bad, 'cause I was still young, so I didn't really know that I wasn't going to come back. To this day I haven't gone back. And now I really miss it. I know how it feels to leave.

TIRED OF BEING SCARED

Dyna Baylon, Makati Philippines
Interviewed by Bryan Logarta

My auntie is very proud of her culture. She is strong, wise, smart, and a great cook. It is incredible that she overcame obstacles in her life that no one can overcome alone. Now she is a proud Filipino-American, living life to the fullest, forgetting her hard past in hopes of a bright future, and encouraging others to do the same. Dyna Baylon has a heart of gold and I am proud to call her my auntie. —B.L.

It's different, life in the Philippines; it's good but it's hard. It's good there when you have money, but if you don't have money it's difficult. Here in California the jobs are still hard, but you can buy what you want. I was born in Manila, but when I was older I grew up in Makati. When I was a kid it wasn't that hard because we had a way of staying alive. But when my dad died it became harder. One time we went to the beach. I fell and I was drowning. It was like that because I didn't know how to swim. I almost drowned. My mama's friend [saved me]. I'm scared [of the water] now, and I think I'll always be scared. I always remember all the fun I had. I would always go to parties. I was a teenager back then. I had a really good time in the Philippines.

I forced my mom [to come to America] because she's a citizen. She was born in Hawaii. I was born in the Philippines. My mom and my dad met in the Philippines. That's why I was born there. I came here by plane. It took sixteen hours. That was my first time riding a airplane. I felt scared.

I went to Chicago because my plane ticket came from Chicago. My cousin, Kathy, had given it to me. I was in the airplane, and when I came out I saw a lot of houses, and a lot of buildings. They were all close together, you know? It was crowded. A lot of stuff was going through my head. How would I get off? Who would be there waiting for me? And what my life would be? All I was thinking about was work. I left my family and my husband's—Ed's—family. They were on their way to San Francisco to start a new life.

My cousin gave me a job. I lived with my cousin for quite some time, almost a year. And every day I would go to downtown because that's where my job was. I worked at American Airlines. I prepared food. I loved working in Chicago. It was better than the job in the Philippines [where] I worked in the factory, a sewing factory.

[I came to] San Francisco because my brother was dying. I went by myself, sad. I stayed here. Before I live on Murray, I lived with my brother, sister, and mom. There was also my nieces and my nephews. Bryan, Rex, Dale, Donna, Michelle, Stephanie. I felt real happy living with them because we all had a lot of fun.

I don't know why, but I don't want to live in the Philippines. I want to stay here. Before, it was good to live in the Philippines, but now it's bad. It's just the way the government is working. I like the government here, but there is a lot of trouble in the Philippines. There is trouble here, but not like the Philippines. There are more crimes there. [Once] when I was crossing the street there was a car that almost ran me over and the guys in that car wanted me to come inside with them. So then I ran back to a grocery store. I was really scared.

Now I am happy. I got a job. I have a great husband and a good family. Life is easier here than in the Philippines. California has big buildings. The Philippines don't have that many big buildings. They don't have that much food. The food here tastes much better and there is so much to choose from. I got used to the food here in America. So when I went to the Philippines I really didn't like the food there. If I was in the Philippines now I would be shopping around, and I would go to the beach, because the beaches there are the best, and I would go to all of the hundreds of islands.

I would always give to the people at the Philippines, especially my family, every time they ask me for something. I like giving to them; it makes me feel good inside. In the Philippines I have a lot of family. I have aunts, brothers, and more.

I want to give to charities in the future. I will do a lot of that. In the future maybe I want to travel, around the world. I have no children, so that's why I want to travel. And I want to see the whole world—but only if I have money!

First of all I thank God. If it wasn't for Him, I wouldn't be in America. I am having a great time here in America. I love it here. Yessir!

Translated from Tagalog

SEEING THE GOLDEN GATE BRIDGE
WAS BEAUTIFUL

STACEY MAYS, JACKSON, MISSISSIPPI
INTERVIEWED BY MAKEEDA LEWIS

I interviewed my mom. She was wearing her pajamas,
and we were in the kitchen. —M.L.

I lived in Jackson, Mississippi, and then I moved to Meridian when I was three years old. I came to California when I was eight years old, and that was in 1976.

[On a typical day growing up] I went to school, came home did homework, and played with my cousins. Childhood was fine, can't complain. Every weekend me and my siblings would go to my grandmother's farm and chase all the animals and help milk the cows. [I remember] Mississippi being very hot. [I miss] my brother, grandmother, cousins, and my father. [I would rather] stay [in Mississippi] because it's much cheaper to live and it's a better environment to raise your children in. I hope that I will return some day.

When I was leaving Mississippi, I was very sad because I thought my mom was just playing around with me and [my] brother and sisters. [That was] until I seen all of our things packed, and realized that we were leaving and my mom wasn't playing with us. [She said] my dad and her was having some personal problems that I was too young to know about, and they weren't getting along too well. So she decided to come to California, where her family was, and she wanted to get a fresh start. But I wondered why we left, and asked questions later on in life.

We came here on a bus, and it took us about two days to get here, but it seemed like a little bit longer because of my age. The bus broke down a few times. Leaving my friends and telling them that I had to go, I was very sad because I would never see them again. [I remember] seeing the Golden Gate Bridge when we first came here, and my eyes lighted up because I had never seen nothing so beautiful before. [We lived in] apartments, but my grandmother and the rest of my family lived in houses.

California is very fast, and Mississippi is very slow and quiet. I liked that you could sit on your porch and watch all the children play outside. But here, in California, that's dangerous, because there is so much going on that you have to watch what you do. Anything can happen. Like where I live, there is a lot of violence, and when you're in Mississippi you don't really hear about things like that because people back there don't worry about that type of stuff.

I like the city life, although sometimes I want it to be quiet. Other times I like it when it's loud, and that you can walk down the street and see so many people that are different from you.

Being a single parent [was hard]. I think that if my kids' father was in their life then they would probably not be the way they are. But I think that I did the best that I can, and I did a good job at it.

[My expectation in life] was to work with children and work with the elderly. I got to accomplish my goals, but I had to wait until all my children were old enough. Mississippi is a better environment to raise your children because the population is much lower, and is much cheaper than California. I haven't talked to my father in over fifteen years, but when I do get in contact with him I will go to Mississippi and will be reunited with him. [I'm] thinking about moving and raising my last child there.

SMALL TRIP TO AMERICA

IRENE CAYABYAB, ZAMBALES, PHILIPPINES
INTERVIEWED BY FREDERICK CAYABYAB

This is the story of a woman who makes the transition to the United States from the Philippines. In the process, she reunites with her husband, prepares to bring their son to the U.S., learns about American food, and gains a new job. It is the warm story of a newcomer and her adjustments to a new life. —F.C.

I was born on April 5, 1962, in the city of Olongapo, and grew up in Zambales, Philippines. I am forty-two years old and a mother of two. I came on April 10, 1992, to the U.S. because my husband petitioned for me to come here. He's a Filipino and a naturalized U.S. citizen, that's why. After we got married in the Philippines and had my first baby, he petitioned for me to come here. We both have stable jobs here and [are] living simply and peacefully with our two kids.

My husband and my in-laws came to the airport and picked me up. I was so excited to see my husband because I had missed him. I saw the glittering lights from the buildings and houses. Because it was my first time when I came here, I was so amazed and so exited to go around the city. My husband lived in an apartment on Van Ness near downtown San Francisco.

Before I even came here, my husband told me that even now that I'd be earning money in the U.S., I [would] still have to spend money here with the house bills and everything. Also, I had to send money to the Philippines because I had left my son with my parents there for one year, so my husband and I could find better jobs. With better jobs, we could work [and] easily petition to have Frederick come to the U.S.

I missed my husband so much because I waited almost two years before he was able to get me here. We just communicated through telephone and letters. I knew I would miss my family, but since I already had a family of my own, I had to take the chance and join my husband [in the U.S] so we could all be together.

When I first came here, I was looking for foods that reminded me of the Philippines, and I found some of them in the Filipino stores here, but [they were] expensive. I still miss the Philippines because I still have my family [there]. I also miss the foods there, [especially] the fruits, like mango, banana, and pineapples. Your uncle and aunt and I used to eat them a lot.

When you're in the U.S., you have to buy everything from the store like the fruits and vegetables. In the Philippines you can just get it from your backyard because we grow fruits and vegetables in our backyards and [on our] farms. I lived in the province where fruit and vegetables are there for picking. I think American foods are good, but Filipino foods are the best, especially *pansit* and *lumpia*.

I was working at Philippines as a stock clerk in a supermarket. My first job here in the U.S was a sales clerk in a KFC store. There is a KFC in the Philippines, but it just happened that KFC was close to our house in San Francisco, and they had available positions [at] that time. So I applied there and luckily got hired.

In the Philippines, I worked from 9:00 AM to 5:00 PM, office job hours, forty hours a week. While here I work different hours. And [it] could be less or more, depending on the availability of hours I could work. It's more flexible when it comes to hours [here], but on the job or work I do, it's almost the same. Although it was hard, my first job here, because I wasn't used to working at nighttime and working fast. Also, because it's a restaurant, so at busy hours we have to work double time. What scared me when I came here was if I could get a job right away because I'm Asian. [I was worried that] people might not like me or might discriminate against me for my nationality. I like my job right now as a sales associate in Payless Shoes, because I like doing customer service and selling, too.

MY FIRST AND ONLY PLANE RIDE

RIC RYAN PALENTINOS, MANILA, PHILIPPINES
INTERVIEWED BY JESSICA BALIDIO

Ric is my best friend. He's really funny and always makes me laugh. I really like talking to him and spending time with him. He is a great person. I love him very much. —*J.B.*

My name is Ric Ryan Palentinos. I was born in Manila, Philippines. I lived with my family: my mom, my dad, my two sisters, and my brother. Life in the Philippines was good because you can just go out and play with your friends after you do your homework. You can play all day and all evening, and go home at night at seven or eight. In our street there were no cars going past. And the food's great, too. My dad did most of the cooking back home, [which] was really good. My favorite food is called *sinagang*. It's a soup with fish, shrimp, or pork. It always has a lot of different vegetables.

I went to a private school in the Philippines, a Catholic school. It's totally different from here. It's harder in the Philippines than here. We start from six or seven, then go till three, four, or five. We used to have a school choir, and we would practice singing and then perform. The teachers in the Philippines were sort of strict. We had to wear a uniform every day. I learned a lot of things in the Philippines at a young age because it's more advanced there at school. We had a lot of homework after school.

I knew almost everyone in our neighborhood, on our street. I had a lot of friends. It's a small neighborhood, so you know everyone. I think it's safer there, because most streets don't really have a lot of cars going past, or gang members passing by. It's like a suburb. I remember we used to play a lot in the streets, and we used to light up fireworks every December to celebrate Christmas.

I came to California in 2001. I was eleven. My mom and dad came to California first, almost a half a year before me and my brother and sisters came here. I was sad. I missed them. We left because my mom and dad wanted to give me, my brother, and my sisters, a better life. I didn't want to leave because I didn't want to leave my home or my family or my friends. We came by plane. It was the first time I had ever been on an airplane. My mom came back to the Philippines to get us. It took us two days to get here. We had to change planes three times, and we made a lot of stops on the way. I thought about the people or how the places were different from here. I expected it to be different from the Philippines.

When we first got here, we went to Los Angeles. We stayed with family members who lived there. We stayed in L.A. for a while, then we came to San Francisco. When I came here, I went to school at James Denman Middle School. I started to go to Denman at the end of sixth grade. There were a lot of Filipinos at my new school. It was easy for me to talk to them in my own language. I really didn't expect anything when I was coming here. I was just scared when I was coming here.

I live in Daly City, over in the Westlake district. Daly City is different from how it was like in the Philippines. I go to Jefferson High School now. I like it over there and I have a lot of friends, too. Now we have a computer, big-screen TV, video games like PS2, Game Cube, and Nintendo. I have only lived here for four years, so I can't really compare. But [in the Philippines] we lived in a normal-sized house, two bedrooms. I had a lot of cousins, uncles, and aunties. I miss the fruit, my family, and my friends.

Parts of this interview translated from Tagalog

ANIMALS COULD GET
SOMETHING TO EAT ON OUR PROPERTY

MARCOS FLORES, EL SALVADOR
INTERVIEWED BY ERICA FLORES

My dad was very unsure of doing this but I insisted. He
was playing with his necklace while I was interviewing
him.   —*E.F.*

My name is Marcos Flores. I was born June 27, 1964. I come from El Salvador, from the city of San Salvador. El Salvador is a small country, but it's a beautiful little country that has the best weather. Like Hawaii—tropical, very nice. I left because it was a crime to be of a young age in El Salvador, 'cause the government thought everybody that was young was a guerrilla. It was against their government. I left when I was fifteen. I would say it was a good childhood, 'cause we had most of the things we needed. My dad and my mom supplied for us, and we grew up on a farm. We had all different types of fruits, vegetables. My grandfather used to plant vegetables and fruits, and we had plenty of food and plenty of trees. The place where we grew up was a big place where we could run around and ride bikes and stuff.

We had land with grass, and next door was a big field. And the circus used to come to town, and they had elephants, horses and everything else. The owner of the circus asked my dad if the animals could get something to eat on our property. In the middle of the night my dad went outside to see what was that noise, and he got scared because there was an elephant right next to him. He said, "Tomorrow I am going to talk to them people because I didn't tell them to bring elephants in here." So the next day, they had the horse in the field eating grass, and one of my older brothers, maybe Mo, he was trying to ride the horse without the saddle, and he jump on top the horse. He was like, "Look, look at me, I'm riding a horse," and I think me or my younger brother poked it. The horse took off running into the fields. My brother was screaming, "Let me off, let me off, stop this horse. It gonna drop. Stop. I'm scared." And when it stop my brother didn't jump. When the horse stopped he lost control, and he fell to the ground and his behind was like, "It hurts!"

There was no conflict [about coming here]. It was just a decision. My mom was already here, and she said come on, 'cause it wasn't safe for us to be over there. I cried a little, but I had to come and be with my family. We got a visa and came on a plane. My brother Mo took care of us when we got here. He was working two jobs and I went to school. I went to three schools to learn the language and I succeeded. It was very hard 'cause I couldn't understand what they were saying. I was going to school and trying to learn the language, so I can make it in this country, because if you don't speak the language, you are not going to make it. You need to learn the language, and when I was going to school I thought everybody was talking about me because I didn't understand what they were saying. But now I do much better.

Everybody in my family came to California because they care more for the migrants in this state than any other state. I left nothing when we left the house where we used to stay. It was destroyed by the government; they bought the land, and they destroyed the farm and made a road. And that happened to most all of our neighbors and stuff. I have left nothing behind but my dad. If I go back, there's no place for me to go back to visit a friend or a neighbor. It's too dangerous for somebody who doesn't know nobody to go back there, 'cause there's a lot of crime and it's not safe.

America was all different to me, big and cars and everything. I thought California was another country, but it was another state. I asked my brother why there's two flags. And he says, "One is the American flag and the other one is the California flag." And I was impressed because they have two flags instead of having one. Yeah, it's easy—you have a lot of opportunity, to do whatever you want to and become whatever you want, to stay in school, whatever.

California is different because you have a lot of opportunity here. In El Salvador you don't have that many options. Either you are stuck with a job to pay for college, or you don't succeed. In California it's a very hard life. It's good, but it's hard, because you still have to work. If you don't get an education here—a high school diploma or a college degree—you won't find a good job. You can find a dishwasher's job or a cook job or helping the cook, or whatever, and they don't pay you that much. I see a lot of racist people here still, I guess. Like they see you're an immigrant, all that, and they see you as some type of an alien. That bothers me.

I would like to say to all the kids to stay in school. Stay in school, study, get a degree. Do not drop out of school for no reason. Go to college, the jobs pay more when you have a degree in something. I'm telling you that because of what I do for a living. It's a hard job [being a MUNI driver]. If I would have went to school and finished college, I wouldn't be doing what I'm doing. As a parent of Erica Flores, I'm telling you, stay in school.

A COUNTRY WOMAN
LEAVES EVERYTHING BEHIND

Diana Carter, Florida, Louisiana
Interviewed by Brittany Carter

An African-American woman leaves her hometown for the big city. I interviewed my loving grandmother at home in San Francisco. —B.C.

Louisiana is a southern state. It's known for its hospitality, soul food, and good churches. You must go to church. My religion started when I was a small child. We had to go to church every Sunday. I attended New Missionary Church. It's a Holy Ghost Church. A Holy Ghost church is praising God, lots of singing and testifying.

The earliest memory I have of my life living there was when I started kindergarten. When it was time for me to come home on the bus, there were so many little yellow buses to ride. My teacher saw me crying that day and she knew the bus that I was suppose to get on, [so] we ran [to catch the bus]. I did not go to preschool because during that time I was coming up there were no preschool. There was first grade, and by me being born in December, that put me a year behind because you had to be five years and so many months. I didn't make it, so I started the next year. But there were no preschool, no Head Start.

High school was fun. I went to basketball games, football games. We had parties, and we had the best basketball team. And the football team, well they were kind of bad. Before graduation we had play day. That was the day the girls dressed up as little girls of six or seven, and the boys would dress up as little boys and play ball. After graduation, some people were getting married, some were going to college, some were going to the service, and some were undecided. So quite a few people did leave. My family stayed. My mom and dad remained in Louisiana.

When I was in Louisiana, which was a long time ago, everything was very reasonable, because of the [economy]. Income was low, so therefore housing, food, and everything else was very low. I lived in a house. I had six brothers—four younger and two older—and a sister in California. I didn't like it a lot because I had to do all the housework. I had to do everything, plus I had to take care of everybody.

When I left I felt very sad and very lonely because I was leaving my friends. I was leaving my family. I was leaving everything and everybody I knew and grew up with. A visit to California is one thing, but moving to California, even though I wanted to come, was very difficult. When I left, I didn't say goodbye to my friends, I just left. If I stayed in Louisiana that would have been all I knew.

I came to California on a Greyhound. When I first came to California, back in 1965, I came for a visit for six months and I rode the cable car. I was very excited. California was very exciting. Things like the lights, the hills, the houses being so close together, all of that was new to me, and it was very exciting at the time, but now it no longer interests me.

It was very cold. It took me a long time to adjust to the weather. Louisiana weather is hot for the summer, no in-betweens. Meaning not hot one week and cold the next week. And we have winter months. When it's cold, it is cold. There is no comparison with California's cold weather, as to Louisiana's. When I first came to California, I somehow lost contact with my friends [in Louisiana] because most of them went their separate ways, some got married and moved away. And I really feel bad about that. Now, out here in California, I have a very good friend, but I have very few friends. I have girlfriends. As a matter of fact, I have two girlfriends that I could call true friends. We've been friends for a long time. We're like sisters.

I was in banking. It wasn't hard because I went to classes [that taught] me all the techniques of how to get a job, how to present yourself, what to say, and what not to say. I also remembered the instructor saying, "It's not always the person with the most experience and the most knowledge that gets the job, it's how you present yourself." I think I present myself very well. There were good and bad experiences. I'm a people person.

I love people so that made it fine with me. There were times that things went wrong, but I didn't take it from people, so I will say overall the good outweighed the bad.

[I have never been to the Mardi Gras] because it's like when you live in a state and there's a Mardi Gras, it's no big deal. Like in California, if you were born and raised in California, cable cars don't excite you. It's something you never really think about. I've never gone. I never had any interest in going.

I plan to visit [Louisiana again], but I don't plan to move back. It's not in my plans. I've been gone away so long, and sometimes it's hard to go back. My family is back there. California is all I know. I've been out here a long, long time, and I like California. That's my home.

GHOSTS THAT WILL HUNT YOU

AUNOA UIAGALELEI, AMERICAN SAMOA
INTERVIEWED BY SASAULI SHARON MALAUULU

My aunt Aunoa, whom I call my grandma, is loving, caring, and very loud. She is a nice person to be around, and she is someone you can count on. When I was interviewing her, she was wearing a traditional Samoan outfit called a puletasi. *I interviewed her downstairs in the garage. It was on a Wednesday and she was getting ready for church.* —S.S.M.

I was born in American Samoa. I came to California in 1967 for my mom and my grandmother. I was only twenty-five years old. I came on an airplane. It was nice because I never been on an airplane. I was so happy because I was going to be in a whole different place. I am happy that I settled in California, but I do wish to go back home. I was happy because my brother is here, my grandma is here, and my mother is here and my father was here. Oh yeah, my kids too. I was happy with the fact that my family would have a better living. I'm not trying to say it's bad in Samoa. But that's what I thought.

It's different here because, you know, over there it's free living. You didn't have to pay for a lot of things that you have to pay here in California—free houses, free food, and free land. It was nice to live somewhere beautiful. I sometimes went with my friends to go do girls' stuff just for fun, but there was a certain time we had to be at like home. Samoa is a place that no one owns. If I had the chance to, I would like to live there and here too. I speak a little English, but a whole lot of Samoan. I was confused when I got here because here there are a lot of roads. In Samoa there is only one main road. People did have cars and they did a lot of running around. There wasn't that many jobs because women stayed home to cook and clean their house and land.

The culture in Samoa is very strict. You had to follow the guidelines that your family had planned for you and your brothers. I miss waking up early in the morning to help my grandma. I did a lot for my family and they did a lot for me. Whatever the family goes through, you go through it yourselves because if you are close to your family and talk to them, you will feel their pain. The family always will have your back if you have theirs.

I did a lot in order to get from where I'm from. Samoa is very hard, especially for the kids. In Samoa there are morals that you have to learn because if you don't then you are asking for trouble. There are ghosts out there will hunt you. The morals and the way you treat people are important because it shows how much respect for yourself and others. There are rules that need to be followed. [The ghosts] will hunt you down if you break any rules.

My mother [helped] me a lot by finding jobs and stuff for me. If it wasn't for her, I wouldn't be able to do anything. I was a nurse aid. I liked working with the people because it showed how much we care for each other. Back at home we helped each other, so that gave me old memories. I did have fun because I got to work with a lot of people. And the fact that I had a job made me really happy.

I do feel sometimes that I want to go back home and just go see my other family and friends that I used to hang out with. [The lifestyle] that I lived was a good one. I had many goals that I wanted to achieve, which I did, just to show that not only one or a few people could do it. That's what I can tell you for right now [laughing]. It may be scary but for real it's not. Just don't do anything stupid. And believe in yourself. [If you] don't, then the ghosts come after you [laughing].

THEY BECAME VERY CLOSE
AND ALSO GOOD FRIENDS

Sgt. Major Elmo Conley, about His Mother Haydi Lovings,
Metz, France
Interviewed by Roberto Ortega

*Elmo Conley is a very easy person to talk to, and will
help you when you need it. He's a very good teacher at
Balboa High School. He talked to me about his mother.*

—*R.O.*

My mother's homeland was absolutely terrible. It was during the war. My father was over there fighting in World War II and my mother comes from Metz, France. Her home was up down and everything was in shambles. It was terrible. There was no food, no clothing, no work, no money, no nothing. It was turned upside down because the Nazis had done a really good job of destroying France at that time. So she was glad to get away and escape the war.

I think the most memorable aspect of her homeland was when she was a young girl out in the countryside with the cattle. She talked so much about gathering the wild berries, and milking the cows, and making all the desserts from the crème from the cows' milk. And she was a milk maiden in France.

I think she misses the camaraderie with the people, because the American people were very rude to her when she came over with her accent and all. I think she misses the closeness that the French people have. She moved here because her family had all been killed in the war, and she married my father, and my father brought her over to this country.

She did not come to California. She went to Wyoming because that's where my father's people had a ranch.

Of course she was happy knowing she was going to get out of Europe and come to the United States, because they thought everybody who lived in the United States was rich, and she would escape the war by coming [here]. So she came, right at the end of World War II, and she was very happy to be here, and she has a lot of respect for this country.

Her journey here was nice because she was coming with my father and he brought her over. I guess she was expecting [the journey] to be much like it was, but once she arrived she was surprised because of the reception she received from the people. She thought she'd be greeted with open arms and she would be able to get a job. She'd be able to work and be a good wife to my father. She was out on the ranch, and it took her about two years to fully get settled in and to where she felt comfortable in this country, and after three years she was speaking English.

She faced many obstacles. Most of it was the rudeness of the American people towards her and the accent that she had trying to learn English. It was very difficult because she did not have the opportunity to go to school. She had to learn English by word of mouth. When she went to the store, my grandma [my father's mom] had to accompany her so she would buy the right things. She thought that people were trying to cheat her when they charged her taxes.

She was married once in France, once in Germany, and then when she came to this country she was married over here. She was married three times because French marriages weren't recognized here so they were married again in a church in Wyoming.

It was very hard for her to get around in Wyoming. First of all, you have to remember that in Wyoming, the closest town to us was fifty miles away, so it was very difficult. Luckily my grandmother was there to help her a lot. My grandmother at this time did speak a little French, so she was able to help my mother with the English language.

She has money, she has a nice home, she has friends. She has more money here in this country but she misses the camaraderie of the French people. [Her most memorable aspect of Wyoming was] when she was learning English from my grandmother and they became very close and also good friends.

My mom is a very happy woman and we are very close. I even call her three times a week. My mom is still alive. She's eighty-nine and she's healthy. She still lives in Wyoming.

THE BUILDINGS GOT ME LOST
JUST BY LOOKING AT THEM

MANA'OMIA TITO MOALI'ITELE, MANU'A FITIUTA, SAMOA
INTERVIEWED BY ROBERT TAGO

My grandfather is a hard-working, church-going man
who never gives up. He is a loving and caring man.
When we talked, he was halfway asleep, in his pajamas,
just thinking about what to say. —R. T.

Samoa is a beautiful island. A lot of green trees, lots of coconut trees, beautiful beaches, white sand beaches, and blue water. Weather-wise it was good; it was around eighty degrees warm and peaceful. Out here [San Francisco], every day you hear people dying over stupid things. But out there everyone gets along, and they do not kill each other. They are strict. In Samoa every parent teaches their kids about respect so if you disrespect there you will surely suffer the consequences.

Samoa is a small place. You go to school, then go home, and do daily things you got to do every day. It's just like [that], day in, day out. Back in Samoa I would go to school, then I would go home, then in the evening I would go to a missionary school after everything was done. School out there was easy because we did not have to take big tests. But out here these days you got to take big tests to get out of school. You had to wake up and do nothing but clean. Then after you're done, you eat, then have free time and then go to sleep and get ready for the next day.

When I first came to California I got lost. Things are so big here. Well I didn't get lost, it's just the buildings got me lost just by looking at them. Every new place you go you have to learn. That's why I was kind of scared, because this is the first time I came to California and was away from home. My family was not worried because they knew I was going to be all right.

I was to join the Coast Guard, [and go to] Hawaii. They brought us to California to take us to training boot camp over here in Alameda. I was traveling with a group of people [who] joined together to get over here. Some friends went to the Coast Guard together. There were some other Samoan guys ahead of me already. I was a happy-go-lucky guy. I always had no problem. I was in the service. That's what I did, spending twenty years in the Coast Guard as a machinery technician. I liked the job very much. That's what I did for a living.

I expected California to look like what I'd seen in books and read about: a lot of land, a lot of foods, like a lot of plantations over here. Only thing is the earthquakes, that's what happens here in California. I was scared for a minute, but now I am used to it. But I got scared the first time it happened.

I just liked it, the way California was made. People were nice, buildings are high, and the cost of living those days was kind of cheap. The houses were cheap, and also the cars, too. That surprised me a lot. The difference between the beaches out here is that it's kind of dirty and muddy, and there's also bad weather.

I didn't really regret leaving. I am glad I came over here [in 1955] because this is what I was looking for: a new life and a place that would give a lot of opportunity to get ahead. I've been back a few times to visit my family. It was nice to see my family that I hadn't seen in many years, and it's still the same out there.

After being here so long now I feel like an American. I know I am from Samoa, but right now I feel comfortable over here. I am satisfied with a lot of people who live out here because there are so many kinds of people. It seems like they live together and get along together, and that's what's the nice thing about [it].

I like to encourage every Samoan-born or Samoan [that] ain't born here. Don't ever lose your Samoan culture or Samoan language. English is easy to learn, but if you lose your Samoan culture, then it's really bad for the kids. So I want all you Samoan kids born and raised here to learn the Samoan culture and speak the Samoan language. That's it.

A LOT OF KILLING GOING ON

TANYA VOQUI, EL SALVADOR
INTERVIEWED BY MARQUITA DAVIS

Mrs. Voqui is a very smart young woman who has been through a lot, and has learned a lot in life. I really enjoyed being with her and listening to her life story. I learned from interviewing her that the choices you make in life are always important, and that you should live every day like it is your last. —M.D.

I came to the United States in 1981, so I was three years old. At the time there was a war going on in Central America. My mom decided to move the kids to America so we would not be exposed to that.

In the country, it's kind of like what you see in the movies. There's no streets there, there's dirt roads, the houses are small, that kind of thing. I really miss the weather though. It was really hot. Long, hot days. There's beaches where you can just go swimming all the time.

There are a lot of differences, you know. Different language, different culture, so I don't see too many similarities. I mean life is definitely harder over there in terms of making money and getting a good job and a good education. Education is harder to come by, you know? Over there, the families are poor, so kids sometimes, they don't finish school because they have to go out and work to help out their families.

I was still pretty young, but from what my mom told me, it was a big change for me to come here. It took me a while to get adjusted to the United States.

We had to get visas in order to come to the United States, so it was a long process. My mom had [to wait] for a year until we got them. When we finally did get it, we took a plane ride to L.A. And we stayed for a couple of months with my uncle, who was already in L.A. He had a house there.

I was definitely shocked. I mean you see cars all over the place, and airplanes and stuff. It was definitely a shock.

There's more opportunities here. I mean it was definitely a good choice. If my mom had decided to stay [in El Salvador], I don't think I would have gone this far in my education. I would go back to visit, but not to stay permanently. I have been here twenty-three years.

It's hard for a young student to finish their education, because they see that their parents are struggling. And the parents also want the kids to work so they can help the family bring in some money. It's just harder over there.

The main reason why my mom decided to come to the United States was because the soldiers in El Salvador were killing people at random on the streets. And they needed more soldiers, so they were recruiting boys that were as young as ten. And she was afraid that they would be dangerous. She thought that one of my brothers was going to be one of those men that was going to be recruited, to be kidnapped to go out and fight. Because, I mean, it was pretty bad.

I came here when I was three years. I was really young. I was educated in American schools, so I feel more American, definitely. But I know my mom introduced the culture to us, our own culture. But not as much as we were exposed to the American culture.

Men and women are created equal. For us, over there at that time, it was the woman who took care of the husband. She took care of the kids and education. [Education] was available for women but not as much as [for] men. Things have changed now, but that's how it was at the time.

I probably would be married and have kids already, or be a housewife or something [if I hadn't left]. I don't think I would have had the opportunity to get a master's degree or higher education had I stayed over there. If anything, I would be a maid or one of those jobs that was common over there for women.

FROM THA ISLAND 2 THA HOOD

JOHN NAUER, AMERICAN SAMOA
INTERVIEWED BY JUSTIN PASENE

*This is my stepfather. He moved from Samoa. He is now
a football coach at Lincoln High School.* —J.P.

I was born in American Samoa. I came over when I was seven years
old [for a] better life, for more opportunities. I flew on a plane over
here. It was kind of scary the first time. Also, back then people were
allowed to smoke on the plane, so it was really scary then. Because they
would stand up. They had a certain area for them to smoke. I flew on a
747. I believe it was the last year it snowed here. Back in '75 it actually
snowed over here.

I miss walking around bare-footed, miss swimming every day. We had
this sliding board at the beach. Little kids would slide on the flat land, but
the older kids would slide from the top and jump into the ocean. It was
cool. I miss that we used to play there every day, but it was dangerous. It
was always known to have somebody that would drown over there
because it was right next to a whirlpool.

I used to make slingshots, loved slingshots, making swords, playacting
with swords. I played sports. I used to love throwing rocks: find somebody
to try to hit, to throw a rock at, and hide. I remember when I was little.
Back then, one of the games that was really exciting was playing hide-'n'-
go-seek in the *dark*! They didn't have any street lights, so it was pitch dark.
Unless you were somewhere in the open where the moon could shine on
you, it would be hard to find you. During those times there were a lot of
ghost stories because a lot of people believe in ghosts out there. I mean
ghost stuff, man. Yeah, when you walk through a graveyard or something,
your mouth would be crooked from getting slapped, but it was cool. We
used to play hide-'n'-go-seek in the dark, that was the best.

There were nine of us, and we used to always have slingshot wars with
all the black kids. There were always more of them than us. They used to
always cap on us about being green banana eaters. We used to pick them
off. We used to use like the real kind of slingshots made out of the
stronger rubber bands. And we used to take carts and take the ball bearings out the carts. So they would be shooting rocks at us, but we used to

shoot ball bearings at them. So you can tag them damn near fifty feet away. *boow*! You know? They used to hide in the empty projects.

We were kids, you know? The only time we'd get in trouble was when someone started bleeding. But when they start bleeding, I mean, that was the whole purpose, right? 'Cause the more they bled the more respect you got. I used to feel sorry for them man, because some of them used to have busted foreheads. I mean they used to get tore up. They never had a chance because they never knew how to make real slingshots. They only knew how to make the hanger slingshots, but they didn't know how to make the wooden ones. See, we learned the wooden ones from the islands—you get the real rubber band, the thick one, and you tie it on, you know? You get you a nice little, wide wood and you tie it on there. And if you're a good shooter, you could shoot and tag somebody a hundred yards away, real nice.

We used to do some stupid things, man. We used to ride a lot of dirt bikes since we didn't have our own bikes. We used to have fun going around taking other kids' bikes from Third Street and other parts of Hunters Point, or go to the junkyard to put them together. We used to do a lot of stupid things… have sword fights with them. We used to use sticks. We used to actually make swords out of sticks. Yeah, we used to cut them and sharpen them with filers.

California's a beautiful place, so it's like being back home. It's hot, it's cool, it's open. I think I'm too used to the fast pace. I think I would like to vacation in the islands, but I think I would rather live here. I don't think I'd be able to make it back home. It'll be too small for me. I wouldn't be able to do anything.

You know, being a kid, it was tough trying to get adjusted. I guess when you're a kid you're afraid of not having any friends, but you really didn't talk to nobody, because nobody could understand you. The lifestyle was different here, culture was totally different here, coming from the islands, you know? I went to Catholic school and they were very strict, disciplined. They would whoop you with rulers and have you kneel down on the cement, you know? They'd just have you do all kinds of stupid things. Coming over here, it was a whole different story. It was like the damn teachers were scared of the kids, you know? Like they would break if they yell at them or something. So it was different.

The first thing you try to look for is identity, and try to figure out who you are. It was kind of tough, though, because you have, as a Samoan in the community, there wasn't no role models. So it was tough trying to figure out who you were, trying to fit in, 'cause the only world, the world that you lived in, was a black and white world, you know? It was always something that was tailored either to the white folks or to the black folks. It was nothing in between for the other folks.

It was like late 70s, early 80s. I guess all the black kids, we got to know each other, you know? All African-American folks and Samoan folks kind of learned each other's culture and it was cool. I mean, a lot of my closest friends were African-American. Some of the guys we used to try to hurt real bad, and they were trying to hurt us real bad, we became very close after we grew older, started finding out who we were really about.

EVERYBODY WANTS
A GREENER PASTURE

VANESSA BUENDIA, TUGUEGARAO, PHILIPPINES
INTERVIEWED BY PJ EUGENIO

My sister is a caring person. We did this interview in our kitchen while she was cooking adobo.   *—PJ.E.*

In the Philippines it's happy and it's pretty. There are a lot of good sights. I said happy because you know your neighbors, you have a lot of friends, and a lot of beautiful tourist spots like the Banawe rice terraces. Especially in our hometown, we have the Callao cave where you climb the eight chambers. And there are a lot of beaches, and places for horseback riding.

I decided to move here to California because life in the Philippines is hard. Although you have a job, you work hard. You work like a *carabao* [water buffalo] but there's no compensation. It's not right for your family, and even if you earn something it's only [enough] for food.

Some good experience I had was people helping each other. And when you have a problem you have a lot of people to talk to or run to, like your relatives and family. There's this bonding that happens when you have a problem. There are some who say Filipinos are hospitable, because when you visit another person's house they will really treat you well. About Filipinos, especially my relatives—if you have a problem you can go to them and tell them what you want. They have the time to listen. Here in California you don't have to listen to the person because you mind your own business here. In the Philippines you have all the time to tell someone about what you are going through.

Once I needed help because my husband and I were not getting along, and my relatives were there to listen. They helped me fix the problem that I had. They are always there willing to help.

Bad experiences? *Abu Sayyaf* [a rebel group], pollution, war, civil war, and exploitation, drug abuse by the children. I didn't experience that. That's what I saw happening.

I enjoyed my childhood because we had the freedom to play and experience what childhood was like. In school you have a lot of friends. I went to elementary at Tuegegaroa North Central School. High School was at Cagayan National High School. It's also in the province. I went to my college at Saint Paul University, with a bachelor degree in science and nursing.

Early memories... some are good, like when I was in high school, when my mom was still there. On the weekends, I always accompanied her to the market and bought food for the whole week. And then we would go to church, go to the parlor, and also prepare the food. I was still in my second year high school when my mom passed away.

I had to go through a lot. First I had to get my passport, have my visa, prepare to come here. Finally, I was here. My plan was to work as a registered nurse here. Also to bring my family here. But before I could work as a registered nurse I would have to pass the exam, the NCLEX RN examination.

Everybody wants a greener pasture. In the Philippines you have a job, but the salary doesn't match what you need. You cannot buy what you want with the pay that you get. The first time I came here I traveled with my dad and my brother [who is interviewing me now]. The second time I went by myself. This is my third time, and I traveled by myself. Finally, it's for good.

A lot of things were on my mind when I was traveling. Like, when you reach the airport, what will they ask me? And did California have any improvement since the last time I came? And then, I couldn't wait to see my brother and my parents, whom I hadn't seen for four years. Of course I thought about how were they going to live without me. And also me, how am I going to go on without them?

To leave the country, there was a lot of preparation, packing the things I needed to bring, gifts, also my stuff. I couldn't bring thin shirts because the climate here is different. It's cold. It's not like in the Philippines where it's hot. You cannot wear the clothes you wear there, here. There was a lot of preparation and also a lot of bonding. I left my kids and there was a going-away party with my friends, relatives, a lot of people coming to the house. And we had a little party, because maybe they wouldn't see me for a long time.

In some ways, I didn't expect a lot because I'd seen California before, but before that, I expected California to be a very beautiful country, very clean. It's a lot better than the Philippines in terms of technology, in terms of the environment maybe, there's no place like home. That's all I can say because here I can't see the things that I saw in the Philippines, like special qualities of the Filipinos. There's a lot of things missing here. Filipinos are hospitable, but also I found California people to be friendly. But like I said, there's no place like home.

Here you have opportunities to grow. You can work, you can have your house, you can have your dream car. You can have a good life here. In the Philippines there's no growth. You just work for now, not thinking of the future. Here your future is good because you can work and save some of your income, but in the Philippines, life is hard.

The only thing is, the teenagers here, they're different. It's a little bit weird for me because I'm not used to it. How they dress. And there are a lot of races and it's very diverse. In the Philippines there is a lot of respect. As an adult you can [get] respect from a kid. It's different here because they exercise the rights of the children, they protect the children. In the Philippines there's exploitation. It's like, as a kid you have no rights.

My hopes for the future are to work, to have a better life. I want to have a house, I want to have a car, and I want to travel to more of the U.S.

Translated from Tagalog

HARAJUKU GIRL

JOANA MENDOZA, DAGUPAN, PANGASINAN, PHILIPPINES
INTERVIEWED BY LORENZO MENDOZA

Joana is unstoppable. She is my sister. She reads Harry
Potter, *and is a little bit of a weirdo, especially in her
sense of fashion.*   **—L.M.**

Some of my earliest memories from the Philippines are way back at
school, when I was still a senior. I was in this group thingy at
school, this dance-troupe. I was a vice president. This troupe at
school, it was an elite organization. So it was a privilege for me. It was so
nice to be a part of that organization, because I met different people, you
know? Talented people, talented students. You could practice your craft,
your talent, especially in dancing, even in acting. They gave you chances
to perform in front of people. There were programs in school. We always
performed. Even out of town. Then we had this place at school and we
usually performed programs there. That's the thing that I miss most. And
those are the memories that I can't really forget. I practiced all my stuffs
there. One of the memories that I can't forget is still in school. As far as
I could remember, I was the girl in school who they always looked up to.
I was known as a Harajuku Girl [one who is always dancing in clubs],
because my fashion sense is really, really weirdo!

We had this counselor who always taught us to be confident in per-
forming, and to do our very best in every performance. They taught how
to be good with others, how to act in front of many people, how to create things, all of that stuffs. It's really nice to be there, you know what
I mean?

What made me decide to move? Not only me, of course; I was with
my family. My dad, and of course my brother. We don't know if we were
gonna have a good life here. We tried to. We tried to have a different life.
But we had a better life than before. We were happy, but still, we needed
to look for a different one.

I thought we were gonna be having a good life here, thinking of our
future. You know, lots of opportunities. We had some relatives over here.
And some of my friends were here. My aunts and uncles and my grandma. She was the one who petitioned for us to be here. She's the reason

why we are here. I could work while studying. I could support myself, and, of course, help my family. They're one of my priorities. But first things first: I need to finish school. We decided to move here because there were lots of job opportunities, and with good pay. Even though there are lots of bills to pay, as long as you have a secure job, you can live. Also I decided to move here because they said I could have lots of options going to college. Even though I couldn't afford it, they had this program where I could get scholarships, loans and other options. I could go to community college if I wanted to! That's it.

When we were moving, of course I was a bit sad at first. I was really, really sad, you know? I was going to miss all of my friends. You know, my homies are there; my friends are there. I was going to miss them so much, so badly. But then, when I started thinking of my future, like I was starting to be happy, 'cause not all Filipino people are given the chance to come here to the U.S.

A lot of our relatives are here. And we like it here, because unlike any other state, here there are lots of job opportunities. Especially here in our place. It's near everything! We're almost living in the very heart of the city... so we don't have any problems.

I traveled with you, my dear brother, and our dad. You know, I didn't really enjoy traveling with you, 'cause you were like pissing me off... when I was still on the plane. You're like, "Oh my gosh! It's our first time to be on the plane!" And I was like, "Sorry for you two. I've been to a plane ride before. I'm used to it."

Our date of departure was July 21, I think, 2004. It was summer here. Back home in the Philippines it was the rainy season. I was thinking, why was it sunny? And I was still catching up with the time change thingy. I hadn't slept for like two days. You know it was nighttime there, and over here, it was daytime. On my first week here, I was so messed up. But of course I got used to it by my second and third week. Now, I'm used to the day, and the weather, of course. It's a bit cold here. Way back at home it's so warm. So it's a total different thing being here.

At first I thought I was gonna study here. 'Cause I had just graduated from high school back home. But hmm... the thing went wrong, and everything got messed up. They promised that when I got here I'd go straight to school. And of course I was expecting that I was really going to college. But then, when we got here, people were trying to tell me that you need to find a job, to work, and to live. I was like so disappointed when they told me that I couldn't study!

You know, what? I'm still a bit mad, 'cause if I wasn't here I'd still be in the Philippines, and for sure I'd be in college, still enjoying my life there. I'm not feeling that I don't want to go to work. But [here], you can't find a nice job if you don't finish school. When still in the Philippines, I had a good life. My mom and dad would do anything just to send us to school, I mean a private school, and they would make sure that we were going to be somebody. But here people were trying to tell us what to do and what was good for us, and trying to control our life! They were pissing me off! I was like, we know what to do! Their point was, we are new here and they're trying to tell us that everything here is way different. But duh! We can live with that! We are independent!

I hate to tell this, but these people that I'm talking about are mean. So I ended up paying the bills and all that stuff, you know? It's so totally different. I don't like this kind of thing. I don't like this kind of world. So my plan is, maybe, to go back to the Philippines to take up college, or earn a bit here. Maybe here, if I'm that lucky, maybe if I will afford it. I want to go to college here, you know?

The number one problem here in Frisco was the high rent, the bills. It's so expensive! We didn't have a place to live at. A house, that was the very first problem. I never had any job before. I was still, like, underage, under twenty-one. I was having a hard time looking for a good job here, especially since I hadn't finished college. I hadn't *entered* college yet. I was expecting that I would be taking up nursing or something. But the thing is, I ended up being at Burger King! I'm working at Burger King right now, as a food server. I was supposed to be at school, you know? But this is life... We need to pay the bills. It's really hard here: go to college, and get a degree. It shouldn't be that way. How can people have a good life, get a good job, if they don't [have] the money to spend to go college? How can they pursue the American dream? That's is so wrong.

I'm a full-blood Filipino "muggle." For now I think I don't consider myself as an American, 'cause I just got here. Maybe when I'm already a citizen. 'Cause I haven't even been living here for five years. Maybe in the future, maybe I will, I don't know....

I BELIEVED THAT WAS DESTINY

CINDY BI, JINAN SHANDONG, CHINA
INTERVIEWED BY EMILY (XUAN) SHANG

When I interviewed my mom under a warm, pale-yellow light, it was 8 pm. She had just come out of a comfortable bath, and she was in her pretty pink pajamas. She looked a little bit sleepy. —E.S.

I was born and grew up in Jinan. Jinan is a beautiful middle-sized city in China. It's also the provincial capital of Shandong. The four seasons in Jinan are very different. The spring in Jinan is windy, but warm. Flowers are very beautiful at that time. The autumn is very short, but the air is very fresh. We always celebrate the Autumn Festival, which is my favorite festival. People usually go home, have dinner together, and enjoy watching the full and bright moon. The full moon means getting together. The winter is freezing. It usually snows two or three times. The summer is very hot. I don't really like these two seasons in Jinan. Jinan is also called "Spring City" because there are a huge number of springs spread all over Jinan. Jinan has been developing very fast during these last several years, and streets have become wider. A lot of buildings have been built, and more and more factories are there. The economy of Jinan has become very strong. Meanwhile, the public security has become much better. My parents told me if I went back to Jinan, I wouldn't know the city.

The people I miss very much are my parents, my friends, and my daughter. However, my daughter has already come here; my homesickness is getting much better than before. I also miss the food in Jinan very much. It's very delicious!

Food is a big part of the culture in Jinan. Toasted sweet potato is the most famous dessert of Shandong. However, Jinan food is not just sweet potato. There's also chicken and pork with a kind of sauce that tastes very sweet. The steaming lotus root is another unique food in Jinan. The lotus roots are grown in Da Ming Lake, which is one of the famous lakes in China. Another favorite dessert is called *Tang Hu Lu*, which is made with haw and sugar. We like those kinds of foods.

I went to primary school, middle school, high school, and medical school in Jinan. I got the best education there. I think the Chinese education is very strict in that students must remember all the knowledge which is in the books, and do a lot of practice to remember it. However, I think Chinese education lacks creativity. It does not fit in with all the students.

When I was very young, the Cultural Revolution happened. The high school students and the college students couldn't go to school, and they had to go to the countryside to work as farmers. Fortunately I was in primary school at that period of time. I stayed in the city and studied in school. When I was old enough to go to high school, the Cultural Revolution was over. I didn't want to leave school to find a job because I thought I would lose a lot of chances to get a good education and find a great job in China. So I studied very hard and got ready to go to a high-level high school. Finally, I did it. I went to the best class in a high-level high school in Jinan. It meant I could go to a good college when I graduated. After I graduated from high school, I went to Shandong Medical School. After that, I became an internist. Even though being a doctor in China cannot earn as much money as the doctors who work in America, we have very good status.

I have a sister who is ten years younger than me. She was feeble when she was very young. The reason that I wanted to be a doctor was to help my parents to take care of my sister.

I came here because I believed that I would get another great life in America, you know? America is the richest country in the world now. But I think it is hard because when I just came to America, I couldn't speak English very fluently, so I couldn't find the right job. However, I didn't want to give in. I wanted to have a good life in America. So I tried to study English very hard. I found my English improved very fast! I thought that I could do anything I wanted as long as I stuck to my goal. Before long I found a job as a private nurse.

I went to City College of San Francisco when I came to America, and had a lot of classmates. After studying together so much, some of us now have very deep friendships. I also go to church. The people in the church are very nice. When you have problems, they always like to come over and help you out. They say, "We are in Jesus, we are one family." We love each other and take care of each other. I also have a lot of friends in my church.

When I was in China, I had never heard about church, because the people who live in China believe in atheism, which is a part of the theory of communism.

Why did I come to America? I believed it was destiny. I really didn't know why I chose to come to California. However, I like living in California because the air is very clean, the sky is very beautiful, and the people are very kind here. I don't want to move to any other place.

I think American education is very good, but it's hard. The students work as hard as they can to get a high score. If the students don't study, they will fail very easily. We also have more time to study by ourselves than in China. I prefer American education, because I feel free here. And if I do what I can do, I always can get a high score here. In China, sometimes even though you did your best to do the work, you might not get a high score, because the teachers just wanted you to give them the right answers.

I've been here for four years. I think I have a nice life. I have a job, which is enough to pay the cost of living. I have a car. In China, people cannot always afford a car. I rent an apartment with my daughter now, I feel the rent is very expensive. So I've decided to buy a house. I believe my life will get much better.

For the future, first, I want to have my own house. Second, I want to give my daughter the best education. Third, I want to go back to China to see my parents. And I want my parents to come to America and live with my daughter and me.

I believe my life will get better and better.

Translated from Mandarin

I STARTED AT SIX YEARS OLD
TO BE THE MAN OF THE HOUSE

MERITA KAULAVE, PAGO PAGO, AMERICAN SAMOA
INTERVIEWED BY JONATHAN KAULAVE

My mom is a strong, loving mother who cares about her
kids' future. She was interviewed in her bedroom.—J.K.

I was born in America Samoa, on a little island called Masosi. We lived
in huts, and my experience there was... We grew our own food. We
had pigs, chickens, all sorts of stuff. It was really laid-back. In our
island, we built our own huts. We made our own blankets and things like
that. It was very, very hot and humid there. Even when it's raining you got
family out there swimming. It just helped us cool off a little bit. We're all
a great big family on that island, and within that one family there were
like twenty families. We worked as a team; we always worked together. We
always took care of each other. There was only one family that had television, and that family was stubborn and would [usually] never share. But
they wanted the whole island to come and watch TV with them. And the
show they watched most was *The Price Is Right*.

The education system in my homeland [involved] a lot of discipline.
If we didn't do what the teacher said, we would get the paddle. They'd
either whack you on the butt, or do the same amount of smacks on your
hand. We have pride. That's basically it, and family virtues. The Polyne-
sian people have only one way of disciplining their kids. You give them a
warning, and then you give a second warning. And if they do it again you
either give them the belt or something else. That's basically how we discipline our kids, so when they grow up they'll have respect for others.
I believe that works. I believe that abusing your kids is not right, but it's
to teach them a lesson not to do it again. I believe that our kids are getting that same message as our ancestors did.

[When] I was three years old, my mom gave birth to my sister Kiki.
And right when she gave birth to my sister, she decide to move to Hawaii,
so she could get a better life. We left our homeland in an airplane. All the
choices were made by my mom, since she divorced my dad. She thought
that Hawaii was a better place to raise kids. We didn't have enough money.
My dad ended up moving to Hawaii, too, where we were, and he gave my

mom a pretty hard time. Actually, my mom came from a very abusive relationship. She was beaten up and she couldn't take it anymore. So she grabbed us and took our family and moved here to California, where she had family. [I was thinking] where are we going to go, and what are we going to do, and how are we going to survive? I started, at six years old, to be the man of the house. I would take care of my sister and my mom. My dad was never there for us. My dad was like a player. He thought he was a man. My dad was always playing around. He was never serious. But my mom was a family woman and she wanted to take care of the kids.

I don't think we prepared ourselves. We just got up and left [Hawaii]. We didn't pack nothing, we just left. The people in the plane, they really treated me nice, my sisters and my mom. When we got off the plane it was cold. It wasn't the same weather as Hawaii. We didn't expect the weather to be cold. We just thought we were moving from one place to another. We didn't expect a lot.

When we arrived, my mom told me that her uncle was picking us up from the airport. But unfortunately, when we got to the luggage area, no one was waiting. My mom, she didn't speak much English, but she did her best to try to get us to where we need to get. I don't know what was the mix-up but my mom went and got a cab for us to get to her cousin's house. After we caught a cab, her uncle was waiting there, and it was a lot of miscommunication. So her uncle finally took us, and we went to his house, and we settled in. The same night they made us a nice dinner, showed us to our room, and right then and there everything was okay.

I miss the ocean. I miss the weather. I miss the little island get-togethers, which we call the *luaus*. A *luau* is like a big celebration where everybody gets together and dances and has fun. Those are the main things that I miss.

FOLLOWING MY HOPES
AND DREAMS FOR LOVE

ANONYMOUS, TORREON, MEXICO
INTERVIEWED BY ANDREA AVILA

*My grandmother is a smart, independent woman who is
full of love, humor, and compassion. While speaking to
her you don't just hear her words, but you feel them, too.
I think that she's a very important woman in this world,
and without her, life wouldn't be complete. I love my
grandma.* —A.A.

I was born in Torreon, Mexico. There were no cars, no nothing.
We—my mom, father, brothers, and sisters—were not too rich and
not too poor. We were in the middle. We studied. There was no TV
when I was little. It's very funny because we didn't have a lot of money,
same as here. My house had three bedrooms and a kitchen. Every day I
went to school 'cause I was very smart in school. School was from nine
to one, then three to about five or six. I went to both. At school I took
all the classes—math, everything. All the kids knew how to crochet, how
it worked, or they couldn't pass to the next year. We learned needlepoint,
everything.

We had cousins who owned a very nice vintage car, and they had a
cousin who had green eyes and looked like Robert Redford, everyone
admired him. We went there to visit Grandma and all them. We all just
really liked being around each other. We used to play with these flowers
that are like little red holly. Smaller than that—they looked like little red
cherries. We used to play with different flowers and make things out of
them. There's a snapdragon flower; if you move it a certain way it looks
like it's barking. We used to call them little puppies. You know, I still like
plants a lot.

I came to El Paso, Texas, in 1958 on the bus. It was maybe twelve
hours from my hometown to El Paso; now it's different. I went there after
I married. Uncle Robert, Auntie Elsa, and Auntie Blanca were born
there in Texas. I lived in Texas maybe two or three years. When I was
growing up I didn't plan on leaving Mexico. I only moved because I got
married. My house had only one room because I had no kids. Your

grandpa and me got married on September 6, 1958. I would tell your auntie how handsome he was (laughs). Grandpa would tell the kids how he would wait for me to get off work because he couldn't believe how beautiful I was (laughs).

We left El Paso for San Francisco because of your grandpa. We used to live in the San Pablo hotel in Oakland, on the main street, well one of the main streets. I remember your grandpa used to commute to San Francisco for work, probably on the AC Transit. It was a nice place, and I remember I used to look after your grandpa and make sure he made it safely. Your grandpa never missed a day of work. Even if he was sick, he never missed a day of work.

Then we lived in the Excelsior apartments. We were on Mission Street. And oh, that was unbelievable. I don't remember how many stairs, but I would go to do the laundry and carry my little cart down those stairs like it was nothing. I would do the laundry across the street, and then I'd bring it back up. It must have been about a hundred something stairs. I was always a very strong woman. I babysat quite a bit of kids. People knew I was a good mother and good with kids. My neighbor, she always would visit me. I don't recall her name, but I know she used to visit me. In the apartment complex, there was a nice playground where I would have the kids go so I could bake. I make a very good cake that has orange zest in it. And I asked your Auntie Blanca to learn how to make it because it would be a nice wedding cake. She made it. It was really very delicious. She made it from scratch.

We moved because I dreamed of having a house. That was in March. I remember it was about four days before your Auntie Blanca's birthday, maybe March 24, 1963. The house was a greenish color, like a pastel greenish color, and your grandpa didn't like that. So he put a panel up right away in the living room. The house had a lot of doors. Your grandpa took them down the same day. I remember he painted Elsa and Blanca's room. When we first moved there, Auntie Elsa and Blanca got the back bedroom. It was so nice because, in the morning, they would hear the birds when they got up; it was spring. Then me and your grandpa [were] in the front where Auntie Elsa is now. We loved the house and we had a nice backyard and the kids would play there all the time. The kids would have water fights with the hose.

Your dad was born here in San Francisco. I had never worked. I just stayed here with the kids. My first memory was of a lot of work that your grandpa worked, for all the four kids and me. I worked as a nanny. I would take care of thirty kids to pay for the house. I only hope my grandson [and] granddaughter go to school in a university. I'm glad I moved here. I love this city. I have lived here for forty-two years, in this house.

Parts of this interview translated from Spanish

BACK AT THE ISLAND

SEGA TUAPOLA, AMERICAN SAMOA
INTERVIEWED BY JOHN TUAPOLA

My mom, Sega Tuapola, is thirty-nine years old. She is a mother of three. She was born and raised in American Samoa. She is really loving, caring, and open-minded to all people. She is also really big on religion.   —J. T.

My name is Sega Tuapola. My birthday is July 30, 1966. I was born in American Samoa. Samoa is a small, beautiful tropical island. It's warm, not cold, but it rains sometimes. It is like paradise. People come all over the world to spend their vacation there. First of all, I want people to know that Samoan people are.... Samoan people are loving, caring, and respectful people. I don't know how other people around the world, how they see Samoans, but from my understanding that is how we are. The other thing I'd like to add about Samoan people is that [they like] hearing what other people say and think about Samoans. Some people think like if they see Samoans are big and heavy, they get scared of them. Some people think that we are monster people. They're scared of Samoans. We're not like that. We are just loving, caring, and respectful people. If you see a Samoan and wonder why they are big and heavy like that, it is because when we were little our parents would feed us a lot of fat food, like pig, chicken, and a lot of starch (laughs).

The other thing that I want people to know is that we are really big on religion. Back home that is one of the biggest things. That is the number one thing back home, for my family and myself. It is bigger than sports, and sports are really big for us. We compete with other villages and see who is the best in every sport—football, softball, cricket, and the biggest one, volleyball. Samoans are really competitive in sports. They really don't like to lose.

The thing I remember the most was waking up every Sunday and getting ready for church. First I had to go to Sunday school, then we would have our service right after Sunday school. Of course any kid back home would love to wake up in the morning to go to church. It is like waking up in the morning to go and see your friends. Going to church back home, it is like going to see your friends, because you mostly know everybody. They all live in your village, so everybody knows each other.

I can remember some things growing up in my village. In those days I would go to school and come home with my older brothers and sisters. I had both of my parents at home, and I remember we had a lot of fun. After school, we would come home and do what our parents wanted us to do, like picking up trash, feeding the pig, and other things. I remember my brothers and me going outside and playing on the swing. We would always swing and jump into the ocean, because our house was right next to the ocean. We would get on the swing and swing as high as we could and then jump into the ocean. Really, every day we would go swimming in the ocean.

I left Samoa when I started to have a family. I had a child. Plus, by looking back and looking how the lifestyle is in Samoa, it wasn't helping my family or me in those days. I know that I couldn't depend on my parents to help me and my family my whole life. So my husband and I made a decision to move to the States, to find a future for my child and ourselves. Something like that. It wasn't easy back home. Samoa wasn't a big island and the jobs were not like how they are in the States, like how I see it right now. If you work over there I don't know how you are going to make it. If you work back home, it is like two-dollars-something an hour, if you compare it to the life out here is, it is way different. I don't think that you can survive life back home. That is why my husband and I talked, said we had to leave our island and our family, and come to the States to find a better life. I'm not saying that Samoa wasn't a good place to stay, but I wanted a better life for my family. Of course my family supports me. They were one hundred percent behind me. They didn't have anything against me, my husband, and my little baby. They just let us know how they felt, and they gave us their blessing to leave Samoa and come find a better life for us. Of course my oldest brother had already left, then my third oldest brother left, and then I left. We all had the same reason. They wanted to find a better life for their families. I felt so sad that I was going to leave my family, friends, and my homeland. But I had no choice. I miss my family a lot, but I have to do what is best for my family and me.

The other thing that I was scared about was that I didn't know anybody in the States when I came here. You don't know how people act, what kind of lifestyle they live here. It is not like how it is in Samoa. You can go from one house to another, go talk to other people around your village. Everybody knows each other over in Samoa. You can walk around the street without people looking at you different, yelling at you, and calling you names.

It wasn't that I really chose San Francisco. It was because my husband's family was over here that we came up to San Francisco. The first thing that I felt was the cold air (laughs). Wow! It was damn cold. It wasn't like how it was back at the island. At the island it wasn't ever this cold. That was the first thing that I felt when I stepped out of the plane—the cold air. I wasn't ready for the cold. I didn't know that it was even cold out here. I looked around, and everything I saw was really big. I had never seen this many people at an airport before. When I got here I saw a lot of different people every day and night, and you could hear how loud they were outside and around your house. It made you scared to go outside of the house, because I wasn't used to it. The lifestyle out here is really weird. At home, not a lot of people would be outside late at night talking loud.

This lifestyle wasn't easy for me to get used to. As the years went on, I had my second child, my son. It was a real important part of our life because we had to find a bigger house for ourselves and we had to find a better job for both of us, since now we had two kids. And now we know that life here is really expensive, even when you have two kids.

The thing that I miss the most about Samoa is my family—my dad, my two brothers and sister that stayed back home with my dad, my friends and my other family, like my cousins and uncle. The last thing that I want to say is I'd like to give thanks to God for the blessing, guidance, and everything that he helped me with, my family, and especially what he did for my three kids. How he guided them and helped them on all their things that they need help on. I still live here in the States, for over seventeen or eighteen years. And yeah, that is all I have to say.

TO A LAND OF CHANGES

ALLAN, KOWLOON, HONG KONG
INTERVIEWED BY WARREN CHOY

*My friend Allan is always worried about others. Caring
for others is what makes him happy.* —*W.C.*

I was born in Hong Kong. In Kowloon, Hong Kong. That's where my mom, my dad, my brother, and my sister was born. We were living in project homes, the government homes, because we were poor. My dad would go to work, and we lived in a one-bedroom place. That's it. There was no living room, no nothing, so five of us lived in one room.

I went to school in the afternoon. They had a morning session and an afternoon session. I attended the afternoon class. I'd go to school at twelve o'clock, and then get off six o'clock. I learned typical kid things like English, math, social studies, and all that stuff. [I was good at every-thing] except Chinese, the calligraphy and stuff. We had to go to school on Saturdays, too, and they're very strict people in Hong Kong. [With] the education, they're very strict. Like, the teacher could slap people, could punish, physically punish us. That's what all the teachers were supposed to do, in a way.

I did not have a social life. I was a kid. Mainly we played in the park. There were no computers. I think there were some, but we never owned a computer, so we usually played with our neighbors, you know? With a project housing, there were about a hundred people on each level. We just played with people around us, and helped around at home a lot.

My dad's older sister got married and they moved to San Francisco. When she got her citizenship, she applied for our whole family. My dad and my mom wanted to come here. We tried to escape 1997, when Hong Kong was turned over from England. Hong Kong at that time, before 1997, was one of the colonies of England. So we thought if Hong Kong turned over to China, everything would be really bad. Living in Hong Kong, it is really hard to go to university. So we wanted to come to America to have my parents said it was for us, a better education for us. So that we could have a chance to go to a university, and to get a good job, and to make more money. It was better than staying in Hong Kong.

The only thing I remember about the government is they used to come to our school to clean our hair and wash our teeth, and we would go to the library. They used to have the library in trailers so we would go to rent books in the trailers.

[In Hong Kong] my dad worked at a dry cleaner's, and my mom didn't work. She was a homemaker and she did stuff like sewing at home to make extra money. I think they made about 1,000 dollars a month for the whole family, every month.

I think [this was enough to live on] because it's government housing and we didn't really live a lavish life. [We had] enough to pay for our books for school, because in Hong Kong, we had to buy our own books every semester. And food every day. We didn't spend money on vacations. We never had vacations, so I guess it was okay. [My parents told us we were going to America] when I was eleven, several months before we moved. [I was] excited. Going to America seemed to be very high-class.

I wanted to come because everyone says it's good [here]. Coming to America, land of freedom. But I also knew that I would miss my relatives, because all my relatives were in Hong Kong. So coming here meant that we had to forsake everything we had, especially our family and friends. So that's the only thing I miss. I expected to be living in big houses, because our auntie here said that she rented a place for us. So we expected that each of us would get our own room, that there would be a kitchen, and that there would be a bathtub, because we'd never seen a bathtub in our lives.

How did we prepare to leave? We did a lot of testing. Like medical tests and stuff. And we had to take a lot of X-rays to make sure that we didn't have anything serious, terminal diseases. Also, we had to take some English classes to equip ourselves with at least the basic level of language skills. And I think that's it.

We had a BNO. I don't know what that [stands for], but it's sort of like a Chinese/British passport. So we had an English passport.

We did not have a house [there]. We lived in a government housing project, so all we did was give it back to the government for people who needed it more than we did. We brought a lot of dishes and stuff. [We came] by airplane—my first time on an airplane. It was 1984.

My parents wanted their children to get a better education, because in Hong Kong, tuition is very, very high. And they wanted us to go to at least the university level because they'd never done that. Education here in the United States is free. So that's good.

My auntie, my dad's sister, was the one who went through all the trouble to get us to America. She applied, got us here, and helped us a lot. She rented us a room. She paid rent, and all that. [My parents' plans were] definitely to get a job quickly, and get to school quickly. I didn't have any plans. I was only eleven years old. So whatever my parents wanted me to do, I did it.

[My first impression of the U.S. was that] it was huge and different. Everything seemed so big. And also, things seem very slow here. The houses looked very old. And people dressed very badly compared to my old country. The people were very nice. People spoke a foreign language. People were very big, huge. People were very conservative compared to Hong Kong.

I lived very close to Chinatown. I didn't know there were so many Chinese people here. We lived there because we didn't know the language, so we could just go to Chinatown and buy our daily necessities. [I went to school at the] Chinese Educational Center. I adapted pretty well into the culture because there were teachers, and my auntie was helping me out a lot, so we didn't have to worry too much. Then my dad got a job very soon [afterward].

[It was hard to adapt to the] time because of the time zone thing. When it's daytime here, it would be nighttime there. Another thing to adapt to was how to use money. We had to keep calculating money. And also we had to adapt to the culture, because in Hong Kong everyone is the same race. Here you could see… I remember seeing all different kinds of people everywhere. People weren't as trendy as I thought they were. I thought there would be a lot more white people here. But there are a lot of Asians here, too, or I guess just in San Francisco. I was surprised that they didn't give homework [in school]. In Hong Kong we had a lot of homework every single day. Here there were maybe one or two home-works each day, and I was sort of upset.

I have lived in San Francisco ever since I moved here. I have learned a lot of stuff. I like the slow pace. I get to enjoy life more here. I go back to Hong Kong every year, but I don't like it anymore. But there's a lot of stuff to buy and look at, so I sort of miss that part of it. [I also miss my] grandma and my relatives.

I guess I've been acculturated into the U.S. I think I'm more of an American, but I also appreciate my Chinese culture. But I'm living in America, so I appreciate those special privileges. I consider myself a Chinese-American.

I AIN'T TRYIN' TO HOP NO BORDER

DIEGO ALVAREZ, COSTA RICA
INTERVIEWED BY ROBERT GAITAN

Diego Alvarez is a quiet, serious person, but he also likes to play around. —*R.G.*

The only thing I remember was that [Costa Rica] was a peaceful place. I lived on a big farm. I had cows and dogs and [stuff] like that. [We left] to have a better life. So I could have more money and a better education, and more freedom. We had to come to school wearing black and white and shiny black shoes. You had to come to school clean all the time or else they would send you home. [For fun,] we would go to the market and steal food and the people wouldn't chase us.

I left because I wanted to be with my mom. I came with my mom, grandma, and grandpa. I came by plane. I ain't tryin' to hop no border.

San Francisco was the first city I lived in. I think the first thing I can remember was going to the Golden Gate Bridge. My grandparents and my stepfather live here. I didn't like [my stepfather] because he wasn't good to me. He didn't like me. [My mom] wanted to come to California for a better life, but I'm not sure why she wanted to come to San Francisco. In school, I got into fights. But I learned [to speak English], because of my surroundings.

What happened to the animals in my farm? I don't know. I haven't been there in a long time. I have been back to Costa Rica only to visit. I only have a little family that still lives there now. I like it here in the U.S. better because we have better stuff over here, so I ain't sure if I will go move back. I don't know.

WHAT WE HAD TO TAKE,
WHAT WE HAD TO LEAVE

Monica Llerena, Lima, Peru
Interviewed by Maurizio Zegarra

My mom is forty-two years old. She's a very interesting, hard-working woman. We did this interview in her bedroom on a Sunday morning. She was very excited about doing this with me. —M.Z.

We used to live in the capital, in a little place called Los Cedros de Villa [within Lima, Peru]. We had a beautiful little house there, and it was painted white. People used to say it looked like a hospital, but I don't know. I always liked that color. The entire house was white. I think I did it so that I could combine the color of the furniture. Depending on the situation, sometimes we had to buy furniture of different colors, but it always went with the color of the walls. My dining room was cardinal red, my living room was baby blue, I loved it. And the little tables in the center were blue, and the glass in the tables were blue as well. Our house was about four blocks away from the beach. Since I was always working I didn't have a chance to visit the beach, but before you and your sister were born I used to walk the dog there. I used to just sit looking at the ocean, amazed at how big it was. The sea was very rough. You could always feel a strong breeze. The coast is all about the sea and the seafood, but you could also appreciate the good weather that we always had. We lived right next to a swamp, which was conserved because many exotic birds that migrate to the south during winter settled there.

I had a good job and we were in what was considered to be the middle-high class. But then we had many debts because the economy started changing. We all had visas because of the good job that I had, which helped a lot. Then I spoke to your father about coming here [to America]. There were many other things that pushed us to come here, but the main thing was the economic situation. I found myself later on without a job, and we had many debts to pay off. The most important thing was to come here and start over, and above all to have a better life.

For us a normal day started at 6:30 AM. You and your sister would wake up and get dressed, the bus would come and pick you up. By then I was already awake and drinking my daily coffee and waving you two off. Then I would take a bath, and my uniform for the bank would already be ready for me. While I was waiting for the little cart to take me to work I would put on my makeup. Every day it was the same thing at work. I worked in an office. The schedule was different to what I have now. I would start at 9:00 AM. Lunchtime was three hours long. At lunchtime I would always go to the mall with my friends. We were usually a group of five girls. After lunchtime we would keep on working until 6:00 PM, unless the boss had an important meeting to go to. Then we would have to stay longer, preparing the slides we had to show during the meeting. But then, when I didn't have to do all that, my job was mainly to see what was needed in our section: pencils, pens, computers, etc.

I liked working there because people were mostly friendly. I worked in a very modern building with high-tech electronics. I had to learn a lot about my job, though, because what I had to do you couldn't learn at the university. This was something you learned at the bank, taking a learning course. There was truly a lot to learn. There were ninety-nine offices in the building, and you also needed to know about the other banks that we controlled—which were about ninety-nine in the whole city. First I was in the lower branch of administration, then I went on to work in the treasury. After that, I went back to administration, but at a much higher— and you could say harder—level. They also bought new software, and since I was the worker with the most experience and the most years working in the bank, I was entrusted with trying the new software and fixing whatever problems it might have. I am also proud to say that that same program is still being used today at the bank.

I miss my job, the food, and the time I used to spend with my friends. But still, what I miss the most is my job. I've never had a good job like that one. I don't think I'll ever have another job like it.

For all Latino people, the United States is the land of opportunities, so I was excited because of the new life we were going to have, and the opportunity you and your sister were going to have to go to the universities here in the States. And everything I ever wanted to have, you and your sister would be able to get it. The main idea was to get a good job. I also wanted to enjoy California and learn more about it. It was very exciting, the idea of moving, but also very hard. It was very sad to leave everything we had ever known. I had many dreams, many ideas. Education is the base of the society and the culture of our country. Sadly, not everyone has access to our education because of money problems, etc, etc.

Coming to America was the most exciting thing. What we had to take, what we had to leave. I had to leave a whole bunch of my books. We were on the plane with winter clothes because in Peru in July it is the middle of winter. So naturally, when we got to Houston, we didn't know that it was really hot there, so we were burning. It was 102 degrees out. Houston to me was the most beautiful city I had seen in the U.S. so far. We had little trouble, except that they were checking our bags while we were transferring from the international airport to the domestic airport. There was a little police dog that started sniffing around the bags and kept on following us. So before there was any trouble, I asked a cop if there was any trouble, and he said no. But I was very relieved because I was scared that they were going to stop us or something. Other than that everything was cool. I was delighted to be in a new country, to hear another language other than my own. It was truly amazing.

California, without a doubt, is very beautiful. I especially love the way the houses are built, trying to keep nature beautiful. Since we are from the coast in Peru, we weren't used to seeing so many trees, all that nature. And of course all the people that have great taste and make gardens—that is what I loved the most. I liked everything that had to do with nature. Also, seeing a lot of beautiful birds—such as the cardinal.

My first job was the most disappointing thing of all this experience. I went to work folding napkins in a restaurant. It was horrible. I didn't want to wake up in the morning. Those first four months of my life here were a nightmare. However, all the people that helped me get that job, I really have to thank them, because it was hard trying to get a job. Time and money were running out.

I'm still not a citizen. I am merely a permanent resident through a marriage that went wrong. My second husband left me and got into drugs, and I suffered a lot. And I'm still suffering, because he left me in a bad economic position that I'm still trying to pay off. Everything I came to achieve in this country almost went down the drain, but thanks to the law and my attorney, I got my residence. We all came with a tourist visa, but after the six-month time limit we had here in the U.S., we had to live illegally. Then came my marriage, then the disappointment, then my attorney, and now, well, I have my residence. I hope things keep on like this so that I can get my citizenship later on. The most important thing I am focusing on is the education of my children.

What surprised [me] the most was the way the bosses in different jobs treated their people, the way they mistreated them so that they could get a promotion. There was also racism I had to endure from some people. I had to keep quiet because at the beginning I didn't know what could happen, since they were people with more authority over my job. I was afraid that they might kick me out or something. People here seem to be only interested in what helps them to get to the top. It doesn't matter who they step on or what sort of damage they might be inflicting upon those people. That was what surprised me the most, and also what disappointed me the most.

Translated from Spanish

GROWING UP IN THE GHETTO

EMILIO MEDINA, BROOKLYN, NEW YORK
INTERVIEWED BY JESSICA QUINTANILLA

Emilio is my youth leader from church. He was really excited about doing this interview. The interview was done at the church. —J.Q.

I come from Brooklyn, New York. The Green Point section of Brooklyn. It's a ghetto. It's actually one of the poorest, little ghettos in Brooklyn. It's an industrial area. They have a lot of old factories but mostly just little houses—tenement buildings.

Growing up in Brooklyn, in the ghetto, wasn't easy. First of all, I grew up watching my brothers and sisters thuggin' and wildin' out. My brother was a drug addict, heroin addict. So I seen him runnin' the steets. And growin' up as a boy, I seen my sisters always fightin' and gettin' high and doin' drugs. And so I told my mother that I would never do that. That I would not make her suffer the way they made her suffer. But I grew up wanting to be in the streets, also. I said, "Mom, let me go to the front of the house," and then I went from the front of the house to the corner, and from the corner I went to the next block. And from there I was lost, you know? I would hang out, and I would run the streets of Brooklyn. It wasn't easy, you know? I started using drugs. Drinking at the age of ten. At the age of twelve I was smokin' weed. I was stealin', robbin', I was thinking it was all fun and games. That's what I was doin'. I was hangin' out with the boys. I was breakin' into houses at the age of thirteen, and I was doin' a lot of things I wasn't supposed to be doin'. So that's how it was. It was hard for me growin' up. I didn't have a role model. My father was never there for me. He left me at the age of one, so I never knew him. My mom, she did the best she could. She raised us, you know? She raised us on welfare. She sent me to school and everything, but it was hard.

Well, I went to public school. I really wasn't so smart in school. I was in special ed. I was real slow at first (laughs). But I kept going to school, I kept learning, and then I left 'cause I got sent away to a home. I got sent to a youth home in upstate New York for bein' bad. I went to high school there. I graduated over there. My education was… it was okay. I could've done better. If I would have listened to my big brothers, and I would've listened to my mother that told me don't cut out of school, I think I would have finished a lot faster. But because I wanted to hang out with the boys, and I wanted to cut class and go to hooky parties, you know, hang out, I think it affected me a lot.

[I left] because they was tryin' to murder me out there in New York City (laughs). I did a lot of bad things. I was into drugs and alcohol. I was into, you know, doin' a lot of things that I shouldn't have been doin'. I had to run for my life. I came out here because I needed… I needed Jesus. I needed God to change my life. So I came to California with hope that my life would change.

Some friends I knew told me about California. They told me there was a lot of opportunity here. And that's why I came [at the age of thirty-one]. [I came to San Francisco] five months after I came from New York. I didn't know what to think. I didn't know what to expect. I was nervous. I was scared. I knew that there was hope. I knew that maybe I was gonna start new here. I felt hope. Coming to California, I knew it was gonna be a fresh start.

There was a lot of challenges on my way here. It was hard for me to leave my family. But I had to leave. I left everything behind. My mom, my family, my loved ones. You know, my old life I left behind also. I've come a long way. Another challenge was that a lot of people, when I came to visit the first time, they didn't understand me because I was of a different culture, and they didn't accept me. It was so hard for me. I didn't have any family [in California], but I had friends. I had a lot of friends and I had "the family." The Mexican family, which were friends, came to help me. They opened up their house to me. They really supported me, and they really didn't even know me. But they helped me a lot, and I'm grateful for them, you know? Because if it wasn't for them, I think, "Where would I be?" Maybe I'd be sleeping in the streets. But they opened their doors, and they fed me, and they did a lot of things for me.

I miss my family in New York City, my loved ones. I miss old friends. I miss the city itself—the sights, the big buildings, and the noise. I miss the fire engines that neva' stop and the police that neva' stop. I miss a lot of things, 'cause I was born and raised in New York City. The good part is I left the old man behind. I left the old things in the past, you know? I left the gangs and the drugs and all that behind. And so today, you know, I'm happy I left all that.

I got here through a friend. I met a Mexican pastor, and he introduced me to a family. I came to California to visit [Half Moon Bay], and when I came to visit, I enjoyed myself. I loved [it]. I saw the mountains. [The family] told me to come back. I wanted to come back. [After] I went back to New York, they helped me [come back here]. They sent for me, and I flew down here. They helped me get on my feet, and everything after that looks good.

A lot of times I've thought about going home. When it's gotten so hard that things weren't working for me the way I expected them to work. Things weren't looking right. At first it was hard for me to adapt to the culture here. I'm Puerto Rican, [and] there was not a lot of Puerto Rican food. I had to learn how to eat Mexican food and Salvadorean food. And I had to learn how to adapt to new people, new cultures. And yes, it was hard for me. Plus, I was lonely. I had no family here. I thought about going back a lot of times. But I kept on hoping that things would get better, and things did get better. And today I'm established, and I thank God. I'm doing much, much better.

California and New York City are the opposite. California's got a lot of mountains. A lot of beautiful scenery. The weather is beautiful. New York City is totally different. Yeah it's got mountains, but it's the fast life. The city never sleeps. New York City is fun, it's exciting. California is more mild and quiet. So I love California! Because the people are even friendlier.

When I was in Brooklyn, man, I was on a mission. I was lost. I was bound on drugs, I was bound on gangs. I was hurtin'. I mean I was lonely, and depressed, and oppressed, and possessed (laughs). I didn't know if I was coming or going. All I knew was that I needed help. And today, my life in California... I have direction. I have hope. Today I'm set free from drugs. I'm stable in all my ways. And I'm learning, I'm growing. Today I'm [a] man of God. I'm a Christian. I was never raised [knowing] anything about God. But God has changed my life—I'm a living testimony. I should have died a long time ago, you know? I could have overdosed on crack cocaine and a lot of drugs. But today I'm a young man, thirty-two years old. I got my right mind. I'm healthy. I got a good job. And it's possible. Things are possible.

PART IV

HERE
YOU FEEL RICH

THE TRAVELER WHO CAME
FROM "THE PARIS OF THE ORIENT"

STEVEN HAN, SHANGHAI, CHINA
INTERVIEWED BY YAN RAN TAO

Steven Han likes to travel. He has traveled through almost all of Asia and the United States. Nobody helped him during his journey. He just worked hard and saved money for his dream. —*Y.R.T.*

I come from China, Shanghai, the most prosperous city in China. Some people called it the Paris of the Orient. There are a lot of people who like to go to Shanghai because they want to know the new China there.

Shanghai is a big city with 1.3 million people. The residents of this city are from different places in China. It is the epitome of the whole Chinese culture.

I grew up in Shanghai, and had a very good education there. Since 1980, China has had a big change. It opened its doors, and there were a lot more opportunities. Now I want to know my hometown more, and to see different parts of Shanghai, see the new buildings. I want to go back. Speaking of my hometown, I want to thank my mother, because she gave me life and she took care of me very carefully when I was a child. I got a very good education because of my parents' encouragement.

I came to the United States in 1980. People had more freedom at that time. In 1990, China had a a cultural revolution. It was called *Wen Hua Da Ge Ming* in Chinese. People lost a lot of freedom. They did not have the freedom of speech. But now it's changed a lot.

When I was very young, I dreamed of being on ships from all different countries. I wanted to clean ships so I could get to travel for free. So when I was a child, I stood at the front of the port—Waitan (which means the "Shanghai Bay")—I saw many different ships from many different countries. I thought it would be a good way for me to travel. This is how I came to America.

I want to tell you another story. When I was in Shanghai, a long time ago, I met a Japanese man. At that time, Chinese could not speak to Japanese, but the Japanese guy I met was very friendly. I said hello to him, and he took pictures for me and I gave him my address. This was in 1987. Then he went back to Japan. Many months later, I got my first letter from another country. He mailed the color pictures to me. He was eighty-six years old, and I still keep in touch with him. In 1998, I went to Tokyo. I called him and told him I was there. Then I saw him. He was ninety-seven years old. He is still alive now, and I want to tell you that friends make you happy and you should give your heart to your friends. This was what I learned from my journey.

I have had many experiences travelling around Asia, America, and other places. When you have a dream, you try to make your dream come true. How do you make it come true? Just do it. Dream it and do it, and believe it. You smile, you give your heart to others, and others give their happiness to you.

Nobody helped me during my journey. I just worked hard and saved money for my dream, and just stayed with my friends in America. I did everything by myself. That way every day was the best day, the first day, and the last day of my life. I think the hard times made me grow up, and the hard times made me learn a lot from people. So I am a student forever and everyone is my teacher.

It was no different when I left my country, because I traveled around the whole of China and so everywhere is my home. So I came to America and it became my home. I didn't have any language problem, so I could easily touch the culture of this land. I traveled around almost forty-seven states in the U.S. I learned many different languages from people, from American Indians to others. Everyone was my language teacher. Everyday was a school day. When I travel around, this is my journey.

I want to tell you about the story of my journey, back in 1995, when I traveled in Alabama. I wanted to take the bus. I was waiting for the bus to go to Montgomery. A very old guy saw me and asked me where I came from. I told him I came from China. Then he asked me which city I came from. When I said "Shanghai," he was very surprised and emotional. He asked me if I wanted to come to his home. I said okay, I have time, so I went to his home and he showed me his pictures. In 1928, he came to China; he was an American soldier. And he fell in love with a Chinese singer, a very famous singer. They both fell in love, then three days later, the American army left Shanghai and went to the Philippines. So he had to leave her. He showed me many pictures from that time and told me his love story. I still keep in touch with him. He is ninety-three years old now.

I traveled all around the United States, so I saw that each state was different. For me, there were a few reasons [for coming to California]. The weather here is good and the Golden Gate is here. And there is more Asian culture here. Also, there are many different foods here. The weather is good and the people are friendly—I think it is the best state. It is very easy to open your heart to exchange culture and it is easy to make friends. I like it here. This is the reason that I live in California.

I want to tell you the truth about my first week in America. I had many pen pals before I came to the U.S. I told you before that I think everyone is my teacher. People gave me new ideas and information, so that changed me a lot. So I thank them. I came to Chicago and saw my friends there. I stayed at their wonderful house. The first week, we went to the downtown area and some famous places. I had a wonderful week and it helped me know how to communicate with American people.

The most important thing I can tell you is to study, study, study. Every day is the first day and the best day and the last day of your life. Learn more from people. Try to smile to other people and show your heart to others. That way you can have a heart-to-heart exchange.

Translated from Mandarin

I KNEW I HAD TO MOVE ON
WITH MY LIFE

Mayra del Carmen Gomez, Corinto, Nicaragua
Interviewed by Freddy Gomez

My mom is a loving mother who cares for her family. She was interviewed in our living room. —F.G.

My name is Mayra Gomez. I am forty-six years old and I came from Corinto, Nicaragua.

Corinto is located in the province of Chinandega. It is the main gate of transportation in Nicaragua. I was not raised with my *mamá*. I was raised with one of my aunts because we were nine brothers and sisters and my mom and dad were not working at the time, so my aunt helped out my mom. My auntie took care of the three oldest—Enrique, Antonio, and me. Because there were no jobs, work didn't come around very easily. My dad couldn't find any work. I went to primary school, I did three years of secondary, then I went to a study course for nursing. My aunt came through with a scholarship and I went to go study nursing for one year.

I got a nursing job at the hospital in Corinto. I had experience in giving shots and offering programs about pregnancy. I also did emergency work—broken bones, flesh wounds and other things. I miss nursing. I didn't do it here because I was afraid of making a mistake and getting in trouble. I have been a janitor for eighteen years. I work as a custodian in buildings downtown. But I just got into an accident and I am not working right now.

I met your father because we were in the same neighborhood. When we were young adults—about seventeen, eighteen years old—we started to fall in love. We were going out for about three years, and we got married on the eighteenth of December, 1976. We got married in Corinto, and there was a little family get-together. There was family from your dad's side and my family right there in our house in Corinto. I had one son, George, born on June 21, 1977.

Freddy, my husband, worked as a welder in the docks of Corinto, and they would come to pick him up in the middle of the night for work. Some of the people who got picked up, they would find them dead in the morning. Some say the guards may have killed them, thinking they were Sandinistas. They would find them dead in the morning with gunshot wounds to the head.

George, my son, fell from a tree [when he was six], and he landed on his knees. He did not say a thing when I saw him limping and asked him what was wrong. He just told me his knee hurt. I took a look at it and it was swelling up. I took him to the doctors. They told me that he needed X-rays, and he needed to go see a bone specialist. From there they operated on him, and they told me that his wounds were infected. We took him to many other specialists. They told me his leg would have to be amputated. So I found another bone specialist in Chinandega, and he was the one who operated on him. He had to take off the kneecap and unite the two bones together. That is the reason that my son can't bend his right leg. That was the second reason I had to come [to America]—to put my son in doctors' hands so he would be able to bend his knee again.

At that time in Nicaragua, there were problems with the Sandinistas. What I knew about the Sandinistas was they lived like normal people; they dressed normally. They did not have a certain dress code until they won; then they wore the colors black and red. The Sandinistas wanted to take the power from the government. They wanted to make it like Cuba, with no liberty and everything under their control. If you said anything bad about them, they would put you on a list called the Black List. That meant that you were the enemy.

I thought the United States was the country of paradise. I thought for the health of my son and my whole family, [we should] live in a free state. Some, not all of my expectations were met, because I still haven't learned the language. I understand it but I can't read, write, or speak it.

We took an airplane. Your grandmother had bought the tickets, and we left Nicaragua in an airplane, straight to Mexico. We took birth certificates, passports, the clothes that we had on, and food. I left Nicaragua on the fifteenth of August, 1984, for Mexico. And I got to the United States two days before Thanksgiving, that same year. I felt sad for part of it, because I knew I was going to miss my family, but I still had to find a better future for them, and a specialist for my son.

We left, all five of us, in an airplane for Mexico. Before that, we caught a taxi that took us to Puebla, where one of my husband's mother's nieces lived. We stayed about three weeks. We had the Mexican identification [papers] for all of us because we had to drive on a bus and pass through a couple of checkpoints. From there we bought tickets to Tijuana. First to Guadalajara, then to Tijuana. There we stayed at a hotel that the *coyote* had told us to stay at. When the *coyote* picked us up at the hotel, we left a little late. We crossed a freeway and we started to walk. We walked really far. We walked until we got to a place where there were a lot of old cars and scraps of metal and wood. We could hear a helicopter looking for people trying to get across. The *coyote* had told us to hide in the old cars. When the *coyote* said it was safe, we kept on walking until we arrived at a village, where a car was waiting to take us to the *coyote*'s house. When we arrived, the *coyote* gave us food to eat. We asked the *coyote* what part of the United States we were in. He said we were in Los Angeles. The next day the *coyote* got in contact with my husband, so he could send him the money for bringing us across and to buy the Greyhound tickets to go to San Francisco. I did not find the *coyote*. It was your dad's brother, your uncle.

I knew I had to work any job that came my way. I wasn't going to come to work as a nurse even though I had studied it. I did not know how to speak English, and I needed to find a hospital that could help my son. I was not scared. I felt weird coming to a whole new place that I did not know. I was not used to it or the language.

The first thing I noticed was the weather; we were dying from the cold. We had to sleep on the floor. We did not have any other clothes, so if we took a shower, we had to wear the same thing again.

At the beginning I missed my family and friends back home. When I got a job, I knew I had to move on with my life and put my son and niece into school. I warmed up to the weather and working hard but I missed my house, our neighbors, and all of my family.

The difference here is the climate, the people, the language, and the things I was used to doing in Nicaragua, like sitting right in front of our home on a sunny day. Here, you're inside from all the danger and all the gangs. The supermarkets over there are different. The main thing was the food. Because back in Nicaragua, when I [needed groceries], there were no supermarkets. You had to go to the corner store with your shopping card, for them to give you a bottle of oil. Or a pound of rice, or a pound of sugar. But here you have everything in different sizes in the supermarket.

It took more than a year to save money to get our own apartment. We found an apartment in the Mission district. It was hard. Our first job was sweeping Candlestick Park when the 49ers or the Giants played, or we would be cleaning other people's houses. Then, when we could not find a job, we would go to church to look for a job. We have been here about twenty-one years. I have three children, one born in Nicaragua, and two born here in the United States. Mayfred, she is nineteen years old. Freddy Gomez Jr. is sixteen years old.

I would go back because my side of the family is over there. And you don't have to pay rent. I'm tired of paying rent. I've spent so much paying rent. I would rather spend money on things over there than on rent. I don't know how the future [is] going to be here, with so many laws, and so many privileges taken away; so many benefits they are taking away. I don't know how everything's going to end up.

Translated from Spanish

HERE YOU FEEL RICH

JOEL CASTILLO, PHILIPPINES
INTERVIEWED BY JAKEY CASTILLO

*This interview took place at my house, in my dad's room,
at 9:00 PM. The interviewee was my dad, Joel Castillo.
He is a mechanic and a pretty funny person.* —J.C.

I lived with my real dad, my cousins, and my auntie [in the Philippines]. [I moved to California] because I got a petition with my mom. My real dad had passed away already.

I didn't have anything when I was a kid. I didn't have toys or anything else valuable, just my family. It's hard because you work all day at the house; you do a lot of work. It's hot and dusty. I didn't like the weather very much because you get all sweaty and hot when you are working. Your body feels like it's burning.

Most of my experiences are just work. That's what I mostly did when I was a little kid. There wasn't time to play or anything like that, just the regular chores that normal kids would do. You know, wash dishes, get water for the household, clean the house, and throw the trash out. I can't say I liked doing it. I just had to do it.

I [understood English], but I couldn't speak it because I was young, so I didn't really practice speaking English in the Philippines. It's a second language [there]—that's why I understood it already.

[In] California you can have anything. In the Philippines you have to work your ass off. Here you feel rich, you know? [Did I encounter] hardships? Nothing really, just getting [parking] tickets from the police (laughs). Everyone treats me well here. Everyone is kind and polite. They treat you like an equal because everybody goes through hardships.

I live here [now] with my mom, half-sister, cousins, and aunt. I enjoy [being] here because it's an easy life, not like the Philippines. I work as a mechanic, and it's an easy job for me because I understand cars well. I have a lot of experience now. I was too young [to work on cars in the Philippines]. I used to work on my bike. [It was] a two-wheeled bike (laughs), five speeds, and ten speeds.

WE AIN'T GOT NOTHING TO EAT

JOSUE DOLE, HONDURAS, CENTRAL AMERICA
INTERVIEWED BY LYEISHIA BLUE

Josue Dole is a funny boy. We did this interview in the United Playas room at Balboa High School. He was wearing a Black Diamond jacket, blue jeans, a white tee, and a pair of white Air Force Ones. **—L.B.**

My name is Josue Dole. [I'm in] eleventh grade. [I grew up in] Honduras, in Central America. It's big, like San Francisco. About seven million people live there, indigenous... like mixing indigenous with Spain 'cause it was founded by Spain.

My mom is kind of the reason [we came here]. We didn't have nothing to eat, like most of the Latinos [who] come to this country. It was hard [in Honduras], 'cause you have a lot of people who like using drugs around you.

I want to go back to my country, but just to visit, not to live again! If I go back to my country, I'm not going to be living the way I'm living here in the United States. I think it is better here and I [am] living way better than I used to live in my country.

Living in my country is really hard 'cause most of the people won't survive like you do here. [The U.S is] just a country where you get opportunities to study, to be somebody. In [my] country, most of the people, they don't survive.

[When I came here, I was] thirteen and I didn't speak English. It took two years to learn. It was like harder [for] me, 'cause I didn't speak no English, and then it was hard to communicate with other people who ask you, or talk trash 'bout you when you don't speak the language.

[When I came here, I knew] just my mom and my sister. I wasn't planning nothing. I just thought that being with my mom and family would be better. She was working here while I was in my country for about thirteen years. The way people live here is way better than in my country.

[The first thing I remember seeing] was the downtown (laughs), 'cause in my country we don't have those kinds of downtown. So it really impressed me to see the big buildings.

In my country you could go anywhere you want. Here, if they see youth, they won't let you go out. In my country, it could be around 1:00 or 2:00 AM and you can be out in the street, and they won't tell you anything. But [in the] United States they go ask you where your parents at, or something like that (smirks).

I miss my friend, my auntie, and my cousins.

It cost my mom 1,000 dollars to get me here because she wanted me to come like [an] immigrant, [with] papers. So it was 'bout twelve or thirteen years until she got some papers and she paid the immigration. And then, after two years, I came to the United States.

In United States you got a lot of opportunities. It's really easier to get into college. In my country you got to pay a lot of money, and it's hard to get in, 'cause only like the smartest people in my country get to be in college. I like the way you live here, and it's better than other countries. You don't have to be born here. You still can get in, be like a governor, like Arnold Schwarzenegger (laughs).

Two of my cousins, they came 'cross the border, and I came in an airplane, so their experiences [were different]. They walked, like, three days [in the desert], and didn't have anything to eat or drink.

[People need to know] that we are not the same, because like some people, not only for my country but from other countries—come to the United States [for different reasons]. The reason you should come to this country is for the opportunities that this country is offering you. But then other people, like with other countries, and my country, they just come to destroy the country instead of helping it.

My mom came first [to the U.S.]. She used to work any job or craft job until [we came], because she just worked for us so she could send us money, so me and my auntie could survive.

I first heard [that Balboa] was the worst high school in San Francisco, but when I came here it was different. I thought it was really bad but it wasn't.

I STARTED WORKING
AT THE AGE OF FIVE

RODOLFO REBOQUIO, MAKATI, PHILIPPINES
INTERVIEWED BY RANDOLF REBOQUIO

*My father is the funniest man alive. He is currently resid-
ing in San Francisco and is working as a parking control
officer. He has a big house with a family of four.* —R.R.

The only reason that drove me to leave my homeland is poverty.
To seek a better future for my kids and family. Jobs are very hard
to find even for college graduates. Overseas employment is the
only way out, and emigration to [other] countries. I am lucky to finish
college and land a police officer's job, but the salary I make is not enough
for a family of four. Policeman's salary is about eighty dollars a month.
Crimes are high there due to many unemployed citizens.

I started working at the age of five by selling newspapers, Icedrops
(candy), and more. Also, just to survive and help our mom and dad. So
seven brothers and sisters, we all walk in the street, in the market just to
sell paper bags. Anything that can make money, I go for it. There are drugs
all over. There are kidnappings, there are killings, and there's really a lot
going on. The crime statistics are really high. In short, the justice system
is only for the people with money, but for those poor, you won't expect
your case to prosper because you don't have money to pay for a lawyer.
You know, there are good times and there are bad times.

In America we have four seasons: autumn, fall, winter, summer. But
there in the Philippines we also have four seasons of our own. Summer,
summer, summer, and summer! I like San Francisco very much. There's
no snow.

During our days it's really hard when you do not have money to pay
for college. It's really expensive! That's why a lot of people, when they
graduate high school, they just look for a job as construction workers,
something like that, because they cannot pay the college tuition fees. In
one class there are about seventy-five kids. There are seventy-five in one
room. The room is only good for forty, but there were seventy-five
because we were over-populated. Secondly there was not much room.

I do not like the political system in the Philippines. The politicians are corrupt, most of them. Ninety percent are receiving bribes. The last president of the Philippines was impeached because of corruption, so corruption is everywhere. The only thing I like here is the political system. I haven't heard any politicians receiving bribes. Probably there are some, but you can count [them] on your fingers. But in the Philippines you can't count them [at] all.

[At] the airport, it was so beautiful. I saw that the people are really behaving. They have... you know, they are in line. The Americans are well-disciplined. Not like in the Philippines; [there,] they are disorganized. And when I see the roads [here], everything is really in good shape. In the Philippines you can see the roads are abandoned. No budget and open manholes and all that stuff.

The only obstacles that really stop me from reaching my goal is during that time I came here as a tourist, I'm an illegal alien. I don't have proper documentations to present to my job. So I got a job, but the job is really low-paying job because I don't have any documents to show. I really work hard and fought hard until I was able to get a city job, which is very much secure. Not really luxury, but I would say the median—we stay right at the middle. My mind was set on... when I set foot in America, my goal was to stay and never leave until I [became] successful in life!

I live in my auntie's house—that's my mom's sister—in Daly City, California. I miss my brothers and sisters there, my nephews and my nieces. I miss them all. And to be honest, I miss my country. I'm a naturalized U.S. citizen, but Philippines remains near my heart. So if I retire I'd like to retire in the Philippines. I have five more siblings in the Philippines—four brothers and one sister. The other one is in Canada. Yes, we are [happy] and, I would say, more than fortunate. Blessed with the blessings of the Lord.

I'm now a parking control officer. I issue citations to illegally parked vehicles violating parking meters, driveways, no parking zones, no stopping. They hate us, of course, because when they get a ticket, they come up to us, you know? It's nothing personal. It's just doing a job. The hardships that I had was when you were still with your mom and you were still in the Philippines. You know I always think of you there. Homesickness is one of those hardships. Plus my mom and dad are in the Philippines. I miss them and my brothers and sisters.

I'LL ALWAYS HAVE FAMILY
IN BOTH PLACES

LI SI JIANG, GUANGZHOU, CHINA
INTERVIEWED BY VINCENT QIU

My mother is a woman who traveled a long journey with her first child to be with her husband, and later on, bring her family to America. —*V.Q.*

After me, you, and your dad looked around the airport, he brought me to a restaurant. The food there looked good to me, but it didn't really taste good. Maybe it was just because I was used to the food in China.

America is better than China. Your grandparents wanted me to come over here so I could bring them here later. At that time it was easy to get people over here, and life was better. There were a lot of opportunities, good education. I thought bringing my family to America was going to be easy, but the first time I tried, I had to sign a lot of papers. So far, I have brought only your grandpa and grandma to America.

I got married, and your dad moved to America; my parents wanted me to be here with him. And they told me I could bring the rest of the family here later. It's not that easy because you have to sign the papers, then wait a few years for them to get passed. Then your family can come over. I'm planning to bring your aunts and uncles over soon.

The first thing I did when I came to America was get picked up at the airport by your dad. We wandered around the airport, and then we went out for dinner at some Italian restaurant. I moved into the house that your dad rented. I had to take care of you because you were crying, and then I had to unpack all my luggage. I did a lot of cleaning and the usual stuff that housewives do.

How did we get to America? First your dad had to get all the paperwork signed. I had to buy train and airplane tickets. I had to catch the train from Beijing to Hong Kong. Then I caught the plane from Hong Kong to America. It was hard [for me to bring you to America] because you were so young. You were only one year and three months old. I had to carry you on my back. There was no room on the train, so I had to stand and watch my luggage. It was hard to feed you because there was no milk.

When I first came to America it was okay. But it wasn't all that good. I remember at the airport in South San Francisco I was amazed because it was so different from the airports in China. It was so much more high-tech than the airports in China.

I like America now because you and your sister can get a good education and your father has a good job. And the schools here are free, too— it costs a lot in China. It's really good for our family right now. We're not having any problems with money, and there's always food. We have a big house to live in, and we have cars to get around with. Would I move back to China? Later on I might, because China is getting better and better. My parents have a house, and they don't have to pay to live there.

I went back to China in 1993, after I had your little sister. I let her stay there while your grandparents took care of her. Then I went back again in 1996 with you, to have some fun and to see my family again. Things were different at that time, it was very different from before because people didn't really care about racial groups.

What are some similarities and differences between China and America? It's easy to make money in both places, and [both] are big. America has weird weather. China is a lot hotter. And America is more high-tech. I still think China is better, though. I'm in school so my English can get better than it already is. I plan to get a good-paying job later, so I can get more stuff for the family, and so I won't feel bad having your just dad work all by himself. He's the one that takes care of all the money. I have my own money, but I want to make more so I can use that to help pay the bills.

Translated from Cantonese

JUST CLOTHING
& SOME JARS OF KIM CHI

EUN CHUL, SEOUL, KOREA
INTERVIEWED BY CHRIS KIM

I interviewed my dad's friend. He lives in the Sunset district of San Francisco. He lives downstairs in his room, where he fixes computers, but he's usually upstairs with his family. —C.K.

My name is Eun Chul. I am forty-three years old. Because of my job I left Korea when I was like… wow, it has been a while, like about eighteen years now I've been here. It was hard for me to find a job here—I had to wait for my friend to get me a job. I worked as a computer mechanic. In Korea, the job competition is really high.

There were classes—high and poor. It is all mixed in California. For an example, like with funerals in U.S., you go to a funeral and you see the person dead in the coffin. In Korea, it is totally different because you see the person or loved one buried, then they throw hay over the coffin, and then you bow to them and pour a drink called *soju* [an alcoholic beverage made from rice].

I think California tends to be more of a melting pot than other states, and there are more of my people that live in California. My expectations were finding the pot of gold and finding the hidden El Dorado. But jobs are very hard here and mostly labor-intensive. If you had some education I think you probably would do better, as I noticed there is still personal relationships where you can get the job.

I traveled here by airplane, of course. I wasn't able to swim the Pacific Ocean. I was thinking of making a lot of money and helping out my family in Korea. There really wasn't a conflict in my homeland—it was just a job opportunity. I didn't travel with anyone but me, [and brought along] not much, just cash in my hand, and bags. Just clothing and some jars of *kim chi* fermented cabbage for my side dishes.

Coming to the U.S. wasn't very challenging at all—just apply for a visa and get a home in California. It took me a pretty long time, around a year and a half, but I was all patience. California is a big state and everything [in it] is big. My homeland is more crowded and not much of a land mass, but here in California it is [so] big.

It is hard for everyone to learn a second language. It was pretty hard because I had a hard time speaking the words. I also felt like I should have brought my family to California with me. It wasn't [very] hard because first thing was to find your same race through contacts, and then you were able to find a place to live. It took me a while because I didn't know where everything was, so I found a house near most of my friends in the Sunset district. Originally I wanted to live in L.A. or San Diego. I like it here in California because you get a better, more decent wage and you tend to have more free time, depending on your job.

SO MANY THINGS TO BUY

EDELIA GALANG, PHILIPPINES
INTERVIEWED BY MARK GALANG

This story is about my mom, Edelia Galang, and her journey from the Philippines to the United States. She's a mother of two, and holds a steady job. She loves her husband, and would die for her family. —M.G.

My name is Edelia and I was born in the Philippines, on the island of Mondora, south of Manila. It is a small town where everybody knows each other. Farming, fishing, and raising domestic animals were our livelihood. My dad worked as a contractor and my mom had a liquor store.

We are five in the family, and I am the youngest. My family treats each other well and respects and helps each other. Everyone in my family was a college graduate. They helped the one [younger] to them to finish their education, to graduate from college. All five of us graduated from college. Three of us were in some type of education, one in dressmaking, and I [studied] chemical engineering.

I am a chemical engineering graduate. I took this course because I received a scholarship grant. I would like to be a nurse, but we did not have the money for that kind of course. But I was [also] interested in being a chemical engineer.

I chose that because I know a lot of people who earn money in chemical engineering. My teacher is a chemical engineer. Some of my professors are chemical engineers, and they earn a lot of money in the manufacturing industry. So it was my dream to be like them. I wanted to have more money and a good job.

In September, 1988, I came to America to join my husband and start a family. I met my husband through my friend. I had never met him, so I guess you can call it a blind date thing. When I met my husband he was so nice. He would open doors for me and everything. That made me think [he] could be the man of my life. He lived in America, so I joined him.

I am starting over. I have a family and a new life here. Finding a job, looking for something better. They said that there are a lot of opportunities here in America

When I came here it was hard to look for a job that I wanted. You have to have a license, you to have to pass the exam, you have to be [accredited,] and everything must pass the requirements.

[My parents] were so upset because America was too far from them. I like it here, but the only reason I would go back is for my family. They need my help because I am successful here in the states.

My number one thing [I like about America] is shopping! There are so many things to buy, and I want a lot of new things. I like that the streets are clean [in America]. They don't have children selling cigarettes.

When I first came here I stayed with my husband. He lives with his sister in the Excelsior district. It was on the bottom of a house. There were two beds and a television. It was color but no cable. There was good food always. My husband's sister was a very good cook. My husband already got a job when I got here, so money was not a problem. He paid for everything. We didn't have to pay for rent because it was my husband's sister. When I got a job we saved money to move out, and live near Balboa at the bottom of a house. Later we bought the whole house and [rented out] the downstairs.

WHEN IT COMES TO EVERYTHING IT IS FAR BETTER THAN THE PHILIPPINES

ELIGIO NOGUERA, AGNO PANGASINAN, PHILIPPINES
INTERVIEWED BY CHRISTOPHER SANCHEZ

My grandpa is loving and caring. Even though he is old,
he still helped me with this story. Thank you for helping.
This is for you, Papang. I love you. —C.S.

I n the war many [people] died. You need luck to survive. They just shot you any time. They treated people like animals. They killed people without mercy. They were very, very inhuman. What do you call them? We call them barbarians.

The Philippines were under Spain more than 400 years. After that came the Spanish–American War. The Americans won the war and Spain ceded the Philippines to the United States, but the Filipinos, who are peace-loving people, didn't like to be under the Americans, so war broke out between America and the Philippines. Unfortunately, the Philippines, being a small country, lost (laughs). So the Philippines was again a colony of America for about forty-one years.

And then in 1941, at the outbreak of World War II, the Philippines fought against the Japanese with the American forces. The U.S. Army and the Philippine Army were overpowered by the Japanese. The Japanese took over the Philippines until 1944. Then about 1944, American U.S. forces returned and recaptured the Philippines, and they liberated the Philippines. Then a law granted Philippines independence after ten years of transition period and became a free country. In 1945, the Philippines won back her independence from America, and the first president was President Manuel L. Quezon. Philippines became a republic again.

My dream while I was growing up was to come over to America because there were many Filipinos who came here before me, and I learned that there are opportunities [here]. So I made my dream [come true]. That's why I am here in California. In America, there weren't specific activities I did. I just enjoyed my pension. I did not work. I did not ask for any work because I was already receiving my pension. So I didn't need to go to work. Another thing is that I'm already old. So I am depending on my pension from the U.S. Army.

I didn't experience any hard times [moving to America]. I was excited to come here. Former members of the U.S. Army came here so there were no difficulties coming here. There is a special privilege to come. I was a member of the U.S forces before World War II. That was the preparation to the U.S. There were no obstacles [to coming here].

When I was in America, I petitioned for my wife and my children so we are all here. My family is all here. Before I came here, I was married there. That's why I am able to bring them to America.

When I was new [here], I experienced extreme cold, cold especially during the winter. We're not used to cold climate because Philippines is a tropical island. It's hot. It was the first experience here—very cold.

The greatest interest in coming here is that I could get my children here, because I know in America there are more job opportunities than we have in the Philippines.

Actually I am now Filipino-American because I've had the right as an American citizen since 1984. I already lost my Filipino citizenship. I could visit there, but I have to come back or else I will lose my American citizenship. I am more privileged than other Filipino immigrants because I can go there any time without any problem. But when it comes to everything it is far better than the Philippines.

AMERICAN WOMEN VACUUM
THEIR HOUSES IN HIGH HEELS

ANONYMOUS, TUDING, PHILIPPINES
INTERVIEWED BY APRIL SAWACHI

I interviewed my auntie in her house during the Super Bowl. —A.S.

I am sixty-five years old, and I was born in a small village in the northern part of the Philippines, in the mountains, called Tuding. I don't think I knew anything about struggling. I thought it was all fun growing up and that when you work hard and do your duties, everything will be fine.

The village is a beautiful and clean place where most everyone is related. My father and your grandpa passed away a few years back. The family was close and strict, but allowed [us] the freedom to be ourselves. The family was large—six boys and three girls. Our chores were specific. There was a calendar on the dining room wall which detailed our weekly duties. Monday we would clean, Tuesday we would wash dishes, Thursday we would sweep. When we worked in the garden, it was mainly to gather coffee beans, to get bananas, to get sweet potatoes, and whatever crop we planted. We also played and laughed a lot. I remember we took care of our dogs, our pigs, and our chickens. We were very fond of [our] hen named Helen, who was always having a lot of chicks.

I went to public elementary school, and I enjoyed going [there]. For us the seasons in the Philippines are divided into rain, rainy, and wet. School at the time started during the rainy season, and we were off during the summer months of March, April, May, and June. I think we started school in July. It was rainy, but I still enjoyed going to school. I loved to read, and I was made in charge of the library when I was ten years old.

When we had extra money, my siblings and I went to the city to watch a movie or rent comic books. I loved to read comic books. I was particularly fond of Wonder Woman and Superman. I also loved music. My siblings and I used to play records on our gramophone. We would put [on] the record, and then we would wind the gramophone until it would start to play. Then it would end, and we would go through another record. We mostly played music like waltz and instrumental, the music your grandma listened to. It was so fun because my siblings and I would try to dance so pretty, but we would end up stepping on each other's feet. We enjoyed doing this, especially during the rainy season.

I went to a private school for girls for high school. I finished high school before I turned fifteen. I loved to go to school, and I [still] love to read. I always did my best on my homework. I started school at five-and-a-half years old. I accompanied my brother who is one year older than me and enrolled at the same time.

One of my first jobs was when I was a teen, and I sold cockfighting tickets. Cockfighting was illegal so I got out of that after a while.

In college I was proud that I was literary editor of our school paper and, in one issue, I wrote about our national hero, Jose Rizal, who is now in the museum in the Philippines. I graduated with a bachelor's degree in education and then went on to graduate school. I also took a course in teaching English as a Second Language because I knew I was going to be [a] teacher in English and composition, and I think that helped me a lot.

I started teaching at a public high school. I taught literature, English composition, history, and economics. The first class I had was a senior class and at that time the students were divided into college preparatory and technical. I guess it depended on what they wanted to be in the future. If they wanted to go on to college and become doctors and other [similar professions], they would take college prep, and if they wanted to go on to something more technical, then they would take the other course. My students turned out well. They became pilots, engineers, nurses, and lawyers. In fact, one of them is a bishop in the town where I come from. As a teacher I was paid forty dollars a month, which was seventy pesos an hour.

After four years of teaching I shifted careers and went into tourism. I started a tour office in my city and organized tours for locals and for foreigners. At that time I was also on the cover of a national magazine. I could be seen weaving on a native loom. I was active in community affairs and worked very hard to promote the city and its surrounding areas as a tour destination.

Before I came to America I thought all the women vacuumed their houses in high heels. When I got here, it was a different story. I don't know, I just saw pictures of women in magazines vacuuming in nice dresses and stuff.

When I was in the Philippines I had a tour office and a fleet of cars. I was being picked up from the house and being brought to my office. You also have people who help cook your food, and wash your clothing. Then you come to the United States, and you're doing all of this yourself. Sometimes I thought, my goodness, I could be doing something else [other] than cleaning and washing my clothes. But, you know, that was very little compared to the stuff I learned in the Philippines. Chores taught me to be responsible. I learned how to cook for myself, and I grew up with seven siblings. I was the second oldest, so that taught me a lot of tolerance and more responsibility.

Your grandma, your grandpa, your uncle, and your father had [already] immigrated to America. I was the only one in the Philippines left because I had my business. But I decided one day to visit them in the United States, and your grandma convinced me to stay. Since I had petitioned [for U.S citizenship] I could not go back to the Philippines.

I came [here] by myself. It was a big airplane and before I came I had to go down to Manila to the U.S. embassy to work on my papers and be interviewed. Basically it was just some council that asked you questions, like who are your parents? Where are they? They were just reviewing what I had written on the application form. When I came to the States I was carrying, like most immigrants, your x-rays so that when they opened it they saw that you were in good health and then that you would not bring in any diseases to the United States.

When I arrived, my point of entry was Hawaii. The immigration officer asked me questions in Honolulu, stamped my passport, and said I should go to the Social Security office and apply for my Social Security number. It went very quickly. Then we boarded the plane and went on to San Francisco, where I was met by your grandparents, your dad, and your uncle.

When I [first] came, it was hard because I thought life was easier in the Philippines. It was cold and windy [here], of course. It was raining [a lot] in the Philippines, but you also had a lot of sunshine and it was warm. It took me a while before I decided to stay.

In San Francisco I saw all these houses on top of one another, and I thought it looked funny because the houses were like little matchboxes that were marching up the hill. I think [when] I arrived, it must have been evening. I thought it was a waste of energy because there were so many lights, you know? In the Philippines you turn off the lights.

I remember a friend and I went to eat at a restaurant, and it was like a steakhouse, and for some reason the waiter took so long. He took our order, but after every order we placed, we had to pay for it right away. We finished our main course and wanted dessert so we had to keep paying for it instead of paying for it all at once. I couldn't understand why because our waiter wasn't doing it to the other customers, who were all white. I didn't know at the time it was racism because I had never experienced it before. [But] I knew something was wrong because he was only doing it to us. I think he thought we couldn't pay for it or something.

When I started applying for jobs, people thought I was overqualified. I went to [a] temporary agency. So the first job I had was working for the credit card section of Bank of America. I was taking calls from merchants on authorization on credit card expenses and credit card charges. I don't remember how long I stayed at Bank of America, but they wanted me to work with them permanently. I said, "No, I'd like to thank you for the offer, but I'd like to go back and try something else." I went back to the agency. They sent me to Crocker Bank, which is now Wells Fargo, and I filed checks, which was kind of boring, but I was good at it. They asked me to become a permanent employee. I thought, this is a nice company, so I stayed at Wells Fargo for sixteen years in various positions, mostly management. I worked very hard, and I made suggestions, which were adapted. I was a useful employee. I retired when I was fifty-five. I believed it was best to stay with one company, and Wells Fargo was a good company.

[When] I was on a Mission bus for the first time, I saw two men kissing and thought, my goodness, what is going on here? I learned to deal with a lot of different kinds of people. There were gays, blacks, Mexicans, and Russians, so it was nice. There was a mixture and I thought people could learn from one another. However, I was not too happy when I heard a lot of kids cursing and using bad language and very bad grammar. I thought you were to be more respectful, especially on the buses. I was raised to be respectful.

When I retired from the bank, I thought, I wanted to do something I've always wanted to do, and that is arranging flowers. So I went to City College and took a course in retail florists. And that's what I do now. I work for various shops who need designers for weddings, for events, or for simple arrangements. I enjoy doing that.

I will be sixty-five soon, and I know I can continue working. When I start collecting my social security, I will spend the summer months here in San Francisco and the winter months in the Philippines, which is the summertime there. I did my best every year that I was here, so I don't have any regrets. I enjoyed learning a lot. I enjoyed my years in the bank, and I enjoy doing flower arrangements now. I am very happy that I'm with the family and with you guys and seeing you guys grow. I know that if I were to still be in the Philippines, I wouldn't have been able to experience and see all the things I have been through.

I THOUGHT I WOULD COME BACK
IN A FEW DAYS

LUO XUAN, HAINAN ISLAND, CHINA
INTERVIEWED BY GU HUI YAN

*Xuan is a student at Balboa. She is a senior. I have known
her for about a year. She is my best friend at Balboa. She
immigrated to the United States eight years ago. She is nice
to everybody and she likes to help other people.* —*G.H.Y.*

Hainan is a very beautiful island. The specialty in Hainan is
coconut. If you pick the coconut at noon it is the best, because
that time it is the sweetest. Hainan is very hot. Most people
don't want to come out in the afternoon because it is too hot. Some stores
just open at night, so people just go shopping at night.

In Hainan there are a lot of rivers. I remember my dad always took
me to catch lobster. One night we sat in a little wooden boat. We went
across the river to catch lobster. We got a big bag of lobsters and we
brought them back home for my mother to cook. It was the tastiest lobster I have ever eaten.

I remember my happiest days were when I was seven years old. One
night at about four or five o'clock in the morning, suddenly I heard my
dad screaming "*Yeah!*" I was frightened, so I woke up to see what happened. My dad was so happy that he had won $50,000 in the lottery. He
pulled me up from bed, and we went to the ocean with fireworks.

Including me, there are six people in my family.

I came to the United States with my father. I have been in the United States for eight years now.

In Hainan we had to go to school from day until night. Every day
I had to be at school at 6:30 AM to exercise. Then school began. At night
everybody had to go to night school, which ended at 10:30 PM. In the
morning we had five classes, in the afternoon we had two or three classes, and at night we had two classes. School was very difficult. They gave a
lot of homework and a lot of pressure [was] on you. Schools in the United States are different. They give you a lot of freedom and they don't give
you a lot of pressure.

One day when I came back from school, Dad asked me to follow him to the living room. He said he had something to tell me. He asked me, "Do you want to go to the United States with me?" I didn't think, I just answered, "Yes." Then he told me there you can get a better education and you can have a better life. I just listened for a few minutes, then I just walked away to play with my friends. I was only eight years old. I didn't know what the United States was and I thought I would come back a few days later. But I didn't.

I went to the United States immigration office in Guangzhou. There were lots of people waiting in line. Lots of people wanted to come to the United States.

When I was left, I felt happy and excited. It was my first time on an airplane. I walked as fast as I could to the plane. I never thought that I could go such a long distance from China. (She looks sad.) I never thought that I wouldn't see my family for such a long time. Now I have been in the United States for almost eight years. I have only gone back to China to see my family a few times.

When I first came to the United States, I felt everything was strange to me. Before I started going to to school everyday, I just stayed at home watching TV, but all of the channels were in English. There was only one channel that was in Chinese. But one channel was not enough for me to watch all day long. Every day I missed my family and my friends in Hainan. The first school I went to in the United States was the Chinese Education Center, a middle school. Luckily, all the students in that school were Chinese. But we could only stay in that school for one year.

When my father and I arrived in San Francisco, we didn't know what to do. My uncle came to pick us up in the airport. Then he took us to his home, and we lived with him for a few months. Then we rented an apartment. For the first year I wanted to go back to China every day. Now I am used to the United States, and I've met lots of new friends, so I don't really want to go back to live there anymore. But I go back once a year to visit my mother and brother.

When I asked my mom why she didn't come to United States with us, she said it was because of my little brother. He is only five years old, and my mom wants him to learn more Chinese in China. If he comes to the United States now he will not have much memory of his homeland. When my brother is older they will come to the United States to live with us.

My mom says she likes the education in China more. Because the schools are very strict, they make sure you do your homework. If you don't do your homework, the teacher calls home right away. The schools in United States are different. If you do not do your homework, the teacher will not call your home.

If I didn't come to the United States, I think I would be busy with homework everyday. I would have to stay up until two or three o'clock in the morning to do my homework. But in the United States I don't have as much homework as in China. I like the United States because I can get a better education and it's easier to find job.

Translated from Mandarin

FROM SLIPPERS TO JORDAN'S SHOES

FATIMA C. MOSQUERA, PHILIPPINES
INTERVIEWED BY JEFFERSON MOSQUERA

*Fatima is an intelligent, responsible, loving, and caring
mother.* —*J.M.*

My homeland, which is the Philippines, was okay. I had a simple life there. I didn't have much money because the government there was poor. It was so hard to find a job there, but I was happy because I had my whole family together with me. Life was simple enough—eat three times a day, to go to school and study. Simple. That was my life in the Philippines.

When I was studying there, I always had to walk from my house to school. It was about three miles away. We were poor, so I wouldn't eat at school. And I went to school with my slippers because we couldn't afford to buy even cheap shoes. That's how poor we were. When I finished sixth grade, I graduated as salutatorian. My mom became a nurse when I was in high school. Then I went to a private school, Saint Catherine Parochial School [SCPS]. I graduated high school as salutatorian.

I started my own family when I was in college. It was so hard for me to look for money while studying. I didn't know how or what to do in order for me to get money. I didn't know where to live at that time because my parents were so disappointed [in me]. However, later on, they helped me with my family, and helped me to finish my medical degree in college. I was dedicated to my studies. You need to have a goal to finish [your] studies and get a good job to support your childrens' education. Also, you need to have patience, love, and you can't be lazy. That's how I got through all of my problems.

After I graduated, I worked as a private physician for a year. After that I had a job in a government hospital as a doctor. Lucky for me, I had a job, because it's really hard to find a job there. After a couple of years I had my own little house next to my parents' house. It used to be my clinic, too. It was so small that we couldn't even fit in there. There was only one room for all of us, a small living room, a kitchen without any plates, no refrigerator, and all that. So we would eat in my mom's house. We didn't have a bathroom, so we would take showers in my mom's house.

We didn't have much money. I think my family was okay with that. However, for me as a mother, the Philippines wasn't okay, because I didn't want to see my kids having a hard time. And it hurt deep inside because I couldn't give them a better place to live. I realized that I had to do something about it, so I thought of coming here to America.

My father petitioned for us to come here. I had to look for money first because, even though I was a doctor, my money wasn't enough for the tickets. Then we went to Manila to fix our papers and stuff. It was so hard to get into the immigration office because a lot of people were there. And I realized that there are a lot of people in the Philippines who want to come to the U.S. because they need money to have a better life and a better future for their kids.

I lived in my brother's house. It was okay, but it wasn't what I expected when I came here. I had to sleep in a tiny bed with my husband. And my kids had to sleep on the floor. But I thought that it was okay because we were just starting and my brother didn't have enough room.

When I was in Philippines, every time I heard of America it was like a very big word. I would think of a very nice country, rich people, snow. When I got here, I felt like I was born again, because everything was just so different. The food, environment, people, and much more.

After a couple of weeks I had a job in a hospital. I worked in medical records and later on I got promoted as a social service assistant. My husband got a job, too. He made sandwiches at Subway, and later on he got promoted as a manager, but he didn't take it. We needed more money so we could pay back the money we borrowed to come here. So my husband and I looked for different jobs. Also, we had to send money to the Philippines for my eldest son who was left there (because he was over-age).

It wasn't a waste of time becoming a doctor, even though I can't be a doctor here. I served people, when I was there in the Philippines, for more than nine years. But of course I miss my work. I miss helping people, treating their illnesses. But here in medical records, it's related to my job before because I work in a hospital. I help old people, so it feels like I'm being a doctor, too. The only difference is I do more paperwork. If they're going to give me a chance to be a doctor here, then I'll be glad to take it.

There are times that I'm happy because I can see that we're having a better life. I see everything's going well. But there are times that I just want to go back to the Philippines, because I miss my son, my relatives, my friends, the food, and all kinds of stuff. Now we can earn more money than we could before. I get to buy things that I want. I can buy my kids what they want, and it's affordable.

I remember the first time I bought the first Air Jordan shoes [for] my son. It was like the first time I saw him with a very big smile in his face— compared back then in the Philippines, where I couldn't buy them what they wanted. It's hard because I have to work nonstop. I work seven days a week. I work at the hospital on the weekdays, and I work as a private nurse every weekend. We barely spend time together as a family. For me, I like it better in my homeland because I realize that being together as family is more important than anything else in this world.

It really doesn't matter to me where I live the rest of my life, as long as my family is complete and happy being together.

Translated from Bisaya

PART V

IT'S ALWAYS
RUSH RUSH

EVERYTHING WITH THE CLOCK

JUAN MARTINEZ, TARIMORO, GUANAJUATO, MEXICO
INTERVIEWED BY JOANA MARTINEZ

Juan Martinez is my father. He is a strong man. He was shy and nervous during this interview, playing with his watch while talking. —J.M.

My name is Juan Martinez. I'm from a small town called Tarimoro, which is in Guanajuato, Mexico. Tarimoro is a little town, like most in the province. It seems like time does not pass in that town. People visit the town and it always seems the same. It is calm; there is not that much noise. There are still a lot of trees, the water still runs through, and the people are very nice. We worked in the field making bricks. I came to California when I was seventeen years old. First I went to Texas, where an uncle invited me to work.

I left like everyone, an illegal immigrant. I went through the mountains running. When I got to the place where my uncle worked in Texas. I started working. I realized that life was different, that there were more opportunities, and I decided to stay for a while. The expectations came later. After five years, I returned to Mexico, I got married, and realized that life was more difficult there. I thought that maybe I would come to California, like everyone who has the American dream. I thought that maybe I would move.

That's what happened. I came to California. It was difficult, running through the desert, although it was not as dangerous as it is right now. I sent money to the family so they would be okay, buy a decent house to be able to live here in San Francisco comfortably. Then, in time, my ambitions would start increasing. If I had a house, I would want it with nice furniture, well-fixed. Well, that was the ambition.

Everything was different here: a lot of traffic and a lot of people, the big buildings, the San Francisco bridges—things that I was not used to seeing. You get to see these gigantic buildings, and it becomes something fantastic. When you first get here, you can get lost, even if you're three blocks from your house or where you live. Life in the U.S. is hard. It's hard to compare to. Everything goes with the time; everything with the clock.

Tarimoro is different. Over there it is very calm. Over here life is faster because of the time that you give to go to work. To get home, maybe you have to take two or three busses. Sometimes the bus takes a long time and basically, you have to run and wake up early to be on time.

But I like life here now because I'm used to it. Now I know. I've lived here for twenty-seven years as a restaurant owner, so now I see it differently. I see that when I leave San Francisco for a long time, I miss my house—something that I never felt before.

Of Tarimoro, I miss… well, the food, the Christmas tradition, *Los Reyes*, New Year's, and the Tarimoro traditional parties that happen every September, which are always a very happy time. I also think of the family that stayed at home—my parents, *los viejos*—who I never stop missing. I consider myself a Mexican and I will always consider myself a Mexican because those are my roots.

Translated from Spanish

IT'S ALWAYS RUSH RUSH

LINDA DE LA CRUZ, NUEVA ECIJA, LUZON, PHILIPPINES
INTERVIEWED BY KYLE PINEDA

My cousin is a twenty-six–year-old Filipina. She can be very, very serious at times, and she often talks about her life in the Philippines. We talked in my living room while watching Fear Factor *on television.* **—K.P.**

O ver there it's very hot and humid most the year, remember? When I was a little girl I liked the butterflies, so I used to go after them. One time I got lost in the mountains chasing them, so I started crying, and I guess my dad heard me and found me. I also remember working in the fields with my dad, helping him plant rice. I also remember walking up and down the street trying to sell caribou milk—twenty-five pesos for four bottles. We didn't have any lights, so at night it was very dark, but the moon lit up the whole area. We also used to play tag at night too. That was fun.

I never really saw [the rebels], but I heard of them. My father used to tell me that they are good people but they just don't like the way the government ran things. I also heard that many of them had military backgrounds, and you could never tell who they were because they always wore masks. According to my brother, [they] used to come over and ask for food or medicine. They had rifles, and my brother had to ask them to take the bullets out. They [the government] never knew [that we were helping the rebels].

The teachers over there were very strict. You couldn't have any dirt in [your] nails, and we had to clean up the schoolyard before school started. In a way it was like how it is here: about fifteen to twenty-five people in one class. We learned about [Filipino] history, English, math, and other things. Where I was from it was very poor. Everyone wore flip-flops. The only time you would see us dress up was for Christmas.

I never did want to come here. At first I went to Hong Kong because there was no work in P.I. [the Philippine Islands]. I was there for about two years. I didn't really like it because I was a housekeeper and have to stay there twenty-four hours a day, with only one day off a week. On Sundays I would go to church to pray. I also would go shopping a lot. I worked for one family who was American, and they were very mean and everything was rush, rush. Over here you have more freedom. In Hong Kong everything is work, unless you have money and you don't have to work. Sunday is the only day that everyone gets off.

While I was over there, my friends would tell me that they had done four years of college. I said to myself, what's the use of going to college if I'm gonna have the same job as them? After two years of college, studying computer science, the family I was working for moved to Chicago. This was my chance to go to America. At first it was hard because my employers couldn't sponsor me. So I asked my family to help. I got a visa to come here by sending a letter saying to let me work in America. I started to work here in the U.S. I did all this to get a better life. The only thing that was a little hard was the immigration test, and processing the papers to get here.

[When I got here] I felt very happy and free, because here, like I said, you don't have to work twenty-four/seven with only one day off. When my employer left I got scared, because I didn't want to go back. I had lots of family here at the time. And California has a little of everything, like beaches and mountains. The thing I like about California is the fact it's so diverse.

[But] I don't like the way things are here sometimes. How it's always rush, rush. Over here, you can't kick back like in the P.I. You have to keep up with the bills, the car, the rent, and taxes. Once you've messed up that, all the hard work you did to get here is for nothing.

Sometimes I do miss the Philippines. The things I used to do there and eating and playing with my family. But that's okay, because I'm still 100 percent *Ilocano*, who still has her citizenship in the Philippines. And someday, when I'm retired, I'll go back. But till then, I'm here.

MISSISSIPPI IS A VERY BEAUTIFUL STATE

Shirley Hubbard, Mississippi
Interviewed by LaCherie Hubbard

My mother is fifty-two years old. She lives in Oakland, California, but she comes from Jackson, Mississippi. She does not like being told what to do, and she is a very confident, strong, loving, caring, forgiving, and powerful woman. —L.H.

Mississippi is a very beautiful state. It's very much behind the times. It's much slower. It's a much simpler life. It's sort of like the Grizzly Adams story in a sense. It's all country. It can hold your thoughts. You can have a clear picture of everything in nature, in its natural state, the natural color, the natural setting. It's not polluted by concrete and asphalt. Mississippi is a state that is very earthy. It's very real. The people are very real, down-to-earth, simple people. It's a hard culture, survival-wise. You have to have an education. You have to have skills. You have to have stability to survive. It's a very elegant, rough life, but it's a good life. It brings the best out of people. A lot of trees, lots of acreage and greens, lot of animals, a lot of bayous and streams and lakes, backwoods, hunting, fishing, ponds. A very organic environment.

It was one of the last places where slavery existed. It was a place where Indians, slaves, [and] Caucasian-Americans came together eventually to form [the] frontier. People own homes, hundreds of acres of land. Farmland, cotton. We ourselves had about three hundred acres of farmland. We was farmers. We work the farm, we had livestock, we did manual labor. We lived our life surrounded by our farm, and our farm was the process of our livelihood. It's what bought the cars. It's what bought the houses. It's the farmers that paid the bills, and we maintained that farm. At the age of adulthood, we leave to go to college or get married and grow our own family.

Then California projected the land of opportunity, everything easy. It was a place where you can accomplish some goals and some dreams in life. I remember the big bonfire of 1969, I think it was '69. I felt that the whole world was on fire. That was in California, and it burn for a long time, and now I realized California is still burning. It's just not over, the fire. It's not time. It's still burning. The people are burning. It's like hell with no fire.

My family did not leave Mississippi—I left Mississippi. I came out here to visit a sister, and never went back to live in Mississippi on a permanent basis. Mississippi is very family-oriented. California is not. California is not children-friendly. Mississippi is very children-friendly. California is all commercial. We work to live, and eventually all you seem to do is work. You don't end up having a life. All your time is spent at your job, maintaining your livelihood. You can be bought for the price of a dollar, whether it be for a better job, better neighborhood, better car, better house.

In Mississippi they're more spiritual. To be a Mississippian, you are still an American. I'm first a Mississippian, because I was born there, and I am an American because Mississippi is within [the] American continent. Because Mississippi is what I eat, the way I dress, the way I think. It's my culture. It's more of who I am.

I do not want to live in San Francisco. I really did not want to move out here to the Bay Area. I wouldn't want to live in L.A. It's a jungle; it's a harsh life. It's not a loving place. It's a very harsh life. California is a concrete jungle, and Mississippi, you know, its people are more real. Whether they hate you or like you. It's simple: you're either right or you're wrong. Or you a man or a woman. You ain't gay; you ain't bi; there is no middle, you know?

[In Mississippi] I cleaned houses, I worked in a furniture plant, and I worked on the farm. The farm was wonderful: We milked milk out of the cows and we drank it, picked the tomatoes out of the field and ate them, busted the watermelons in the field and ate them. It was wonderful. It was nice. I learned how to make furniture.

It was a little humiliating when I was cleaning someone else's house, making up somebody else's bed, washing someone else's dishes, sweeping someone else's floors, but I got a chance to read a lot. [If I could start over] I would come out here and meet my husband, have all of my children, and go back to Mississippi. Probably I would start having a good life at an early age.

LIVING IN THE 'SCO
ISN'T AS EASY AS YOU THINK
RONALD MARTINEZ, SAN SALVADOR, EL SALVADOR
INTERVIEWED BY MOISES MARTINEZ

My uncle is very funny. When I interviewed him, he was wearing dark blue Old Navy jeans, a white T-shirt, and some "cocaine forces" (white Air Force Ones). —M.M.

When I first came here I used to miss [El Salvador] a lot, but I got used to living up here and now I like it here more than down there. There was a lot of cute girls down there. I went out with a lot of them.

I was fifteen years old when I left El Salvador and my aunt brought me up here with my mom. When we came up here, we stopped in Guatemala for about a week with some friends of my mom. Then we traveled to Mexico, where we were in Mexico City for about five days, and then we stopped in L.A. for a day. Then we came to the 'Sco.

We used to live in the Fillmore district. I went to Everett Middle School. At first it was hard because people always tried to pick on me. I had to take care of myself. The first day of school was tough and just making friends helped me a lot.

My first experience [in the Fillmore district] was kind of rough. I was going home one day and we got jumped by a couple of guys. So that was a kind of rough experience.

In the early 60s, growing up in the Fillmore, nothing was really settled with guns. It was more fistfights than people getting shot. I don't think I knew anybody who carried a gun at school. If you had difficulties with anybody or if you had a beef with somebody, you had to take care of it with your hands.

I went to John O'Connell, which is a school of technology. We learned trades there. That's what kind of kept me out of trouble then, going to school and stuff. When I first started going to high school we lived in the Fillmore. Later on, my aunt bought a house down in the Mission district. We lived there for a while. And so I was closer to my school then. While in school I learned how to play sports. I played basketball.

I thought it was crazy [in the Mission], but it is crazier now, you know. Now, if you're from a different block, you have to be careful where you walk. You see the young homies out here, carrying guns, wearing red and blue, calling you names because you're wearing the wrong color. Sometimes people call me O.G. [original gangster]. I'm more like a blood. As old as I am, I got people wearing blue looking at me crazy. They throw their gang signs at me, but I just ignore them, feel me? That's how I learned to live in my 'hood. Just try to be peaceful and don't back down from no one.

[When] I graduated from high school I was fortunate enough to have met some people who helped me make the decision to go to college. I went to San Francisco State, where I got my teaching credentials.

One of the opportunities here that a lot of people should take advantage of is education. Back home, you know, if you don't have a lot of money, you can't really do anything. You can't go to school. When you're young you have to work to support your family. But in California there's a lot of opportunities. The government helps you to go to college. They have scholarships. They have grants. These opportunities they don't have in El Salvador. A lot of the Latin American countries don't have these opportunities. Living here I have been able to better myself, and I think back home I wouldn't have had these opportunities.

I visited my family a few years back, and they was really different from what I remember. I felt pretty much lost in El Salvador, trying to find my way around. If it wasn't for my family I would have been totally lost. It was kind of nice to visit, but the way the situation is right now, it's probably worse than it is here, with all the gang problems they have. And as small a country as it is, they have a lot of drugs smuggled in. A lot of young people can't go to school, so they join a gang and sell drugs. In order to survive, they have to do something. A lot of the young people I know are selling drugs. They either end up dead or in jail.

Some of the differences [between here and there] are basically the way of life. I think a lot of the times we take it for granted, like being able to go to the store, buy a soda, buy some bread. Even, like, taking a shower, you know? They have areas down there where, [because of] the political system in El Salvador, they don't have any water. They only have water sometimes. It's a lot easier living here than down there. Sometimes you can't even buy a loaf of bread because the electricity went out. Up here we don't even think about that. You can go to Safeway and Cala Foods and buy whatever you want.

The hardship I have is being Latino. A lot of the people find it hard to believe that there's still racism in this country. But I couldn't get a room at a hotel because of the color of my skin. I get a lot of racism sometimes.

The political system here is more diverse and more open. Down there there's always the corruption with the political system. The political system is very heavy still.

I have a lot of family here. Most of my family here lives in California. I still have relatives that live back home, where my mom was from and where my dad was from; I still have uncles and aunties that live there. But probably like eighty percent of my family lives up here in Cali.

WORK! WORK! WORK!

Loreta C. Halili, Quezon City, Philippines
Interviewed by Felisha Anne Juridico

Loreta Halili is my grandma. She is from the Philippines and her sister-in-law brought her here. If she hadn't come, I wouldn't be here today. —F.A.J.

When I came to the U.S. I thought that all the streets would have a lot of trees and a lot of snow, like I had seen on the Christmas cards. I thought that we would be in heaven. I did not think that I would have to work, like when I was in the Philippines.

I went to school in the Philippines. I did not finish high school—only went until the third year. Then my father was in a strike at the Rizal cement factory. He could not get me a good education [because] he lost his job. That's when I started working with a band. I was helping my parents. That's when I met your grandfather. You know, I was a bandleader, and your grandpa was a musician. He played the saxophone.

The teenagers there are not like here. They help their parents *and* they have fun. If your mother tells you, "No, we cannot do that because we have no money." What can you do? You don't have money. You just stop asking. That's the teenager there, if the parents say no.

We had a small store in the Philippines. I was helping Grandpa there. Your grandpa was a musician. He was always going to a *fiesta*. I was always going to the market to buy something to put in the store, some goods—drinks, oil, eggs—so that we could sell something. I had a small minibus business with your grandfather, too. We had two minibuses going to Manila from Rizal province, our province.

We came to America on April 6, 1978. All of our family was here. All my children were already here. Your grandpa's sisters and brother were already here. So we chose to stay here. We lived in your great-great-grandfather and grandmother's house.

Here in America I would sew some dresses. I could make anything. Like right now, I made some covers for a dining room chair. No one told me [how to do that]. I did not go to school to learn how to sew. No one taught me how to do that. I just learned it by myself.

When I came here I didn't have a high education, but I was talented.

To tell you the truth, I knew a lot of things. I did sewing. I did house-keeping. I thought, "I'm going to be rich, I'm not gonna work, I'll be like a princess." But it was very hard. Your mom and me and Grandpa could not just stay home. We just had to find a job because we were a big family. When we came here, we needed to feed your mom, Auntie Elma, Auntie Joy, and Uncle Chris, and so it was hard. But by May I had work already. I went to the social service agency and they gave me a job. I worked four or five hours a day taking care of an old lady. Then your grandpa [got] a job in June.

My job was very easy. I would just go to the lady's house—her name was Mrs. Gunther—and I'd said, "Mrs. Gunther, good morning!" I would wash dishes. Then after I washed then, I would clean and fix her bed. Then I dusted, every day. Mrs. Gunther would tell me to go to the laundry to pick up her clothes. She ate ground beef and potato, every day. Every other day I would go to the grocery to buy food for her, like cookies, ground beef, and potatoes. After that I would go back. I would peel a potato, boil it, and all of the ground beef I would put in foil. They paid me $2.99 per hour. That was in 1978. I just worked there for six months. She was a very nice lady. The only thing I didn't like about it was that, you know, I would have liked to work a full-time job. I like to work eight hours, but I only worked there for sometimes four or five hours. And every time we had to eat, she wanted me to join with her, but I could not stand to, especially if I saw her nose was bleeding.

Auntie Yaye had a friend who knew how to sew. She was a supervisor in a fabric department, so I said, "I know how to do sewing." Because, I told you, I was talented. I knew how to even if they didn't. No one had taught me how to do sewing, but I learned by myself. I tried to learn how to use the power machines because the machine in the Philippines were different from here. The machines here were electric, here the machines were faster, and I learned how to use them. It's very easy to learn how to. After that, because the sewing work was always at the end of the year, I didn't have work. I got laid off. So I tried to find work in a hotel. And I found some at the hotel in Campton Place. I worked there for eighteen years. I worked as a housekeeper, then I became a seamstress, and then I became a supervisor.

I liked working in the hotel. It looks like a very hard job, but you can earn a good bit of money. And it's not really a very hard job. I earned more money there than I could in the Philippines.

I think I can make every kind of food dish I want to here because all the things that I want from the Philippines are here. The only thing that I miss from the Philippines is *ayungin*. It's a small fish. I like to make it like in a *sinagang*, like in a soup. That's the one thing I miss because I've never seen that kind of fish here in America. I miss the *ayungin*, the food, and the fruit because it's fresh. And I miss some of my friends.

I like it here! I want to stay here in San Francisco because I told you, your grandfather's family is already here and all of you are already here. I just want us to go on vacation to Las Vegas and Hawaii, and go shopping.

Translated from Tagalog

PART VI

I DIDN'T WANT
TO COME

FOREIGN STATE

PERRY GONATICE, EWA BEACH, HAWAII
INTERVIEWED BY KHANH TAO

I interviewed my friend Perry. He is an emotionless fif-
teen-year-old Filipino kid who takes an excruciatingly
long time to answer questions, and that's what makes
being his friend so difficult.   —*K. T.*

A lot of people think that [Hawaii's] a paradise, but it's not a foreign country, it's just a state. I'd wake up at six-thirty in the
morning, dress up, and walk to the bus stop on Renton Road at
the church. When I got to school, I went to sleep, or I waited for recess.
I had a lot of friends there. I went to school not to learn, but to socialize
with my friends. We went out to eat or go to Starbucks. I liked to go to
Jamba Juice and order a White Gummy Bear. Usually I would go out the
minute I got home. I would hop on my bike and go to my friend's house.
It was like ten blocks away. We'd just hang out and ride our bikes. I like
biking a lot. I biked all the time in Hawaii. We had races a lot and I always
won, like ninety-nine percent of the time. We had this one dirt hill, like,
close to our neighborhood. Me and my friends would call it Dirt Mountain. That's where the dirt bikers and the quad riders, or whatever you call
them, those ATV things, would go.

Usually every weekend me and my friends Gilbert, Mark, and Bran-
don would go fishing at Kaneohe Bay, at the Marine base. One day
I caught three *papios* [jackfish]. They were, like, four pounds each. It was
like the happiest day of my life. My friends were jealous of me that day
because I was the only one that caught fish. It was really just a good day
because I caught a lot of fish and I was just around my friends.

I liked diving because I got to see a lot of underwater life. The greatest creature underwater is the octopus, or what Hawaiians call the *tako*.

I remember one time I was in the hiking club, and we went on this
hike. At the end of the hike there was a waterfall, so we went swimming
in the waterfall. It was so clean and amazing. It was about twenty-five feet
high and ten feet deep. It was fresh water and was surrounded by rocks
and plants.

I moved to California around the beginning of [last] August. It all started when my dad and mom got separated. They were separated for about a year. My dad moved to Washington with his brother to start a new life. [Then] me, my sister, and my brother went to visit my dad in Washington. When I was there, [it] was great. I'd go bowling a lot, sometimes even four times a week. We were there for about three weeks, and after the second week my dad and my mom were talking over the phone and they decided to, as a family, move to California.

Yes I do [have regrets about moving]. I had to leave my friends without saying goodbye to their faces. And it was hard telling my friends that I wouldn't be going back to Hawaii. When I told them the bad news, they were shocked. I had to leave my house, leave my neighborhood, and basically leave Hawaii. Hawaii has more country and California has more city. They both have beaches, but Hawaii's beaches are nicer and Hawaii's parks are nicer than California's. I try not to think too much about leaving my friends in Hawaii. I basically just want to start all over, to do my best in school, and to do the best in everything I do. I am going to graduate high school, move back to Hawaii to go to college there, and buy a big house somewhere close to the beach.

JUST LIKE THAT

YongHong Chen, Zhuhai, China
Interviewed by Yu Fei Huang

My aunt is forty-five years old. I can always find a smile on her face. She was an immigrant who came to the United States two years ago. She is the cook of the family. We did this interview in the living room. She was wearing blue jeans and a red shirt, and looked excited. —Y.F.H.

I come from Zhuhai. Zhuhai is a city near the South China Sea. It is a very small but beautiful city. The air is fresh. A Taiwanese businessman once said you could put the air in a bag and sell it in other cities. Zhuhai is a city full of immigrants. The people in Zhuhai came from all over the country. It became a city in about 1980. Before that, Zhuhai was part of Zhongshan. In 1980, it became a "special economic zone." A lot people moved to Zhuhai at that time because they had more opportunities for success.

The things I liked about Zhuhai were the transportation and the business area. If I needed something, I just went downstairs and I could get what I wanted. In a department store, I could shop all day. They are very big there and have all kinds of things. The things I disliked about Zhuhai are the people who came from the Northwest because they were poor, rude, and they could not find normal jobs. They would steal people's wallets and cell phones. I hated those people.

I was born in Wuhan but I do not remember a lot things about Wuhan. The only things I remember are, when I was young, I would always go to the Yanzi River to swim and catch frogs. I miss the food in Wuhan from that time. I have been back to Wuhan to see my friends, and I have found the food I wanted, but it tasted different.

After I finished high school, I had to go to a village called Qian Jiang to work as a farmer. I grew food, and made and sold *tofu*. The reason that I had go to work as a farmer was because of the Culture Revolution; all the people with education had to work as farmers. The Culture Revolution was a revolution against the people who had education. They said the people who had it needed to go to the villages to work as farmers and do hard work to know what the life of the people who lived at the bottom was like. All students finished high school. All the people could go to high school, but very few people could go to college. There were only a few colleges at that time. I never had a chance to go to college because only the people who had relatives in government could get in.

The first time I heard of the United States was when I was in school. They taught us that the U.S. was bad. We had to fight against the U.S. When I grew up, I knew that the U.S. was a developed country, that it was a rich country, and kind of rude. It was like an international policeman. I heard these opinions after the year 1990 because before that time, the Chinese government controlled all the news and newspaper. You could not find out about the things the government did not want you to know. After 1990, we began to know about things outside of our country. And I also heard it from my parents.

In 1993, my parents moved to the U.S., and we decided that when they became citizens, they would let the family go to the U.S. I came because I wanted to live with them. They were old so I wanted to take care [of] them. Another reason was that I wanted my daughter to attend college in the U.S. so she could have a better education. I did not do special things to prepare. It was like we just moved. We just picked up all the things we needed. Just like that.

When I was on the airplane, I was very excited because I would see my parents very soon. I had not seen them for three years. I saw San Francisco was just like a village. I did not see any tall building. San Francisco did not seem like a modern city; it just looked like Zhuhai ten years earlier. The first week I just stayed at home. I did not know the streets or English. I was afraid I would not find my way back home.

I was a little bit disappointed when I touched the land, because the airport was very small and old. Zhuhai airport was bigger and newer than this one. It was not as good as I thought. And it is colder than China. The things I like about San Francisco are that the air is fresh, it is always sunny, and the streets are very clean. I do not like the transportation here. I always have to change busses. And there are fewer stores in my area. Like, if I want to buy some food, I need to take a bus for an hour to get there and then come back. It takes too long, and I am a little bit afraid about safety. Sometimes I hear people get killed or robbed in some neighborhoods. And in Chinatown, a lot of people steal stuff. I think safety is not very good here.

I was very disappointed about San Francisco. It was very different than what I had thought. In my mind, San Francisco was a very modern, rich, beautiful city. But San Francisco did not look like a modern city at all. There are some things we have in Zhuhai tht you cannot find here. Life here was boring, not as good as I thought it was. Even worse than my life in Zhuhai. But I do not really think about going back to China. My parents do not want to go back to China. And my daughter is studying in college. I just do not think about going back to China.

I cannot communicate with other people who do not speak Chinese. I am trying to blend into society. I am studying English. I take ESL class in the community college in San Francisco. I do not think I will ever live comfortably because the language is really against me. I am not young. I cannot learn English very well.

I always think I am Chinese and I am happy about being Chinese. My blood is Chinese. I never consider myself an American.

Translated from Cantonese

WE USED TO PLAY A LOT ON THE STREET

MARIA ELDA LAFARGUE, SÃO PAOLO, BRAZIL
INTERVIEWED BY STACY LAFARGUE

My mother is a very soft-spoken person. We sat on her
bed late at night as I interviewed her. —S.L.

I am from Brazil, where I lived in the largest metropolitan city, the city of São Paolo, which is actually comparable to New York. Brazil has twenty-two states and four federal districts. I would say about 150 million [people live in Brazil]. They are mostly Portuguese, also a lot of Italian and Japanese. I think one of the most important things is that when Brazil became independent from Portugal, they did so without a war. There was no bloodshed, and I thought that was very interesting.

Actually, I was born in Portugal, but I moved to Brazil when I was about five years old. I went to school in Brazil, and that's where I have all my memories. My earliest memories in Brazil are from when I first arrived in the country. My dad had bought us a beautiful house by the beach. There was lots of sun (laughs)... We used to play a lot on the street. All the kids played on the sidewalk, and it was a lot of fun. I went to Catholic school, but I didn't finish high school because I came here when I was seventeen. My grandfather had came here from Portugal, and he brought us here. Then he asked my dad if he wanted to come and my dad said yes, and that's how we came here. We just packed our things and came.

I was very sad because I was seventeen and I had all my friends and family in Brazil, and I had to leave school. It was a hard thing for me, but I had to [do it] because I had to come. I did not want to leave my mom and dad, so I had to follow them. So that was pretty much that. I came by plane (laughs). My grandparents were here, and I had some aunts and uncles, but since I left Portugal when I was so young, I really did not know them well.

I planned to go back to school and finish high school, which I did. But my first impression [of the U.S.] was not very good, because in Brazil the weather is tropical, very hot, and when I came here it was very cold. And there were no kids on the street playing, and everything was so different, so I did not really like it that much. The first thing I remember seeing when I got here was this big green house that I came to live in. The first week I just spent with the family. As the days followed I was home-sick. I just wanted to go back to Brazil, no matter what. But then I enrolled in school and things got better because I made new friends.

Right now I like it a lot. I have gone back to Brazil to visit, and the truth is I couldn't wait to get back here, even though [Brazil] is beautiful. But I got used to this lifestyle. It's very difficult, very difficult. But it depends where you go, because if you go to São Paolo it's very fast-paced, but if you go to Rio it's a different thing altogether—it's very relaxing. I miss the weather, I miss the beaches, and most of all, of course, I miss my friends and my cousins. I still have cousins in Brazil.

BLOODY MARY

DENISE COLLIER, WASHINGTON, D.C.
INTERVIEWED BY VINNIE COLLIER

My mommy is a wonderful woman who is very caring—
and at times can be very loud! —V.C.

I lived in Washington, D.C.; I lived in the Northeast. Well girl, let me tell you, when I was young I used to hang out with my friends. We used to go out to parties on Friday and Saturday nights. Then I had to work. When I got off of work I hung out with my friends. We would kick it all the time. We would go to the park, chill out, smoke our little cigarettes, then talk mess to people and stuff. It was me, Tanya, Brenda, Chubby, Angie, and Wanda. They called us the "wrecking crew." Well, they weren't bad, but I was bad. I was the bully of the team. I would do things to people, and then if somebody wanted to fight my girls then they would have to fight me. Oh, honey, I done been in so many fights I couldn't even count 'em on my fingers.

[In] one of my fights I had to fight this big fat girl, KK, and she chased me, and I was scared 'cause she was big, but then one of my friends told me, "Stop running and fight her." So, when I stoped running, I got one good punch on her, and then I took off running again. Man, KK, she was a big girl.

When I wanted some money and stuff, I'd go to KK, or I'd go to any-body, and tell them to give me some money. Well, they'd give me some money, but KK, she wouldn't. So sometimes I would threaten KK for her to give me some money, or I would throw peas and stuff over at her table.

Sunday nights me and Brenda would get together and stuff. It'd be boring and everything, so then we'd go get Clyde and Anthony and go to the park. We'd walk up there, sit in the park, chillin' and stuff.

When I'd see [Michael] coming down the street I'd tell Brenda we gotta split up now, 'cause my baby's here now. I had a crush on him. He had these tickets once, and he wanted to take me but then his momma was like, "No, she too young for you to be messing with, Michael" and stuff like that. He asked my sister if she wanted to go, and he took my sis-ter. I got mad, then me and my sister got into a fight. And then my momma said I could go [out]. I went over across the street and me and my girl, Angie, we went to the movies. The movies we would go to, you got to stay in there all day and watch them three or four times.

One time when I got in trouble hanging out. My momma used to tell my stepfather, "If you keep letting Bunny hang out like that, she gonna get pregnant." My momma thought I was gonna mess around and get pregnant. [So] I introduced my momma to the guy, Charles. I sometimes would call my momma and let her know where I was at. But this partic-ular [time] I came home from somewhere and my momma was sitting in the living room waiting for me. All the lights were out, and I thought that I could sneak in the house, but soon as I got to the house my stepfather, Zeke, opened the door. And as soon as I got in the house he opened up his big mouth, talking about, "You were out with boys," and all this. My momma, she said something to me and then she smacked me in my face. And it being dark in the house, I didn't know whether my nose was bleeding or the snot was running from my nose. But when I kept rubbing it, it wouldn't stop. I found out my nose was bleeding and I wanted to cut the light on, but my momma told me not to turn that light on. She pun-ished me, but she only punished me for a day. I was a good sneaky per-son. I tried not to let my mother catch me do anything wrong. If some-body said something to me I'd curse them out, as long as they didn't [tell] my momma.

I always travel by bus. Some people say it ain't safe on buses, planes, trains, or whatever, but I feel a little safe on buses. Plus, I can get to sightseeing and see different things. [On the way to California] our bus broke down on us. And we were out on the highway, waiting for another bus to come. It took us about two and a half hours for a bus to come, so that kinda made us late getting here. I came up here with my three kids: Chunkey, Fatman, and Peanut. Yeah, I was happy, because we got to stop at a lot of different places on the road and stuff like that. So I was happy when I was coming up here. One place we went had these little bugs crawling across the street. I seen deers, horses, possum. Some of the places we went through [were] Chicago, Delaware, Baltimore, Vegas. It took us four days to get here.

I left [Washington] because I wanted a change. I'd been up here probably about three or four times, brought my kids to visit. Well, I thought California was gonna be a nice place where I could meet some celebrities and get to go out to different places, but it ain't what I thought it would be. I want to meet people like singers and actresses, like Patti Labelle, Diana Ross, all the oldies, Stevie Wonder, Smokey Robinson, the Four Tops. And then some of the latest, like Usher and Ludacris. I love me some Ludacris.

I do I miss D.C. a little bit. I thought this was gonna be a better place for me. The kids might like it, but I don't really like it because people here [are] antisocial and stuff. So I'd rather be in D.C. any time of the day. [My sister Renee] loves it here though. After she got out the military, she moved here. She would come visit us in D.C. a lot, but she said she would never leave S.F. because it's more better here for her than down in D.C. I came here because I wanted to see if the weather was nice, and to see what they had going on—if people can help people and stuff. I came up here because I had my sister up here. I thought that things was gonna be better for me. I thought that it was gonna be better than Maryland.

[I came to] San Francisco trying find a job here, trying to find a place to live [for] me and my family. I came from Maryland when I was forty-three. I don't like it here because I don't like the hills they got. And where I live, I don't like that area either. I do like the school system up here. Tell you the truth, I'm not sure which state I want to go to. I don't know if I want to go to Maryland, where I came from and have more friends and family, or if I want to go to Philadelphia. I'm not sure. But I'm traveling. I never got a chance to travel like this, and I want to see different places.

HERE IS TRANQUILITY

YING LIU, CHINA

INTERVIEWED BY HAOYI (JACK) LUO

*Ying Liu is a good, kind woman who spends half her
time making money for her family.*   *—H.L.*

I come from Neijiang. It is a mid-sized town. The population is about 400,000. It is famous for fruit, sugar, and tangerines. Because the tangerines are very sweet, the town is also called "sweet town." It has a long history, about 500 years, and there have been some famous people from there like Daqian Zhang, the famous artist. My town is a good place.

There are so many things that I miss that I cannot remember them all. But I do miss my son, my family, my friends, and homeland's food. I left because I wanted to look for new, nice everyday life. I wanted to learn something new, to know the world.

I was alone in my travels. Sometimes I wanted to have a friend—I was always missing my family and friends. I was twenty-three years old when I began my travels. In ten years, I went to Shenzhen for a new life there. I went to Chile also for a new life, and for work. I was scared in my travels. I just do not want to say why.

Shenzhen is in China. I went there because I wanted to have a new life. I had divorced my husband. I felt if I stayed in Neijiang, I could not make much money. I had friends in Shenzhen, and they told me that there I could make money. It was easier than in Neijiang, but I was worried about my son. He was too young to look after himself. My friend said that it was okay, that I could ask my mother to take care of him. And I had to make more money if I was to take care of my parents and my son. So I went to live in Shenzhen.

Chile is a very quiet and beautiful country. Their fruit is very delicious. The work I did was import goods from China and sell them in Chile. In Chile, life was too plain. I went to work at eight o'clock in the morning and studied at night. Every day like that, work, study, work, and study.

I came to the U.S. because I wanted to have a new life, and this place for me was a novelty. I said novelty because I had never been here before. So I came. It took me about one year to get here. Why? because it is not easy to get here. You must get a visa first. It took a long time, and I had to work during that time.

I had no plans for what I would do when I got here. I do not know why. It is true; before I came here I really had no idea. I came here because my boyfriend—he was here in San Francisco. I thought here, everything would be different than in China. Here is tranquility, not like China. China is very tedious. I married again here. I felt happy, I liked living here.

Life here is so-so. I work, make money, and eat—like other people. My boy came here to live with us, I really feel happy about that. My heart feels too old to leave here. I only want to have a smooth and stable life. So I do not want go on my travels again. I only want to have a good life here with my husband and my son. Since I was born, it has been more than thirty years. I still like my homeland, but now I am taking care of my family. When I am older I think I will go back to China to spend time with my family there, because my brother and sister are still in China.

Translated from a dialect of Mandarin

MY LIFE SHOULD NOT BE LIKE THAT

TAFFER NG, HONG KONG
INTERVIEW BY SIU PO KINGSON NG

My brother is a sixteen-year-old boy. He was born in Hong Kong. He is funny, but he is lazy at school. He always sleeps. He was playing computer games during the entire interview. —S.P.K.N.

I think Hong Kong is great! Hong Kong is an international city. There are many great things about Hong Kong, you know? Hong Kong is called the "City of Food" and the "Heaven of Shopping." I am so proud that I was born in Hong Kong.

Hong Kong was fantastic. Every day I would wake up at 7:00 AM then go to school. When I had free time, I would go to the library after school. Later I would go back home and do my homework. Sometimes I would also borrow some books from the library to study.

Sometimes people in Hong Kong are very busy. They work from nine to five and there is little free time to relax. That's enough to make people crazy. And for students in Hong Kong, school life is not good. There is much homework every day. Luckily, Hong Kong has many ways to help people take a break, like going on picnics, riding a bicycle, or going fishing—things you can do on weekends or holidays to relax.

Hong Kong has many tall buildings and it is hard to see the blue sky. The pollution is very bad. California isn't like Hong Kong. It has a blue sky all the time—except when it's raining—and the air is fresher than Hong Kong's. California also has many cars because you need a car to go to work or go to school. The difference is Hong Kong is a small place, so the cars made the air pollution very bad.

In school, there are so many classes, and you can't sleep in class. Sometimes I would play with friends in class if the class was boring, like talking with each other or eating food. Here it is not the as same as in Hong Kong. The classes are so free here, and sometimes I will sleep in class when we are studying something I have learned before. Sometimes I will copy some homework from my friends, because I don't want to do it! The teachers are very nice, not like Hong Kong's teachers. There, they always give students lots of homework. The school rules are almost same, but in my school in Hong Kong, students needed to wear uniforms to go to school. Not like here. We can wear jeans and T-shirts.

I'm very angry about coming here. I'm angry about leaving my friends. I love Hong Kong very much because Hong Kong is my *home*. I choose Hong Kong. But I was forced by my mom to come here. I have a lot of friends in Hong Kong. I lived there for such a long time that I didn't want to leave it.

But I choose California for work because I can earn U.S. dollars here and U.S. dollars are better than Hong Kong dollars. Don't you think I am right? The money exchange ratio is one to seven.

The difference between Hong Kong and here? I think work is the same because the working hours are almost the same, so I think the difference is the wages. I told you, the U.S. dollar is better than the Hong Kong dollar, so many people may think working in the U.S seems better.

Translated from Cantonese

HERE, YOU MAY HAVE A BETTER LIFE

XIAO QUAN DI CHEN, CHINA
INTERVIEWED BY JIE CHEN

My father, Xiao Quan Di Chen, is forty-eight years old. He came from China in 2002. Even though he is strong and courageous, he is a weird father and always has a different idea about me than other people do. —J.C.

When I was a kid, the Culture Revolution happened, so I didn't get an education because all the schools were closed. When the schools were opened, I only went as far as middle school, and then I went to work because my family had economic problems. My father was a land owner and the communists took all my father's land away from him. Since they took most of the things we had, my family became very poor. I went to work at a young age. When the Culture Revolution was over, I went back to school, but soon I dropped out because my family needed me to help them make money.

After I graduated from middle school, I went to an army camp. At first I wanted to join the army, because they gave you free food and a place to live. But I couldn't join them because my father was a land owner. But I worked very hard, then they finally accepted me.

Soon life in the army got very boring, so I chose to leave. Then I worked with steam machines at a factory. As I grew older I began to fix machines for the factory. I lived in the factory for a few years. But then I left the factory, and found a new job.

I felt I didn't have enough money to spend, and I decided to leave for a better life. At first I found a job transporting things to and from different cities. I borrowed lots of money from relatives, bought a car, and began a new life as a taxi diver in my homeland, Fu Zhou. I repaid those debts in a few years.

Life became more interesting. I had more money and my own family. Everything was going well. But a typical day was just working and nothing else. People like me who want to make a lot of money must work all day long.

I came to the U.S. for the same reason I had quit my old job: because I wanted a better life. I had heard many people say that the U.S. ccould make your life better, that if you went to the U.S., you would be rich in a short time. So I thought that I would go to the United States and make my life even better. My mother and sister were already in the U.S.—of course I had to come. Another reason was that my family had economic problems. We needed more money, so I had to find a place where I could make lots of it.

But the United States is different than what I had expected. Everything is difficult because I do not understand English. I worry about our life here. When I first arrived, life was pretty simple but hard. I lived at my sister's house, and I worked with her husband. I was fixing houses with him.

Of course I always want to go back to China. When I feel homesick I just work harder. I think that is the only thing that can make me not to think about my homeland.

In China I had a good job, and life was pretty easy for me. In the United States, I can't communicate with people, and life is hard. I'm not very happy that I came here, but at least it is good for my children. Here you may have a better life.

Translated from Mandarin

I DIDN'T WANNA COME!

DIANA, OLONGAPO, PHILIPPINES
INTERVIEWED BY MICHELLE TRUONG

The person that I interviewed is my co-worker at Waiters On Wheels. She is a twenty-eight–year-old Filipina. She was wearing a gray pair of pants, a striped, pink and blue-purple short-sleeve shirt, and a white long-sleeve T-shirt underneath. She had slippers on and had her hair tied up.　　　　　　　　　　　　　　*—M.T.*

I was born on March 25, 1977 in Olongapo City, Philippines. We had nine [children in my family]—six brothers and three girls. I'm one of the oldest, the fourth. My life [there] was very sad. My dad's not here and my mom's not here. My dad has another family. My mom also has her own family. We talk, but not like *that* talk, you know? Not like mother and daughter talk. [Back then] it was just my brothers, my sisters, and I. I was like the mom and my brother was like the dad. I was serious about [them]. I had to iron their shirts and everything. I had to pick them up from school and stuff.

[In the Philippines] it sucks. It's hot, really hot, there. We did pretty well—uh, half-and-half well, I mean. Like, we ate three times a day, so we were fine. The bad thing was when it was raining. We had a small house on the seashore. This one time it rained [and] we had a flood all the way to our roof. I almost died then. I was crying; I thought I was going to die. But the rain stopped when we were on the roof. I was so scared; it was in the middle of the night, and I thought it was my last day (she laughs).

I came here in 1996 with my dad and my two sisters. My dad, like, worked at the embassy, for American people, so that's why I came here. [We were], like, special immigrants. You had the chance to go to America without going to the embassy, you know, and asking for ticket thing.

[I came here when I was] nineteen. [When I first came] I wore a casual dress in the airport when I shouldn't have. My dad said, "Wear casual dress in America," but when I got here it was so cold. So dang, it made me mad. The first week sucked, the first month sucked, but by [the end of the first] year I was okay. At first I didn't have friends and I didn't know anybody. I was so lonely. It's not like in the Philippines where you can always go outside and talk to somebody. I'm still not really happy because I don't really wanna be here. It's just that my dad pushed me to be over here.

I never went [to] school here, so I don't know [the difference between the schools here and there]. I went to the PhilAm Center. I was supposed to go to school but I didn't. I worked at Nordstrom as a night shift supervisor. It was in a mall and it was really hard, especially when I just got here.

My friend, when she first came to America, she kissed the floor, because she was waiting to come here for a long, long time. Everyone wants to come here, and they don't even know if it's good or bad. They just wanna come here because of the money. The dollar is higher than there, and when you work here and you go back there you're like a rich person.

The Philippines was so poor. It was hard to get a job. There was no money, and it was hard, you know? I believed that people who came here were rich when I was still there, but now I don't. They feel that they're rich there but they're not (laughs). Man, I wanna slap my dad for making me come here. He just said it was fun to be here and a lot of money. One dollar there is like fifty-two pesos. That's why all the people there wanna go here, because of the dollar thing. I know it's good money, but if you're asking me, I don't want to be here.

I have two [kids!] (laughs), one boy and one girl. One is four and one is two. Marlon and Angelica. They both were born in the Philippines. All the good things I know are the kids. In the morning I have to pick up my kids, and sometimes I work at McDonald's, and I work seven days a week on the night shift. I have no choice, man. I have two babies [and] I have to take care of them. When you have a kid, no matter how tired you are [even if] you don't want to show up at work, you have to, because you have to pay for a lot of stuff and you have two kids who have to live.

No, [I haven't been back to the Philippines] yet. No, I don't really [talk to my family over there]. [We came over here] because my dad said it would be better for us. But all I know [is] I don't want to be here. He said that it'd be better, but s***, no! I wish I never came here. My life's worse. I want to go home and don't want to come back here.

IF YOU GIVE ME A CHANCE,
I WILL STAY IN HONG KONG

Yuk Ming Edmond Tang, Hong Kong, China
Interviewed by ZhuoJun Paul Lei

Edmond Tang is an immigrant who just came to the United States ten months ago. He is very nice to his friends, and always has a smile on his face. He is a senior at Balboa High School, and he is going to college next year. Now he is going to tell us his story.   —Z.P.L.

In the 1980s, my family moved to Hong Kong and I was born there. I spent most of my life there. My life was pretty busy when I was in Hong Kong, especially at school, and I could feel lots of stress around me. My family was not very rich. We lived in a small house with six people: three sisters, two parents, and I (sighs). It was so terrible. On the other hand, I never complained. We did not need to worry about our food and we did not need to worry about any other things. All we had to do was study well. Moreover, I had lots of friends there. That was enough for me.

Basically, my family decided to move to the United States about eleven years ago, and they did that without asking us kids, so it was not our choice. I believe my parents made that decision because they wanted us to have a better education and better lives here.

I felt sad when my family decided to move, because I did not want to leave Hong Kong. I love it there so much. In my family, I am the only one who disagreed with the move. But finally, my family convinced me.

I like to travel to other places in the world in order to open my eyes. But I never thought I would move to another place to live for a long time. I expected I would travel all over the world but just live in each place for a short time, in order to touch all the different cultures found in the world.

The date when I left Hong Kong was March 21, 2004, and I will remember that date forever. About twenty friends came and saw me off. Those friends were my best friends, and I have known some of them since I was six. That was a very emotional moment. I felt very bad at the time. I almost cried, but I did not, even though I would miss them forever.

There were two things in my mind on the plane. First, one was I remembered all the time I spent together with my friends. I hoped I could keep those memories in my mind forever. The other thing was the anticipation for my life in a new place. I hoped I could learn more things. It would be good for me to try another kind of lifestyle in a different country.

As I remember, it took thirteen hours to get here. Most of the time I was awake because I could not fall asleep. Sometimes I watched the movies on the plane. I didn't really want to fall asleep, because it would make me feel bad if I awoke and found myself already in America. Therefore, I kept awake most of the time.

I knew I was going to stay in San Francisco, but I did not know much about it. I thought the living conditions should be better than they were in Hong Kong. I thought I was going to live in a tall building like I did in Hong Kong, and the environment should be better as well. I wanted to make diverse friends, because there are lots of different cultures in the United States, and that means there are lots of different people here too.

Now, I have been in San Francisco for ten months. I think there are not too many differences between my old life and my new one. I still live like I did before—there are trees, roads, and cars, all the same. However, the environment is different. The population of Chinese people in San Francisco is so big that I could not believe it at first. I could find Chinese everywhere around me. Most of my friends are Chinese. That was totally beyond my expectations. My lifestyle is still the same: go to school, go to class, do homework, watch TV, and go on the Internet. Nothing has changed. However, the environment is different. The air is much better here.

The advantage of having so many Chinese people in San Francisco is that it makes you feel warm when you see people who are like you in a foreign country, and you feel safe when you can communicate with them. I feel free and happy when I am speaking Chinese with people. On the other hand, you miss the chance to practice your English. Basically, I do not speak much English in San Francisco. If I was in another place in America, I would get more chances to speak English, because I'd have no other choice, and my English would be much better.

I feel warm and safe when I communicate in Chinese in San Francisco, because I can express myself clearly and other people can communicate with me clearly by using Chinese. In my opinion, my English is not very good, so I think I cannot express myself. I worry that other people will misunderstand me and maybe I will not understand what other people say either. That would just make me feel frustrated. Moreover, it is hard for me to feel safe in a foreign country in such a short time. I need some time to feel safe with people. Everything has to restart again in a foreign country.

After living in San Francisco, I think life here is pretty busy, even though when I was in Hong Kong I heard life here would be relaxed. Especially at school—I think that it is almost the same. We still have much homework to do. And then, the transportation here is so terrible that I have to be very patient, waiting for the bus. I never thought that I would depend on the bus so much, and I never thought that I would have to wait for a bus such a long time. Even when I want to take a taxi, I have to wait for a long time. Transportation is much better in Hong Kong. And here it is so boring. We do not have many things to do to kill time. Also, I think it is too quiet here, and that makes me feel very lonely.

I think after I moved here I became more reserved than I was before, because now I put many secrets in my heart that I do not tell anybody else. It is very hard to get to know true friends here. It takes years of time to build up true emotions between friends. When you have a true friend, you tell them everything, no matter what. In the last ten months, most of time I have felt empty. I prefer to care for other people instead of having other people care for me, because I think I can solve my problems by myself. But I always seek to share my love with my friends.

My family? Both of my parents are very busy. My mother comes home just once a week, and my father comes very late at night, so I communicate with my parents less than before. Sometimes I think if we could just have dinner together, that would be enough for me. I feel the relationship between my sisters and me has been improved, and we know we will support each other. I think it is very hard to have a perfect family, but know I should try my best to repay my parents by working hard.

Of course I miss my homeland. I like Hong Kong very much. If you gave me a chance to go back to Hong Kong at once, I would be willing to do that. Especially during holidays, I call my friends and use email to keep in touch with them. I think if we can keep the friendship, even though I departed from them, that we have a real friendship. I miss them so much. I even dream about them at night.

Translated from Cantonese

PART VII

OH, I WOULD
FOR SURE GO BACK

OH, I WOULD FOR SURE GO BACK

JANET DEAN, FIJI
INTERVIEWED BY TYLER FRAZIER

During this interview, Ms. Dean, who works at Balboa
High School, was very happy to tell me her story and
talk about her homeland. —T.F.

I moved when I was twenty-five, to the U.S. I've lived here half of my life. Ha ha. I'll be fifty-four in April. We came in 1976. We took a flight to Samoa, spent a night there, then came to America. The Fiji islands, it's located near New Zealand, but closer to the equator. The main religion back home is Christianity, the second largest religion is Hindu, and the third largest is Muslim. The Hindus and Muslims came from India as indentured laborers to work the fields, and when their contracts were up they chose to stay. They were brought there as indentured labor workers to work the fields in the mid–1900s. I think the most famous person from my country is Vijay Singh, a golfer who just out-stroked Tiger Woods out of the number one spot.

My husband's parents migrated to the U.S. By tradition, the oldest son, he has to be responsible for the parents. So once they migrated to the U.S. we had no choice but to come. When I was growing up I spent a lot of time at the mental institute, and I always wanted to work with people who had mental disabilities. And that's what I'm doing now.

We now have three grandchildren, but we came here with three children. We had our children already. They are two years apart. When we came, the youngest was three years old, so they were three, five and seven. I have a sister, but she didn't follow my footsteps. She married an American, and she lived in New York, and now she lives in San Francisco. [We're] very tight. All our families are tight; that's how we are. All my children speak other languages. I speak English, Fiji, and Hindu. My husband is from India and he speaks Indian. My children, they all speak English, Fiji, and Hindu. My youngest son speaks Chinese, and my oldest speaks Spanish.

Right now the U.S. currency is low. I went home in May of last year, and the exchange rate was one U.S dollar for two dollars in Fiji money. It's dropped a lot, the U.S. currency. Oh, I would for sure go back, when I get too old and retire.

UNDER A SUMMER RAIN IN VIETNAM

BINH THAI NGUYEN, HO CHI MINH CITY, VIETNAM
INTERVIEWED BY HANNAH GIAO LINH NGUYEN

During this interview, my father was sitting in the living room watching TV. He looked a little tired, but he welcomed me with a gentle smile. He's a really funny and honest person. —*H.G.L.N.*

I was born in Cambodia because my parents used to live in Cambodia, and my mother gave birth to me at the time they were living in Cambodia. My parents at that time didn't have any job in Vietnam, so they worked as coolies on rubber farms in Cambodia. Life was extremely hard for us. When I was born, we had the war with France in Vietnam. French soldiers took all of our farms, fields, and houses. They forced us to obey them. If we worked for them in fields, factories, or in the military, that meant we had to betray our country. But then we would have a better life. Some people chose working that way because of their hungry stomachs.

However, most Vietnamese people, including your grandparents, didn't choose that way. Many young people, including women, stood up and fought for our country. Your grandfather had an injury in a fight, and he couldn't fight in the army again. Still he worked in the army as a nurse, and so did your grandmother.

Two or three years later, my parents received news that my eldest brother was starving to death in North Vietnam. They were so upset. After the Declaration of Independence was released, North Vietnam got their freedom, but South Vietnam didn't. We, who lived in South Vietnam, were still controlled by France. French soldiers began to be crueler, and my parents didn't have any jobs then. So they had to escape to Cambodia to work in rubber farms, as I told you.

Life was also hard in Cambodia. I have seven brothers and sisters, and it was really difficult for my parents to raise us, but they did it well. We were well educated in Cambodia, and all of us graduated high school there—that's incredible. I met your mother at high school.

After our life became better, we went back to Vietnam. My brother and I went to the army after that. I was in the army for nine years. When my father died, I couldn't be with him. I couldn't even go back to join his funeral. That is one of my biggest regrets, that I couldn't see him that last time. Your mother also had to wait for me for nine years before we could get married, because I was in the army all that time.

I don't regret fighting in the army for the independence of my own country. Some of our people don't like our country, but I do. I think it was because of their bad and tragic experiences that they have bad views about Vietnam. That is my own opinion. The reason why some people don't like Vietnam, I think, is the political condition. At that time, Vietnam had two different groups, known as the communists and the anti-communists. The communists were people who loved and fought for Vietnam. The anti-communists were people who didn't like it and [were] against the communists. Let me tell you this: I'm neither communist nor anti-communist. I'm neutral. I fought for Vietnam because it is my country, and when my country was in danger, I had to do something for it.

It took us more than twelve years to get here. We couldn't come here because of the immigration conditions at that time, but eventually we did make it here to San Francisco.

We left Vietnam and came here to be with my wife's family members. All of her brothers and sisters lived here in the U.S. At first, I was considering if I wanted to come here. The main reason why I came here was because of my child's education. We want you to receive the best education, and we want you to find your best future here. I was thinking a lot before I came here. I was thinking if we could have a good life here, and if I could find a job that would provide enough for our family. I was also thinking a lot about the future, about what I would become after coming here.

I came here in July, 2004, which means half a year ago. I was surprised when I came here. Everything was different from Vietnam, from the language, to food, to climate, etc. I couldn't sleep when I first came here. I couldn't eat American food either. I only ate Chinese and Vietnamese food. I didn't go out for a few weeks because the weather was too cold. I felt very lonely because I couldn't communicate with people. I hardly spoke English and was almost silent at that time. I was also very homesick and thought about Vietnam, about my relatives, too much.

My first impression of the U.S. when I came here was that the U.S. is a very big and civilized country. The roads are large and the cities are big.

Public transportation is also developed here. I was worried about communication. I could hardly speak English, and I was worried if I could find a job to provide enough for our family. And because the city is so large, I was worried I would get lost, which really happened. In Vietnam, we went by motorbikes. It was fast and convenient. But here, when I didn't have a car yet, I had to go by public transportation. And if I got lost, it would take me a day to get back home. So I was worried a lot when I went out of my home (laughs).

I have to work hard, not like when I was in Vietnam. In Vietnam, people can work and... play around at the same time (laughs). Now I'm working in construction, and my wife is working as a waitress at a Vietnamese restaurant. The salaries are enough for us to live and provide for our usual lives here.

I miss the time when we were with our relatives and friends most. Every week, we visited others, gathered together, talked, went out to eat or play, etc. I really miss that time. I will consider myself Vietnamese always, because my homeland is Vietnam, I'm carrying Vietnamese blood, and my first language is Vietnamese. Although I wasn't born in Vietnam, and I had a very difficult time there, I'm still Vietnamese.

I want to live the rest of my life in Vietnam. I have my family and relatives in Vietnam. I like eating food and fruits there, very fresh, very tasty. I like the feeling of just being there under the hot sunlight, or under a summer rain in Vietnam. I miss those feelings.

Translated from Vietnamese

FROM MEZCALA TO SAN PANCHO

RAFAEL ROMERO, MEZCALA, JALISCO, MEXICO
INTERVIEWED BY STEFANY ROMERO

*I interviewed my dad over the phone, since he lives in
Mexico and I live here. He's a short, funny man, and I
love him very much.* —S.R.

I was born on August 6, 1939, in a small town called Mezcala, in the
state of Jalisco, Mexico (bird screams in background). I lived there
until I was thirteen years old. I only went to school up to the sixth
grade because I had to start working. My mother died when we were very
young, and we had to make money in order to eat. My mother died in the
year of 1955. She was about thirty-six years old. She died of cancer. We
were really little. My mom left us the house, and we took care of ourselves.
My older sister cooked for us, and all we ate were *frijoles y sopa de fideo*
beans and noodle soup because we didn't have enough money to buy any
meat (sighs). There was no one to take care of us. My oldest brother was
the one who took care of us, until he got married when he was sixteen
years old and left us. We struggled a lot to live. I didn't have shoes. I had
guaraches [sandals], and if they broke I was barefoot.

When I started to work, I started off by planting corn and beans and
I also had to milk the cows with a man who owned many cows (laughs).
There were five of us in total—your *tías* Emilia and Chayo, and your *tío*
Polo, and our brother Elias, who died when he was eighteen months
old—very little. He died of a sickness. I don't remember much of what
kind of sickness he died from but since there were no doctors to cure him
he died.

The first years of my life were really hard, because back then the
countryside of Mexico was very hard to live in. There was no money, no
jobs, and the amount of food produced was very low. The life in Mexico
was not like the United States, *mija*. I got 30 pesos per week and two liters
of milk. And my older sister, Chayo, worked in a *tiendita* [liquor store] and
received only two pesos per week.

My father was already living in the Unites States, and by being in the
United States he forgot about us. I met my father when we came to the
United States. But back then, when my mom died, my dad went to the

Unites States and married another woman. And that woman found out he had kids. She was the person who brought us to the United States.

Back then, there were men called *contratados* [hired men]. They would get hired for a total of forty days to sixty days to pick fruit that was taken to California. One of those men came to Mezcala, my home town, and he had seen your grandpa in the United States. We somehow began to talk to him and he gave us your grandpa's address in California. Then my sister, Chayo, wrote him a letter. And my father's wife found the letter but she didn't tell my dad, your grandpa. In the letter my sister wrote that our mother had died, we were very lonely, and were very poor (sighs). She sent back one hundred dollars and she asked us to send her pictures of us. So we sent them to her. Your grandma, Josefina, showed the pictures to my dad and said, "Look, Manuel, these are your children and they're in Mexico—very poor." After that happened, they were separated for a while, but later on they got back together. And that is when your grandma, Josefina, brought us to the United States.

We left for the United States in the year 1959. Our trip up there was by train. We went to the city Guadalajara, and we took the train from there to Mexicali. I remember the train ride was very long. It took five days to get to Mexicali from Guadalajara. When I saw my dad (long silence), I looked at him and looked at him because he was my dad but it felt really weird to say I had a dad. Because he wasn't really with us, and I never knew him.

We got here all dirty—*todos tisnados de rumbadera*. The trip to the United States was very, very long. I went with my sister Emilia and a man from Mezcala who only rode with us until we got to Mexicali. My sister Chayo and then your *tío* Polo came later on. On the train we would fall asleep and watch as we passed by the different places we never knew existed because we'd never left our hometown, except for a small place about fifteen minutes away called Tepa. That's as far as we had gone back then. From Mexicali we went to Tijuana, and your grandma, Josefina, picked us up in Tijuana. We were not scared because we knew that man from my hometown and we felt comfortable and felt really happy to finally come to the United States. Your grandma, Josefina, was the one who fixed our papers. When we came to the United States we all had our papers and came to a home; we didn't suffer coming over here.

We thought that we were going to come and meet my dad and were going to finally see what the United States was like. Also, because a lot of people from Mezcala, my home town, had already come to the United States, we had heard that in the United States you earned money and you lived a good life. I wanted to have a better life, a better future, and earn money because I never really had money.

Well, my thoughts were to come to America and work and move on to a better life, earn money. You see how well I had you and your brothers and sisters living when you were all born? You were living in a nice home. But unfortunately your mom and I decided things were not working. We fought and we separated and it has hurt me a lot because now I'm here alone [in Mexico] and I suffer without you guys. I expected to find more jobs and I thought that by working I would succeed.

We stayed in a small town near Fresno, California, called Fowler with my stepmother, your grandma, Josefina, who always treated us very well; I loved her very much. Yeah, she picked us up from Tijuana and was very much like a mother to us. I remember she would tell her friends when they came over to the house that we were her children. She never said we were her stepchildren. She always said we were her children. What I remember the most is going to a store and buying cold milk because we had never tried cold milk before. And eating at Wendy's, because they didn't have a McDonald's or Burger King back then. We liked them so much because we had never tasted them in Mexico and they were very delicious. I also remember tasting ice cream. Oh man, it was very delicious; in Mexico we only had *paletas* [popsicles].

I worked on the ranch with my dad, picking grapes and peaches. The money we earned, which was about $1.25 an hour, my dad would collect our checks and keep the money. He would give us only $5.00 per week. This was when I really didn't know about money. I didn't even know how to go to the store because I didn't know how to speak English.

When I moved to San Francisco to work as a scavenger, I moved to a house on Bayshore with a total of six or seven men who also worked as scavengers. Our rent was one hundred dollars. I only had my sister, Chayo, and her husband, Gabriel, and friends who worked as scavengers that were from my hometown. I remember buying a car. It was my very first one, a 1958 Chevy. It was black and, *¡uy!,* I loved it. I washed it every day because it was a very pretty car and I felt really good after I bought it with my own money. The only thing I had to do was never give up and work hard.

Some of the things I left behind were poverty and the place where my mom died. I went to the United States in search of a job, a good life, and to buy new a pair of shoes because I never owned a pair of shoes, *mija*. I did feel bad because we didn't have shoes but I was used to it, and the money I earned was not all that much—30 pesos—and I had to give it to my sister so she could buy food.

In the United States I never felt discriminated against, except for one day when my car broke down and I got on the bus. I had just come from work in my work clothes and a lady plugged her nose because she said I stunk. The bus driver asked the lady why was she plugging her nose, that I was the one who picked up the garbage and she should be grateful. What I remember is that it was a beautiful city, very clean, and I really liked living there. I never moved to another city after I moved from Fowler; I always have lived in San Francisco until I went to Mexico and married your mom. I fixed her papers for her and when we got there we bought our own house and raised you and your brothers.

I came back to Mexico because it's my country and I love it (pauses). I also consider the United States as my country because I lived there for a long time. I like that everyone there works and has money and everything about it because it's a beautiful country. From Mexico, I would bring to San Francisco the beautiful climate and the people, because all the people in Mexico say "hi" whether they do or don't know each other. In San Francisco, the people are nice, but not like people in Mexico.

Translated from Spanish

PEOPLE ALL AROUND,
CLOTHES, SHOES, & TREES

Anonymous, Samoa
Interviewed by Teuila Failauga

The person that I chose to do my interview with is my aun-tie. She moved to California from Samoa. She was the first person I ever thought of doing an interview with. —T.F.

My country is real big. It's like a house that has a lot of rooms and bathrooms put together. It's like you're living in San Francisco and you are traveling from San Francisco all the way to China. Well, actually, almost to China. In Samoa we don't have that many cars in the streets, and we don't have people who go around treating people like their enemy.

My homeland doesn't have many good jobs. Yes, I did have a job in Samoa. I was working as a screener. When I was twenty-five I had to move to Frisco because I didn't have anybody to live with. My mom had moved to Western Samoa and I was living with my grandma. A year passed by. My grandma was very sick, and passed away. [I left] because I wanted to see how my life would be like if I lived in Frisco. I wanted a better job. There's more opportunities over here than they have over there in Samoa. I expected to have a good job that paid better, and to live a better life. I wanted to be able to be in a country that I would feel a lot more comfortable in, that I thought that I would be safe. I prefer to live in California because I have a lot of new friends who I can talk to.

When I first came to Frisco it felt so weird. It felt like I was going to prison. Going to a whole new, different country feels weird because you are surrounded by different personalities. To me it felt weird because where I come from I was surrounded by a bunch of huge Samoans. Everything [here] is different. I mean the time, the people all around, clothes, shoes, and trees.

It wasn't hard for me to get a job. To tell you the truth, I expected to have a good job that pays better, to live a better life. I had to go through a lot of stuff. But it wasn't hard for me to get a job out here because I had worked at the airport as a screener.

I want to be able to be in a country that I will feel a lot more comfortable in, that I think that I will be safe. I prefer to live in California because I have a lot of new friends who I can talk to.

IT'S ALWAYS PRESSURE

GLORIA USI, MASANTOL, PAMANGA, PHILIPPINES
INTERVIEWED BY ROBIN USI

This is a story of a woman who made the decision to come to the United States, leaving behind her old life and starting a new life with her husband. —R.U.

My name is Gloria Usi, I'm, uh… forty-seven years old. I was born on August 7, 1957. Our province was Pampanga, and our town was Masantol. The Philippines is beautiful; it has natural resources and moral values.

The village—we call it a *barrio*—the name of our *barrio* was Maluali. Many lived there. Some of them belonged to poor families. Their main occupation was catching fish and planting vegetables. My father was a farmer during the harvest time. I helped him, like bringing the food. [My parents] were busy and they could not go to the house to get their food, so I just brought the food to the fields. No, we didn't have a rice cooker. We had a small pot to cook the rice in. There was no electricity yet at that time in the Philippines. If you were a hard worker you would be successful in your life. But if you were lazy, I think you would not become successful in your life.

Our house was very small. There was only one bedroom, a living room, and the kitchen. There was no restroom. When we needed to use the restroom we had to use the backyard (laughs), 'cause bathrooms weren't that popular back in the Philippines. When we had to take a shower we had to boil water and go in the backyard. Luckily your grandma had a lot of plants or else people might have started watching us. Even though our house was small it was always clean. Remember when we went to the Philippines, like about five years ago, that house we stayed in?

That's where we used to live. Now it has one room for a bathroom and one for a shower. It now has two bedrooms, which are very big. Uncle Bong has a business, and he gives money to them. He's the one that helps out over there. They have a big swamp where they grow their fish, shrimp, and crabs. When these are big, they start selling them, and that's how they earned enough to get their house so big.

On normal days, when I was not going to school, I was playing hide-'n'-seek with my friends. We played at the shore, and we also played *sunka*, a game with a carved board. On Sundays I would help my auntie clean the church to make it extra shiny (laughs). I like to clean!

In the Philippines, I was always happy. I had a good-paying job that I always loved to do. I didn't have to work that hard and I wasn't stressed out. Here, it's always pressure—very tiring. In the post office where I work it's always pressure. I have to carry packages sometimes that are very heavy.

When I was teaching, I woke up early in the morning, like 6:00 AM. Then I would walk to work and catch a ride in the *banka* [boat], and then go to work!

We're Catholic, and every Sunday we always went to church. We just walked to go to church because we really didn't need a car. But we were always sweaty because it was a long walk.

I have only one brother and five sisters, and I'm the oldest. I'm feeding my youngest sister and doing household chores.

When I came here, it was a very long journey. I needed sixteen hours to get from the Philippines to San Francisco. It was my first time seeing an airplane. I was scared because sometimes the airplane shook, and if something happened… I might not be able to see my husband.

First he had written me a letter. Then he introduced himself after that. We became pen pals, and it was the beginning of a beautiful relationship.

I decided to move here because my husband was here and he wanted me to live with him. I resigned from my job and moved to San Francisco.

If I apply [to school] here I need to study because I think you need more units. But I think I don't want to go back again to the teaching profession because I have high blood pressure (laughs). I can't handle the kids here. In the Philippines, oh my God, they are so well behaved and nice. But here, oh my God, you just can't handle them. I miss my teaching profession because I love teaching. There is no place like home.

When I arrived, the first thing I saw was the international airport! When I saw the airport I was amazed because everything looked so clean. I was thinking of how I would adjust to this kind of technology—I mean, taking transportation. Instead of using boats, here we use cars and buses.

He [my husband] was the one who picked me up. After that we reached home. I saw his relatives and friends, and they all stayed with me until midnight. The next morning, your dad took me out and he showed me the Golden Gate Bridge. We stayed there for a couple of hours.

I speak English, but I was still kind of nervous coming here. And it was very cold here. It's a change of weather from the Philippines. It's so hot [there], and I'm used to hot weather.

My first job was as a clerk at the post office. When I got the job I thought they wouldn't accept me because I was new here. Your dad used to pick me up from work at around midnight, and you would come with your brother and would sleep in the car with your blankets. Our car at that time was a sports car and you both had to be in back.

Then I got homesick. I received a letter from the Philippines, and as I read it, I started crying because I missed my parents and my sisters. When your dad came home from work he told me that I could go to the Philippines. Yeah, but I had already gone back when your grandpa passed away. That was the first time I went back, and you went with me. You were only six months old, and it was hard for me to take care of you in the airplane. You were so small. You were always crying, and your dad did not go because he had work. Yeah, you got sick, and the doctor was very far away, like in Manila, and I didn't know what to do. So it was hard for me because when your grandpa passed away I was two months pregnant with your brother, Roy. Oh, I don't want to remember when your grandpa passed away.

Well, your grandma came here. I petitioned her to come here because I needed help raising all of you, and your dad and I were busy with work.

I think the similarity between here and the Philippines is when you work hard you will be successful here. If you are lazy at work you will be unsuccessful in your life. The difference is, in the Philippines, even though [you] like to go to school, you can't because you can't afford the books and the uniforms. Here, if you like to go to school, you can because there is a public school and high school. I went to elementary school. I went to the closest one to my *barrio*. [I] went to the high school in my town. In college I went to another town because there was no college near my town. So I moved to the nearest town, Macabebe, and I finished there. My degree is Bachelor of Science in elementary education, which is for [teaching in] elementary school.

Did you know, in the Philippines you have to walk to where you want to go? Here you're always in the car. There, when you're working, you feel comfortable doing your job. What I'm trying to say is that I think I like it better there than here. It's always pressure [here]. Like, when you go to sleep at night you have to arrange the hours to sleep. Probably when my husband and I retire we might move back there to the Philippines. We're going to get a house made there, and then we'll just [visit] back here.

Yeah, I'm very happy that I have my own house, which is very big. We have three cars; one is my husband's Cadillac Escalade. I was very angry when your dad bought a new car and he didn't tell me. But as long as he is happy with it I'm happy. We have a happy family. You guys are getting so tall and big. I'm happy because [you're] growing up so fast. It just amazes me. I want to thank God for blessing me with a wonderful family.

Part of the interview translated from Kapampangan / Tagalog

PART VIII

MY THUG LIFE
CALIFORNIA DREAM

WHEN I SHOT THEM FOOLS

ANONYMOUS, PHILIPPINES
INTERVIEWED BY MARC MORALES

*I interviewed my uncle, who came here straight from the
Philippines. He lives near Geneva Street with a beautiful wife and three wonderful children, and another one on
the way. He works very hard to look for a job, but to me
he's just a straight-up ghetto gangster.* —M.M.

In the Philippines I was young. I was like nine years old [and] I traveled here by myself. People say, of course, it's [the Philippines], not
California. It's way different in the Philippines. It's hot there, and the
food and cars and the houses… It's, like, s***, it's way different. I was by
myself 'cause my dad, mom, and brothers, they're all here. They sent [the
plane ticket] to me. [There] were a lot of people in the plane, of course.
I ain't got no choice, 'cause this where my parents at. I wasn't scared. I was
happy to see America.

When I moved to Sunnydale [housing project], I was going to Balboa
High School. But I wasn't going to school because I was cutting, drinking, hanging out with friends, gang bangin'. I was doing that. Nobody
used to go to class. Yeah, it was different back then. Back then it was a lot
of gangs. It was Filipino gangs like SC. That means Satan's Child. They
got MG, that's means Mag Tangol. And they got BNG, that's Bahal Na
Gang. There's a lot of gangs in middle school [too]. A lot of gangs, yup…
I was in lots of gangs; I think three gangs. I was SC, and I used to be RPB.
I was in Vigilante Boys, [and] I stayed with them the most. I say from
about 1988 until 1994 or '95. I… I used to be with them. Of course we
used to go out and drink. So we go to a house party. We'd see some different gang and s***, we like, we start, you know. Of course you're going
to start shooting, like, "Who's that? Who's that dude lookin' at?" You
know, "What you lookin' at?" You know you gonna get conflict. We started fighting, you know what I mean. Shooting, stabbing, you know.

[To get initiated in the gang] I had to get burned by a cigarette. I was
the first generation, so we didn't [get jumped by thirty people, to join a
gang] but it was the second generation, the third and fourth [that did]. We
used to beat 'em up. You wanna get in, you gonna get whooped. You

know, if a girl wanna get in, they gonna get lined up by like six people... uh huh, the Vigilante Girls.

We used to do drive-bys. I shot a few people; some of them are paralyzed. We did a drive by, and then a week later they knew who did it. And it was us, and soon some of my friends got caught, and they told on me. They snitched on me, so I went to, uh... I denied [it] at first, but you know, the one I shot, he said he seen me, so I went to, uh... He was Samoan and one of 'em was Filipino. See, I didn't shoot for no reason, you know? They did something, so I got 'em back. Three of his Samoan punks tried to jump me on the fourteen/Mission bus. I was a Vigilante. They didn't get along with Vigilante boys. 2V, Visitacion Valley, that's what [their gang's] called. We got them back, uh huh. When I got jumped, we got them the next day. We came back rolling two or three deep; three guns, every car got a shotgun. I had an Uzi, and my boy had a forty-five.

When I shot them fools, [I was sixteen so] I went to juvenile hall. They gave me three years, so they send me to CYA. That's the junior prison. So when I got out from CYA, I went back to the same old stuff again. I hung out with the gang again.

We'd go party, we'd go steal cars, you know, rob the liquor store... So I get caught. I wasn't sixteen. I was nineteen, so they didn't send me back to the juvenile hall. I went to prison. Altogether, about nine years. I went to San Quentin, Folsom, Soledad, Solano, and Pelican Bay.

[Prison was] crazy. It's about the respect, see. It doesn't matter how tough you are, or if you're a big guy, or if you be a killer. You have to have the respect. You have to know how to carry yo'self. I seen people getting stabbed—there's a lot of gangs in prison.

They treat you like a dog. They tell you when to eat, they tell you when you want to take a shower, they tell you when you go out of your room. You're like a dog, like a slave. If you're not going to follow the rules they gonna send you to the hall. The hall mean when they send you, like, for a month in a room [and you] never come out. You only come out to eat and that's like ten minutes a day. I followed [the rules], 'cause [if] you go to the hall, you gonna go crazy. You don't come out (laughs). There's no light. You don't see a sunlight [for] a month.

When I was in prison I met a lot of people. [It's] like a big town. [There was] a mafia, a drug dealer, a big-time drug dealer. So I gave them my address. "What's your name? If you get out [and] I get out, we gonna get hooked up on the street."

[When I got out] I didn't join a gang, but it was different stuff. I started slangin' drugs, start selling drugs, yah! I didn't get caught. I was so, so, so secretive.

My first job was as a dishwasher [in] Stonestown. It was an American restaurant. Back then it was like five dollars an hour. [Then I was] a waiter, in a restaurant in the Holiday Inn [downtown], a waiter and bus boy. After downtown, I got laid off. So I went to a printing company. It wasn't paying a good amount, so I kept applying, applying.

I missed my country, you know, like the food and the girls, stuff like that. And the places, the province. I miss all that. My wife, she got a good job and I had a good job [until] I got laid off. We bought [an Expedition and] a house together. Working, paying bills, car payment, house payment, grocery bills. I wish I [had] wanted to go back to school. I wish I finished high school. I want to go to college—I'd get a better job that way.

I still see them [gang members] once in a while, in the street driving. We say, "Aye, wassup, man. Oh, where you goin'? Are you working now?" You know, they ask me a question, "Are you working, you got kids or what?"

It's kind of hard right now. I… I don't have no job, I got laid off. I'm still lookin' for a job. I get interviews, they gonna see all my tattoos, my tear drop [gang tattoo], you know? They gonna get scared, so they don't call me back. It's hard. I got a lot of bills to pay, car, house payment. My wife's working, she make good money. We [got] a letter [saying] we have [extra loan] money in the bank, plus savings. The mortgage is like 2,500 dollars a month; car insurance, 800. We get money out of savings. That's how we livin' right now.

I did [sell drugs] one time last month. crystal meth. I was broke, you know? My homie, I still had his number. He's a big-time baller, so I told him to hook me up one time. I made a couple thousand. I'm just drinking, smokin' cigarettes now, but yeah, I used to do drugs.

But I don't wanna stay home, cleaning the house, dropping [my wife] off to work. I don't like the way I'm living right now. I'm just where I am, I just keep applying, keep applying. I'm too old for that [drugs and gangs] s***. I don't want to go back to prison. I went to prison all my life, so I just try to do good things. I don't wanna rob or sell drugs. Actually

I don't wanna go back there [to the Philippines either] because all my family is here. [If I] got a choice, I'd stay here.

MY THUG LIFE
GREYHOUND CALIFORNIA DREAM

MORRIS LUMAR, NEW ORLEANS
INTERVIEW BY SHANTELL LUMAR

My father is a nice guy. He came from a hard life.

—S.L.

My name is Morris Lumar. I'm a single parent. I'm a bus driver for AC Transit, and I've been in California now for about seventeen or eighteen years. I'm a hard worker, and I'm a good person to get along with, and I love my daughter, which is you. Also, it's a lot of opportunities here. I decided to move here to better my education. I wasn't a very nice person where I was from. I was always getting into trouble, so I decided to come out here and finish my education. And I was hoping to get a family and just better my life, and California is a good place to be to do those types of things and to meet a lot of different people from different countries.

My grandfather, he raised me to the age of nine years old. I was living in New Orleans, Louisiana, a country boy raised around a lot of pigs, chickens, and cows, walking around in bare feet and everything. I didn't really know my mom until after I was nine. We lived in the projects, so I grew up to be a thug and I did a lot of thuggish things that I'm not proud of.

He died, my grandfather. He got old and he couldn't really take it, so my mom, she decided to come and raise me on her own by herself. I never knew my dad until I got a little bit older, and me and my mom we didn't really get along that good because by me staying in the projects I had a lot of thug inside of me, you know? I had a lot of hatred and stuff like that. So it took us a long time to really get along. We talk a lot, you know? So that's about basically it. I was happy sometimes, but most of the time I was a very sad kid.

I went to several schools [in Louisiana]. My first school was kinder-garten. I was at this place called William J. Guste. Then I went to this school called O.P. Walker. I went to a high school called Thomy Lafon. I didn't do too good because I was the clown of the classroom. I thought that was the way to go at the time.

Some [of my] early memories [include] being with grandfather, and until I left I had a good friend of mine. We were very good friends. He was murdered when I was, um, must have been twenty-three or twenty-four years old. I really miss him, you know? I fell in love with this little girl named Sandra. I was twelve years old, in love with this girl name San-dra. She was a beautiful little thing. She had long gold and black hair. She was just beautiful and pretty. I really loved that little girl, man. I used to tow her books and everything. I used to pull her hair [and] I did all type of boys' things. I used to love going to parties, too. And we used to go to a lot of skating rings [rinks]. And Christmas was a very exciting day, [and] Halloween—I remember those days.

[To get to San Francisco] I just saved my money, [and] just decided to come out to the West. There wasn't any jobs [and] stuff like that [in Louisiana], you know what I mean? So I used to hear a lot about Cali-fornia, you know? That it was a great place to better your life. I got you [my daughter] in my life that I love so much and the rest is history, I guess.

I stayed out here with my aunt. Yes, I forgot I lived with my aunt for a while. She's now deceased, but I lived with her about a month or two. She was a very sweet lady, you know. She sheltered me, and I left from time to time to seek employment. I also decided to finish my education. I went to school out here. I finished my education as far as getting a high school diploma. I went to college, but I didn't stay in it, though. But I was shocked, knowing me, even going to college.

I had to put in a week's notice to inform my employer that I was leaving Louisiana to go to California. I said goodbye to a lot of my friends. I went to buy me a suitcase. I didn't have that much clothes, you know—about five pairs of drawers and four shirts and T-shirts [and] a few pairs of pants. I was like a broke person when I got out here, but everything was okay.

I didn't travel with no one. I came out here all alone by myself. I came out here on [a] Greyhound bus, yes I sure did, and I will never do that again, no way. I had a hundred bucks in my pocket, and I was a hungry jack—I ain't telling you no lie. I was a very hungry jack, you know? I couldn't use the bathroom or none of that, you know. Three thousand miles. Could you imagine that? All cramped up in a dirty, rusty seat, with this man on the side of me snoring and making all that noise, "Rrrr. Rrrr..." God, I just hated that. Really, I would never do that again. I didn't take a bath for three days, man—three days—because they didn't have nowhere you could take a bath on that bus. So I was so glad to get water. I didn't know what the hell to do. I would go to the bathroom and take a bath in that little birdbath sink. I'm not proud of that. I'm not used to being stank and funky and crispy.

This was my plan [when I got to California]: get me a good job, be some type of performer. I wanted to be that, or a comic, because I love making people laugh. And I wanted me to have a home and be married and have a family. And I have a pretty good job now. I mean, I could do better, but I'm happy.

I [was] so tired and wore out, especially going through that desert, man. I was so hungry, you know? 'Cause a hundred bucks in your pocket is not enough money traveling that far. I was really, really happy to get to my destination. When I got to California, I got off the bus and kissed the concrete. People laughed at me, seeing me doing that, but I didn't give a damn about that 'cause I felt good. That was the longest ride I ever had, you know? It messed my back up. Sitting down like that makes you get, oh... you don't want to sit down for a long period of time like that. It's not good for your circulation.

I felt good, like I said before. I mean I felt *good*, you know? California. I used to hear about it and read about it. Coming out here was a very refreshing thing. Seeing all these mountains and the Golden Gate Bridge and all this beautiful weather. I loved the weather where I'm from. It's very, very hot, and when it gets cold, it gets very, very cold. Out here it's like a neutral thing. I love it out here. I love all the beautiful ladies out here, so many beautiful ladies out here. Man, I love it out here. [In] about five more years, I'm going back home, though, 'cause it costs too much to live here.

WE WILL LIVE FOREVER

Gregory Morton, Miami, Florida
Interviewed by Teonna Moore

My cousin is a very smart young man who I think is going to make it somewhere in life. He's eleven years old, and has been through a lot of things in his short life, conquering all obstacles that came his way. I just want to say to anybody who's in a situation like this, just remember: "What doesn't kill you will only make you stronger." —T.M.

I'm Gregory Charles Morton III, eleven years old, [an] African-American [from] Miami. My dad had five kids, and my mom has two. My mom is [alive], but my dad died. Raygenae [is my girlfriend]. I have more girlfriends than that. You want me to name them? Shaketha, Raygenae… nah.

[We left Miami] because my mom was getting beat up by my stepdad a lot. Yeah, a lot. My mom was tired of it, so we moved here with my Auntie Toska, [in] South San Francisco. Because he was abusing my momma, he hit her in the head with the tank. Then he pushed her into the sink. I punched him. Then he punched me in the nose. Then I started bleeding with blood and snot. Then I wanted to kill him—I wanted to kill her husband. I thought he was nice—he used to buy me everything, take us out to eat dinner, you know? Like the first day I met him. But the second day he was mean. I guess he was just acting nice so he could move in [with] us because he had nowhere else nice to go. And our house was so big—had a big backyard for, like, BBQs and stuff. I was like, "I'm about to kill [this guy]."

Yes, [I was scared] because her head had a big knot, and she used to wear hats that covered her whole forehead. When she came up to the school people used to stare. Yes, [I was mad] because they made it seem like something was wrong with her face. But she was still pretty to me.

We stole that man's car [when we left Miami], and we drove out here. It took two days. The car stopped on the side of the road, and we had to get so many bottles and fill them with oil, and then we went back on the road. It happened twice. I was thinking, was he [stepdad] going to bust out our house windows or something? Because we stole his car while he was sleep. We came early in the morning. We was packing and then he heard [a noise]. I know because my suitcases started falling down the stairs, and then he woke up. Then mom gave him some water so he could go back to sleep, and then we went out and got in the car and was gone.

It was bad [the trip] because his car had a lot of problems. We kept having to stop and get this and get that, but my mom was in a big hurry to get here. We did what we had to do. We saw, like, little animals. Yes, we saw a skunk and reindeer and a new animal called Jaquan [Jaquan is his cousin.]. When we got to my auntie's house she was stressing and tired. My mom slept from like 12:00 in the afternoon all the way until the next day.

[We stayed at] my Auntie Toska's house. She threw us out, and we had to sleep in her garage for about a month. [We ate] fish, spaghetti, and BBQ. She had a little bed, a fridge with a little food. We ate all of it in one day or two, and that was that. Then my mom put some coats on me and put me to sleep and read me a book. Then I woke up and put her to sleep. Then she slapped me, then I slapped her, then we slapped each other and went to sleep. [We were playing!]

She [my aunt] moved, to get four bedrooms so we could live with her. She got my mom a new job cleaning the buses that everybody catch. You know, MUNI. We don't live in South San Francisco anymore. We stay in the Sunnydale housing projects with my Auntie Toska, my Uncle John, my mom, and my baby brother, Kaylan. I saw my grandmother for the first time in California.

I thought [when I came here], like, everybody would be asking me questions. Like: "I know your dad, Travis," and "Dadadada." They was like, "Where's your dad?" And I was like, "He's dead." And they were being sarcastic, like, "Where he at?" I was like, "He at heaven."

He was going to the store and he was going through the alley—like in the "K.O." [in the Fillmore]. They have one in Miami, Florida. He was across the street and then they shot him in the head. He was going to get me some canny [candy]. Someone told us, and then we went to the hospital and my mom was crying, like, "No, don't go..."

Yeah, [I like it here]. Here there are better people, like more for me to fight with, than in Miami, Florida. They have, like, the boys out here, like "totally bro," like "cool dude," like skateboarders: a California person.

[I attend] Harvey Milk Civil Rights Academy, fifth grade. Um, yes,

[I liked school when I first got here] but I be getting slapped up by some kids. [School now is] much better because I'm used to everybody, and I have two new best friends. We kind of are the popular boys at school, you know? We get all the girls. The girls... duh! Nah! But for real, I love my math teacher. [She] is so easy and she let us eat in her class, too. I get As all the time, like every Friday on our tests. [But] I hate when we go outside for recess because sometimes I be cold and then I get sick. But the teachers don't care. They never let me stay in or drink hot chocolate.

Guns [scare me]. I'm scared. I don't want to get shot. Because they're killing for sport, they love to kill, but when someone dies, they go and kill the next person. I'm mad about that. That's not even cool. I want to be a doctor because I like to help people, and when someone in my family is sick, I can help them before they die. And that way we will live forever.

HOW DID IT HAPPEN?

MICHAEL APOLONIO, WASHINGTON, D.C.
INTERVIEWED BY AJ IBANEZ

Michael is a typical teenager of today. He came from Washington, D.C., to the city of San Francisco just two years ago, in 2003. He is one of my friends. I met him at Balboa High School. Here's what I found out when I asked him a few questions. —A.J.I.

Washington D.C. is very different from San Francisco; a lot of white and black people. It's pretty boring living over there. There's not as much transportation as in San Francisco. Like, here you can get anywhere, like, in a couple of minutes, and in D.C. it'll take, like, half an hour if you don't walk. It's not far and stuff. It's, like, since we're young we don't have cars to drive, not unless our parents drive us. So, like, the buses, they take a lot longer compared to here. My school was far away so I had to take the bus because, like, the school was pretty much two or three miles away.

The education over there in D.C. is a lot better than here in San

Francisco. San Francisco schools are, like, for retarded people, and Washington D.C. is, like, smart. Like the stuff I learned in eighth grade was the stuff I learned in ninth grade here. So that's why I take honor classes. And then their middle school starts at seventh grade, because of their schools and stuff over there. They teach more advanced subjects. The stuff that they teach here is the same as over there, but they just teach a lot faster back in D.C.

My childhood would've been a lot different if I lived here, 'cause I had a stepdad over there that was kind of strict, but he taught me my manners, and he taught me how to play sports, ride bikes and stuff. And yeah, I wouldn't be nice. Or probably I would've been mostly rude, because it's just a different lifestyle here, more gangsters, more thug life, it would just be a really different environment over here to grow up in.

Friends and stuff here is all cool but then, like, the houses and stuff is really sad, like weak. I just wanted to see what it would be like to live here and also, like, I'd been living with my mom, and I just wanted to see what it would be like living with my real dad. And that was like the biggest mistake ever, because he's a dork and then my stepmom is, uh, too overprotective. They just don't really pay attention to me or really discipline me— they just piss me off.

The trip over here wasn't really planned. All I came over here for the summer to visit the family, and like, at the end of the summer I kind of decided to stay here. So it was all of a sudden. Transportation wasn't a real big issue. I didn't really know what to do, except pack and go. I just took a plane because it was the most reasonable form of transportation.

The school here is cool, and there's better transportation. But there's, like, this hard life here, because there's hella more people here, more taxes, more gangsters. Well, you can't really tell over in D.C. who's in a gang, but over here it's kind of easy. In D.C., there aren't a lot of gangs even though there's a lot of stereotypical teenagers and thugs and stuff.

And the Filipino culture is, like, you can hardly see one, unless you see a whole bunch of them, at a Filipino restaurant or a Filipino gathering. Which is pretty rare in D.C., because, like, the only type of Asians are Chinese and Korean. I guess it's kind of okay.

I brought my clothes and my shoes. I traveled by myself, because my mom lives in D.C. and my dad lives here. So I came here to visit and that's it. And turns out, I stayed here. Kind of miss my mom, though.

I WANT THEM TO KNOW
WHERE THEIR DADDY CAME FROM

BRYAN LOGARTA, CANDELARIA, PHILIPPINES
INTERVIEWED BY DEXTER PASALO

Bryan is a good person. He thinks he's a pimp and he
thinks he's all that.   —D.P.

Candelaria is one of the poor islands with kind of like a farming industry. Our, like, closest neighbors was like a mile apart, so it was kind of an isolated island. My homeland was like when you are just by yourself and don't hear anything else. My land is like the ultimate peaceful land, and I think that it's kinda better than America, except for [not having] things that we really need, like money and education.

When I was in the Philippines, I learned Tagalog [as] my first language. I learned to walk, I learned to talk, and I even learned how to farm a little bit. My dad would always take me to the farm, 'cause I had no babysitters. He would just take me to the farm and watch me while I just sat there and watched him. Our surroundings was all farming: trees, grass, plants, and just dust everywhere. No buildings, nothing. We had to walk around and get groceries by foot. No cars at all.

Farming is hard. It's really sticky. You had to get down and dirty. It was messy and the animals were really stinky. We farmed rice. We grew a lot of vegetables that kept my family strong. We raised a lot of animals, like chickens, pigs, and cows. We sold them, but we mostly ate them all. And we also ate dogs because dogs were, like, misbehaving, so we hanged them and we ate them. We ate more dogs than we ate chickens, because we had more dogs than we had chickens.

I was there when I was a baby. I would go outside, I would play with animals, I would play with dogs. We didn't have that much money, so I would play with stuff around me. I would play in trees with, like, parts of pens. I was amazed by pens. I was just amazed by them because to me they were fancy. We never had that much toys, so that's what I did. I went crazy on pens. I drew with them. My mom bought me markers, oh man, with different colors. I was, like, wow. I felt like an artist with pens, but I would make a mess. I would draw on the floor, and my mom would get mad at me. But man, I was really into drawing with pens and markers, because we didn't usually have them in the Philippines.

I came to the U.S. when I was like two or three. The U.S. is much better than the Philippines. The life in the Philippines was a hard life. I remember my parents struggling for money. It was really hard. Here my parents are doing okay; I'm doing okay. I'm learning. If I was in the Philippines I wouldn't be learning like I'm learning today.

I wanted to leave the homeland because my parents wanted me to have a better life, a brighter future, and I was their first kid. If I wasn't born, [they would] still be in the Philippines because my parents really love the place. And I love the place, but I know I couldn't have a bright future if I didn't move here.

When we were about to go to the U.S., my parents were trying to teach me English. We went to all these cool places, like the carnivals and stuff. And we walked around and said goodbye to the neighbors, and yeah, that was pretty much it.

I remember I was really confused [before we left]. I didn't know where I was going. My mom packed all my stuff for me and said we were going somewhere. It was really confusing for me, and at the airport and I thought it was like a carnival or something 'cause I was really young, and I, I really didn't know what I was doing.

When we got here, I expected, like, buildings and stuff, because my mom told me we were gonna go to a better place. It's gonna be like Manila, that's what she told me. When I came here the first [thing] I saw was [it was] crowded. It was like buildings stuck together, like people everywhere. And one thing I remember is that it was cold, really cold, and I had my *tsinelas* on—my slippers. I was freezing and my foot was like a Popsicle.

I experienced new things that I didn't know how to use, like spoons and forks and stuff. And cars, that was a big thing for me. I experienced new food. I think we went to Pizza Hut on my first day here, and we ordered a lot, a lot of pizzas. Back at home, there wasn't any Pizza Hut and no other fast-food restaurants. So I think the new food that I've experienced were fast foods, and I also tasted popcorn for the first time. Yeah, I was really liking it here because of the food.

When I first got to America, we all lived in this one big house; it was like three families in it. Every day, every night when my dad and my uncles came home, they brought food and put it on the table. And that was, like, every day. It was like a party, like a feast.

I would go back to the Philippines, but I wouldn't stay and live. Here is much better. I'm more comfortable here. I would spend the rest of my life here. I really like it here. Except for when I start a family, if they don't like it here, then I'll move.

I expected my life [to be] like it was [before I came to America], but now it's better. I never expected to have these jerseys on. I never expected to have a wonderful girlfriend. I didn't expect to have nice friends. But you know, God blessed me and I'm thankful that my parents came here.

In the Philippines, I [would] usually wake up to the sunlight because we had windows. And my mom always cooked food and I would help her. I would get, like, the vegetables from the garden, and I never saw my dad from the beginning because he would go straight to work. We had no television, no toys. I also went outside to walk around, and it kinda hurt because my slippers were small and I needed new ones.

My only friends were my cousins, but they were my best friends, and I had a lot of them. So we was like a group. Every time I went out, I would knock on the neighbors' doors and just hang out and play.

It was like four years ago when I went back to Philippines. We didn't go back to the place I was born in because we gave money to our families that were living there and they had moved to a better house. When I first seen them, they was like, "Who's this?" You know? Because it had been a long time since we'd seen each other. When I went there I was wearing big clothing, big jerseys, and my pants was down to my knees. They was like, "What are you doing?" And I said, "This is the American style."

And when we went there, we brought like these big boxes full of great stuff. We brought a lot of candies, towels, pillows, and other stuff. There was also shoes and jackets. As soon as they opened the box, man, their faces was like *wow!* They were really amazed by what they seen. So they was, like, wanting to get their hands on it, 'cause they had never seen these things. So, yeah, they were really amazed. This made them want to come to America, too. So I said to myself, man, when I have the money for them to come to America, I will bring them here and just, like, give them what they never had before.

My parents actually did not want me to know about my past because they don't want to remind me of the things we had, and didn't have. I still found out ways to figure it out and remind myself about my past. I asked my grandma about it. I wanted to know what my past was like because

I am proud of it and where I came from. When I have kids of my own, I would never not tell them about my past. I want them to know where their Daddy came from and why I had to come here. I take pride of being a Filipino-American, that's who I am!

PART IX

I MISS
THE SIMPLE TIMES

IT'S A BEAUTIFUL PLACE TO GO TO

SUSAN AYESH, PALESTINE
INTERVIEWED BY YAZAN TAHA

Susan is very nice and respects everybody. We were at her
house. —*Y. T.*

Susan Ayesh is my name. I am from Palestine. Palestine is a great place to go to. It has so much history and it is a nice place to live. The population [is] 5,248,155 (looks it up on the Internet), but I think that was estimated in the year of 2000. It's a gorgeous place to go to. It's very green. It's mellow without the war. It's a nice place to raise a family and, you know, learn history. That's where Jesus was born. It's got so many things going on, and it's pretty. People there always welcome you. You can sit down with your neighbor and have a cup of tea or a cup of coffee, and it's a nice place to be. It just has so much history to it. It's hard to describe with words without you actually going there to see it.

I wasn't there for very long but I did go to kindergarten there, and I remember my grandparents, and my great-grandparents. When I was a child we didn't have that many wars. There were always conflicts going on, but it wasn't as bad as it is today. My grandmother would get up early in the morning, and we'd have fresh bread and what they call *sayg, potet sayg*. We'd eat that with the bread my grandma used to make, like pitas— she'd stuff the bread with meat or spinach. We'd have a glass of tea, and then we [would go] off to school. We came home and we had lunch or snacks, whatever you guys want to call it. [When] it was dinnertime we had guests coming in and out [and the] family was in and out. I mean you saw your family every day.

I did attend kindergarten there, and when I went back in 1986, I did second grade. [It] is just so different than it is here. They got so much discipline there. I mean, school uniforms. I think it's better than here, where kids is running around doing whatever the hell they want. We came here because my parents wanted a better living for the kids. At the time there was no money. It wasn't bad but the thing is, my dad was one out of six brothers, and my grandfather wanted a better life for his kids—to have them learn discipline, also responsibility, and make a better living for them. To find a better future with school and education, better than we could back there— that's why we moved here.

Everybody cried when we left. We had a big dinner. All the family was over: uncles, great uncles, aunts, grandparents, and everything. I mean, it was nice. It was, I think, March 22, 1978. I knew was gonna miss all my family and friends there, so it was hard. We flew by plane. It was hard on my parents. I mean they had to go through customs, go to a place where they didn't know the language, and everything for all of us. It was kind of hard for everybody. My dad's oldest brother was here—my uncle—and my dad had his uncles. We had some family here. We all wanted to go to school because we came as a big family—my uncles, my younger uncles and my aunts, and me and my dad—and we all wanted to finish school and get a good education out here. Yeah, basically half of the family on my father's side [came here].

Well, everything about it here was different. Back home we cooked our own food; here it's done by restaurants or caterers. [At home] people are covered; here they wear whatever they want. The music is basically still the same Arabic music, but the way they dress is different. The way they danced back home, the men had their own place to dance and eat and the women [were] by themselves. But here it's a mixture of man and woman. They both dance together. I prefer back there, because I think it is nicer, actually. The girls could dance the way they want, without a man or anyone judging them. It's just so traditional.

It was scary [here], with people dancing on the street on cardboard boxes. You had loud music; people would carry music boxes. I mean, it wasn't as bad as it is today. I prefer back then. Actually, back then, I liked it, it was calmer. Now you got drugs, you got girls sleeping with everybody, you got guys doing all kinds of crap. You got weed, you got drinking, you got cocaine. I'd rather raise my kids back then than raise them now. You guys got too much freedom here. In Jerusalem, you yell at your child or you spank him. Here you get Child Services on your case. When kids [are] doing something wrong, you blame their parents for it.

Everything just surprised me. New rules, new customs, new everything. It was hard at first to learn a new language. We wasn't taught to speak English. It was just basic Arabic, so it was pretty hard, but once we got to know our neighbors and our community it was pretty nice. And we got to know kids our own age and we went to school here. I got to meet some of my family that I never got to see before. It was pretty nice. We went to a wedding the first week we were here, so we got to see how the weddings are different than back home.

It was more peaceful [in Palestine then]. There wasn't that conflict with the Jews. It wasn't as bad as it is today. Yes, right now, if they see a kid walking down the street by himself, they shoot at him. If somebody wants to leave, they won't let him. Like today, in the news, in Jerusalem, [a] lady went to labor, and they wouldn't let her leave. Yeah, they wouldn't let her cross the border. She had the baby in the car.

Actually, I prefer back home more. I mean, even with all the war going on, at least your kids can play in your neighborhood without you worrying about them. Here you got to watch your kids be kidnapped, or somebody selling them something, giving your kids drugs. So I prefer back there. I mean, if I had a chance to take my daughters and go back there, I would. I like it back there better. Here in the United States there is more freedom, but you guys here [are] teaching your kids that it is okay to do things that are nasty: to make out on the streets, to feel up on each other, to do drugs, that it's okay to have sex. Back there we had more rules and regulation, so it's much better back there. Here we barely get to see family unless [it's] a big occasion or a funeral, but back there you sit with your family, you got family coming in and out of the house, you got friends coming over. I mean, basically, it seems like every day is just a big party over there compared to here, where there is so much stress.

I don't want to be an American. I like Palestine better. I recommend that anybody who gets a chance should go back there. Because I think it's a better place for kids to grow up more civilized. You can trust your neighbors. You can walk down the street without being scared. Here you got to watch who you talk to and who you deal with. Too much drugs and stuff like that going on, here.

IT DOESN'T REALLY LOOK
LIKE AN UMBRELLA

AUNG CHAN, BAGO, BURMA
INTERVIEWED BY KIMBERLY CHAN

*He is a fifty-year-old Chinese man who was born in
Burma. He now lives in San Francisco and works for his
family. He is a really good dad who never does or says
bad things, and always tries his best.* —K.C.

Burma is a small Southeast Asian country. It has hot weather. The
population of Burma is about sixty million. There are many ethnic groups but the main groups include Shan, Kachin, Mon, and
Kayin. Most people speak Burmese, but some people speak different
dialects in their different states. The main dialects are the same as the main
ethnic groups.

Most Burmese are Buddhists. There are many pagodas in my country.
I liked to go to the pagodas to pay homage. I like those places because they
are peaceful. I could meditate well. I enjoyed learning about Buddha.

Burmese pagodas are very sacred statues. Most are made of wood,
cemented rocks, or bricks. The base of a pagoda is big and the top is
steep. They are like the pyramids from Egypt, but not the same. The
upper part has a lot of staffs, and at the very top, there is a thing called
"umbrella," but it doesn't really look like an umbrella. We call it a "pagoda umbrella" in my country.

I enjoyed my childhood. I was really happy and felt free. I also liked
to go to school with my friends. I got free education until eighth grade.
Later, I had to pay money for school, but it wasn't much. My sisters and
brothers went to the school too. I think it cost about two or three dollars
a year. My parents supported us.

We ate rice with curry. Most Burmese foods are spicy. We ate two
times a day, for lunch and dinner. Farmers ate three times because they
had to work hard. They ate rice for breakfast too. There was also a popular ethnic food called *Mohingar*. It's kind of like soup, and it's made of
fish. So we ate that fish soup with vermicelli. If you liked chili or lemon,
you could add them into that, too. It's very delicious. It's a popular breakfast in Burma.

In Burma, I owned a rice mill. I had to control and manage the mill and the workers in it. I was a supervisor. In the evening, I taught high school students math and science, and also taught college students. I was kind of like a tutor.

Life in Burma was okay but not really good. If one person worked in a family, the whole family could eat. However, people couldn't make much money. But there was no stress. If you didn't make a lot of money, you didn't need to worry too much. There wasn't much pressure. We didn't need to have insurance. When people got ill, they would go to see the doctor, but it wasn't expensive, about one or two dollars. If people are poor, the doctors don't make them pay. Even if people go to the hospital, it would only cost about three to five dollars. As soon as you get ill in Burma, you can go see the doctors, but here in the U.S., we have to make an appointment to see the doctor.

I remember the time I was ill in the U.S. By the time I could see my doctor, I had already recovered from my illness. Here, if people don't have medical insurance and they get a serious disease, they have to pay a lot of money. When your grandmother had to go the hospital, she would have had to pay about 30,000 dollars if she didn't have medical insurance. If we didn't have insurance, how could we pay that much money? Here we have to worry about insurance and jobs. But living conditions are better here.

Burma is a country which is neither too rich nor too poor. [At the] time [I left], people wanted to come to the United States or other well-educated countries, because parents thought that their children couldn't get a good education in Burma. Everybody wants to get a better future. So most Burmese people wanted to leave their country for a better life.

Before I came here, I thought America had a lot of good things and also bad things. One good thing was that people could get a lot more money than in Burma. I heard that the weather was good in San Francisco. Another good thing was there are not many insects, like mosquitoes. [One] bad thing was that it was hard to find jobs. Another was the expense of renting a home and living. But I also liked San Francisco because it was beautiful. I thought here my children could get [a] better education and future. I got the idea [to move here] because your grandparents live here.

Oh, of course I had [difficulties coming to San Francisco]. It was very difficult to get the visa (pauses). I think we waited about seven years for your grandparents to call us. After waiting that many years, finally we went to the American embassy in Burma, and tried to get a visa. Unluckily, the American embassy was closed for a while because of 9/11 in New York. After three or four months, we were contacted by the embassy. We had to go for an interview, and they asked for a lot of identification and paperwork that we didn't have.

We had a hard time about our names at the embassy. Our names were spelled different from how we pronounced them and how they spelled the names in English. We had to explain that they are the same. We had a very hard time there. But after one year we got a visa for our family. But we had another problem: that our passports were expired. They said that Burmese passports were valid only for six months. So we had to extend them. But finally, everything was okay. I was really happy at the time, but I was really tired. Finally, we could come.

I felt both happy and sad. I didn't want to leave my country and my relatives. But I was happy that I was going to a better, improved, democratic country, and my family would have a better future. Everything was okay on the day of my departure with my family (laughs). We had no difficulties at the airport or on the flight.

The time zones were different from Burma. So here, at night, I couldn't sleep. And during the daytime I wanted to sleep, because it was nighttime in my country. But later I got used to that.

First, when I went around the city, I went with my relatives. They told me about the streets, buses, and city, and I memorized as much as I could. And then I went by myself and took a map with me. Later, I took a bus and BART. I remember when I took the BART with your sister and brother. As soon as they got onto the train, the door closed, and I was outside of the train. I was really afraid and I didn't know what I had to do. I just pointed my hands to the next stop. And luckily, they understood what I meant, and waited at the next stop. I took the next train and met them at the next stop. I was really happy when I met them. It is really funny, when I think about it now, but at that time, we all were very frightened.

San Francisco is a beautiful and great city. The people are nice, kind, and great. When I first came here, I couldn't speak English well, so it was difficult to communicate. When I first I came here, sometimes I got lost. I had to ask people for directions, but they couldn't understand me. But people in San Francisco are nice and kind, and even though they couldn't understand me, they tried to listen patiently to what I was telling them. Finally, they understood me, and directed me to where I was going. Also, I didn't know how to pay for the BART ticket when I first came here. [But] when people saw I was having trouble, they helped me to do it. I like the people of San Francisco.

The thing I most miss about Burma is my house. It was big, with a large compound and a garden. Here I can't live in a house like that. Houses are very expensive. If I had a permanent job, a house, and medical insurance, I would stay here the rest of my life. How could I live without those?

Translated from Burmese

I MISS THE SIMPLE TIMES

ERIC WALKER, TUSKEGEE, ALABAMA
INTERVIEWED BY DASHENA BURKE

Eric went through a lot in his childhood, but he has made it through with flying colors. He is a very intelligent man who knows his history. We were at Balboa High School in his classroom, having a great time, and bringing up good and bad memories. —*D.B.*

I was born in Tucson, Arizona. My father was stationed in the Air Force there, and I was born July 15, 1957. I was twelve and I moved out here [to San Francisco] from Tuskegee, Alabama, which is where my family is originally from.

I had a very good childhood in Tuskegee with my uncle and my grandfather. My grandfather had a small piece of land, his property that he owned, and I would help him with the hogs and milking the cows (laughs), just doing things that a kid would do on a small farm. Now, he didn't have a farm, but he had a couple of acres, and I helped him to plant corn, and he showed me how to plant the greens and all kinds of stuff, you know? And my uncle showed me many different things. My uncle was like a father to me—he was more like a father than my biological father could ever be. My mother was a strong woman, but my uncle and my grandfather early on taught me how to be a man.

I took a train to New Orleans from Tuskegee that went through Montgomery on to New Orleans, and then I took a plane from New Orleans to San Francisco International Airport, and that's how I got out here. And what I brought out here was my Southern roots and my pride.

Probably what I miss most about [my homeland] is of course both my grandfather and uncle, who are gone now. But I also miss the simple life of being in a world or a place that is not urban—as some folks call it, the country. I guess not being able to just go fishing, or to just walk next door to a neighbor and just hang out for a minute and just not have to worry about anything, not have to worry about people coming up and harassing you or bothering you. The easy times back when I was a kid in the South, I miss those quite a bit. Yeah, I miss that a lot.

[Tuskegee] was segregated, as they called it back then. They had public facilities that were marked "colored water fountain," "white water fountain," "colored swimming pool," "white swimming pool." Even though Tuskegee was predominately black or African-American as far as population was concerned, there was still some segregation of public facilities and whatnot, that was very, very visible to the public. You could tell that racial line was definitely there. I remember the Ku Klux Klan threatened to blow up our community pool. I thought they would and I was afraid that they would.

I felt real angry even as a nine-year-old. [In] my generation, you weren't too young to be politically aware, because there was so much happening to our folks at that time that even at the dinner table this was the subject of discussion—about how the movement towards civil rights was going on, and what happened that day, and what we thought would happen in the future, and so on. These things were talked about every day with my uncle at the dinner table when we would sit down and eat together, and even as a young kid, as a young child, I was politically aware of what was going on. We had to be, all of us, because so much was affecting us at that time directly.

When I moved out here to California I went to a school, a junior high school, Jordan Junior High School [now it's called Jordan Middle School] in Palo Alto. When I was twelve years old I had been predominantly around schoolmates that were black. Now all of a sudden I was thrust into a school that was predominately white, and I didn't adjust too well (laughs). I didn't adjust too well at all. I had a really hard time, my grades were like Cs and Ds, and, you know, I rebelled against a lot of things, against a lot of people. I rebelled against my father for sending me out here in the first place, you know? Bringing me out here. I didn't have too good of a year in my first school that I attended. I didn't have [a] good time at all.

I [talked to my father about the situation] and he didn't listen to me very well. My father and I did not have a very good relationship. We don't have a really good relationship now. He didn't give me any credit for having an opinion, you know, because the way he was raised is that children ought [to] be seen and not heard. Many of my relatives tried to talk him into leaving me down in Alabama, and he didn't listen because with him it was all about image, how you look in the eyes of people.

I wanted to go back so bad, wanted to go back so bad, Dashena. Many nights I would cry because I missed my uncle, my grandfather, my friends. I missed the South, I missed everything about it, even though there were bad times going on down there. But you know, the community had a way of being strong together and helping us get through those bad times. It was helping out your neighbor, it was looking out for your folks, man, it was a different time and it was a different attitude all the way around, and I miss that, I miss that a lot.

The kids here would pick on me because of my accent, or they would go out of their way to just be mean because I was new and I was different, and for a while it was hard to make friends. But the next year, in eighth grade, I went to a junior high school, a middle school in East Palo Alto. Which is predominately what? Black. I saddled in. And I had this principal, I'll never forget this principal. His name was George Smith, from Tyler, Texas. He was a big, light-complexioned black man with a heavy voice. He must have been—man, Dashena—this man must have been about 6'5".

I became a teacher officially in January of '98, [but] I actually started teaching at a youth center on Third and Quesada Street in Bay View/Hunters Point. I did that from '94 to '98. I really enjoyed that job because it introduced me to Hunters Point. I learned more from that job than any college could ever teach me. That was where the real education started for Mr. Walker.

THE SKY IS VERY BLUE
& THE MOON IS VERY BRIGHT

EMILY (XUAN) SHANG, CHINA
INTERVIEWED BY YAN QUN HUANG

Xuan Shang is a seventeen-year-old girl. I met her at Balboa High School. The reason we became best friends is that we both come from China and have the same cultural background. We were eating McDonald's while I was interviewing her. —Y.Q.H.

Hi! My name is Emily Shang. This is my English name. I come from China—Shandong. My Chinese name is Xuan Shang. Do you know what the meaning of Xuan is? It means "beautiful jade." The reason my parents gave this name to me is they want me to be a beautiful girl. In fact, I am a beautiful girl.

I was born in Jinan. Jinan is the capital city of Shandong. This city is not big; it's a developing city. There are 500,000 people [that] live there. Jinan has many scenic spots, like *Bao Tu Quan Spring Park*, *Qian Fu Shan*, and *Da Ming Hu*. The north of Jinan developed some new scenic spots which are very fun. The young people like to go there with their lovers, the old people like to go there to take a rest, and the children like to play there.

When I was in elementary school, the school was very far from my home. My parents would take me to school and I would return home by myself after school. When I was in middle school, I did not have lunch at home; I just stayed at school. High school was completely different. My high school was located in a small village. The foods in school were not delicious. After going to school for a week, I would lose weight. I could have gone to another canteen for lunch, but I'd have to pay for it, because we couldn't use our lunch card there. In high school I had to get up at 6:00 AM. I got back to my dormitory at 10:00 PM. After they turned off the lights, we used a flashlight to do homework. I went to sleep almost at 12:00 AM or 1:00 AM. My time in high school was very hard.

In China, the students are like ducks. Teachers put all the knowledge, just like food, into their mouths. After the ducks felt full, the teachers would stop, and then students could graduate. Teachers told you all the information in the textbook and we didn't have many activities. Education in America is free. And, if you want to increase your knowledge, that depends on yourself. Teachers tell you one point, then you have to develop another point. I think American education is very good, but it's hard. The students work as hard as they can to get a high score. If the students don't study, they will fail very easily.

I miss the Mid-Autumn Festival and the Lunar New Year most of all. The Mid-Autumn Festival has a story about two people, Niulang and Zhinv, who are Valentines, but can meet only on that day every year. That is very romantic. People always go back home, have dinner together, and enjoy the most beautiful moon of the year together. I have happy memories of the Mid-Autumn Festival. When I was in high school, living in school for the first time, everybody missed their home. On the Mid-Autumn Festival, my best friend's father made a phone call to her. We were very happy, but after the phone call, we were all missing our families. We promised not to cry on that day, but we cried. And then I made a phone call to my grandma. I said I wanted to go back home, I missed her so much! After I said that, she cried, too. At that time, I felt how the love between family members is very important!

Many children like the Lunar New Year because they get the lucky money, they can buy new clothes, and eat delicious foods! We celebrate with all family members.

I am a Christian. My mother and I believed in Christianity. My father and grandparents believed in the communist party. I rely on God, so I thought God would give me what I want in my spirit. When I was a child, I always got sick. By chance, my grandma's friend introduced Christianity to my grandma and then my grandma prayed for me [to] get healthy. It doesn't matter if religion is good or not; it only matters if you believe. Many people believe in Buddhism. In China most people believe in Buddhism. In their opinions, Buddha is very important and always in their mind. You cannot say they were wrong even though you believe in Christianity. Religion is their freedom. The government told people religion is free, but if you are a Christian you have less freedom.

Before I came here I thought the United States was very big and rich. The sky is very blue and the moon is very bright. After I came here I had proof that this was true.

Why did I come here? Because my mother was here. My mother

works as a private nurse. In China, she is a doctor. My father does not plan to come to America because China is a wonderful country.

When I first came here, I was afraid. I heard that the society is chaotic. Everything is good now. I thought Balboa High School was a bad school, but in fact it's a good school. I want to learn English, so that I can be part of society here. I think [that to learn another language] if you try your best, you will succeed. I feel very tired these days because I have much homework to do and many things to think about, such as how I will go to college. But when I have time, I'll go shopping with my friends.

Translated from Mandarin

CHINESE AIR,
NOW THAT STUFF IS THE BEST!

VICTOR CHAN, CHINA
INTERVIEWED BY ROGER LE

Victor is a good friend of mine who lives a few blocks away from my house. He lives sometimes by himself, and sometimes with his brother and grandma in a house in the Sunset district. —R.L.

I'm eighteen. I'm not even twenty-one yet. You know, in China you can drink and smoke at this age. Pretty much most of the world is like that except for the U.S. I'm an American. I'm just playing. The U.S. isn't that bad. I guess it's better then some places, like China. We were pretty poor in China, but than again, so was everyone else. Communism isn't that bad if you're not greedy and you know how to do your part of the work. If you have a nation that is very unfair to the lower class and neglects to see them as humans, a commie nation is nice. [In China] I would be working hella hard and get nowhere, but here I can work hella hard and I might get somewhere. I used to be happy with just my family. Now I need my car, my TV, my computer, this, that, those, you know?

Money, cars, a house: (laughs) that would be nice. You know, living the high life. No worries, you know, stuff like that. I'm pretty sure that if I was still in China, I wouldn't really be happy. But there are some good things about China, like how everything is cheap and stuff. If you have money, that is. I don't think I would have learned how to break-dance, and most likely I would've ended up working in some sort of labor camp... or a Nike factory, yeah. We were not as poor as some other people. We had enough money to get out of China.

When we came here, we moved in with my relatives in a downstairs part of the house. It was cool. We had some nice fresh air, but not as good as Chinese air. Now that stuff is the best!

Well, my mom and dad don't really know English, so I'm pretty sure they didn't give me my name. I'm pretty sure some white person gave me my name.

THE ONLY OBSTACLES

Harrison Khanh Tao, Vietnam/Texas
Interviewed by Perry Gonatice

Khanh is a stylish turntablist and guitarist from the jungles of Vietnam, the deserts of Texas, and the womb of an awesome mother. No, not really, but it's something close to that. —P.G.

My name is Harrison Khanh Tao. I'm from Saigon, Vietnam, and I was born on April 19, 1989. Where my parents lived, it was in shambles because of the war. America is what they had in mind. They knew that any life they could make in the U.S. would be better than Vietnam. I don't know [what Vietnam was like]. I was only there for three weeks after I was born, and then shortly after that I moved to Texas.

I moved to Dallas, Texas. I lived in a one-story house with my parents and my younger brother. Dallas was an okay city. I had lots of friends, and I had a nice school. The most memorable aspect of Texas would have to be... the neighborhood I lived in—all the people there, the people I grew up with, my friends.

[In my neighborhood] there were a lot of big houses and a lot of trees everywhere. I used to ride my bike every single day. There was a creek that a lot of people used to go to. We used to go fishing down there, and we'd just hang out there and throw rocks, mess around, whatever. There was also a tree house that we had built and, like, during the summer when I was like in fifth grade… um, it was a really nice tree house. It was like, two stories, and there was carpet, and there was electricity running through so you can plug in a TV, you know? Stuff like that. We'd spend the night there. We'd eat there, and we'd make a bonfire, all kinds of stuff. Me and my friends built it. It was Ryan Salazar, Saleem Ali, Derrick Hampton, and me. Ryan's dad would help us with the electrical wiring and stuff like that, but we put it together, the wood and practically everything else.

The house that I lived in with my stepdad, it was a really big house, and I had so many friends that I'd just gotten to know over six months, and they already had become my best friends. I [still] keep in touch with them every single day, calling them and through instant messaging. I always thought I would still be living in that house, since, I don't know, my mom loved it so much (pauses). I never imagined that I would move to California. I always thought that I would stay in Texas and live in that house, and that's it.

I had to move because I lived with a stepdad I didn't get along with. All my family members didn't live in Texas, and it wouldn't matter if they lived in Texas anyways because I don't know any of them. And I knew I had to, I knew I had to get away from that house, so the best possible choice I could make was to move in with my grandma on my mom's side [in California].

The teenagers here, a lot of them seem to be carefree. Everybody cares about clothes and shoes. Everybody wants to be trendy or something like that. Everybody just seems to wanna have fun all the time. The schools in Texas are… are much more serious than over here. They would constantly try to push you to do well and do all your work. It seems like education is really important over there because you're trying to get out of Texas. A lot of people wanted to do that. San Francisco is much bigger, it's dirtier, and I live near a beach. There was nothing like Golden Gate Bridge, stuff like that.

[My expectations I had for California were] good weather, the beach, lots and lots of people—just like a busy city. I guess you could say that what I saw in the movies is what I thought California was gonna be like. And I thought there would be a huge number of gay people—I don't know, like, rainbows and s*** everywhere (laughs). I was worried about that. I'm serious.

[On my journey] I tried not to think about anything, really. I just wanted to see how things were gonna be, right when they happened, right when I got to California. I'd thought about all my friends back home as I was packing, but that happened way before actually going to California. I moved here in May, yeah, May of 2004.

I remember right after I came to the San Francisco airport, my uncle picked me up and he drove us to the apartment that I'd be living at. And I walked in and I looked around. I was just surprised at how many apartments there were around where I lived. And, like, everywhere, there's restaurants—everywhere. I don't know. I was just used to living in neighborhoods, like real neighborhoods, and it was just different.

School took a while to get readjusted to. It was just difficult. I went to Mission High. That school, like, sucked, big time. I didn't really have any friends. That kinda sucked. [I found my peace] in my room (laughs) and hanging out with my friends. [They] give me all the peace I need. I mean it's the closest thing to what I would do in Texas.

[Here] I stay home a lot, and I don't know where to go if I'm bored or something. I didn't know how to use the bus and everything. I just tried to do good in school, and I don't know, I just really want to go back home. Um, I just really want to work hard. That way, when I grow up, I can just take my brother and sister and move back to Texas. The only obstacles that I would consider obstacles at all are probably... (pauses). They're all emotional, and it's sad to be here.

WHY AM I A GIRL?

ANGEL, GUANGZHOU, CHINA
INTERVIEWED BY NICKI WEI

Angel is my good friend. She always wears a green coat.
She is like her name: Angel, because she likes to help
other people.   *—N.W.*

In China, I studied in nursing school and lived in a dorm there. It was funny to live with my classmate, and many interesting things happened. When it was night, there were always some strange sounds from outside and we would share ghost stories. There were some students who said they really saw them sometimes in this dorm. One of the students on the second floor was so scared that she was forced to go to the mental hospital that was near our school. She said that she found and saw something strange in the back room of that floor. A long time before, someone died in that room, and from then on people were always scared to walk around the room.

I like to experiment. We did many experiments in our school. We would inject some medicine into the bodies of animals such as mice, rabbits, frogs, etc. We could see what happened to the animals. But after that we had to kill the animals because they may have caught some bacterium. Once I saw a baby specimen that was nine months old in a small bottle. It made me want to vomit.

I think many people would like to come to San Francisco, because it might bring more property to people and they could make more money than in their country. So every year, a lot of new immigrants from different countries came to the U.S.A. They always leave their relatives, their parents, their friends, and their own life to go to America. Maybe they will get more wealth in their future, but at the same time they lose some valuable things too, just as I did.

My dream of going to the U.S.A. forced me to be separated from my mother. My mother is still in Guangzhou, and I live with my father in the U.S.A. now. My father and my mother divorced when I was young. After that I lived with my mother in Guangzhou, and sometimes went to Father's home for two days a week. The relationship between my mother and me is much better than my relationship with my father. But I wanted to have a better future, so I followed my father to America.

My mother is the most important person in my life. I think my mother is very tough. After she divorced my father, my imperfect family influenced me very much. My mother worked hard to provide for me by herself. She had to work, take care of me, and handle the housework. I often helped her and tried not to let her worry about me, although I had some unhappiness. But she always could find out and care for me patiently. She is a really good mother and I'd like to be as good a mother as her when I have a baby in the future. After I came to the U.S.A., she got married with another man and I am happy for her. Because I think she needs a man taking care of her, instead of me.

When I came to the U.S.A., I had many problems. I lived with my father, my stepmother, my grandma, and my grandpa. I think they didn't like me because I am a girl. In China, some families still care if their child is a girl or a boy. They want to have a boy because they think a boy can represent their family better. The main reason why my parents divorced is that my mother couldn't bear a boy for them.

My family is very traditional and I always get a cool treatment from them. My stepmother doesn't like me either. In Guangzhou, when I went to my father's home, she once threw my clothes outside. I was very angry and asked her why, but she said nothing. I know the reason was she didn't like my father to have communication with my mother. After we came to the U.S.A., she treated me better in front of my grandma, but she always looked angry with me when nobody else was present. I felt very helpless because my dearest mother was back Guangzhou. I would call my mother and I would tell her everything. She was the only one who could understand me because I didn't feel any warmth from this family.

I want to go back to China to be with my mother, but she said my future is more important. Although my mother has a new family there, she still cares for me, and I love her very much. She is the most important person in my life.

In my future, I will finish my college and continue my nursing course here because I want to be a nurse when I grow up. I enjoy this job and I will apply for my mother to come to the U.S.A. later. I will continue my American life with my dear mother.

Translated from Cantonese

PART X

DON'T FORGET
WHERE YOU COME FROM

IT'S A NEW BEGINNING IN MY LIFE

Guo-jian Ou, Canton, China
Interviewed by Sharon Ou

My dad, Guo-jian Ou, is the nicest and most hardworking person you could know. He's very dedicated to family and work.   —S.O.

I was born in Canton, China. Canton is a really beautiful place. There are four seasons there: fall, summer, winter, and spring. We also have an ocean, a big park. We usually went out and played in the park. Canton is a really big city. It's nicknamed "Flower City." The kind of flowers that bloom there are beautiful and of all different kinds. In spring the flowers bloom and it is beautiful.

Another nickname for the city is "The Five Goats." A long, long time ago, Canton was a really poor city and people had nothing to eat. Then there were five gods who saw that the people there were starving. And [the gods] became goats, held a bundle of wheat, and gave the wheat to the poor people so they could have rice. The people in Canton said thank you to the gods by nicknaming Canton the The Five Goats.

In the spring comes the Chinese New Year. It's the biggest holiday in China. Usually on this holiday people get four to five days off from work, or a week. They have a festival, where they just sell flowers, and during the festival the streets are blocked off. People are always happy to go to the festival, and during the festival there are flowers all over. The festival lasts a few days. On Chinese New Year, the children always get red envelopes from parents and married grownups. When they get the red envelopes, they're really happy, and they save their money for school (laughs). Chinese New Year is the biggest holiday, and the happiest.

It's Chinese peoples most important holiday. This holiday is almost like America's Thanksgiving. What I mean is, family members who live very far away come back home to have dinner with their families. After dinner, everyone would be so happy. The people who are married would bring their children along, and the whole family would get together and have a big dinner. After dinner all the family would go out to the festival to buy flowers and put them around the house. And at midnight we would play with firecrackers, and celebrate the new year.

On the first day of the new year we would only eat vegetables—no meat on this day. Then, on the second day of the new year we would go out and visit all the relatives and friends. We would bring candy. And the following days are the same. The new year's celebration lasts for fifteen days, and the fifteenth day is called Chinese Valentine's Day (chuckles).

Then summer begins in July, and around this time the schools would go on break. And around our house there was a big park. Usually, when it was really hot people would like to go out to the park. When it's too hot to go to sleep, people would bring their stools and something to put on the floor, sit together, and talk about everything. And some families had bamboo fans to cool themselves down.

When fall came, the weather would get colder. But no matter how cold it would get, there would be no snow. When winter came, it would be really cold, and we would stay home and put a little stove on the middle of the table. Inside it would have a pot where we would put the vegetables and meat to boil them and for eating (makes boiling sounds).

Well… in China the income is mostly from the parents when they go out to work and earn it. My mom was a waitress in a restaurant and my dad worked in a canned food factory. They would earn just enough for us to live by. I wouldn't say we were rich, but we were okay.

When I was seven years old I started school. I had six years of elementary school, three years of middle school, and then three years of high school. Then I turned eighteen and I went out to work. When I graduated from high school, at that time I was supposed to go to college, but instead I went to work on a farm. I lived with the farmers and learned from them. I worked there for three years, then I went back to the city to go back to school. But this time I went to a construction school, and stayed there for two years, and then worked at a factory as a mechanic. I got paid forty dollars a month, and the money that I had left over, I would give to my parents.

When I first came to San Francisco I was about twenty-three years old or so. I didn't choose to live in San Francisco. My wife had immigrated here with her family, because in China there's not as much freedom as they have here, and so your grandma's sister applied for them to immigrate to the U.S. Because her parents were coming and she was still young, she had no choice but to come with her parents. Then after a year she came back to China and married me.

Your mom and I, we met in high school. We became really good friends when we graduated. Then after I came back from working on the farm for three years—your mom and I kept in touch all that time—we started going out to dinners and movies and then started going out. And, well, you know what happened next (laughs). After going out for a while we got married. [She had to return to San Francisco to be with her parents], and then two years later I immigrated to San Francisco.

I took the train from Canton to Hong Kong, and then I took a plane from there to San Francisco. [When I got to the airport,] I was like, "Wow!" The airports were really big, and the airplanes were so big as well. Everything was new to me; it was my first time. When I got on the plane, I was so scared, my heart was beating so fast (laughs). And I kind of panicked a little bit because when the plane was taking off it was so rocky and shaking and I was just so scared. But the stewardess came and calmed me down, and she just told me to sit down and put on my seat belt and relax, and that there was nothing to be scared of. And then she went and got me a drink. After fifteen to twenty minutes I got more calm and relaxed. Then I enjoyed the ride, and then I said to myself, "Whoa, there's a TV on the plane?" (Laughs.) And then from there I was relaxed for the rest of the plane ride.

I felt sad when I left Canton, but I had to go to my wife, and I felt really happy when I finally saw her. I missed her. But I still felt scared, and I didn't understand the language, and I didn't know anyone here or how to find a job.

My first job was at a Chinatown grocery store, as a sales clerk, and my second job was as a painter, and I worked at a laundry place. Then I started working at a sewing company.

When I came here, my wife's parents had already bought a house, and we've been living here ever since. After I got here the weather was good, and everything was fine (laughs).

I've been in America for almost twenty years already, and I'm used to it now. But I'm really homesick, because my parents and two brothers are still in China. Hopefully one day I can go back and visit China, and see my family and friends again.

Translated from Cantonese

DIE WIELAND

SUSAN EMMERICH RITTER ABOUT WILHEMINA JURGENS,
HAMBURG, GERMANY
INTERVIEWED BY MILES MIDDLEBROOKS

*Ms. Ritter is a teacher at Balboa High School. I have no
relation to her except that she is my Modern World History teacher. She is a strong woman who likes to talk.*
—*M.M.*

There was my great-grandmother, Wilhemina Friederika Dora
Kruger Jurgens; her husband, my great-grandfather, Hans Jurgens; their small son, Peter Jurgens; and Hans' brother, Wilhelm
Jurgens. So all together there were four of them, including my great-
grandmother.

I think the person we should talk about is my great-grandmother,
who came to America in 1893. She lived a long time, and I knew her well,
and listened to all her stories about her life back in Germany and her
journey to America. My grandmother told me this story so many times
I know it by heart.

She lived in a village on the outskirts of a big city—Hamburg, Germany. She left at the age of twenty years old.

The problem did center on money, and the lack of it. Her husband,
my great-grandfather, Hans Jurgens, was the oldest son of a family of five.
He would have inherited the family land when his mother died except
that she had remarried. When she died, the stepfather was very mean and
would not share the land with her children. [In Germany] unemployment
was high, and when my great-grandfather did not inherit the family land
when his mother died, he wasn't making enough money. My great-grand-
ma did not work. She stayed home with the babies. My great-grandfather
told my great-grandmother that they needed to go to America so that he
could find work and earn enough money to support their family.

Hamburg and the Schleswig-Holstein region of Germany are in the
far north, where it gets very cold in the winter. They decided to leave in
the winter, and actually made the voyage from Hamburg across the
Atlantic Ocean in March. They went by boat. I'm sure it was pretty
cold—a lot colder than the weather is in San Francisco.

They went on the final voyage of a very old ship. She called it Die Alte Wieland, but "alte" means old, so the actual name of the ship was Die Wieland. They left the port of Hamburg sometime in late March or early April, and arrived at Ellis Island in New York Harbor on April 26, 1893.

I do know that my great-grandmother suffered from morning sickness and seasickness throughout the voyage. She was about five months pregnant with my grandmother at the time of this voyage. She said their tickets weren't cheap, so they went "steerage," which means they rode in the bottom of the boat. I am sure she spent most of the trip nauseated.

Part of the voyage was a long train ride across the country. They rode the train from New York to San Francisco. They had only German money, and they understood very little English. I know they were very nervous about spending their money, for fear that someone might take advantage of them and either charge them too much or fail to give them the accurate change. Maybe they bought less food and ate less on that journey, and suffered a little from hunger in that way.

My great-grandmother said she was so homesick when she got to America that all she could think about was going back to Germany. [When] they got to California, their little two-year-old son died suddenly. It made them both so sad that they just wanted to return to Germany. My great-grandmother would buy coal for the stove only one small bag at a time, even though it was cheaper to buy the big bag. She said she was NOT going to stay in America long enough to use a big bag of coal. But in the end, she never left. She never went back to Germany, not even to visit.

When they first arrived in California, the train dropped them in San Francisco. The city is very much like Hamburg, also a seaport town. However, they came over to live with Hans' sister, Katerina, who was living in Newman, a small town in the San Joaquin Valley near Modesto. When Hans and Dora went down to Newman, it was not like Hamburg at all. It was hot and dry and they did not like it. When their son died in Newman, they decided that they could not stand to stay any longer. They went back to San Francisco, near the water, to earn enough money to purchase passage back to Germany. But soon my grandmother was born, and they stayed in San Francisco.

When they left Newman and came back to San Francisco, they went to the part of San Francisco that was populated by German immigrants.

This area was called "Butcher Town," and is now known as Hunters Point or "H.P." There they were able to speak in German and get help from others who knew English better than they did.

I am sure that life was much better for them in America than it had been in Germany. My great-grandmother was already quite old when I knew her, so much of what she told me was the thinking of an old woman. She was a twenty-year-old woman when she came, but those memories had changed over time. She loved Germany to the day she died. But I do believe that she and my great-grandfather had a better life here than they would have had in Germany. I am sure glad they stayed, so I am an American!

THE BEST CLEANEST UNDERWEARS

AMATAGA TALANOA SELU, PAGO PAGO, AMERICAN SAMOA
INTERVIEWED BY SHARON LAFAELE

I interviewed my uncle in his room. He was with his friends when I was interviewing him. —S.L.

Well, it started on a sunny day in San Francisco, Mission and 24th Street. Me and my family was walking, and yeah, I saw a lot of people sagging their pants. I didn't think that they were really mean. But they were staring at us all stupid, and I didn't like it. But my brother said, "Leave it," because I was about to beat one guy. I couldn't stand them boys walking by us, mugging, talking all they crap. They acted like I couldn't hear them. So I looked at them to see who looked tougher than the rest. I spotted him, and they all asked me what the f*** was I looking at, and the tough guy called me [a word in Spanish] which I knew was something bad. So I said my Samoan words, and said stuff in English though I didn't really know what I was saying. So he walked up to me, and yeah… (laughs). I beat the f*** out of him, and then I asked if any of the rest of them wanted a piece of me. They all backed up. And that's when I knew that you should never be afraid of anybody bigger or smaller than you.

Samoa is a place of respect, where people honor and sustain the law. People that are not Samoans, like Chinese, Asians, do a lot of good things for you. I mean they dance for you, they shake their butts for you, and a lot of stuff, and they make a lot of food. The best you ever ate, like *palusami, pilikaki, fai* [green banana], *mulipipi* [cocktail], *fasipovi* [corned beef] and fish. I like fish and pig, which they call *pua'a*. Stores in Samoa are cheaper than the stores down here. That's pretty much it.

The schools are filled with disciplined kids. They show a lot of respect and they speak pretty good English for Samoan kids that have never been to America. They speak mostly Samoan in school, but yeah they speak English. The schools were pretty strict, you know? Once a month the girls lined up in one line, and the boys had to line up in one line, and the teachers checked their underwear to see if they were dirty, *kaka*-stained, or if they had any holes in them. If any of those appeared, they sent them home. If not, they spanked them on the behind. It's funny to say, but I was rewarded for the best cleanest underwears (laughs). Every time I pulled down my pants it was amazing how my underwear came out clean and shiny (laughs).

The schools, they started at around six o'clock in the morning and went until three o'clock in the afternoon. The boys didn't do anything in the morning, they just woke up. But what the girls had to do, they probably had to wake up earlier than us. They had to clean the whole house before my parents woke up, and cook breakfast.

The homes were funny-looking because they had no windows. The bathrooms were outside, but they're nice. You got fresh air, and... boy, I gotta tell you something: Samoa is really fun. I mean, mango trees, coconut trees, and running the wheels down the hill. In the *faleo'o* [a little house in the yard] we would play bingo, tingo, and have some fun. We would even do prayers, welcome ceremonies, and a lot of dances and stuff. And a lot of hands-on activities.

My *teine* [girlfriend] is moving to Samoa, and I gotta go only if she is really moving. We are getting married pretty soon. And the other reason is so I can get used to my culture again, because I forgot all about it. I mean, I know a lot, but I know less than I used to know before. But yeah, if I had a chance to go back to Samoa, I would go.

Well, years gone by, people got really used to Samoans, and now when I go to the Mission, all they say is, "What's up, dude?" And yeah, I made a lot of friends that I beat up. And they started selling weed (laughs), just playing. And right now, as always, I'm still in a gang, but it's hard for me to be a gang-banger and have a job at the same time. The gang really changed my life. I mean, I'm not really the same person anymore. I'm actually free. Free.

I THOUGHT PARADISE

EPATI MALAUULU, AMERICAN SAMOA
INTERVIEWED BY DAMIAN TUATAGALOA

I've known this person all my life. I thought I knew him, but after this interview I have more respect for him as a man, as well as a grandfather. —D. T.

I'm from Nu'uli, Nu'uli village. The houses there were made of wood and leaves from the coconut tree. We tied the roots for the roofs. Now we have houses like Americans. [I did] much of the work in the banana plantation, pulling the weeds and cleaning up, feeding the pigs, basically everything a person does on the island. We used a *fale umu*— a stove we made with rocks—[to] cook all types of things. But you had to take time; if you didn't, your food wouldn't cook right.

Back then, Samoa was different. I just came back from [visiting] the island of Samoa and everything has changed. People over there started living like American people instead of living their own customs.

I came here [at] the time of the war. There was a lot of workers, but in California there weren't that many people—but not like nowadays. The population grows every year, people from all over the world. But in my day there weren't that many people, so it was easy for us to get a job. I came with my "mom," Futino, and family. We visited our relatives in Hunters Point, stayed there for a week, then went to do paperwork [to] apply for housing, and while we were waiting we visited more family in L.A. We took the Greyhound. We had a lot of family all over San Francisco, San Diego, and L.A.

When I was going to school, in junior high, I seen Samoans come to the island and they were dressed nicely. They had nice uniforms and I liked their clothes, so all my life I wanted to be in the Army. Since I was a kid I liked the stars, especially the Marine Corps. In 1968 I got laid off of work. The Vietnam War was on, and people were drafted in the war. They sent me the letter and I went over there to take the exam, but I wasn't drafted. I joined.

I never knew my mom. That's why I call my sister my mom. I never saw my mother. I like mixed foods, like Samoan food today, Chinese food tomorrow. You know, mixed. I can't eat one food all week. Only the old people like Samoan food all week.

I'd like to stay and make San Francisco my home. It's easier because I know where to go and I get around a lot easier. I know a lot of people. A lot of people don't like living in Samoa. It's too hot. I have lived here a long time—that's why I'm not used to the weather there. It's hard to live out there 'cause it's hot. The only thing I miss is the clean air, the ocean, and the way every house has its own beach and people go work and come back to the beach and hang out with whoever is there.

IN MY COSPLAY MEMORY

Rainbow Wan, Hong Kong, China
Interviewed by Wai Wa Ada Tang

Rainbow Wan, my fifteen-year-old friend who is now studying at Balboa High School, is a vivacious girl who always smiles. She looked mature when she was telling the story.   —*W.W.A.T.*

I immigrated to California from Hong Kong. Hong Kong had been ruled by Britain for ninety-nine years. Hong Kong gradually developed from a fishing port to an international city. Hong Kong is now a special administrative region of China. As an international city, Hong Kong is affected by Chinese and Western ideas and cultures. People are traditional, but at the same time they are open-minded.

We learnt English when we were three years old. People in China learn English when they study in high school. But I have been learning English for twelve years.

I was very happy when I was living in Hong Kong. I'm very proud of my identity because I have a superior feeling when comparing myself with people in other regions of China. We had a sense of fashion, and we were always willing to improve ourselves. Hong Kong people are free to express their discontent toward the government. We could have demonstrations and blame the government without the fear of being arrested. I'm also proud of my city because the people are brave and can face many uncertainties. Although many people say Hong Kong people are indifferent, if anything happens, they will be willing to help each other.

I really liked the life in Hong Kong. However, there were many problems in Hong Kong at that time. We had just overcome the problem of SARS [Severe Acute Respiratory Syndrome], and many incapable officers of the government resigned. The problem of SARS affected me a lot. We couldn't go to school during this period. When we were able to go to school, we needed to wear facemasks for a few months. Hong Kong was very unstable at that time, and the change of the educational policy made me lose confidence in Hong Kong. I think our education standard was lower after 1997 [the year that China regained control of Hong Kong]. I didn't think I could find a decent job after I graduated from university. Therefore, I sought changes.

I have dreamed of immigrating here [San Francisco] for ten years. I'd been in San Francisco on holiday before, and I thought that it's very different from Hong Kong. That made me want to try something new and start a new life here. When my parents received the letter from the immigration department that said we could go to San Francisco, I was very surprised and I was happy and sad at the same time. I was happy because immigrating to America had been my dream for many years, and now I was able to fulfill my dream. However, I needed to leave my friends.

I always played cosplay with my friends. Cosplay means "costume play." It's an emerging activity among people who like reading comic books. People wear the costumes of the characters that they like, or they create a new character themselves. They always wear the costumes and participate in the game shows. It satisfied my desire to be special. The most impressive activity was the last cosplay activity that I joined before I immigrated to California. It's because we knew that was our last time to play together. We all treasured this activity. Many friends took photos with me.

I immigrated here in March, 2004. I've been here just for one year. I was fourteen years old at that time. I needed to prepare my clothes and all the necessities in a month. I didn't have enough time to prepare. Therefore, I didn't take my school examination before I left. It was just like preparing for a war.

I think that America is not as free as what I thought before. For example, my school tells me that I can't wear a blue or red shirt. Now I am afraid that someone may hurt me if I wear a certain colour jacket. Also, not all the people are rich here. Some of them are quite poor.

It's not difficult to make friends here, but it's difficult to have true friends. People will be your friend because you came from the same country or city—it's not because you have the same interest. Fortunately, although they don't know Cantonese, my friends who are studying in honors class will speak slowly and play with me. However, my friends in Hong Kong know what I like and what I think. I regard them as my true friends. True friends are people that can cry and laugh with me.

I remember when I was in Hong Kong, I was angry with my best friend, and we didn't talk for six months. I had other friends, but I felt lost because I had lost my best friend. Finally, we became friends again, and we now have a better relationship than before. However, something has changed between us. For example, I don't know what is happening now with my school in Hong Kong, and sometimes I don't know what my friends there are talking about. It seems that there is a wall between us. But we write letters, or communicate through MSN or by phone.

I think that Chinese immigrants are discriminated against by people from their own country. For example, when I go to Chinatown, the Chinese are rude to me, but when they see the white people, they will smile and treat them nicely. My father had some problem with his job, so he went back to Hong Kong to find a job. In fact, my father found a job here, but the Chinese employer exploited the labor. He asked my father to work for twelve hours a day without taking a rest. My father stood for a whole day and his feet hurt when he was working. Mother and I didn't want him to suffer, so we asked him to go back to Hong Kong.

The relationship between my father and me is different from other people's with their fathers. We are like friends. He is an honest man and he loves his family. When I was young, I was not good at mathematics. One day my mother told me that if I got one wrong answer for the math question, she would hit my hand. If I got ten questions wrong, she would hit my hand ten times! Finally, I got some questions wrong, and my mother really wanted to hit me! My father asked my mother not to hit me, but my mother didn't change her mind. But, my father shared half of the hits with me. He is my idol.

I've never lived without my father before, so my mother and I were living in sorrow in the first week. Especially my mother. Her attitude was not stable at that time.

My mother is a good and gentle woman, but if I do something wrong, she will act like a monster and blame me. When I was small, I was naughty and I would not say hello to any people. My mother taught me and asked me to say hello to relatives, but I still refused to do it. So, my mother took her cigarette lighter out, and said that she would burn my lips if I didn't say hello to relatives. Therefore, I will say hello to people now. However, I am not afraid of my mother.

My mother doesn't have a job, so we depend on my father to send money to us. Our deposit in the bank is gradually decreasing, and I really worry about the financial condition of my family. In fact, my mother has tried to find a job, but I don't want her to work because I want her to stay at home and see me growing up.

Through this immigration experience, I have learnt that I should be strong so that I can support my parents. I should be happy in order to make my parents happy. On the other hand, I recognize my Chinese identity and think that I am a "real Chinese." In Hong Kong, I didn't have any special feelings toward my identity. Here, I see different people of different colours, speaking different languages. This reminds me that I'm Chinese.

Translated from Cantonese (using British spelling as used in Hong Kong)

THE PRINCE THAT NEVER WAS

Antonio Siaos Ama Te'o, Sr., American Samoa
Interviewed by Paradise Vaovasa

*Antonio is bright and caring. And he's very easy to talk
to because this guy is very encouraging and very inspira-
tional in his own ways.* —P. V.

It was difficult to leave my homeland, 'cause it was the place where
I grew up and called home, and I had to come into a new environment with different people and culture. Yeah, it was difficult. It was
like a jungle back home, without Tarzan (laughs), because of the palm
trees and banana trees. And it was beautiful. People lived off the land.
They fished, there's an ocean around the island—and you could just grow
your crops and eat your food that you grew.

[I liked] being around my family. And back in the islands everybody
was calm and so relaxed and it was not so stressed out. It was like a laid-
back atmosphere. [I miss] the scenery, you know? They have beautiful
waterfalls.... And being with the family, also—hanging around at the
beach. Which was nice and clean, not like New Jersey.

But sometimes it was hard to get transportation [over there], and
I mean public transportation, you know? Here can get on a plane, on a
train. There, you could not do anything unless you got relatives that have
a vehicle.

You know, they say America is the land of milk and honey—a place to
come for new opportunities for a new to start in life. Well, I guess I got a
new start, because in the islands, when you wake up, you go work in the
fields—there's really not much to do—and in California you got more
opportunities and better education. You know, opportunities to get employment in fields and learn trades and things like that.

The difference between California and my homeland is the multicul-
ture. There's more cultures here. We [did] have different nationalities—
Polynesians, Tongans, Hawaiians, and New Zealanders. [But] in California
it's just a whole different world. It's like you're saying apples and oranges
are the same, but they're not.

To be honest to you, it feels different, but not as a culture shock. Let
me correct that. One, I had to speak English, and two, the streets are dif-

ferent from the jungle. It is a big culture shock. But I feel really good here now, since I know the culture here in America—I get it. I'm more Americanized now. But I would choose to go back [to my homeland] because with the knowledge that I have, and the education, I could probably go back and help my people prepare themselves before making the move to America.

I see [my homeland] as paradise because it *is* a paradise; it's beautiful. I mean, people [here]want to get away, to get some serenity and some space, and that's where people go [to my homeland].

Oh, I traveled [through the U.S.]. I went to college and worked on my music to get my music degree. And from there I went into the U.S. military. Then after that I ended up in the Southeast, and I played a lot of music there. And then I ended up in Branson, Missouri, the home of the country singers and stars. It was great doing music in Florida, too. Florida is wonderful. I lived fifteen years there.

My spiritual life is wonderful, you know…. When I gave my life up to God, it made me recommit my life to doing the right thing. Instead of… you know, wandering around like a lost soul. [But if I had to choose between being a music director or a pastor in a church] I'd rather be a music director, because I know what I can do. I know my limitations and I know my strengths. And my strength is music, playing music and singing.

Music to me is like a passion. I love music. If I had to choose between eating a nice piece of steak or playing the piano, I would play the piano (laughs).

I played music with Jessie Dixon, who is a famous recording artist in Europe. He's a gospel writer. I have played with Stella Parton, who is the sister of Dolly Parton. I played for Gary McStand who used to play with the Gators. I played with the Johnson's and then I played with Jim Bakker, who used to be the brother of P.T.L. [Praise the Lord]. And I met a lot of famous stars. Oh! and Barbara Fairchild. Well, right now I [work] for Lowes and that's my job now, but my first job, was playing music for church.

I always love [everything] I do. I do it because I love it, not because I have to. I'm a person who stays in my own realm. I don't bother anyone; I just mind my own business and I do what I want to do. And I go and I come as I please. But I would be the first one there if you need me.

I've been away from [the Southeast] for thirty-something years. That's a long time. When I left for California I was nineteen. It was a journey that was special; I felt like the prodigal son going out into the world and coming back. Because he went out to the world and, you know, I'm not saying that I'm broke and I'm nothing in the world. Because I have my children and my family and they make me a wealthy man.

[The people that influenced me the most] were my father and my stepmother, who raised me. My real mom had passed away. So then my aunt and uncle raised me. My real father was a happy, loving man, and he was always a musician. And everybody loved my father and my mother. She instilled music into me, and the value of music, which I hold on to [till] this day.

The first thing I wanted to do [when I came to California from Missouri] was look up and see the fog and smell the smell of the fog, feel the breeze, see Fisherman's Wharf, and see the two bridges. It's just like Tony Bennett said (sings), "I left my heart in San Francisco." I was back home.

Do I believe in destiny? Hm… Yes, I do believe in destiny because a destiny has been destined by God for every individual. You see people walk this world but they're still lost, you know? Because they don't take the opportunity that has been provided for everybody to step up and get an education. That is your destiny if you want to get somewhere or you want to be somebody. You heard that saying before, "step up?" It's a cliché, you know? I mean, it was said in *Sister Act*, you know? You got to step up. Step, and don't be afraid to fail. And when you fail, that's a part of your destiny, because you learned from what you did and what you went through. My destiny, I'm still trying to fulfill it.

FROM THE SOUTH TO THE WEST

Felita Clark, Tucker, Arkansas
Interviewed by Solomon J. Webster

Felita is African-American. She knew me before I knew myself, and has been a part of my family for a long time. We did the interview in her living room. —S.J.W.

I am originally from Arkansas, which is in the South. I was born and raised there. My grandmother delivered me. [Tucker] is a small town. During the time I was there, there were about five hundred people. The streets were not paved, and there were no streetlights. I stayed on a farm with my grandmother, aunt, and four uncles, with a smokehouse and an outhouse. [That was the most memorable part], staying on the farm with all my animals.

I dealt with causes [problems] from the KKK. As I was growing up, I dealt with causes, and signs that said the, ah, the *N*-word, "Keep out," "Don't let the sun catch you down," and things of that nature. It was a very strict community, as far as blacks knowing their place, and whites knowing their place—and I knew my place.

This was in the 60s. My mother left to find work in New York, so therefore I was taken care of by my aunt. And one night she stayed up late at night and she got caught out in the fields. And we saw the KKK riding down the road, and she and I had to hide in a pile of grass. And I looked at her and asked her, "What's wrong? Why you pulling on me?" I was talking loud, and she covered my mouth. "Those are the KKK, and we cannot be caught out here," she told me.

I would not say that that kind of thing has stopped. I would say that people are more aware, and they know what places to go and what places not to go to. I was just there last year—2004—and white people still call the black men "boy." Or you have the blacks getting off the sidewalk to let the whites walk on the sidewalk. So there is still racism as of today.

Before moving to California, I lived in Chicago. I moved with my mother and father because Grandmother was deceased at this time. Mother got me to move to Chicago, to the West Side. With me being raised in the country, I did not know nothing about city life. I used to get beat up; kids used to take my lunch money. I did not like the city life. I was not used to wearing shoes. I didn't like the city life at all. So I made a goal for myself, that when I turned seventeen [and got] out of high school, I would go to California [and live] with my aunt, who moved here before I graduated from high school. [This was] the aunt who raised me in the South. I had this feeling that my aunt was my real mother, rather than my biological mother.

In the South, which is the country, I still had my country accent. I really liked that. The majority of my family is still in the South. I liked the freedom, I liked the open air. It wasn't cold. And racism was right in your face. In Chicago, and California, there is still racism, but it's hidden racism. I prefer to know if someone doesn't like me, instead [of] them keeping it hidden.

A typical day for me in Arkansas? My grandmother would wake me up, and we would always have cooking sessions. There was no such thing as cold cereal. We would always cook a hot breakfast before school. My grandmother was very religious, and we prayed each and every day, for everything. We went to church maybe about three or four times a week, choir rehearsal, meetings, and all that good stuff.

After my grandmother passed and I moved to Chicago, breakfast was whatever you could find, because my mom was not really a cooker. So that's why I had cold cereal, milk. For dinner I would open up a can of pork and beans, and what have you. Once I moved to Chicago, my mom had to work and my dad had to work, so basically I raised myself, and my brother.

During my last year of high school, my mother and I were not getting along. I thought I was grown and she told me I was just a child, but I figured that as soon I turned seventeen, she could no longer tell me what to do, so therefore I was going to California. So she bought me a round trip airline ticket to come to California. But I traded it in. I got the money for it and hitchhiked to California. It took me about three or four days— that's when hitchhiking wasn't bad.

I arrived in California on June 20, 1980. I moved in with my aunt who lived in Berkeley, and [I] began looking for a job. My first job was at Sears in Oakland. I told myself if I did not get a good job by December, which was Christmas—I was going back to Chicago. But I did get a good job, and saved up some money. I have been here ever since, and it been, like, twenty-four, twenty-five years.

The day I left Chicago, I had no feelings. I was glad to leave Chicago behind. 'Cause for one thing, there's no snow in [this part of] California. So coming to Northern California, I really liked it. But I should have chosen Southern California, because they have more warm weather than Northern California. I had no ties. I mean, I loved my parents and all, but it was time for me to move on.

Really, I did not know what to expect. I thought when I first came I see all the movie stars, but that was a myth. There were no movie stars where my aunt lived. But I enjoyed it. I didn't have to work, I didn't have to go to school, I didn't have anybody telling me what to do. But I felt guilty living at my aunt's house without paying any bills, so I did go into a depressive state because I wasn't doing anything with my life.

I expected it to be very hot, very humid, because I like the heat. I expected the mountains, the trees, and the greenery. I did not know it was this expensive to live in California. I did not expect that. Which is one reason I was think about moving back to Chicago, getting an apartment, and sharing it with one of my friends. But as I stayed and looked at the benefits that are here in California, I decided to stay and struggle it out.

What I don't like here is the hidden racism. I don't like the tall buildings in San Francisco because they block the sun. I like sunshine. The same thing in Chicago—the tall buildings. But you have variety here in California. You can go up to Tahoe and get the snow if you want. You can go to Southern California and get all the heat you want. And that's what I do like, the diversity here in California. There's more diversity here in California than in Chicago.

I wouldn't use the word happy [to describe myself here], but I'll use the word comfortable. I'm more comfortable here. Chicago is not be a place I would like to move back to, but I like going to visit during the summer and maybe during the fall just before the snow hits. Arkansas, I go back because my grandmother left me a home there. So I go back and check on my home and I see my relatives there.

I have family members there who are too needy. Just for the simple fact that I live in California, they think I'm rich and have money. If I moved back there, they would always want to come to me [and] request certain things, like I can help them out. But I'm living from paycheck to paycheck, just like they are. Moving to California made me independent; I do not depend on my family members any more.

IT'S LIKE GOING TO A CARNIVAL

ALEX DE GUZMAN, BULAKAN, PHILIPPINES
INTERVIEWED BY ALJED DE GUZMAN

My dad always wanted to know what it was like in California. Now he knows because he worked so hard to get here, and all of his hard work paid off. My dad is a kind person. He will make you laugh when you are feeling down, and he will always be there for you. —A.D.G.

I lived in the Philippines. I went to school there. I played on my high school basketball team, and I worked during school break. I worked as a helper in ice delivery.

We came here at 1996. You were only six years old when we first came here, and you were so little. I moved [here] because we were petitioned by your grandma to live with her in the U.S. It was so exciting because I had never been to America and we were going to start a new life.

I left my parents, brothers, and sisters. It was hard to leave knowing I'd be traveling thousands of miles away. I was not paid that much; the money was not enough to support the family. I took extra time selling truck chassis even though I did not have any experience in marketing. I did it to have extra money to help the family.

I had mixed emotions—happy because of the new challenges in life, and sad because I had to leave my family (sighs). I had to do a lot of paperwork, like getting a passport and police clearance, and having to pass the physical exam and interview. I was working on a ship [at] a ship terminal. It was a twenty-four/seven job, very busy, mostly because I was dealing with passenger and cargo ships.

I was awake during the entire trip because I couldn't wait until we arrived. I was so happy; it was like going to a carnival (laughs). I like it here because my job pays well, not like in the Philippines. I wanted to come here to live a good life and to a better job so I could support the family. I wanted to see new things around me. Coming here was so exciting.

The first things that I wanted to see when I got here was the Golden Gate Bridge and Alcatraz. The first things that we did see was where your aunt took us, around downtown and Pier 39. That was so fun because I'd never seen seals before. That was a new experience for me (laughs).

My first job was as a re-stocker at Macy's. I got the job by myself. I remember it was a group interview, and they told us to sell anything that [they were] selling, and I did well on the presentation. When I got my job at Macy's, I was hired as a re-stocker [in the] lingerie department, and I was the only guy working in that department (laughs).

My life here is better than in the Philippines. No traffic, no pollution, and it felt really good when we first came here because of the new challenges ahead for my family and me. I felt like a new man. My life did change when we came here to America.

I miss my homeland a lot, and I miss my family and my friends. But living here is good, too, because we came here to start a new life. I don't know which one is better. All I know is that I will never forget where I came from.

WHEN I GOT TO SEE THE OCEAN, I GOT TO FULFILL ONE OF MY DREAMS

PATRICK GENE WAITES, DALLAS, TEXAS
INTERVIEWED BY DESIRE THOMPSON

My dad is a very nice man and we have a real good relationship with one another. We did the interview in our kitchen at 9:30 at night. While we were interviewing, my mother cooked us some chicken. She is very helpful. And so is my dad for doing this interview with me. —D. T.

I lived [in Texas] until I was nineteen. I loved going fishing and horseback riding, and riding my motorcycle on hot summer nights and cloudy days. I had a lot of fun [with] my childhood friends, you know, people you grow up with till you get older and go off on your own. And the you think about all the crazy things you used to do, like playing basketball in the rain, riding bikes, and helping Grandmother cook.

Then I moved to Saginaw, Michigan, to play college basketball. I didn't really like it [Michigan] because it was very cold and far from home. But I enjoyed it while playing basketball.

[One time] my wife had to come to San Francisco for a family emergency regarding her grandfather's sickness. He needed someone from the family to be with him. So my wife and me moved our family to San Francisco just for a certain amount of time, till her grandpa got better. But instead we made a home.

I went a lot of places with my wife. She and my kids showed me around the city. We went downtown and I got to see all the big, nice buildings. Then we went to Pier 39, where I got to see the ocean. When I got to see the ocean, I got to fulfill one of my dreams. It had been one of my special dreams since I was a little boy.

Well I met a lot of people through my wife and some of my cousins and friends, also at my job. I got to know the town and the friends of my wife's family. I also learned that you need to have money to do anything because things are very expensive out here.

I miss all the fun I used to have with my friends and my family. I miss the hot summer nights, because it is very cold sometimes in San Francisco. The weather is so-so, and the streets are very long. Though, the weather out here seems much better now. I get to see the ocean, and they have places where I can ride my motorcycle.

[In Texas] they are very hard on people who break their laws or anything the government will have a problem with. The laws are very different and the younger kids act growner than what they are. San Francisco laws are very different than the laws in Texas where they don't let you get away with anything. It's like they always got their eyes on you there, and with you knowing that someone is watching you, you can't go do anything.

We also lived in Sacramento for two years before we came back to San Francisco, and I like the weather out there because it can get very hot. Every time my wife and me would take the kids swimming and they swam for a minute, soon as they get out it still be really hot. Usually when you go swimming it gets kind of cool when you get out.

I like Sacramento too because we lived in a very nice neighborhood and it was quiet. The kids' school was right down the street from the house, and my wife worked like three blocks away. There was a lot of things for the kids to do when they got out of school. And on the weekend they had two swimming pools around the house. And for the girls they had a mall right down the street.

They also had this after-school program that helped the kids with their homework, and they would play games and go on field trips. That was good for the kids because they had somewhere to go and it was free for the whole community. They also went to Bible studies every Wednesday, and church on Sunday. They had a lot of fun, and I think that they were upset that they had to leave.

I would like to thank my daughter, Desire Thompson, for doing this interview with me because it gave me a chance to think back about how many times I've moved in the past and how much fun I used to have. Even though I don't really feel like I miss home, by doing this interview it made me think way back.

SALVADOREÑA FOR LIFE

ANONYMOUS, CUSCATLAN, EL SALVADOR
INTERVIEWED BY MAIVE MENDEZ

My young aunt is a joking person, always dancing, who never gets mad. I interviewed her in the living room. She was wearing her T-shirt and baggy pants. —M.M.

El Salvador is the smallest country in Central America. The population is six million Salvadorans. It's a country with different cultures and different customs. The most important cultures of El Salvador are La Griega, La Maya, and La India.

I was born in El Salvador, in the department [province] of Cuscatlan. I remember when I used to go with my friends to the beach, to parties. I did activities with them. We had a lot of fun together.

All of my family—my sister, brother, mom, nephew, and niece—went to the United States because they wanted to have a better future. They wanted to give us a better life. I missed them a lot. I came to this country with the help of my brothers and sisters. They were the ones who helped me. I also wanted to get to know the United States. I was alone with my dad in El Salvador, so I made the decision to look for somebody to help me to cross the border, the United States. I had strong faith in my personality. I got here by boat, walking, and in cars.

When I came to the United States, I thought it was a very beautiful place. The very first thing I saw was central Los Angeles. I saw how different life is here from the life we had in El Salvador. Over there, I didn't have any luxuries or the opportunity to do the things I wanted to.

The first few weeks, I felt weird. After a month I started to feel better. But it's hard to get used to your surroundings and another language. Although I was with family, I still missed my country and the things I used to do. I missed everything. And I think that right now I still miss my country, because even though I have a better life, it's not the same.

In the United States, I have a future and I can live all my wishes. In my country everything is difficult. In El Salvador there is a lot that you can never experience.

After a year here I was starting to feel much better. I knew more places in the United States. I made a community when I started work, and my family had friends. I have luxuries I didn't have over there. I can work and have many things I want to have.

I consider myself a Salvadoran because that is my origin, I was born there, I grew up there. I have many memories there.

Translated from Spanish

WE WANT *PISUPO* AND *FAI*

POULIMA MALEPEAI, AMANAVE, AMERICAN SAMOA
INTERVIEWED BY TEPORA MALEPEAI

My sister is a mean person in some ways, but most of the time she can be nice.   —*T.M.*

I was born in American Samoa, but raised here in California. I love my island because of the way it is. They have *pilikaki* [ocean mackerel], *kalo* [taro], *fais* [green bananas], pig, octopus, fishes, *pisupo* [ground beef], *esi* [papaya], and coconut. Mostly the food on our island is the same food here in America.

One of my childhood memories is going swimming in the ocean with my cousins on a hot day in the afternoon. We would always go swimming, when we came home after school, or when we finished with our chores—cleaning around the house, raking leaves. And, like, there was this old house behind the bathroom house, we always had to go there and clean it up. It took forever to clean it up. But me and my cousins would only spend an hour or two just picking up the little things, and then we would go wherever we wanted to go. After we finished swimming, we would head back to my auntie's house and ate some food, like *pilikaki*. After we finished eating, we washed the dishes, then we would go outside and play tag. Then we would go and get the kids from the village to play tag together. After all that, we would go to the store and get some candy to eat.

School was kind of hard because we would get hit every day. Well, not every day, but some days. If we did something bad we would get hit on the hand, or if we caused any trouble we would get hit on the hand, with, like, a stick or a ruler.

It wasn't that big of an island. I don't know how big it is in miles, but all I know is it's bigger than Frisco. My guess is, like, seventy-seven square miles. It is run by a governor, but we are also under U.S. rule. I mean, President George W. Bush is our president. There are mostly Samoan people, and a few white people coming in to visit.

We came here because my dad had a job here, and he wasn't sure if he was going to come back. The people that came to the United States was me, my mom, my dad, my brothers, and my sisters. We came on the airplane. I saw the airport, and half of San Francisco and Oakland. When me and my family got off the airplane, there was my dad's auntie standing there waiting for us, and then we hopped in the car. When we got in the car the first thing I remember coming out of my older sister's mouth was, "I'm hungry!" So we went to this place called McDonald's, and my dad's auntie asked us what we wanted to eat. We said in Samoan, "We want some *pisupo* and *fai*."

[Here there are] too many wars, too many killings, and people getting hurt. Before, there were not a lot of rumors about wars and stuff, but all of a sudden there is.

I miss my family. I miss the ocean, and everything over there. I mean, I grew up in Samoa, and it's hard for me to let go of a memory from a place that I knew.

I have aunties, uncles, cousins, and [a] grandpa [here in the United

States]. They like it because they think it's free. It's not. I'm telling the truth. I mean, what's free in the United States, other than getting shot out of nowhere? I mean, you have to pay for the rent, bills, and the clothes you have on your back. California is not free because we cannot go outside. Every time we go outside [there] is either shooting or something else wrong going on out there. Back on the island it's peaceful and it's not really dangerous. Like, for example, I remember my older sister going somewhere with her friends and sometimes with my cousins. My parents wouldn't even trip or be over-protective. But now that we moved to California, my parents have to have my sister at home at all time. Like on the weekends, my cousins come and ask my parents if she can go with them somewhere, but my parents make up excuses to make her stay home.

When we first came to the United States, I thought, cool, you know. The buildings and the lights. It was fun because my aunties would take us to places just [to] explore the place and spoil us.

You have to pay for a lot of expensive stuff here; everything over there is cheap, cheaper than here. The clothes are probably, like, ten dollars for a *mu'u mu'u* [a Samoan dress]. [Also you can] walk around anywhere all day and anytime you want [in Samoa] without anything happening or anything wrong going on. There is less violence there than here.

THIRD WORLD COUNTRY

ZERINA BANGAWAN, PAMPANGA, PHILIPPINES
INTERVIEWED BY MICHAEL APOLONIO

*I interviewed my mom's co-worker in her pajamas, right
before she went to church.* —M.A.

Back in the Philippines there are a lot of ethnic groups. I mean, like, there are ten to twenty dialects. And I belong to the Kapampangan, about an hour and a half from Manila. We were *Pampangan. Pampangas*, that's what they called us in our hometown. We speak a dialect called Kapampangan. I came to S.F. in 1989, when I was about nineteen.

I miss the food, but we have all the foods over here now because of the Asian store. So we could can them, but it's still different, you know? I miss the hospitality of the people, too. It was very quiet. I mean, people talked a lot. You knew your neighbors, because, as I said, people there are very hospitable. You would go to their house and would they give you food, then they let you use their house. But over here, it's kind of restricted. I miss the hospitality of my neighbors. My sister, our eldest sister, still lives in the Philippines, and my niece and my nephew [still live there too]. When you go visit for about two weeks, then you leave, it's like you wish that they were all here all the time.

When I was younger, I went to a public school where I lived, and I miss the place, running around and going to the principal's office a lot. I was always in fights. Yeah, that's true. They [teachers in the Philippines] were a lot stricter. And you had more respect for them. Not that I miss that, it's just that, you know, it was just fun running around in the school.

It's different living over there, because over in the Philippines we had curfews. My mom and dad was here in the Bay Area while I was growing up in my teens, so it was only my sister I lived with. I had my driver's license and I had what you call a yaya, our maid. In our Filipino culture, as long as you're not married, you still live with your mom and dad. We are very clean. We all still live in the same house. I was still living with my mom at the age of twenty-two. I lived with my mom and dad until I got married at the age of twenty-six.

In the Philippines, there's no red light that they follow, and there's no four-way stop. They don't follow four-way stops, they don't follow the red lights, and then they don't use the lanes. If they see a part of the road to go on, they just go. It's easier driving here. You just follow the rules, you follow the law. My brother taught me [how to drive]. I drove a car that had stick, and I used to drag race too. When I wanted to buy my first car here in the States, I wanted to buy a stick, but my brother and sister said, "No!" Because they didn't know how to drive stick like me. They only know how to drive automatic.

When I got married, I moved to Seattle, Washington. I stayed there for two years, but the weather was so bad and I didn't like it. Yeah, it rains 360 days a year, and for five days it won't rain. So I didn't like it, and I missed the diversity [of San Francisco]. Over here there's a lot of, you know, the cultures are all mixed. You have Filipinos, Asians. Everybody is here, but over there it's limited.

I also missed the food. They don't have many Filipino stores [in Seattle]. You have to drive like an hour to just see an Oriental store. So I moved back here in the Bay Area.

My sisters were the first ones to come here, and I came here with my brother. I stayed for a couple of months, and then went back home to continue my college. I experienced a big culture shock. I mean, in terms of what I said, like driving in the Philippines.

I found a job as soon as I came [again] because I graduated in the Philippines. I took the exam two months after that. Then I was able to work as a nurse already.

All I brought were my clothes and all my memorable things, all the pictures, and everything from college with friends from Philippines.

I had family here in the Bay. My friends were leaving the Philippines too, anyways. I mean they were in the same situation as I am. They all have families here in California. They go to the Philippines, and then they came over here.

[The hardest part] was meeting new friends because when I was in the Philippines, I had many friends. We were college friends. But I met new friends when I started working. It took me a while to meet new friends.

I don't see myself [moving back to the Philippines] because I have family here now, and I have adapted here, too. I would visit every once in a while, but I wouldn't want to move back. Life is too hard there because it's a third-world country.

IT'S STILL CHAOTIC

ANN BARNETT, MANILA, PHILIPPINES
INTERVIEWED BY JOSHUA BARNETT

Ann Barnett is a hardworking mother who moved from the Philippines to have a better life at a young age. I interviewed my mom during her working season. It was late and we were both tired.　　　　—J.B.

I felt really sad about leaving the Philippines, but I thought about how wonderful it would be to live in America. I was so excited and couldn't wait to leave at first. I thought to myself, wow, we're going to be rich. We won't have to wash clothes by hand because they have this machine that will do it. They call it a "washing machine." And because we didn't have television back home, I thought it was great, we would have our own.

My name is Ann Barnett. I'm from the Philippines. [The Philippines is] located in East Asia. The language is Filipino—mainly Tagalog, and second is English, even though there are over eight major dialects and about 500 dialects overall. I remember the climate being hot most of the time, and it can get over 100 degrees. When it rains, it pours, and that causes the area to flood. That's when everyone goes outside and takes a shower, or just plays out in the rain.

Back then all you hear about was how great it was to live in America. It was the land of opportunity. My auntie, who was already in America, made it sound even more exciting when she wrote to tell us how easy it was to live in America.

Honestly, it didn't dawn on me how much family meant to me until I moved. That's when I felt so empty and sad. I was saying goodbyes to all of my friends that I grew up with and went to school with. There were so many tears shed. I was really going to miss my families. I care so much and love them. I don't know if I will ever see them again.

I have such fond memories of my childhood. What I can recall is the closeness of my friends, how we could stay out late at night and be able to play, tell stories, and gaze at the beautiful, bright stars. My friends and I didn't have to have money to have fun. Most of the toys we had were handmade. We made our own kites, made paper dolls, and made them paper clothes. We made paper boats when it rained and ran along the curb to see which would reach the finish line. There were just so many things you can make or create, and have fun with.

I could be wrong, but I didn't feel much hardship coming to America compared to other families who struggled and had difficulty coming here. My parents were organized, and that made it easy for us to move. I remember having to get our immunizations before we could leave the country. We hated that.

It was exhausting, due to the long flight. Everything was new to me, and I had difficulty understanding the English language. It wasn't hard at all to learn how to read, write, or speak English—when you are young you can learn quickly to do almost everything and anything. One thing I do remember is being laughed at when I couldn't enunciate a word, but that's children for you. I'm sure they didn't mean it. And I didn't let it bother me.

[The hardest thing] at that time, I would say, was adapting to the taste of American food, and to the climate. I thought I was going to starve in America. I didn't like the food. I hated pizza, for example, but in time I grew to love it. And as far as climate, I was so used to the hot climate and the humidity, so when I arrived in America, I didn't think I could adapt to the cold, foggy weather. I really thought I would freeze to death. Snow was new to me.

I don't really care much about our government. However, I do read articles and newspapers enough to know about the government. And if the government in my previous country was any better, then I'm sure my parents would not have considered moving to America.

Living here in America is good. [I miss] the food, like *lumpia*, adobe chicken, *pancit*, and fruits—they are so sweet and tasty. Filipino foods are very delicious. I love people from my country. They are warm and fun-loving. They have fiestas, parties, and celebrations. When we have celebrations, everyone is welcome, and it lasts more than a day.

I miss the Philippines. I have not returned or visited my country since I left, back in 1970. Several times I wanted to visit, but at those times, there was always some chaos [to stop me]. I would go back if it I felt it was safe to travel. It's still chaotic.

LEAVING EVERYTHING BEHIND

FENGMAN CHEN LEUNG, KAI PING, CHINA
INTERVIEWED BY ELIZABETH LEUNG

*I interviewed my mom in her bedroom. She was wearing
her pajamas. She's a caring and loving mother who loves
to play video games.* —*E.L.*

I was born and raised in Kai Ping, China. My dad didn't live with the
family. He went to a farm somewhere else in Kai Ping. I lived with
my mom, my grandmother, and my brothers and sister. When I was
seven, my family had to go to a farm really far, far away. China wanted a
bunch of us to go there. You could call it a city, but it was a very small
city. My parents, my brothers and sister, and I went to a farm. I was too
young, so they let me go to Toi San because I had an aunt living there.
I lived there for a year. They didn't have enough food to feed everyone,
so I went back home.

My greatest memory is of catching fish and shrimps with my hands.
During winter we would go to the river to catch fish and shrimp. There
were a lot of rocks and dirt. During fall and summer there was a lot of
water, but in winter there was less water. So it was easier to catch [them].
Since there was less water, we used rocks and dirt to block the river from
flowing. [When] all the water stopped flowing my brothers, sister, and
I would collect the fish and shrimp. We would bring them home, and my
geen-geen [grandma] would cook them so we could eat it. My geen-geen
used to try to feed me. I never wanted to eat. She would chase me around
the house just to get me to eat (laughs). I loved her so much. She was
very important to me because my mother died when I was only a
teenager.

We didn't have any electricity. We played all kinds of games to pass the
time. Like with rocks: we would take five or seven rocks, you were supposed to throw them and catch them with the same hand, but you
couldn't put the rocks in your other hand or else you would lose, almost
like jacks. Then there was another game. You took a chicken feather and
some cardboard. You cut the cardboard into a small circle. Then you took
a nail and poked it through in the middle of the cardboard. You used it to
kick it across and another person would kick it back to you. We used to

kill chickens for food, so we always had feathers. We would take the prettiest feathers, clean them up, and use rubber bands to tie them to the circle. We also played hide and seek. And we picked vegetables and fruit for fun too. We had so much fun when we were young.

My parents wanted me to have an education, and I did. Over at the school, there was only one class. I went up to second grade, and then I had to go to a school further away. It took at least an hour to get there; we had to walk. It would be a group of students walking to school together. Some were a lot older but we were all in one class. Just one teacher taught all of us.

After middle school I still had a semester to finish before I could graduate. I went to Kai Ping to finish up middle school. I had to live at the school. We slept on top of tables. When the teacher told us to sleep, everyone would put the tables together so we could sleep. It was just on the tables so it wasn't soft or anything.

During high school I had to walk to school and get there by 6:30. When you got there you had to do morning exercises in front of the school. Then you went to class. At noon you got out of school to go home to eat lunch. At 1:30 you went back to school. Around 4 to 4:30 you got out of school again and ate at home. Then you had to go back to school *again*, and then you got out of school around 8:30. You went to school six days a week. And you got a lot of homework. There wasn't any time for fun and games.

China had no freedom. Like, if you said you wanted to kill [a government leader], then you could get killed for that or they might beat you. Also, if you wanted to go visit your relatives, you had to write a note that said you were going to visit that person, your name, and how many days you were going to be gone, before you got a bus ride there. Then when you left you had to tell the people that you were leaving before you could go home.

In China you couldn't get married at the age of twenty-one, but since I was moving to America I was able to get married. In China, you had to be twenty-six and over before you got married, because China was overpopulated. You could only have one child. If you had more than one child, then you had to pay 10,000 Chinese dollars for each child you had after the first.

I came to America because it is a lot better, with more wealth and freedom. I left everything behind in China. The only thing I took with me were blankets.

I got here by plane. My husband came to America first, and then he came back to China to marry me. After he married me, he went back to America to find work. I was still in China when I had my first daughter. Then I was able to immigrate to America. My husband came back to China to take our child and me to America.

San Francisco is different. It has all different types of people. It's bigger here, and there are buses. Back at home there are buses that go from city to city only. It wasn't too hard to learn English because I was still pretty young, but as you get older and try to learn English it's harder. My first job was as a seamstress. I didn't know how to sew (laughs). It was hard to find a job. But we had no money problems because my uncle let us live in his basement without paying rent. After a whole year we moved to Linda Street. Then about two years later we moved into the house where we live in right now.

Translated from Cantonese

LIKE A GOLDEN COUNTRY

Glenn Setiono, Jakarta, Indonesia
Interviewed by Spencer Rodriguez

Glenn is a full-time student who has lived in San Francisco since the first grade. He's brave and smart, with a sense of humor. We did this interview in his living room.
—S.R.

Hi, I'm Glenn Setiono. I'm fifteen years old and I was born in Jakarta, Indonesia. [I remember] the weather, the food, and the people there. Well, mostly my family, but they were, like, really awesome. We had nice people, just like right here in America. They had high family values. They were very humble. They would help a stranger who looked like they needed help. I remember one time my family saw a man on the street who had gotten lost and looked like he was gonna die, so my dad pointed him in the right direction and gave him some food and money.

[We spoke] Indonesian, of course, a little bit of English, and... I don't know, but Indonesia has a lot of different styles of languages. The weather there is very hot and very humid. In Indonesia there are two seasons: the sunny season and the rainy season. Rainy season starts around April and goes through October or September—around then. During the rainy season I usually played with my little toys, although they weren't as modern as they are here. Indonesia, I believe, is a third-world country or a second-world country. I'm not too sure on that one. School was five days a week, same as here, except, you know when we move to a new grade and we have summer vacation? You know how we have two months off [here]? Over there we only had one month off. We started school at seven something and ended around three something.

Jakarta, the capital of Indonesia, is where I was born. But my mom and dad decided they wanted to start a new life in America, so, well, they left me in Indonesia. My mom and my dad, they came over here without us because they thought that if they came with me and my sister, then we wouldn't manage the money and we'd end up having to go back anyways. So they just left me and my sister there in Indonesia. So my mom and my dad came all the way over here until they had enough money, then they sent me and my sister over here. And that was when I was six years old. I guess they saw a better life in America. They saw it was something like a golden country. I didn't know why they wanted to leave, though, 'cause we had a good life in Indonesia.

I was so young that I actually didn't even know my own mom. I had very faint memories of her, and when I saw her again I didn't think she was my mom. Honestly.

Twenty-four hours in an airplane [was] torture, but my parents wanted to have a better life—even though we already had a good life in Indonesia. I guess they wanted to explore, so why not California? They heard so much good stuff. Plus, family problems were slowly breaking out, so they needed to leave before things got rough. And so they moved. It's kinda personal, but my family was having problems with money and my parents didn't wanna be in that.

Well, [in] our food usually we all use spices 'cause Indonesia is meant for spice. We have food that is good, of course. You know what? We have one dish in the kitchen that is called *rawon*. It's beef. It's like a small beef stew with carrots and such. It's really good. Actually, the soup color is black, but it's *good*. You don't see that in many stews and soups. We have these things called *goreng*, which are fried; we fry things like ducks, lambs, ox tails. What else? Um, this might not seem appetizing, but cow's tongue. Yes, taste like chicken. No, haha. Well, I only ate it 'cause at the start my mom tricked me. She said it was chicken, I believed her, and I ate it. I thought it was really good. And then we have, uh, sheep skin. It's all dark—fried stuff. Actually it's fried so you can bite it off in one bite.

I revisited Indonesia for three months over the summer because I had not gone there in six years. Oh, no, actually nine years. 'Cause we haven't have the time and money for it, so I hadn't had a chance to go. I finally saw my family after nine years. It was kinda weird, because when I went to Indonesia everything looked so much poor than I last remembered it. The lifestyle there now is so far from me now. It was so long since I remember what it was like there. It felt funny, but my family was there to help me. They showed me the old places I used to go to, like the parks. The parks are in great condition, unlike the ones here in San Francisco. But there it's always hot, so not too many people go out. Also, you know how usually you talk [on the phone] here? Over there the big thing is texting. It's cheaper than talking. This way the phone is easier to use. Also, every place is air conditioned.

The first time I went there to revisit, I was freaked out 'cause there were lizards everywhere. They were on me, and it was weird. Oh yes, they have the Komodo dragon. They only live on the islands of Indonesia. They are the last relatives of the dinosaur. They lived during the dinosaur age. And when I went over there last year, I started messing with one of them, you know? Poking it with a stick and stuff. For the record, don't mess with the dragons. They're very dangerous.

Although there is a bad side to our country, in which—how can I say this?—they rob you with knives. It's just threatening. I remember one time I was in this truck with my mom and dad, and they were driving with their window rolled down. We stopped at a red light. All of a sudden, a guy grabbed my dad's arm. [My dad] started laughing, he punched the guy, the guy fell on the floor, and we drove away. But I'm just telling you there are bad, bad, bad people there.

You know, I thought my new life would be like, cars, ideal movie-star life, but I was wrong. I thought I would have a huge house with a pool and a lot of money because on TV they showed families with huge houses and maids. But yeah, I was hella wrong. Learning the language was the hardest. Mostly just learning the English words. Like, you know, the alphabet [here] is "Ay—Bee—Cee." Over there it is "Ah—Bay—Say." Over there everything is an "Ah," and everything here is an "Ay."

My grandma, she was the one who cared for me and looked out for me when I was alone. Also she was like a mom to me. I couldn't remember my mom, and since my dad wasn't with me, she posed as a mother and father. She was basically all I had there while I was alone. I love her and I miss her.

DON'T FORGET
WHERE YOU COME FROM

KELLY DANG, DAO PHU QUY, VIETNAM
INTERVIEWED BY DUYEN NGUYEN

My aunt Kelly immigrated to the U.S. twenty-five years ago. I interviewed her in her kitchen in San Francisco. She was preparing for the Lunar New Year.   —D.N.

I grew up in Vietnam. I came from an island called Dao Phu Quy. It was very beautiful, not too big. I think the population on the island was probably around 10,000 people and it had four towns on it. We were all Vietnamese. But the big difference was that the people, they had different accents based on what town they lived.

In 1979, the country was under communists, and a lot of people left by boat to seek a better life, speaking of the United States as the country of the free and that kind of stuff. So a lot of people from our island left by boat to Malaysia or other islands that would take them as refugees, and then immigrated here to United States.

I was too young to decide whether I wanted to leave Vietnam or not. It was my parents and my uncles who decided. They wanted to have better education for their children's future—for their generation and the generation after. And that's the reason why we left Vietnam. Because we knew that we could seek a better place for the generations ahead.

When I was on the boat going from Vietnam to Malaysia, at the age of seven or eight, I was very scared. I wondered where my parents were going. You are nowhere in the sea on that boat. Back then if the communists knew that we were leaving, then they would put the whole family in jail. So I didn't know [we were leaving] until, like, I think maybe two days before. My parents and my uncles put away oil and gas in the boat to get ready to go. And that night, around midnight, my parents came and got us. My mom and all my siblings walked probably at least three or four miles across the island to meet my uncle and my father, because we couldn't go out at the main gate. So we had to sneak out of the middle of the night, and it was dark. For a kid, I mean, it was pretty scary.

I always remember the journey. It was a long journey. Traveling by boat wasn't like you could get into the airplane and go, have a fun ride. It was like five days and four nights in the sea, and we went to Singapore. They didn't let us in, and then we journeyed another day and night to Malaysia.

The camp was called a refugee camp. They had all the refugee families there. We were very well taken care of. I mean, we were set aside some goods each week. We went and got our food; each family had a certain amount, like vegetable, meat and water. So we were fed very well. The Malaysian government took care of this. Basically the camp ran very smoothly, and they offered classes as well that taught a little English. So that was really nice. In terms of the camp, it was very good experience. My parents and I stayed there for, like, a year.

My family and I were sponsored by a church in Kansas City, Missouri. The church came to the camp in Malaysia to interview us. Once we were interviewed, we got all our immunizations, got our paperwork filled out, and we got the tickets. The church organization already had a house for us. They had people that helped us, like, shadowed us and showed us the grocery store.

I think the most difficult thing when I arrived here in 1979, was that there weren't that many Asian people, let alone Vietnamese, living in Kansas City, Missouri. They were all Caucasian-American people. So the most [difficult] things were adapting to the culture and language, and understanding what everybody was trying to say to you. So it was more than a year for me and my brother and sister to actually understand what everyone was saying.

I think what most surprised me was all that people we didn't know, and they cared for us so much like we're their family. That's one thing nice about these church people. I also looked at blond hair and that kind of stuff and I was like, "Wow," you know? I had never seen anything like that. People are very friendly. I think that's the same thing in my country. I mean, people were also very friendly, but basically [here] you're free. People who are strangers to you and they don't know you, we were introduced to. They greeted us and they said, "Hello." So I think that's probably one of the things I was most impressed about.

On the first day of school—the first few months of school—me and my brother and sister were surrounded by a lot of students. They loved to hang out with us, to check us out, because we were the only Asians in that school. There were no other Asians. It was all American, blond hair, blue eye. So we were the only Asians and they were so nice. They were like, "Oh, can I help you with this?" Of course I didn't understand anything, but now looking back, I probably knew what they were saying. So that's how it was for the first week, month, and, eventually, year. But it was a lot of fun. They took care of us and they pretty much let us do everything.

I consider myself as a Vietnamese-American. We celebrate Christmas and the Lunar New Year. We hang out with friends and celebrate the New Year here, also our Lunar New Year. We take great pride in celebrating our own culture and where we came from. There is a tradition the day before the New Year, or the week. We clean up the house and dust everything to make sure everything is clean.

Life is always different, but that's how we see things, at least. That's how I consider myself as a Vietnamese-American. I adapted to both [cultures] and I cherish both of them. That's what makes me a Vietnamese-American, not just Vietnamese or just American. I know the country that I live in; it's a country that I'm thankful for and its freedom. And the country where I was born and raised for eight years, I wouldn't forget that.

I think me—coming from a poor, underdeveloped country at that time, and depend on the farming and fishing all our life, and then you an have opportunity to go to another place—you don't take things for granted. So no matter where or what you do in life, you always work hard, help people when you can, and just be a good person and a good citizen.

The most important thing is that you don't forget where you come from and where you were born. Throughout your life, tell your kids where you come from.

GRACIAS A DIOS SI LLEGAMOS TODOS BIEN

ANA, SONSONATE, EL SALVADOR
INTERVIEWED BY CYNTHIA OSORIO

My mom is a very funny person. She's giggling at the fact that I'm recording her. Her laugh is contagious, so I laugh too. I interviewed her in her room while we were watching her novelas. *—C.O.*

I'm from Sonsonate, El Salvador. I was born near the coast, in a place called La Barra De Santiago, near the beach. That's where I'm really from, where I was born. I grew up in the city of Sonsonate. In La Colonia Angélica.

I lived with *mi mamá* and my siblings. We were a family of six kids, three women and three men. I grew up and lived there until I was (thinking, looks up at the wall) seventeen, eighteen, or nineteen years old, and then I migrated over here to the United States.

Well it was a very small house. Um, very poor, we didn't have electricity. We used candles, *¿no?* Yeah. With that we had light, since we didn't have any electricity. I was raised there with my five other siblings. No, with three, because two of my brothers left very young from the house.

Mi mamá would tell me, after I had Fernando, it would be better if I come here to the United States because Fernando's dad could have been looking for me and *mi mamá* didn't want me to have any more kids with him—especially if I was that young. That's why I was sent over here. Because, you know, I had a son in El Salvador [your older brother].

I came from El Salvador to the border of Guatemala, to Mexico, and from Mexico I came in through Mexicali. On, *como se llama...* on a bus. We boarded the bus in El Salvador to Mexico. *¿No?* Then from El Salvador to Veracruz, and from Veracruz to Mexico, *el D.F.* [the capital].

I left my son because I had him at a young age. I left him with *mi mamá* and I also left all my beautiful dreams I had in El Salvador. They were to go to school and to graduate with a degree as a bilingual secretary. Those were my goals for El Salvador, and I never got to accomplish them.

Mexicali is almost at the border of the United States, I think. *¿No? ¿Sí?* I don't really remember since it was a long time ago. It was in 19... 1982.

I didn't have anything except for just 100 dollars, and with that money I ate. I bought food—little things like candy. That was it for food.

We paid *el coyote*—a man that guarantees you will make it to the U.S.—in El Salvador. He was a friend of the family. My sister and *mi mamá* talked to him about me migrating over here. I migrated here with a group of about maybe twenty people. We paid *el coyote* 300 dollars in El Salvador. And when we got here to Los Angeles we had to pay him another 300 dollars.

That *coyote* gave you another chance with that same money. Let's say that *la migra* [border patrol] did get me, and sent me back to El Salvador. That *coyote* would have given me another chance to come if I wanted to try again, a second chance.

Well, that *coyote* had other *coyotes* to help him in Mexico. So those Mexican *coyotes* would help us get to the United States. From Mexicali we went to Tijuana, and from Tijuana to Los Angeles. It was somewhat easy and somewhat hard. Well, from El Salvador to Mexico it was easy. But from Mexico, to come into the United States, it was hard, because we had to walk for five days through mountains to Tijuana.

We had to hide from *la migra*. We walked for five days, day and night. We didn't rest, only for a couple of minutes, and then we would walk and walk again. When we heard airplanes or helicopter, *el coyote* would tell us, "*tírense tírense*," to the grass because, "*ahí viene la migra*." And that's when we had to throw ourselves to the grass. It was a big group maybe of twenty people. And almost everyone was Salvadoran.

Well, the only thing that I was thinking of was that I wanted the journey to finish—*que llegáramos sanos* [that we all arrive safe]. And my only fear was that I always heard that on the way the men raped the girls. All I wanted was to finish the trip because all I wanted to do was to stop walking. I didn't really mind walking but I just felt like it was never going to end. Well it was somewhat hard and somewhat easy, but I didn't suffer as much as I thought I would.

Gracias a Dios sí llegamos todos bien. [Thank God we all arrived well.] After we were walking for five days we passed by a fence. It was barbed wire. We had to hop over it and on the other side there was a white van waiting for all of us. And once we had passed through it *el coyote* opened the door and all twenty people went in. We were stuffed in there. The person that was driving the van was another *coyote*. And we all got in the van like we were animals. It was hot and I felt like I couldn't breathe, like there was no air. We were all on top of each other. And from there they took us, and I didn't know anything the whole trip until we got to L.A.

Anyways there's other ways you can enter the U.S. Many choose to hop the border and cross the Rio Grande. We decided to go the back way and our feet got swollen and they had blisters. That was the hardest thing for me.

In L.A., I was in the house of the wife of *el coyote* until my family came to pick me up. My cousins came. A lot of the other people were going to Houston, Washington, D.C., and all over the place, so everyone was waiting for their families to come to pick them up.

Well, the lady gave us a place where we could take a shower since we hadn't taken one in like five days. We didn't even get to change anything, *ni los calzones* [not even underwear].

When my cousins came to pick me up in L.A. I stayed with them for like eight days. Then my sister went to pick me up from L.A. to go live with her in San Francisco. And that's how I came here to San Francisco, to go live with my aunt, *niña* Olin.

I didn't have any goals. All I wanted was to be a citizen and be able to bring my son with me, but I never could. Even when he was older I still couldn't because he was in school. I wanted to go back so bad. I missed El Salvador, *mi mamá*, and my son. I would sit and cry every night, wishing I was back at home.

I was here for a couple of months [before I got homesick]. Well after that, I went to sign up for free classes at City College campus, the one that's on 23rd. I went to go sign up for an English class since I went three months without working. I went to take classes at night.

After I lived with *niña* Olin, I went to go live with my sister and I was helping her since she worked in a cleaners. It was hard for her.

I would help her take care of her daughters, Tere and Claudia, after they came from El Salvador. I would feed them and take them to school. I kept on going to school to learn some English at night from 6:00 PM to 9:00 PM. And as time went by the girls got older and my sister didn't need me anymore. I decided to look for a job, and I found a job in a McDonald's. And that's where I began to work.

In McDonald's, I worked for three years. After that I went to go work at a Burger King only making $3.50 an hour. For three years, the most that I was paid was $5.25 an hour. In a month I made maybe at the most 200, 300 dollars. And from that I had to send money to *mi mamá* in El Salvador.

Since I lived with my sister, all I had to do was cook. That's really it because my sister never charged me rent for living with her. She always helped me. After that I decided to leave my sister and find a room of my own. I never lived outside of San Francisco because all my family was here. I was already getting used to living in San Francisco. I've lived here for twenty-three years now.

What I had to do was work hard, study a lot, and be smart about things. Well, you know I studied and went to school and got a degree, right?

When I was working in the cafeteria in U.C.S.F., I met your dad. But it's funny, because I knew your dad from El Salvador. We were boyfriend and girlfriend a long time ago, and it's like we were reunited. After we found each other we got back together, and we started living together. We were living together for about six years, then we had your brother, then you, and then we got married when you were one year old.

Then we began our life as a family. I wasn't working because I dedicated all my time to you and your brother. Your dad worked for a long time. I found a job when you guys got older. I found a job at Pacific Marine Yachts. And from then I haven't had another job because I've been working there for almost ten years now. And that's my life. *Calabasa, calabasa, cada qien para su casa. Y este cuento se a terminado.*

Parts of this interview translated from Spanish

ABOUT 826 VALENCIA

MISSION AND HISTORY OF OUR ORGANIZATION:

826 Valencia is a non-profit organization based in San Francisco dedicated to supporting students ages 6 to 18 with their writing skills, and helping teachers get their students excited about writing. Our work is based on the knowledge that strong writing skills are fundamental to future success and that great leaps in learning can be made when skilled adults work one-on-one with students.

826 Valencia offers free one-on-one tutoring, writing workshops, class writing field trips, extensive and professional student publishing, and an in-schools program where tutors go into schools to help teachers and students with reading and writing projects during the school day.

Named for our location in the heart of San Francisco's Mission District, 826 Valencia opened on April 8, 2002, and consists of a writing lab, a street-front, student-friendly retail pirate store that partially funds our programs, and a satellite classroom. We have developed programs that reach students at every possible opportunity, whether it is in school, after school, in the evenings, or on the weekends. All of our programs are challenging and enjoyable, and ultimately strengthen each student's ability to express ideas effectively, creatively, and confidently, in his or her individual voice. Since we opened our doors, 650 volunteers—including published authors, magazine founders, SAT course instructors, documentary filmmakers, students and other professionals—have donated their time to work with students. This incredible resource allows 826 Valencia to offer our services for free.

OUR ACTIVITIES:

ONE-ON-ONE TUTORING: 826 Valencia is packed five days a week with students who come in for free one-on-one drop-in tutoring. We serve students of all skill levels and interests. We host a thriving English language learner program.

WORKSHOPS: In the evenings, 826 Valencia offers free workshops that provide in-depth instruction in a variety of areas that schools don't often include in their curriculums such as college entrance essay writing, SAT preparation, cartooning, bookmaking, starting a 'zine, writing your own opera, or producing films. Experienced and accomplished professionals teach the workshops. One of our overall goals is to connect professionals working in the field with young writers. For example, during our Sports Writing workshop, which was taught by a sports writer for the San Jose Mercury News, students were able to spend a day in the press box at a San Francisco Giants game and interact with journalists who cover the Giants on a regular basis. Our workshop teachers have included authors Dave Eggers, Erika Lopez, and Stephen King, and filmmakers Spike Jonze and Melissa Mathison.

FIELD TRIPS: Three or four days a week, 826 Valencia welcomes an entire class for a morning of custom-designed curriculum. Students may experience a round table discussion and writing seminar with a local author, or they may enjoy an active seminar focused on poetry or journalism. The most popular is one we invented called the Storytelling & Bookmaking Workshop in which students write, illustrate, publish, and bind their own books within a two-hour period.

IN-SCHOOLS PROGRAMS: It is not feasible for all classes to come to us, so we dispatch teams of volunteers to go into local schools and provide one-on-one assistance to students as they tackle various projects such as school newspapers, basic writing assignments, and college entrance essays. Teachers are in tremendous need of support in their classrooms with their enormous class sizes. 826 steps in to support them and their students. This school year we've worked shoulder-to-shoulder in over 250 classrooms.

PUBLISHING STUDENT WRITING: We see that students work much harder when they know their work is going to be publicly celebrated, so we are committed to professionally publishing student works. We are proud to produce approximately one new student publication each month, all of which are offered for sale at our store, on Amazon.com, and in bookstores across the country to help offset a portion of the costs of production and our programs in general. Works produced out of 826 include *826 Quarterly*, our regularly published volume of creative writing by students at the writing lab; *Talking Back: What Students Know About Teaching*; and *Waiting To Be Heard: Youth Speak Out About Inheriting a Violent World*.

THE WRITERS' ROOM AT EVERETT MIDDLE SCHOOL: We have also realized one of our goals in San Francisco of establishing a permanent,
dynamic space on a campus in which to offer our intensive services to
students during the day. The Writers' Room at Everett Middle School is
designed to foster students' critical thinking, problem solving, and active
learning, while bringing the successes of the work at our writing center
directly to students in a high-need school.

ACKNOWLEDGMENTS

826 Valencia's tutors go en masse to San Francisco's public schools to work shoulder to shoulder with students on writing projects. For several years we've worked with Lisa Morehouse at Balboa; tutors have always left impressed with Lisa's energy and her students' intelligence. Lisa is a boundlessly energetic and committed teacher whose sassy and warm classroom presence is simultaneously disarming and engaging. She inspires the best in young people.

We asked Lisa if she would work with us to publish her students' work. She agreed, and we teamed up with her sophomore classes this year as they delved into an oral history unit on immigration and migration. In jumping into this larger publishing project, Lisa knew that she would be adding significantly to her enormous workload, yet her enthusiasm remained unchecked. 826 is fortunate to have collaborated with such a talented and organized teacher.

Lisa's colleagues at Balboa, Mark Heringer, Karen Malm, Cheryl Nelson, Frank Viollis, and Dee Wu, offered their invaluable help with this project as well. Rachel Reinhard, Amy Standen, and Tuyen Tran also provided support to Lisa and her students. Thanks also to Balboa High School principal Patricia Gray.

The book emerged from the study of immigration and migration to California. Before students began their interviews, they learned how to develop open-ended questions and other techniques of successful interviewing. Jonathan Kiefer and Eliza Wilmerding, authors and oral historians, created a lesson plan and worked in the classroom to share interviewing techniques. Prepped with the requirements for outstanding oral histories, each student recorded at least an hour of interviews. Their interview subjects included family members, fellow students, faculty, community leaders, and friends who told their personal stories of coming to California. We thank all of the interviewees for sharing their experiences with the students and with us.

Over the course of four and a half weeks, 826 Valencia sent tutors to Lisa's students as the audiotapes evolved into polished, personal stories of immigration and migration. During these many days the large, light-filled high school library was filled with students and tutors chatting, reading, writing, editing. Students typed the transcripts—in some cases also translated them from Tagalog, Spanish, Cantonese, Bisaya, Arabic, Korean, Cambodian, Vietnamese, Kapampangan, Burmese, Mandarin—and worked with 826 tutors as they selected the most compelling moments and determined whether additional interviewing was necessary. Tutors gave encouragement and asked questions as the students wrote introductions for their subjects. We would like to thank the in-schools volunteers for their dedication to this project. They are: Lessley Anderson, Darcy Asbe, Nicole Bender, Rebecca Blatt, Carolina Braunschweig, Sara Bright, Shannon Bryant, Brenna Burns, Sekai Chideya, Kathy Cohn, Shannon De Jong, Katrina Dodson, Norman Patrick Doyle, Kristen Engelhardt, Alison Ekizian, Doug Favero, Linda Gebroe, Sarah B. Gibson, Heather Hax, Pamela Herbert, Justin Hughes, Gail Jardine, Craig Kelly, Sasha Kinney, Lisa Lee, Frances Lefkowitz, Chad Lent, Lynn Lent, Jenny Lovold, Amber Lowi, Eric Magnuson, Amy Miles, Keri Modrall, Talia Muscarella, Walt Opie, Leslie Outhier, Jina Park, Charlotte Peterson, Brian Pfeffer, Mark Rabine, Lily Rosenman, Karen Schaser, Heidi Schmidt, Gordon Smith, John Snyder, Kim-Lan Stadnick, Constanza Svidler, Joey Sweet, Chris Taylor, Shawna Thompson, Caitlin Van Dusen, Josh Wein, Peanut Wells, Matt Werner, Brandt Wicke, Sinclair Wu, Liz Worthy, and Chris Ying.

Students then continued their work at the 826 lab. A small group of extra-dedicated students met, after school and during spring break, for over five weeks, accomplishing a great deal of hefty decision-making. Their task included identifying central themes, selecting a title, designing a cover, and finding a balance that allowed the oral histories to be edited while maintaining the true voice of the interview subjects. The students on the editorial committee were: Jackie Chen, Vinnie Collier, Jimmy Meas, Mikko delos Reyes, Roger Le, Tepora Malepeai, Roberto Ortega, Sharon Ou, Gabriel Padilla, Dexter Pasalo, Kyle Pineda, Jenny Tran. The following outstanding 826 Valencia volunteers formed the adult part of this committee: Darcy Asbe, Nicole Bender, Kathleen Cohn, Norman Patrick Doyle, Doug Favero, June Jackson, Craig Kelly, Frances Lefkowitz, Walt Opie, Mark Rabine, Lily Rosenmann, and Karen Schaser.

Huge thanks also go to the volunteers who helped edit the manuscript. They are: Shannon Bryant, Ian Carruthers, Sekai Chideya, Katrina Dodson, Norman Patrick Doyle, Alison Ekizian, Doug Favero, Linda Gebroe, Sarah Gibson, Heather Hax, Pamela Herbert, Sasha Kinney, Chad Lent, Eric Magnuson, Amy Miles, Keri Modrall, Walt Opie, Brian

Pfeffer, Mark Rabine, Lily Rosenmann, Heidi Schmidt, Gordon Smith, Maya Stein, Caitlin Van Dusen, and Liz Worthy. Erin Neeley, 826's energetic programs director, manages the in-schools projects and coordinated tutoring at Balboa. Alvaro Villanueva oversaw production, as well as the editorial committee. Alanna Hale, Jonathan Keifer, and Maya Stein assisted with book production. We would like to thank the following people for general assistance with this project: Alison Alkire, Aran Baker, Caitlin Craven, Marie Cavosora, Melanie Glass, Les Hanamaka, Abigail Jacobs, Dominic Luxford, Amanda Machi, Talia Muscarella, Susanna Myrseth, Amie Nenninger, Rick Opaterny, Kelly Pretzer, Mark Ristaino, Lily Rosenman, and Jon Sung.

John B. Snyder, Kim-Lan Stadnick, Joey Sweet, and Brandt Wicke, interns at 826 Valencia, and Tracy Barrerio, Jory John, Leigh Lehman, and Anna Ura, staff members of 826, were essential in bringing this book to fruition.

For their years of support for oral history work at Balboa High School, we would like to thank the San Francisco Education Fund. Their grant this year allowed Balboa High School to purchase tape recorders, headphones, audiotapes, and the resources to print the Immigration/ Migration readers used in this class, as well as in Susan Ritter's Modern World History class. Members of their staff, Te Guerra, Robin Mencher, Jennifer Nguyen, and Mark Triplett, also volunteered with the students.

Ninive Clements Calegari, Executive Director, 826 Valencia
Dave Eggers, Founder, 826 Valencia

THE INTERVIEWERS